SPARKED

HELENA ECHLIN
MALENA WATROUS

Published by Inkshares, Inc., San Francisco, California
www.inkshares.com

Edited by Staton Rabin | Alexa Wejko | Jessica Gardner
Cover Design by M.S. Corley | Interior Design by Kevin G. Summers

Paperback ISBN: 9781942645641
eBook ISBN: 9781942645658
Library of Congress Control Number: 2017938049

First edition

Printed in the United States of America

No man chooses evil because it is evil; he only mistakes it for happiness, the good he seeks.

—Mary Shelley

FRIDAY

1.

THE KNOCKING woke me up from a dead sleep.

Whack, whack.

I sat up, blinking myself awake. The sky outside our port-hole-shaped window was still dark, the silhouettes of the redwoods just a shade blacker. Rain lashed at the glass. Wind rocked the Airstream back and forth.

Whack.

There was that knocking again. I leaned over to wake Ivy. Our beds were so close, they practically touched—

But Ivy wasn't in her bed.

Whack, whack.

She must have snuck out and forgotten her key. I needed to let her in fast. Our mom was a heavy sleeper—especially if she'd smoked a "medicinal" joint before bed—but there was a limit to what she could tune out.

When I eased open the accordion door to the bedroomette, a river of cold air whooshed over me. I hurried to the front of the trail-er where the door was wide open, banging in the wind.

I stepped out onto the top cinderblock stair, straining to see through the rain. "Ivy?" I called into the darkness, but no one answered. The icy wind cut through my pajamas and I shuddered, wrapping my arms around myself. Ivy must have left the door un-locked, and the storm had blown it open.

Still, it creeped me out.

I wasn't used to living in a tin can on the edge of civilization. Our new property bumped up against the state park. We had no neighbors for miles, but hikers, poachers, and the occasional homeless person liked to use our land as their playground. Mom said that we were safer out here than if we lived in some apartment in town. Statistically, there were fewer weirdos in the vicinity.

But all it takes is one.

Get a grip, I told myself. I would've woken up if someone had dragged Ivy out of the trailer in the middle of the night. Our beds were like two feet apart. Besides, this was the third time since school started this fall that I'd gotten up before dawn to find her stuffed lion strategically tucked under her quilt, its yellow mane arranged on the pillow as a decoy in the unlikely event that Mom checked in on us.

I shoved my bare feet into my boots and ran around to the other side of the trailer, where we always parked "Spud," our beat-up VW van. But the key was in the ignition as usual and the tires were submerged in troughs of rainwater. The hood felt cold, and I didn't smell the scent of french-fry grease coming off the engine, so it was clear Ivy hadn't driven anywhere. Some friend must have come over to pick her up.

I trudged back inside and closed the door, leaving it unlocked in case she had forgotten her key. It wasn't like her to be careless, but she'd been acting so weird lately that anything was possible.

I was too worked up to go back to sleep. Besides, I hated being in the bedroomette by myself. It would've been cramped for one person, but somehow, when Ivy was there, she made it feel bigger. I couldn't risk waking Mom by turning on a light. But the sky outside the window was already fading to a steely gray, and I thought I could see well enough to write while I waited for Ivy to get home.

I grabbed my notebook and sat down at our red Formica dining table, uncapping my gel-tip pen and flipping to the first blank page. Writing always calmed me down. I'd filled a whole row of marbled composition books with journal entries, poems, and short stories. But right now all I could think about was where on earth Ivy might be.

The clock on the stove read 6:14. The last time she snuck out, she'd crept back in around three thirty, waking me up. Ever since we moved into this trailer, my ears were on hyperalert, especially at dawn, when the underbrush rustled constantly, owls screeched in the trees, and wild dogs howled back and forth across the park.

Ivy always laughed when I complained about the spooky noises, reassuring me that I had nothing to worry about—just like she used to when I'd wake up from a nightmare after binge-reading horror novels. I imagined her walking through the door now and reassuring me in just the same way: teasing but affectionate.

Feeling a little better, I decided to make some coffee. After staying out all night, she was going to need it. But as I held the carafe under the tap, I realized I had no idea how much coffee to put in the machine. Ivy was our family coffee maker. She took pride in it, groaning at the amount of milk and sugar I dumped in mine. I measured three spoonfuls of grounds, filled the carafe to the three-cup mark, and set it to perc, hoping for the best.

As the water burbled and splurted, I decided: *Ivy will be back by the time this coffee is ready.* I used to play this same game when we were little and Mom left us alone at home. But when the coffee had filled the pot, there was still no sign of Ivy. I ran water on the dishes that Mom had left in the sink. *She'll be back by the time these are cleaned.* I scrubbed each one slowly and thoroughly.

Nope again.

I went to empty the trash, which was full of Bryan's empty Coors cans. This brought back memories of the horrible fight between Mom and Ivy the night before. Bryan, Mom's gross boyfriend, had practically moved in with us. He had a habit of coming over during the afternoon, when he knew Mom was at work. Apparently, he was allergic to clothes. He'd take a shower and then strut around in a towel, showing off his hairy ape chest. Needless to say, Ivy and I weren't thrilled about this. Last night, Ivy had finally snapped and called him a pervert to his face.

"If you hate it here so much, you should leave!" Mom had screamed.

Maybe Ivy took her seriously.

Rain pelted the trailer, and I shivered.

If only I could just call her. But no—that would've been too easy. People in the African bush had cell phones, but not us. Mom claimed that cell phones were part of a corporate scheme to zap brain cells. Convenient, since we couldn't afford the plans.

A sour taste rose in the back of my throat as I stared into the trees, which stretched for miles in every direction.

If someone came to pick her up, why haven't they brought her back yet?

The question morphed into full-blown panic.

"Mom, get up!" I burst into her room. She grunted, pulling the Indian bedspread over her face. "Ivy's gone!"

"What? Go back to—" she mumbled.

"She's not in her bed, and the front door was wide open when I got up." The panic was rising, and fast. "Anyone could have come in and taken her!"

She threw on her old chenille robe and followed me to our room, squinting at Ivy's empty bed.

"I woke up before five and she wasn't here," I said, as Mom flung aside the quilt Ivy had sewn from scraps of our grandma's old dresses.

Mom pushed her fingers through the snarls of her blonde hair, her face pale. "She must have snuck out again." She narrowed her eyes as if daring me to defend Ivy. "Yes, Laurel, I know she's been going out at night. I didn't say anything because things have been so tense recently, I wanted to give her some space."

"But the door was unlocked. It was wide open. Don't you think that's weird?"

Mom shut her eyes and massaged the bridge of her nose like she felt a migraine coming. "Bryan must have forgotten to lock it. He left last night because he was so upset with Ivy after what she said."

I exhaled sharply. "Bryan was upset? Well, boo-hoo. It's our home! *Ivy* is the one who should be mad."

"And I'm sure she'll come back as soon as she cools down." Mom tried to push a frizzy red curl out of my face, but I ducked away.

"How? The van is still here! Do you think someone picked her up?"

Mom nodded. "Does she have a new boyfriend?"

"No." I shook my head, marveling at how little she knew about our lives. "The guys at school are all completely lame."

"Then maybe she met someone at Ritual Roasters."

"She would've told me." But I couldn't help remembering how Ivy had looked away when I asked where she went in the middle of the night. "I just drive around," she'd answered. But drive around where? Maybe she *had* been sneaking out to meet a guy she hadn't told me about.

Mom tugged back the tie-dyed curtain at the window and peered out. "She'll be back any minute. I know it."

"What if she got in some guy's car, and she thought she could trust him, but she was completely wrong?" Suddenly, I was sure that this was exactly what must have happened. Ivy was a good judge of character, but I'd heard that true psychopaths could be incredibly charming. I imagined how some guy had chatted her up at the coffee shop where she worked on weekends, and she'd sneaked out for a couple of dates. He'd spent just enough time with her to win her trust, so that she would run out and get into his car, no question. By now, he could have taken her anywhere. Who knew what he was going to do to her? The trailer lurched under my feet.

"We need to call the police," I said. "Some psycho could be torturing her!"

"You're torturing *me*," Mom said, "and you know it's a bad idea to involve the cops."

I felt a twinge of guilt, knowing that Ivy wouldn't want me involving the police either. We couldn't risk it. Not unless we had to.

Mom wasn't a bad person really, but she was only seventeen when she had Ivy, and it's like she never fully grew up or something. Three months before graduating from high school, she ran away from home to follow her favorite band, Phish, around the country. She painted faces to earn money for concert tickets, and eventually got to know the musicians, who paid her to design one of their concert posters, a psychedelic sunrise over silhouettes of the band members.

That was her proudest accomplishment, proof that she could make it as an artist. We still have that print, framed and hanging over our kitchen table. Unfortunately, right after that she got pregnant with Ivy. Our dad was another groupie who'd barely finished high school. He and Mom moved to Eugene, where they stuck it out until she got pregnant with me. That's when he decided to head up to Alaska to try and make some money. He promised to send her child support as soon as he got his feet on the ground, but that never happened, and we hadn't heard from him in years.

Mom kept painting, but since that didn't pay the bills, she had to clean houses on the side, which she hated. She couldn't afford a babysitter, so when she went to work, she'd leave us in the apartment, locking the door and telling us to keep quiet. But I guess we didn't listen, because one day, a neighbor heard us crying and called the cops. When they saw that two little kids had been left all alone in a filthy apartment, Mom got charged with negligence. We were put in foster care until Grandma came to sort things out, bringing us all back to Cascade to live with her.

But even though Grandma was basically a mom to us all, a social worker was still assigned to our case. For years, this woman named Joan would drop in every month or so, to make sure that we weren't being neglected. We lived in a tidy ranch house, and as long as Grandma was around, Joan was happy. Eventually, when I was ten or eleven, Joan's visits stopped and we almost forgot about her. But after Grandma died last year, and we had to sell her house to pay the medical bills—using what was left to buy this trailer—we got a letter from Child Protective Services letting us know that they were reopening our case. We weren't sure what that meant exactly. No one had been out to visit the trailer yet. But Ivy and I had agreed that it didn't look like much of a home for two teenaged girls. We didn't want to give them any further cause to find our mother negligent.

Our life may not have been the textbook definition of stability, but it seemed impossible to think that they could take us away. After all, Ivy was the same age that our mother had been when she had us, and I was about to turn sixteen. It's not like we could be placed in some Dickensian orphanage. Still, I had three years of high school left, and I was not taking chances. The only thing I remembered about that brief period in foster care was the fact that I'd been separated from Ivy because they couldn't find a home to take both of us.

No matter what, I could not let that happen again.

So I told myself that Mom was right. Ivy was old enough to come and go as she pleased, and super responsible. Maybe she wanted Mom to worry about us for a change instead of the other way around, and that was why she'd stayed out all night.

"Look," Mom said. "When she gets home, I'll talk with her. But right now, I need you to lay off." Her hand shook as she poured herself a mug of coffee. She sat down heavily at the table and took a sip. Her nose wrinkled.

"It tastes like boiled dirt, doesn't it?" I said, collapsing across from her.

She gulped down half the mug, forcing a smile. "It's fine," she said. "Now go get ready for school."

I took a shower, lingering under the lukewarm dribble. *She'll be back when I finish getting dressed,* I told myself. But when I came out of the bedroomette, Mom was still alone, pulling eggs out of the mini-fridge. The clock said 7:21.

"Mom! Where is she?"

"She must have gone straight to school." Mom cracked an egg against the side of the pan, smashing it so hard that she crushed it. Instead of looking at me, she concentrated on picking out the bits of shell. "If she wanted to give me a scare, it's working. You tell her that when you see her there."

"But how am I supposed to get there?"

"I guess you'll have to drive."

"But I can't!"

"Sure, you can. Ivy's been giving you lessons all year, and you have your permit. It's basically the same thing."

"Not in the eyes of the law," I said, but she wasn't listening. "You could drive me," I suggested.

"That's not a good idea." Mom fingered her Eye of Ra pendant. She stroked it whenever she was stressed, convinced that its "ancient wisdom" would rub off, even though she'd found it downtown on Miner Street, at a store called Forbeaddin', in a bin with dozens exactly like it. "If I got caught, it would be a misdemeanor. I could end up in jail, and then I'd lose the two of you for sure."

I sighed, knowing she was right. "But what if I get caught?"

"I don't think it would be that big of a deal, since you don't have any kind of record and you are about to turn sixteen. Just be extra careful and don't get pulled over."

"Thanks for the helpful tip." I wanted to roll my eyes, but without Ivy there, what was the point?

I had zero appetite, but I managed to choke down a few bites of Mom's "eggs scallopini." This was practically the only thing she ever cooked—just eggs scrambled with whatever wilted vegetables happened to be lying around—but she always presented it with a flourish, like it was something truly special.

As I ate, I told myself that Ivy would be at school. After all, she never skipped class unless she was seriously sick. But when I went to grab my coat from our tiny closet, Ivy's favorite black denim jacket— the one she wore like a uniform—was hanging there. I knew Mom would say this didn't prove a thing, but I bit my lip so hard I tasted blood. I just knew that something was wrong.

Something was really wrong.

2.

I WAS A NERVOUS DRIVER even with Ivy in the passenger seat, coaching me through lane changes and turns. Alone, I crept along the highway at fifteen miles per hour, gripping the steering wheel with slick palms. I winced every time a semi whooshed past, leaving a tsunami of rainwater in its wake. I kept glancing in the rearview mirror, expecting to see red and blue lights spinning behind me.

Although Mom claimed she wanted to stay under the radar, it simply wasn't in her nature to blend in, and Spud was a total police magnet. Not only was the ancient VW van plastered with bumper stickers like *Visualize Whirled Peas*, she had also hand-painted it with a wraparound forest scene. Worst of all: the biodiesel that it ran on smelled like old french fries.

Hence the nickname.

WELCOME TO CASCADE, POPULATION 8, 474, a sign informed me as I crossed back into city limits.

Minus four, I thought with a pang.

Even though Cascade wasn't much of a city, I missed living there. I missed our grandma, who had acted like a mom to all three of us. I missed living in a normal house instead of a trailer on the edge of a state park, eight miles out of town.

"The edge of heaven," Mom liked to call it, having skimmed some book on the power of positive thinking. She was determined to see our downsizing as an opportunity. But her version of positive thinking meant turning a blind eye to problems. Such as the fact the redwoods surrounding the trailer were prone to come crashing down in storms, and any one of them could crush the Airstream like a soda can. Or that the septic tank flooded whenever there was a rainstorm, which was just about the only time Bryan didn't come around.

When Mom got pulled over for speeding last summer, the police discovered an ounce of pot in the glove compartment. She claimed that it was Bryan's, that she never touched the stuff herself, but a blood test proved otherwise. She ended up with a DUI that cost her $6,000 (which she was still paying back), and a suspended driver's license. Unfortunately, this happened right after we moved, so Ivy was forced to become our chauffeur, running all of Mom's errands and driving the two of us to and from school. She never complained about that, but I felt bad now that I thought about how she never got a break.

Today, as usual, it was pouring. Only one of Spud's windshield wipers worked—if by *worked* you mean that it swished the rain back and forth—making me squint to see through the smeary glass. Having lived my whole life in Oregon, you'd think I would have gotten used to the unending rain. But it still had the power to infect my mood, which was already dire. Sometimes, I wondered why we hadn't all evolved to sprout gills.

There were almost no parking spots left when I finally pulled into the school parking lot, and I was soaked by the time I made it, panting and drenched, into the building. The bell had rung, and the halls were thinning out as the last stragglers hurried to class.

I was pretty sure that Ivy had PE first period on Fridays, so I sprinted to the gym and pressed my face to the window in the door. I watched as a dodgeball game began, hoping she would appear.

Ten minutes later, I finally gave up, a dull ache in my stomach.

"How nice of you to honor us with an appearance, Ms. Goodwin," Ms. Owen said as I slipped into sophomore English. I muttered an apology, keeping my head down to avoid her look of disappointment in me. By now, I was all too familiar with that look.

The only empty desk was in the back row, next to a new kid named Jasper Blake. With just four hundred students in the school—

most of whom I'd known since kindergarten—any recent arrival at Cascade High was bound to stick out. This guy was particularly noticeable among the thick-necked jocks dominating our social scene (or lack thereof).

I'd seen him around the halls, but never in this class before. He looked at least seventeen, so I wondered why he'd suddenly been transferred into sophomore English. Maybe he wasn't that bright, which would have been only fair, considering how he'd scored in the looks department. He was tall and lean, with olive skin and a mess of dark-brown hair that flopped in his eyes and over the tops of his ears, like it hadn't met scissors in months. He wore faded jeans, a black T-shirt washed to a tissue paper thinness, and a hoodie the color of the storm clouds brewing outside the windows.

As I slung off my backpack, I managed to knock his copy of *Frankenstein* off his desk. Flustered, I bent down to pick it up. It wasn't the school-issued paperback—it was a hardcover with a dark-brown leather cover and gilt-edged pages. It reminded me of the first editions I'd seen behind a glass case at a used bookstore in Portland, and fantasized about collecting someday.

"Sorry," I mumbled as I handed it back. "Nice book. Is it an antique?" I bit my lip. "I hope I didn't damage it."

"It's ancient, but don't worry about it," he said under his breath. "Books were made to last back in the day."

Ms. Owen cleared her throat, crossing her arms over her generous bosom. "You two back there! Laurel Goodwin, and—what did you say your name was?"

"Jasper," he said. "Jasper Blake."

"Save the sweet nothings for after class, please."

As the other kids tittered, I felt my cheeks get red and blotchy—an unfortunate side effect of redheadedness. (As if being covered in freckles weren't bad enough.) I pulled out my paperback *Frankenstein* and tried to tune in, but my mind kept veering back to Ivy.

Where is she?

"Peyton, can you read for us?" Ms. Owen said. "Chapter five. Page one hundred and two."

In front of me, Peyton Andersen's white-blonde hair was styled into loose curls, so she looked like a Disney mermaid. Peyton was the head Skittle, a nickname Ivy and I had made up for these two sophomore girls who acted like conjoined twins, always wearing the same skimpy outfit in different fruity colors. Her best friend Mei was Chinese American, but somehow she and Peyton still managed to look alike, maybe because they both wore identically vapid expressions most of the time. The Skittles lived to make my life miserable, but only if I was by myself, since even they couldn't fail to recognize that Ivy had them lapped in the cool department, with actual talent that money couldn't buy.

Peyton read the passage in which the monster comes to life, managing to make it sound as riveting as a grocery list. While she droned on and on, Ms. Owen paced the aisles. With her tapestry vest and Birkenstocks, and her gray hair pulled into a bun, she looked like a hippie grandma—but behind her glasses, her gaze was pure steel.

"Laurel?" She came to a sudden stop, looming over me. "What motivates the monster to kill?"

"Uh . . . he's a monster," I said. "I mean, that's what monsters do, right?"

"Did you do the assigned reading?" she asked.

I nodded, looking down. I'd just gotten started when Bryan swaggered out of the shower yesterday. We'd been alone in the trailer, and even though it is ridiculously small, I felt like he went out of his way to brush against me as we passed each other. So I shut myself in the bedroomette, where Ivy found me later, still shaken. That's what triggered the blow-up with Mom. My eyes prickled at the thought of how Ivy had my back—then and always. But if Ms. Owen noticed that I was upset, it didn't move her one bit.

"So that's your in-depth analysis?" she said. "He's monstrous because he's a monster?"

I tried to remember the movie but came up blank. "Um . . ."

"He just needs a date," Jasper spoke up. Relief spilled over me.

"Excuse me?" Ms. Owen said.

"He's lonely," Jasper continued. "All he wants is a girlfriend, and Victor Frankenstein—the only person who can make him one—refuses. Seems like that would be enough to make anyone mad." I threw him a grateful smile, noticing the way his shoulders filled his old T-shirt. He seemed at ease in his own skin in this way that made me realize how awkward and jerky the other boys in my class were.

A few kids giggled, and I expected Ms. Owen to get pissed, but she was actually nodding for a change. To my dismay, her laser-beam attention shifted back to me. "That's right," she said, peering over the rim of her glasses at me again. "The power of a great writer like Mary Shelley is knowing that for characters to be convincing, we must understand the thing that drives them. For the monster, it's his yearning to find a mate." I felt myself blushing again as she went on. "Speaking of unfulfilled desires . . ." She paused, shuffling away to her desk and then returning to hold a paper under my nose.

I recognized the story I'd turned in a week ago, "Heart of Stone." I had been really excited when Ms. Owen said that anyone who wanted to earn extra credit could submit a piece of creative writing. English was usually my best subject, the one thing in which I consistently got all As, but so far I was off to a rocky start with Ms. Owen. This had seemed like my chance to show her what I was capable of.

The prompt was to create a character who wants something they can't have. I stayed up all night, writing about this girl who falls for a boy who turns everything he touches to stone. In the end, she decides she'd rather turn to stone than remain untouched by him. When they finally kiss for the first time, she turns into a statue beneath his hands, her lips frozen in a pucker. I wrote from the girl's point of view, so the last sentence trailed off as her mind turned to stone as well. I was pretty happy with it, especially after I read it to Ivy and she said that it gave her chills.

"This was a clever idea," Ms. Owen said, "but I'm afraid the characters never came to life." She dropped the story on my desk. The words—*my* words—were covered in so much red ink, I could barely read them anymore. I hoped she'd move on, now that she'd embarrassed me in front of everyone, but she seemed to want to rub salt in the wound.

"I mean who is this girl *really*?" she said. "What does she see in this boy, aside from the 'sparkle of his ultraviolet eyes'?" Lest I miss her sarcasm, she put those words in finger quotes. I shrugged, my face burning. "And what about him?" she pressed on. "If everything he touches turns to stone, then how does he eat?"

Ouch.

"I don't know," I finally mumbled. "I didn't really think through that part. It's just, like, a fantasy story."

"Well, I think you can do better," she said sternly. "A lot better."

My eyes prickled with tears. I tried to ignore her, hoping she'd just go away—but Ms. Owen was like a pit bull, jaws locked on its prey.

"If you're serious about becoming a writer, then I suggest you spend more time thinking about what makes people tick," she said. "Use your real-life observations to create fictional characters with a pulse. This girl feels like a statue even before she turns into one."

My vision filmed over and I tried not to blink, knowing that would make the tears fall. Normally, I wouldn't have broken down like this in English over a stupid story, but I didn't know how much more I could take today.

Everyone was staring at me.

Except for Jasper.

He seemed to be gazing at some point at the front of the classroom, oddly focused, although there was nothing in particular to see there.

Then I smelled it: very faint at first, but unmistakable.

Burning.

Behind Ms. Owen, a curlicue of smoke rose from the garbage can. Something crackled very quietly, like a twig snapping in the woods. Then a flame shot up over the rim. Half the class screamed, not so much in fear as in delight that something was happening for a change. As the flame whooshed up, Ms. Owen scuttled backwards, as if hoping to use the students in the front row as a buffer between herself and the fire.

People leaped to their feet. Uber-jock Stu Sheers smashed the glass on the fire alarm, and the air filled with the pealing of the bell. Everyone rushed out the door, pushing and shoving. Ms. Owen yelled at us to hurry and I grabbed my backpack. Only Jasper didn't move. When I left the room, he was still pinned in his chair, staring at that blaze as if he didn't want to get an inch closer to it. He couldn't have had anything to do with that fire—I was sitting right beside him, so if he had, I would've seen it—but still, I couldn't shake the feeling that he was behind it somehow, that he'd come to my rescue.

3.

WHILE THE ENTIRE STUDENT BODY huddled in front of the school in the rain, waiting for the firefighters to give the all-clear, I milled through the crowd, still searching for Ivy. Everyone was discussing how the fire might have started. Someone speculated that an idiot must have tossed a cigarette into the garbage can. Another popular theory was that the window had somehow magnified a ray of sun, igniting the balled-up paper. Never mind the obvious facts that a) no one had been smoking in English class, and b) the sun hadn't made a cameo in weeks. I glanced around to see if Jasper was there, but he must have taken off.

Talk shifted to the big party that Stu Sheers was throwing that night, and I quickly tuned out the scintillating discussion of how long it would take to tap out three kegs. I cornered a few of Ivy's friends, asking if they'd seen her, but no one had since volleyball practice yesterday.

At last, the principal came out and herded everyone back inside with his giant megaphone. Instead of heading to class, I headed straight for Ivy's locker, just in case she'd been by to drop off her stuff, and spun her combination:1-0-3-1. When we set our locks, we'd chosen each other's birthdays. Mine fell on Halloween, which was a week away. There was going to be a lunar eclipse that night, and the hall was plastered with posters advertising the "Dark Side Dance" that would take place in the gym.

Ivy and I were planning to go together. When she'd first brought up the idea, I'd informed her that the high school gym was the last place on earth I'd willingly choose to spend my sixteenth birthday. But when she offered to make me a dress for a birthday present, I found myself wavering.

"All eyes will be on you," she'd promised.

"That's kind of what I'm afraid of," I said.

I finally gave in. She'd never designed a piece of clothing especially for me before, and I'll admit it—part of me was dying to see what she'd come up with. But even though my birthday was just a week away, I hadn't seen Ivy sewing anything, which was strange. Usually she was working on multiple projects at once, our table buried under piles of fabric. Our grandma had taught her how to sew, and by now she was good enough to make her own designs. She earned a little money doing alterations for Second Act, the local vintage store. The school's new guidance counselor, Simone Sinclair, had even been encouraging her to try out for *Project Runway*.

Ivy first met Simone at summer camp, which had been a huge disappointment to her. It had been billed as an arts and crafts camp, and fashion design was one of the featured activities on the flyer. But it was funded by the Faith Center—the megachurch run by Peyton Andersen's dad—and according to Ivy, tie-dying camp T-shirts was the closest they came to fashion design. But at least she had gotten to know Simone, who'd recently moved to Cascade from New York City. Ivy told me that it was Simone who'd given Ivy her black denim jacket when she was cold one night. She wore that jacket almost all the time now, which was why it freaked me out to see it hanging in our closet.

When school started up in September, Ivy had been thrilled to find out that Simone had taken a counselor position at our school. She'd started going to talk to her during her free periods. "Things have been so crazy lately," she'd tried explaining to me. "It helps to talk everything over with someone who's trained to listen, you know?" I'd nodded, but I didn't really get it. Sure, I hated being squashed in a trailer, especially with Bryan around. And when I tried to wrap my mind around the fact that we'd never see our grandma again, it felt like a concrete block was crushing my chest. But I couldn't imagine opening up about any of this stuff to a stranger.

Still, Simone wasn't a stranger to Ivy. Ivy trusted her, talked about her like they were friends. Ivy said that Simone had told all of the kids who came to see her in counseling sessions to call her by her first name, but it always sounded weird to me. Maybe I was just jealous because I didn't have anyone to open up to besides Ivy.

Then, it hit me—maybe Ivy was with Simone.

At the other end of the hall, I could see that Simone's office door was shut. A light shone underneath it, which meant she was probably in a session with a student right now. Maybe it was Ivy! I flew down the hall and burst in without knocking.

But the loveseat facing the counselor's desk was empty.

"Can I help you?" Simone said, getting up from behind her desk. I'd never seen her this close before, and I was taken aback by how tiny she was, so young and stylish compared to the other members of the Cascade High faculty. She had a glossy mahogany bob and wide brown eyes accentuated by thick streaks of eyeliner. Her gray dress flowed like molten silver, set off by red stockings and high-heeled black boots. She looked like a different species from the teachers in their orthopedic shoes and appliquéd sweatshirts.

"I'm, uh, looking for my sister," I said, feeling stupid to have barged in.

"Ivy Goodwin?" she guessed, and I nodded, surprised that she'd made the connection. "You have the same eyes," she said. This was true—we both had our grandma's hazel eyes—but otherwise we were total opposites. Ivy had inherited our mom's blonde curls and permanently tan skin, while I had the skim-milk complexion to go with my red hair. Ivy was athletic and curvy, whereas I was what Grandma called a "late bloomer," meaning that at fifteen, I barely needed a bra. Ivy was just thirteen months older than me—"Irish twins"—and I joked that she must have soaked up the good stuff in utero.

"Have you seen Ivy today?" I asked Simone hopefully.

"No, I don't think so." Simone crossed the office, shutting the door. "Why? Is something wrong?"

"Maybe. I don't know. I'm afraid she might be in trouble," I said, surprising myself with this admission. I never confided in strangers, not about anything having to do with our family. But her sympathetic expression was too much for me, and I was so tired that I sank down onto the loveseat, giving in to the tears that had been on the verge of falling all morning.

She turned on a space heater, and as the blast of hot air enveloped me like a warm bath, I told her about waking up to find Ivy missing. I explained Mom's theory that Ivy was trying to teach her a lesson because she refused to see what a creep Bryan was. "But she would never have left without telling me. I'm sure something's wrong."

Simone sat beside me, listening so intently that I started to understand why Ivy liked coming in here and talking to her. But as her face shifted from sympathy to worry, I realized that the thing I wanted most—for someone else to take this as seriously as I did—could get us into a different kind of trouble. Even if Ivy considered Simone a friend, she was actually a guidance counselor who worked for the school district. If she believed that Ivy was missing, it would be her duty to go to the police, wouldn't it?

As she jotted something down, all of the saliva in my mouth evaporated. "I'm sure I'm just freaking out for nothing," I said, backpedaling as fast as I could. I wiped my eyes and forced the corners of my mouth up. "She probably just met up with her new boyfriend last night and fell asleep at his place. I don't know why I got so worked up."

"Her disappearance is very troubling," she said, tilting her head to one side so that the blunt edge of her bob brushed her shoulder. "Do you think your mom's boyfriend—Bryan?—poses a real threat?" She picked up a notepad.

Much as I wanted to get rid of Bryan, I couldn't give Simone any reason to go to the police. "No," I said quickly. "He's kind of annoying, but he would never hurt her." I wasn't one hundred percent sure of this, but I needed her to back off.

Why had I been so stupid?

"I'm sure she'll be home this afternoon." I hugged one of Simone's silky pillows to my chest, wishing my heart would stop pounding. "Please don't call the police," I said. "I really don't want Ivy to get in trouble."

Simone took a long inhale, a worry line still creasing the skin between her eyebrows. "Well, it's only been a few hours, and there was no sign of a break-in, right?" I shook my head, and that line seemed to fade slightly. "I don't need to call them yet. But if you haven't tracked her down by this evening, you should call them yourself."

I nodded, wishing it were that simple, and then reminding myself that I did have a habit of getting worked up over nothing. When I got home and Ivy was there, I'd be very glad that I hadn't done something regrettable.

"I know your mother," Simone said. "Sheila, right? We went to school here together."

"You grew up here?" I asked, surprised.

She nodded. "I was a few years ahead of your mom, but I recognized her name when I saw her show of paintings in the coffeehouse last spring. I was visiting Bill, trying to decide if I should move back to Cascade or not, and part of what persuaded me was this incredibly beautiful art on display. I told her he absolutely had to hire this phenomenal local artist to do the backdrops for his museum."

Everyone knew that Simone was dating Bill Sheers, the closest thing we had to royalty in Cascade. He'd made his fortune in lumber, but now that the last old-growth forests were under environmental protection, he was doing his best to reinvent Cascade as a tourist town. Under his influence, Miner Street was starting to look like a Disneyland attraction, with fake bullet holes in the swinging saloon doors, a gallery that sold beaded moccasins and dream catchers, a gold panning "crick" behind the antique store, and—scheduled to open in just a week—a museum of natural history, housed on his very own property. I remembered the day he'd called, asking if Mom wanted to paint the backdrops for the dioramas, how thrilled she'd been to finally get paid for her art again.

"You got her that job?" I asked.

"She earned it. Bill couldn't be more pleased with her murals." She smiled. "Artistic talent clearly runs in your family. I keep telling

Ivy that she's going to be the next Coco Chanel. And I hear you're quite a writer?"

"Not really," I said, cringing at the memory of how Ms. Owen eviscerated my story. Ivy was the only person who truly believed in me, and she pretty much had to say that she liked my writing, since she was my sister and everything.

Simone reached out for my hand. "It's going to be okay," she said. She squeezed my fingers, and even though I didn't have any reason to believe her, I did feel a tiny bit better.

4.

AT LUNCH, I asked the school secretary if I could make a call home, and Mom picked up on the first ring, sounding disappointed to find out it was just me. Ivy wasn't back yet. I trudged into the cafeteria, hoping against hope that my sister would be having lunch with her volleyball team. I could almost see her waving me over. But she wasn't there.

"You're in luck today. Tamale pie," the cafeteria lady said, hacking off a square that landed with a thump on my plate. I tried to smile. She was nice, always remembering that Ivy and I didn't eat meat, and if the entrée wasn't vegetarian, she'd give us extra sides. But the tamale pie smelled like BO and I couldn't stomach it.

"I think I'll get a yogurt," I said.

"That doesn't come with the free lunch," she reminded me, right as the Skittles blew past the hot food line. Mei Rosen made a gagging noise, and I heard Peyton Andersen pretend-cough the words, "Trailer trash."

Trying to pretend I hadn't heard, I looked around. As usual, every table was already claimed: turf staked, lines drawn. The volleyball team would let me sit with them, even if Ivy was gone, but I didn't feel like having to explain where she was, so I decided to take my yogurt to the library, which was in a separate building on the other side of the football field. As I hiked across the grass, the mud sucked at the soles of my biker boots.

The school's new library was more like a computer lab. I knew I should be grateful, since it was the first time we'd had a library in Cascade since the original burned to the ground in some huge fire long, long ago—even before Grandma was born. Mr. Sheers had donated the services of his construction crew over the summer, and the building was all glass and steel, with solar panels in the roof. The whole collection was digital, which begged the question of why we needed a librarian.

Mrs. Bennet—who'd worked the bookmobile before this—was old school (not to mention just plain old) and strict about enforcing library rules. But there was a note on her desk saying that she'd be back in five minutes, so I seized the chance to eat my lunch at one of the glass-walled study pods before she returned. I tore the foil off my yogurt and logged in to my email to see if Ivy had sent me anything.

Nope.

I was checking her Facebook page in hopes of a new post when I heard the voices of the very girls I'd been trying to avoid. My stomach sank as I watched Peyton and Mei drape themselves over the scanner in the aisle. I'd forgotten that last week, they'd written *Mrs. Bennett is a virgin* in Sharpie on one of the library's glass walls, and as their punishment they had to scan old issues of the *Cascade Tribune* into the digital archive. They had their backs to me, so they didn't see me sitting there, but they made no effort to keep their voices down.

"Are you going to Stu's party tonight?" Peyton asked her conjoined twin.

"Duh. I pretty much have to go to my own boyfriend's party." Mei combed her fingers through her black hair, which was as shiny as patent leather. She was the star of every school play; she loved to be looked at, and everyone obliged.

"I thought you guys broke up," Peyton said.

"Why would you think that?" Mei asked.

"Jamal is telling everyone that Stu got tired of waiting for you to put out."

"We have too done it!" Mei squealed. "It was amazing. It *is* amazing. Trust me—we do it all the time!"

"You slut!" Peyton made this sound like a huge compliment. She paused, and then declared, "If that new guy shows, I am totally going to hook up with him."

"What new guy?" Mei asked.

"The new guy with the incredible green eyes? Jasper Blake? Let it be known that I claim him."

I felt myself tense up, even though I hardly knew the guy.

"You can't 'claim' someone." Mei laughed.

"Watch and learn." Peyton was acting like she already had his head on her pillow. And that was where it would surely end up, since she got everything she wanted, like the red Mini she'd gotten for her sixteenth, wrapped in a giant silver bow in her driveway.

The bell rang and I ducked out of my study pod, hoping I could slip past without them noticing. But no such luck. As I barreled toward the exit, Peyton stepped directly in front of me. "Laurel! Ooh, I love your outfit. And what is that—yogurt?" She pointed at a smear on my sweater. "It adds a nice splash of beige." When I didn't answer, she shook her head at me disapprovingly. "How is it even possible that you're Ivy's sister?"

I opened my mouth, but as usual a snappy comeback failed me. This was one reason I liked writing: it gave me time to find the perfect words.

Mei took over the attack. "Where *do* you get your style inspiration—Mrs. Bennett? Since she's, like, your best friend, do you get to raid her closet?"

Peyton squinted at me. "That sweater actually does look familiar. Wait—was that my mom's? No, seriously—she always gives stuff she's throwing out to the maid! She must have given it to your mom before she fired her!"

Suddenly it felt like my skin was crawling with fire ants. The worst part was, Peyton wasn't imaginative enough to make this up. Mom did used to clean the Andersen house, and I *had* taken this particular sweater from her closet. I'd just assumed she'd scored it at the Goodwill. I was dying to rip it off and throw it in the trash, but I couldn't give Peyton the satisfaction of seeing how much she'd bothered me.

All I could do was march out of the library to the soundtrack of their laughter.

By the time the dismissal bell rang, I was desperate to get home. *Ivy will be there,* I told myself, *with a simple explanation.*

I'd just slammed my locker shut when I saw Jasper leaning over the water fountain. "Hey," he said. As he straightened and our eyes briefly met, I had to admit that Peyton had a point about this one thing. His eyes really were incredible: bright green with flecks of gold, offset by his olive skin and dark hair.

A guy that good-looking has to be a jerk.

"Laurel, right?" he said, and I nodded. He seemed to be about to say something else, but before he could, Peyton and Mei were back, surrounding him and cutting me off. With their pale down jackets and skinny legs, they looked like marshmallows on sticks.

"Jasper Blake," Peyton trilled. "That's such a cool name, Jasper." She twirled a blonde curl around one finger.

"Thanks." He strode through the exit while we trailed after him. I didn't want to tag along, but Spud happened to be parked by Peyton's Mini at the back of the lot, as far from the faculty spots as possible.

"Where'd you come from, Jasper?" she went on. "Have we met? Because you look kind of familiar. Have you done any modeling?"

Could she get any cheesier?

He shook his head. "I'm from here, actually, but I've been away for a long time."

"Details, please," she said.

"Maybe another time."

My heart skipped. *Is he actually brushing her off?* If so, she couldn't take a hint.

"How about at the party tonight?" she persisted. "You are going to Stu's, right?"

"I didn't know about it," he said. "Are you going to be there?"

"Of course." She giggled. "It's going to be epic."

I knew I was probably kidding myself, but I'd had this feeling that he'd been speaking to me. He glanced at me over her head again, and for a moment I couldn't tear my eyes away. Peyton seemed oblivious as she surveyed the parking lot. "So, which one's your ride?" she asked him.

"I don't have a car," he said, shrugging.

"That's weird," she said, which made me roll my eyes. Lots of kids didn't own cars. Only the rich ones like Peyton took it for granted that they'd be given a car on their sixteenth birthday, not to mention that their parents would pay for their insurance.

"Well, this is me." She gestured at her lipstick-red Mini. "Want a lift?"

"No, thanks," he said.

At her look of shock, I felt like singing. *No, thanks!* I couldn't help smiling as they pulled away. But I should've known better than to gloat, because when I turned the key in the ignition, Spud's engine refused to start. The geriatric battery died a lot, but Ivy could always persuade someone to give us a jump. Unfortunately, I'd never paid attention to what she did with the cables. I didn't even know where they were stored.

"Come on, come on," I muttered, as I kept turning the key. I didn't even realize that Jasper was standing there until he knocked on my window. Feeling humiliated, I rolled it down, and suddenly the delicious scent of autumn bonfires wafted over me.

"Want some help?" he offered.

"That would be great," I said, swallowing my pride. I turned to the passenger seat and lifted the cushion. "The battery's under here. It's this weird quirk of these old VW buses."

"Got it." He walked around and opened the passenger-side door.

"But you'll need . . ." I was going to say that to give me a jump, he'd have to have jumper cables and another car, but he didn't seem to be listening. He was gazing at that battery with such intensity that I wondered what exactly he was seeing.

"Try it now," he said, and when I turned the key again, the engine sprang to life.

"Whoa, that's incredible," I said. "How did you do that?"

"It's no big deal." He looked down, picking up a half-empty package of Red Hots that had fallen in the foot well and placing it on the seat before he shut the door and walked around to my side again.

"Seriously," I said, speaking to him through the open window, "this thing dies all the time, so I'd love to know your trick."

"I didn't do anything," he said, looking down and scratching a frayed patch on his jeans. "I guess it wasn't dead after all."

Obviously he didn't want to discuss it any further. "Well, thanks anyway," I said. "I mean, whatever you did or didn't do, it worked. I'd offer you a ride, but I'm in kind of a hurry. I need to get home and see if my sister's there."

"Ivy, right?"

I nodded, surprised that he knew her name. "Do you know her?" I asked. It wouldn't have been that surprising if he did, since Cascade High was so small, but she'd never mentioned him.

"Just a little." He shrugged. "I've seen the two of you driving home together. You're usually with her, aren't you?"

"She's my best friend," I said, swallowing hard. "I know that sounds corny, but it's true." As the words came out, I felt my throat cinch up.

"I get it," Jasper said. "That's how I feel about my older brother."

"Does he go to Cascade High too?"

"No. Toby's much older than me." He shoved both hands in the pocket of his hoodie. "He left home when I was a kid, but we've stayed close. I'd do anything for him."

"I'd do anything for Ivy too," I said.

"So where is she today? Is she sick or something?"

"No," I said. "I mean, I don't think so. I guess she snuck out last night. She was gone this morning. I called home at lunch and she wasn't back yet." My feeling of panic returned, high and tight in my chest.

Jasper frowned. "Can you think of any reason she might have taken off for the day?"

"She and my mom had a fight about my mom's boyfriend. Mom thinks that was it."

Jasper nodded. "I bet she'll be home when you get back."

I hoped he was right. The rain was taking a break for once, and a little watery sunshine filtered through the clouds. Jasper was standing very still, like he was waiting, watching for something. His face was close enough that I could see his eyes more clearly now, and they were as green as leaves freshly washed by the rain. I couldn't forget about the way he'd stared at the engine. The same way he'd stared at the trash bin in Ms. Owen's class.

"Thanks again for coming to my rescue," I said. "That battery was totally dead before you got in here. You must have done something."

He shrugged, just one shoulder lifting and lowering. "It was just a coincidence."

"Just a coincidence, like the way you saved me in English class?"

Jasper raised his eyebrows. "What are you saying? You think I started that fire?"

I laughed, trying to make it less awkward. I glanced at his eyes again, which were looking into mine so intensely that I had to look down at the car door handle. "Yeah, that's what I'm saying." I'd meant it sarcastically, but it didn't come out that way. "You can make things burst into flame with your eyes."

Instead of responding, he just stared at me like he couldn't believe what I'd said. Which, I now realized, sounded like some kind of totally cheesy pick-up line. His eyes were admittedly gorgeous, but they were just regular eyes.

"Uh, see you around," I said, my cheeks burning, now desperate to get away.

"I'm supposed to meet Ivy at Ritual tomorrow morning," Jasper said. "Tell her that I'll see her there, okay?"

I gulped.

It was so obvious. Why hadn't I realized this as soon as he asked about her?

Clearly *he* was the person she'd been sneaking out to meet all fall. It made perfect sense. Here was this gorgeous new guy who didn't fit in. Neither did my super-talented—and did I mention, *gorgeous*— older sister. It didn't take a genius to see why they'd be attracted to each other.

But why didn't she tell me?

The cliché goes that people who are really close can finish each other's sentences, but Ivy and I always joked that we could *start* each other's, meaning that when something was important to one of us, the other instinctively knew it.

If they were seeing each other, why was she hiding it from me?

Maybe she wanted to spare my feelings, since none of the guys at Cascade High noticed me—not that I cared.

Or maybe she liked having something to herself for a change.

I drove home with a pit in my stomach, Spud's one working windshield wiper fighting against the rain. I couldn't decide if I was upset because she hadn't mentioned something so huge, or because it meant that he was officially off-limits. Either way, I'd never felt this alone.

5.

WHEN I GOT HOME, I rushed inside, sure that I'd find Ivy or at least some sign that she'd been home, but the place was empty. The bedroomette looked exactly as I'd left it. I kicked off my boots, wrapped Ivy's quilt around myself, and wandered into the kitchen, which was where we always hung out after school.

Mom had found diner chairs with glittery red seats to match Grandma's table. She'd strung fairy lights over the cabinets, and we'd covered the fridge with our favorite photos. I stared at one of Ivy and me doing cartwheels at the Oregon coast last summer. We were upside down, our wet hair falling in our faces, and you could tell we were having a blast.

Please come home. I willed the thought to reach her.

I don't know how much time passed before I heard a car pulling up. I jumped to my feet, but it was only Mom getting dropped off by her best friend, Poppy. They'd known each other since high school, and Poppy could be counted on to take Mom grocery shopping when Ivy wasn't available. Normally I would've run out to give her a hug before she drove off, but right now I could only think about Ivy.

"She wasn't at school!" I pounced on Mom before she made it through the door. "She's still missing."

For a minute, she just stood there in her paint-spattered overalls, swaying slightly. "I was sure she'd be there." She pinched the space between her eyes again. "I don't know what to do, Lolo."

I didn't have a clue either, but I knew that someone had to take charge. "I'm going to make you some coffee," I said, because Ivy always said that caffeine would stave off a headache, and I needed to keep Mom on her feet. "And then you have got to call the police. I know you don't want to, but it's been almost twenty-four hours. Something is seriously wrong."

She gave the tiniest of nods, which chilled me to the core. If Mom was willing to call the police, it was officially time to panic.

But as I grabbed the carafe from the coffee maker, I noticed something. Tucked underneath it was a sheet of lined paper, neatly folded.

"Oh my God!" I opened it up. "Mom!" I breathed. "I think it's a note from Ivy."

She huddled beside me so we could read it together.

Dear Mom,

I'm sorry for taking off like this, but I think we both need to cool down. I hate the way you always put Bryan first. He is a total creep, and I don't know why you can't see that. Don't freak out. I'm just going to visit my friend from camp. She lives up in Portland. They've got this week off for fall break, and she'll give me a ride home on Halloween. You don't need to worry about me.

XOXO
Ivy

"Well, that's a relief," Mom said at last. "I was getting really scared."

I reread the note several times, squinting at the words as if they were written in a foreign language. "I can't believe she wrote this," I said.

"What do you mean?" Mom said. "It's her handwriting."

"But I made coffee this morning. I would've seen this note, I'm sure."

"It was the crack of dawn," she reminded me. "You were exhausted." She sighed. "I wish you two wouldn't be so hard on Bryan. He hasn't called, has he?"

"What about your missing daughter!" I exploded. "Don't you care about her?"

"Of course I do, but she's not missing. She's in Portland."

I began to pace, looking out the window at the dark sky and the darker forest beyond. "But how did she get there? It's three hours away."

"Laurel, her friend must have picked her up."

"What friend?" Doubt washed over me in waves. "She hated that camp! She said she couldn't relate to anyone." I ran to our room and came back with a postcard, brandishing it in front of me like a weapon. "Look!"

> *This so-called art camp sucks. Wish you were here, or even better—wish I WASN'T! I truly don't know if I can make it through a whole week. Ugh.*
> *Ives.*

Mom skimmed it, then once again declared that the handwriting was the same as on the note. I studied it more closely. "No, it's not," I said. "Look—there's no stars on this note."

"What are you talking about?" It was clear that Mom was fed up, and her expression didn't soften as I tried to explain that Ivy always dotted her *i*'s with stars.

We had nearly matching birthmarks on the inside of our wrists—hers was on her right wrist, and mine was on my left—that looked a little bit like stars. As kids, we used to pretend that they were the source of superpowers that we could activate by holding hands. In our notes to each other, we always dotted our *i*'s with stars.

"But this note wasn't for you, Laurel," Mom pointed out.

I sat down, crossing my arms on the table and resting my cheek on them. She sighed and sat beside me, placing her hand on the back of my head. "You know," she said more gently, "I was seventeen, just like Ivy, when I went on the road to follow Phish. I thought I had to get away from everyone who knew me, to discover who I really was."

"But Ivy knows who she is," I protested.

"Don't worry, Lolo. She'll be back on your birthday, just like she said."

Halloween. My birthday. I hadn't even registered that this was when she said she'd be getting a ride back.

As a little kid, I didn't like it that my birthday fell on Halloween, because it meant that everyone was busy trick-or-treating, and it wasn't really my special day. But Ivy managed to turn this to my advantage. We'd go trick-or-treating together, and at every door, she'd announce that it was my birthday, so I should get at least twice the candy. By the end of the night, my pillowcase would be so full that she'd have to help me lug it home.

This year, we were supposed to go to the DMV right after school. She was sure I'd pass my test, even though the mere thought of it was enough to give me a panic attack. Of course, this was before I'd been forced to drive myself to and from school. Maybe this was part of some twisted plan she'd hatched to make me spend the rest of the week practicing? But Ivy wasn't sadistic. She wouldn't have wanted to freak me out on purpose.

Something's wrong, a voice inside me said.

Or she wasn't thinking of you at all, another, sadder voice said.

The rain started up again. On a good day, there was nothing cozier than the sound of rain striking the metal roof. But right now, that same pinging noise sounded hollow and hopeless. I shivered, forcing myself to admit something. Maybe I was struggling to accept the note because I didn't *want* to believe that Ivy would have left of her own free will, without even telling me. I couldn't deal with the fact that Ivy needed to escape from me in order to be herself—because without her, I didn't know who I was.

6.

Mei

MEI WASN'T IN THE MOOD to go to Stu's party, but she was desperate to get out of her house. It was excruciating sitting at the dinner table with her parents, trying to pretend that tonight was a night like any other.

"How was rehearsal this afternoon?" her dad asked.

"Fine," she said, although it had been amazing. Mr. Dominguez had told her that she'd brought an incredible *"va-va-voom"* to her performance, and she was "on the verge of a serious breakthrough."

Those were his words, exactly. *Serious. Breakthrough.*

"We're really looking forward to seeing you play Anne Frank," her mom said.

"Great." Mei twisted a clump of noodles around her fork. She knew that her parents—both doctors—wished that she spent more time on schoolwork instead of drama.

Her dad cast her a reproachful look. Earlier that afternoon, he had taken Mei aside and said, "Remember that it's a hard day for your mom, so be extra nice, okay?" That was the only time he'd brought up the fact that this was the day that their first daughter was killed in a car accident, when she was sixteen years old. Just a few months later, they had gone to China to adopt Mei as a baby.

She caught her mom gazing sadly at the rivulets of wine trickling down the side of her glass, pressing her lips with her fingertips.

Mr. Dominguez was right. "You can capture someone's essence by mimicking things they don't realize they're doing," he had taught her. "That's the key to being able to embody them onstage."

Embody. That word gave Mei the shivers. Although her parents were nice to her, she couldn't help but feel like Daughter #2, the understudy brought in to play the part of their real child. They never talked about their dead daughter, but Mei sometimes felt like she was supposed to *embody* Rachel, to live the life she'd been deprived of, in a way she couldn't really fathom, let alone pull off.

In her room after dinner, Mei shook out her freshly shampooed hair, as if doing so could shake the morbid thoughts out of her mind. She put on a one-shouldered pink dress with tiny black polka dots, slipped into her peep-toe heels, and applied sparkly lip gloss on her mouth. She was swiping on eye shadow when Peyton texted that she was in the driveway. Mei ran downstairs, once again eager to leave. When she saw her mom hunched at the kitchen table, still nursing that wine, she felt a twinge of guilt. But she swept the feeling aside, kissed her on the cheek, and darted out the door before her mom could tell her to put on a jacket and ruin her look.

Rain lashed the windshield of the Mini, and Mei felt like grabbing the steering wheel from Peyton, who was driving with one hand, scrolling through her phone for music with the other.

"Tonight's the night," Peyton said. "If Jasper is there, I am going to pounce."

"Totally," Mei said, making a sexy meow sound and clawing the air.

"You and Stu can sneak up to his room for some serious quality time—nudge nudge, wink wink."

"I guess," Mei said. The feeling she'd been trying to escape at her house pricked her again. Peyton shot her a puzzled glance. "I mean, hell yeah!" Mei amended, trying to inject the proper note of desire into her tone.

Mei hadn't meant to lie about having slept with Stu, but Peyton was always going on about how it incredible it had been with this camp counselor named Remy, and Mei didn't want to seem like a prude. But the truth was, it had been six months since she and Stu first got together, and although they sometimes kissed until her lips felt all pruney, he'd never once tried to feel her up. At first she'd appreciated that he was taking things slow, but she was starting to think they just didn't have any chemistry.

Everyone said that Stu was so hot, that she was so lucky to be with him—a popular senior and quarterback of the football team—but sometimes she felt like she was playing a part she didn't want anymore.

The driveway leading up to the gate was already packed with cars, so they had to park in a muddy ditch and dash through the rain. Goose bumps covered Mei's arms and legs, and she could feel the throbbing bass beat rising up through her toes as they sprinted toward Stu's house, which he called "the shack," his idea of a hilarious joke.

Perched on a bluff overlooking the Klamath River, it looked like a ski lodge made of giant Lincoln Logs. By day, the floor-to-ceiling windows captured the view of the pine trees covering the hillside that plunged down to the river. Now, the glass flashed violet and black, violet and black, in time with the music.

Climbing the front steps, Mei took a few deep breaths. For a moment, she felt resentful that Stu had chosen to throw a rager tonight of all nights. But, she reminded herself, he had no idea what this date meant to her. She'd never mentioned Rachel to him, as they never talked about anything that mattered. But as she reached the front door, her irritation lifted and a current rippled through her, reminding her of the jittery excitement she felt right before curtain call.

The mansion already swarmed with kids: filling the hallway, bobbing to the music, crowding the enormous kitchen nobody cooked in. Stu's mom had died when he was a baby, and he'd been raised by nannies. But now that he was a senior, he took care of himself, living on Taco Bell when his dad was away on business trips, like tonight.

"I'm going to get us refreshments," Peyton yelled, pushing into the kitchen.

Mei nodded and wandered into the great room. Above the fireplace, a sixteen-point stag head scowled at the kids lounging across the white leather sectional. Stu was sitting beside Jamal, playing quarters. He was wearing a baseball cap backwards, and the high school's purple tracksuit pants—not Mei's idea of how a guy should dress for a party. When he spotted her, he jumped up and grabbed her by the waist, sloshing beer on her dress as he pulled her down onto his lap.

"My leading lady," he said, lifting a fist to muffle a wet burp. She perched awkwardly on his knee, yanking down her hem. Stu offered her his cup, but she took one look at the inch of warm backwash and shook her head.

"How's the acting going, Mei?" Jamal slurred. The words were neutral enough, but his tone was somehow sarcastic. Jamal didn't have a girlfriend, and Mei often got the feeling that he resented her for monopolizing Stu's time.

"Pretty good," she said.

"Opening night is this week," Stu informed him. "Next stop, Hollywood!"

"You're playing Anne Frank, right?" Jamal asked. "But you're not Jewish."

"Yes, I am," she said. "Besides, a real actress can embody anyone."

"Would you ever go topless?" Jamal asked.

"Um, I guess, if the part required it, if I thought it was going to help my career." Mei crossed her arms over her chest, resenting how defensive she felt.

"Would you do a sex tape?" he pushed. Stu cracked up.

"No way!"

"Why not?" Jamal smirked. "I mean, everyone who's famous has made one."

"No, they haven't," she said, but Jamal and Stu were too busy listing the D-list celebrities who'd made sex tapes to listen.

"Doesn't your dad have, like, professional video equipment?" Jamal asked. Stu nodded. "You should totally do it!" He turned back to Mei. "For your career," he said in a falsetto that sounded nothing like her.

When Stu failed to leap to her defense, Mei stood up. "Do you think Meryl Streep made a sex tape?" she asked angrily.

"Who?" Stu asked, burping again.

"There's no point even talking to you!" She stalked off, expecting Stu to come apologize—but he let her go. He was probably pissed that she'd yelled at him in front of his friend. Well, she didn't care.

Still fuming, she wandered into the hallway to break free from the crowd. Her scar—the one at the small of her back—which never bothered her, was driving her nuts. She must have nicked it with her zipper. The lady at the orphanage had told the Rosens that women in China who gave up their babies often marked them so that they might recognize them later. As a child, Mei sometimes fantasized about a beautiful Chinese woman showing up at their door, asking to see her back. But life wasn't some Disney movie. She'd faced the fact that this was never going to happen.

Searching for a place to scratch it in private, she drifted through a set of heavy wooden doors and found herself in the newly remodeled wing of the mansion. A wide corridor lined with dioramas stretched before her. The lights were low, and the scent of fresh paint hung in the air. She jumped at the sight of an enormous mountain lion, its yellow eyes flashing, crouching at the base of a tree as if ready to pounce. Then she came to her senses. The tree was real, growing from a planter. It gave off a piney fragrance, the energy of a living thing. But the mountain lion, statue-still, did not.

She had stumbled into the new museum of natural history, which was full of stuffed animals—not of the cuddly sort, but taxidermied, preserved as they were in death. She saw a wolf, lips retracted in a snarl as it prepared to attack a petrified fox. But her attention returned to the cougar, which seemed to be eyeing her in particular.

This place gave her the creeps. She felt sorry for the animals, unable to stretch or twitch or run. Then she shook herself. The dead didn't care what happened to them. Why couldn't the living wrap their minds around that fact?

Her scar was pulsing now. Listening to the thump of the music from the great room, she decided to get out of here and dance. Maybe that would help.

The party was heating up. Someone had tossed a baseball cap over the stag's antlers, and everyone was competing to decorate it like a Christmas tree. They tossed anything at hand: Mardi Gras beads, plastic cups, jackets.

"BRAS, BRAS, BRAS!" Jamal started this chant, pumping a fist in the air, and soon all the guys joined in. Peyton pulled hers out through the armhole of her shirt and hurled it up. Mei couldn't help but laugh. Maybe she just needed to cut loose. She tore off her belt, swung it like a lasso, and let go.

"Atta girl!" Stu yelled. He was standing next to Jamal, trading swigs off a bottle of apple schnapps. He flashed her a grin, and she found herself smiling back. This was his party, and he deserved to have fun. She made her way to him, wrapping her arms around his waist.

"Sorry about before," she said. "I don't know what's up with me tonight. You know what I'm in the mood for?" *Dancing,* she was about to say, but he spoke first.

"Oh yeah? Right now?" He cleared his throat. "You, uh, want to go up to my room?"

Mei froze. They'd never been alone in his bedroom when his dad wasn't home. Maybe that was why things weren't progressing. Her scar was still pulsing, and now her skin was tingling too, as if a feather floated along its surface.

Maybe this is what it feels like to be turned on, she thought, nodding before she could change her mind.

Maybe they had chemistry after all.

Maybe everything was just as perfect as it seemed.

As they started to kiss, Mei kept pulling away, trying to show him how she wanted it—gentler, less slobbery—but he couldn't take a hint. While his tongue probed for her tonsils, his arms hung slack at his sides. *Doesn't he like my body? Why isn't he touching me? Why can't I turn off my brain and get into it?*

She flicked off the light so she wouldn't have to stare at the swimsuit model tacked over his bed, with her platinum hair, orangey tan, and breasts as round as grapefruits. Maybe the issue was that he was into a different type of girl: one who looked nothing like Mei.

Stu stumbled into her. "Whoa," he said. "I think I need to lie down." Not knowing what else to do, she lay down beside him, and the mattress sloshed and bucked beneath them. "Issa waterbed," he slurred, as he climbed on top of her. "Old school, right? It was my mom and dad's."

Mei could feel the chill of the water through the thin plastic, and she shivered. Stu's parents' tragic romance was legendary. They'd been high school sweethearts, crowned prom king and queen, married after graduation. But Stu's poor mom had died when he was just a few days old, going into some kind of coma as a result of the pregnancy. His dad had mourned her for years, never even dating until Simone moved back to Cascade.

But it wasn't exactly a turn-on lying under Stu on the waterbed where he'd probably been conceived. His breath reeked of alcohol and guacamole, and Mei felt seasick. She tried rolling out from under him, but he was six-three, and must've weighed over two hundred pounds.

"Hey, you're squashing me," she whispered. But he wasn't listening, too busy drooling on her neck and making a rhythmic snorting noise in her ear. *Is that supposed to be sexy?* She felt increasingly angry as he ignored her subtle and then not-so-subtle signs that she wasn't enjoying herself.

"Stu, I'm serious! I can't breathe. This does not feel good!"

But he didn't move an inch, and as he emitted a snore, suddenly she realized why.

Now she was really desperate to escape, but she didn't want to yell in case someone opened the door. She'd die if word got out that her boyfriend had fallen asleep on top of her while they were getting it on.

Her whole body felt like it was itching. Itching on the inside. Her scar again. To comfort herself, she pictured her drama coach. Mr. Dominguez believed in her. He gave her tough parts, convinced that she could embody anyone.

What would he advise in this situation?

A breathing exercise. That was key to clearing her mind.

She breathed in and out, in and out, and as her lungs inflated, she felt a sudden, strange gathering of strength, followed by a shocking numbness. A horrible thought flashed into her mind. Had someone slipped her a roofie? Then a feeling of tightness enveloped her, like she was sheathed from head to toe in Saran Wrap.

"Get off," she muttered into Stu's ear. Her voice sounded hoarse. He stirred and started to nuzzle her neck again, as if the nap had invigorated him. But she was way too insulted to keep up the charade. She put her hands on his chest and shoved him off. He flew backwards, landing in a heap on the floor.

Whoa.

How did she manage that? He was staring back at her, his look of shock mirroring her own.

"Oh my God," he said, as he scurried backwards. "What the hell are you doing in my bedroom?"

What? Now he doesn't want me anymore? Mei tried to get up, but Stu clutched the bedside lamp to his body, holding it like a shield. "Don't touch me! Don't come near me!"

Mei's head was spinning so fast she couldn't speak.

"I don't know what just happened," Stu panted, "but we will never, ever, talk about it. Got it?"

He bolted from the room and Mei slid to the ground.

What did I do to make Stu so afraid? She rested her head on her giant, knobby knees.

Wait. These aren't my knees.

"Omigod!" Her voice was different too—strong and deep. Looking down, she saw thick, sinewy forearms.

She groped at her face. *Is that stubble?*

She rushed into Stu's bathroom, switching on the light to see Mr. Dominguez staring back at her. She held up one trembling hand and her drama coach waved back. She raised her thick, dark eyebrows, and he did too. Her heart jackhammered from behind her toned chest.

Is this really happening?

Then a wave of fatigue hit her and she collapsed.

Peyton's voice woke her up. "We have to go! Mr. Sheers is home, and he's pissed!"

Mei panicked. Peyton could *not* see her like this. But Peyton was acting like nothing was wrong, and Mei felt a rush of relief as she looked down and saw her own slender legs and pale skin. The whole hideous episode must have been a nightmare. But when she stood up, her cute pink dress was weirdly stretched out, hanging like a sack.

They ran downstairs to find a furious Mr. Sheers in the foyer, lecturing Stu. "It's going to take weeks to fix the damage to the museum! At least one animal was stolen!"

"I'm sorry," Stu croaked. "I didn't think things would get out of hand." He glanced at Mei, who clutched her dress to her body.

"Let me give you girls a ride home," Mr. Sheers said, throwing them each a fleece. Mei took hers gratefully, glad to cover up before she flashed a boob.

"I'm fine to drive," Peyton said, but she could barely walk straight.

"Not a chance. Your parents would never forgive me if anything happened to you," Mr. Sheers said, shepherding them out the door with a hand on each of their backs.

As she passed him, Stu stared down at his feet, his face almost purple.

Maybe it really happened.

Mei knew that it couldn't have, but she also knew what she'd seen.

SATURDAY

I'M SWIMMING. Up, up, up through thick tar. Just when I think I'll never make it to the surface, I push through with a gasp. The air tastes sour. It smells like wet soil and ashes. My face feels numb, my eyelids glued shut. I force them open, but it makes no difference.

The bedroomette is pitch black.

My body aches all over and my brain is sludgy. I must have a fever. I'd kill for a glass of water.

"Mom?" I croak. Pszft.

The skin around my neck prickles like it's been snapped by rubber bands. There's something around my throat. I try to reach for it, but my wrists are caught behind me. The slats of a chair dig into my back.

Wait a minute . . .

If I'm sick with a fever, then why aren't I in bed?

We don't have a chair in our room.

And it's never this dark.

"Laurel?" Pszft. *There's that snapping again. It feels like I'm getting an electric shock. I try to stand, but my arms are wrenched backwards and I can't get up.*

I scream, and there's no mistaking the jolt of electricity that shoots up my neck, branching into my skull and making my teeth rattle in their sockets. I'm hyperventilating now, trying to push the fog from my brain, trying to remember what the hell happened, how I got here—wherever "here" is—when I hear a scraping overhead.

Something heavy is being moved.

I shrink back against the chair as a pale square of light appears in the ceiling—it must be a trapdoor—and I see a rickety ladder leading down to a room that looks like it was scooped out of the earth. I twist in my seat, looking around frantically. There are no windows in the walls, which are so grimy that I can barely see the shape of bricks beneath the dirt. Aside from this chair, there's nothing but a bucket and a mattress. The sight of it makes me want to run and hide, but I can't because my wrists are trapped behind me in handcuffs, chained to a metal ring jutting out of the wall.

My chest feels packed with ice. A foot appears at the top of the ladder, then another, as a man descends, his back to me. He's a big man. He's moving slowly and carrying a lantern. He appears in pieces that seem disassembled—heavy brown boots, dark-blue jeans, a green polar fleece—or at least that's how I perceive him, as if I could take him apart in my mind, keep him from reaching me.

His clothes look so clean and normal.

Is he coming to save me?

But when he turns around, a black ski mask hides his entire face—except for his glacial blue eyes.

"There's no point screaming," he says in a muffled voice. "You'll just get shocked, and there's no one up there to hear you."

My whole body clenches as he wedges himself behind me. The chain rattles, the lock clicks open, and I fall forward, landing hard on my knees. He pulls me roughly up by the arm, turns me to face away from him, and unlocks the cuffs.

I claw at my wrist—my body suddenly feels like it's covered in hives—and glance at the ladder. Could I outrun him? But before I have time to make a move, he's got a knife pointed at me. It's bigger than a butcher knife, with a black rubber handle and a foot-long blade that curves up at the tip.

"Please don't hurt me," I cry, gritting my teeth through the shock.

"I'm not here to hurt you," he says. "This is your chance to go."

Go? Adrenaline floods my body. Is this some kind of twisted game where he gives me a head start and then chases after me? Or has he had a change of heart? Is he setting me free? I'm about to sprint toward the ladder when he points his knife at the bucket.

"I said, go! I can't wait all night."

Suddenly I get it.

"I can't," I whisper. By making my voice so quiet that even I can barely hear it, the shock is bearable. "Not with you watching."

He squints at me. His blue eyes seem familiar, but he looks down before I can get a closer look and figure out how I might know him.

"Fine," he says. "I'll give you three minutes, but I'll be right up there the whole time, so don't try to run." He sets the lantern down and climbs back up the ladder.

Once he's gone, I walk over to the bucket, but I can't bring myself to pull down my pants. Not with him up there listening. Probably watching too.

I'm still wearing the flannel cupcake pajamas that I put on before bed last night, only now they're soaked with sweat. The last thing I remember was saying goodnight to my sister. I must have been drugged. But how the hell did he get into the trailer and drag me out of there without waking her up?

I scratch my wrist again, but it only makes the itch worse. I know what would make it go away, but it's the last thing I should be thinking about right now.

Something drops into the cell and I jump. But it's just a roll of toilet paper, still in its paper wrapper, decorated with dancing teddy bears. The expensive kind we never buy. It rolls to the far corner of the cell, out of reach.

I rake my fingernails against my wrist, desperate for relief.

I remember the first time the itch flared up. I was at that stupid camp, and I became convinced that I'd been bitten by something venomous—a scorpion or a snake—something way bigger than a mosquito. The itch seemed to be concentrated in the star-shaped birthmark on my wrist. The more I scratched, the worse that spot throbbed, until I started to worry that I was going to dig a hole in my skin. I used it as an excuse to hide out in the cabin. I was alone, trying not to scratch myself bloody as I stared at my sewing machine, wondering why I'd lugged it all the way there, when I realized that the needle was moving up and down, lifting and lowering the thread in perfect stitches through the fabric of the dress I was dying to finish.

There wasn't even electricity in our cabin.

"One more minute," he calls from above.

I catch sight of that roll of toilet paper in the far corner. I shouldn't even be thinking about doing this. I hate this freaky power. But I hate this crazy itchy feeling even more.

I take a few jagged breaths, trying to clear my mind, and then I flex my eyes. Everything else fades, until the toilet paper seems to be illuminated by a spotlight that's glowing from inside me somehow. Then it starts to roll. Very slowly at first, and then faster and faster, all the way across the floor and into my waiting hand.

Thunk. Thunk.

He's coming back. For one sweet moment, I'd managed to forget about him.

I drop the toilet paper. The itch is gone, but so is the adrenaline. As the power drains out of me, it takes every ounce of strength just to stay on my feet. He moves the chair aside, and pushes the mattress into its place.

"Lie on your back," he orders me.

"Please don't hurt me," I say, and a shock crackles through me. "Please just let me go. Please!" Maybe if I keep begging—if I'm really, really polite—I'll get through to the tiny part of him that isn't a monster.

"I can't do that," he says. "I'm sorry, but I need you."

He kneels beside me, uncapping a bottle of water and pouring it over my chapped lips. I hate drinking from his hand like a pet, but I know I need to stay hydrated, so I swallow great gulps, coughing half back up. Once the bottle is empty, he rolls me onto my stomach. I mash my face into the mattress, wishing I could burrow inside it and disappear as he snaps the handcuffs back on, then chains me to the wall again. I brace myself for the worst, squeezing my eyes shut.

But instead of feeling his weight crushing me, I hear him start to walk away.

"I'll be back to check on you tomorrow," he says. "Sorry the sleeping arrangements aren't more comfortable, but you should try to get some rest. Otherwise it'll be a very long week."

7.

I SAT BOLT UPRIGHT, panting and rubbing my throat. That thing I'd had around my neck in my nightmare—was it one of those electric shock collars they put on dogs?

No, not my neck. *Ivy's* neck. I wore her pajamas, the ones covered in cupcakes. I called out my own name for help.

I surveyed the bedroomette. After reassuring myself that I was safe at home—not in some horrifying underground lair—I got out of bed, shoving my fingers through my curls. Last time I'd seen Ivy, we were getting into bed and she had those pajamas on.

But it was only a nightmare, I told myself. *It couldn't mean anything.*

I went to the bathroom to splash some cold water on my face. Instead of a mirror, the Airstream had a sheet of shiny metal on the front of the medicine cabinet. As always, it made my reflection look wavy and distorted, but today it reflected the fuzzy way that I actually felt.

That dream had been so vivid, it made the real world seem blurry. Even the craziest parts had seemed totally real. I could still feel that flexing sensation in my eyeballs as I rolled that toilet paper across the floor. *Telekinesis.* I'd always thought the name for this power sounded scientific, like it had to be real.

But of course it's not.

As a kid, I'd fantasized about having some kind of power, devouring books with any kind of magic in them. By now, I was perfectly clear on the distinction between fiction and nonfiction, fantasy and reality. But I still couldn't resist staring at my chewed-up old toothbrush, willing it to fly into my hand, until my eyes started to water.

As I emerged from the bathroom, I saw that Mom's door was open. She was sleeping all the way at the edge of the futon, obviously leaving room for Bryan, who hadn't been back since the night Ivy disappeared. I felt a prickle of suspicion. Why was he suddenly AWOL? Could he have kidnapped her? Remembering how I'd reassured Simone that Bryan didn't pose a real threat, suddenly I found myself less sure.

Get real. Bryan wasn't together enough to kidnap anyone. Anyway, the reek of his cologne alone would've been enough to wake me up if he'd set foot in our room.

I switched on the light and opened the blue canister where we kept our coffee, but we'd finished the last of it yesterday. Normally, Ivy would have brought fresh grounds home from work today, along with a mocha for me, a latte for Mom, and a bag of pastries. It was a great perk of being a "barista," a pretentious title that she pretended to mock, although she loved the job itself, especially after having worked the guacamole gun at Taco Bell all summer. Unfortunately, she had to spend pretty much everything she made on groceries, since Mom needed the help.

Suddenly, I had an idea for how I could put my mind at rest. I was sure Ivy would never have left town without asking her manager for the time off. I could go to Ritual and talk to him. Once I found out she'd let him know she was going to miss her shifts to take this trip to Portland, I could relax until she came home. I scribbled a note to Mom, telling her that I'd be back soon with coffee. I felt so much better now that I had a solid plan, I didn't even worry about having to drive into Cascade again.

When I got to Ritual, Ivy's friend Ava was working behind the counter, filling a plastic pumpkin with fun-sized candy bars. Her dyed black hair and smudged eye makeup made her face look even paler than it already was. She stopped when she saw me.

"Is Ivy sick?" she asked. I shook my head. "So what's the deal? Where is she?"

I bit my lip. "I guess she's, um, visiting a friend from camp up in Portland. Didn't she tell you she'd be missing work?" I asked, desperately hoping the answer would be yes.

But Ava shook her head and scowled. "The milk-delivery guy called when he couldn't get in, which meant I had to come in on my day off."

Hope leaked out of me, and the panic from my nightmare came seeping back in. "Are you sure she never mentioned that she was going out of town?" I asked.

"Not to me." Ava jutted out her lower lip, blowing a strand of hair out of her eyes. "But we haven't talked much lately." She paused. "I'll bet she told Chad, and he spaced it. You know how he is." She pantomimed smoking a joint and I nodded. Ivy always complained about how flaky their manager could be.

"Can I speak to him?" I said.

She shook her head. "Not until tomorrow. He's got a busy day surfing, which is why I had to drag myself in here with a hangover. Hey—are you okay?" Her look of irritation turned to concern. I nodded, but my head was suddenly pounding, and spots swarmed in front of my eyes.

"Whoa," said a voice at my ear. A hand gripped my elbow. I turned, finding myself staring into a pair of bright-green eyes flecked with gold.

Ivy's secret boyfriend.

I shook Jasper's hand off. "I'm fine," I said, although I was still light-headed. "I just didn't eat breakfast." And barely anything besides a yogurt yesterday, I realized.

"You almost fainted," Jasper said, looking concerned.

"No, I didn't," I said. "Who does that, outside of a Jane Austen novel?"

"Laurel said that Ivy's up in Portland," Ava informed him.

"For a moment, I thought you were her." He jutted his chin at me and I looked down at myself. Instead of my usual jeans and a sweater, I'd put on black leggings and a dress that Ivy made from a pinstriped men's shirt, taking it in at the waist and adding a red belt. I'd wanted to feel closer to her, if only by wearing her clothes.

I pulled off my knit cap, freeing my frizzy red hair so he could see that it was just me. "So you guys had like, a date, or what?"

He shoved his hands in the pockets of his black hoodie. "We've been . . . hanging out."

Yeah, right.

"You should sit down," Jasper said. "I'll bring you coffee and something to eat, and we can talk for a minute, okay?"

Too disoriented to protest, I made my way to the back of the coffee shop.

A few minutes later, he joined me, setting down a mocha topped with whipped cream and an apricot scone. I took a bite, but the scone tasted like cardboard. "So you and Ivy are, like, together," I said, needing to be crystal clear.

But Jasper shook his head. "Not in the way that you mean."

"Oh," I said, newly confused. "Then what's the deal? How do you know her?"

"I've been tutoring her."

"Seriously?" I asked, and he nodded. Yeah, right. If Jasper was her tutor, then I was the queen of England. Ivy didn't struggle in school. She got straight As in every AP class our school offered. I raised an eyebrow, but instead of clarifying, Jasper just raked his dark hair back and it stayed that way—perfectly tousled. He had that bedhead look that most guys spent hours trying to perfect in front of the mirror. Everything about him was kind of perfect—more so because he didn't seem to know it—but I didn't want to be thinking about that.

Clearly there was something going on between him and my sister. But why would he lie about it?

And why wouldn't she tell him about her trip to Portland instead of standing him up at the coffeehouse?

"So who's this friend she's visiting?" he asked.

"Some girl from camp." I sighed. "At least that's what she said in her note. Did she ever mention a friend from camp to you?"

He shook his head. "In this note, did she say when she'd be back?"

"On Halloween."

"What time?" His knuckles turned white as he gripped his mug of coffee. Did they have a date that night or something? I couldn't believe she'd do that to me. It was my birthday, after all, and we had plans.

"We're supposed to go to the DMV in the afternoon," I informed him, "and then to the dance that night."

"There's a dance?" he said, his eyebrows bunching up. "Where?"

"Uh, at school?" Hadn't he noticed the ubiquitous posters advertising the Dark Side Dance, to take place during the lunar eclipse? If he and Ivy were together, then why weren't the two of them going together? Maybe they weren't dating after all. Suddenly, I remembered her complaining that she'd received a B- on a trig test. I knew she wanted to keep a perfect GPA so that she could get a full ride to college out of state.

"You're tutoring her in math?" I said, and he nodded once. "Is that why she's so stressed out? Is she, like, failing or something?"

"I wouldn't say that," he said. "She just needs a little help."

"And she does not like admitting when she needs help," I said.

He nodded again, and suddenly, I felt a little bit better. If he was just her tutor, then there was no reason she would have told him about her plan to run away to Portland. I could picture her there, revisiting that cool fabric store we'd discovered on a trip with Grandma, with bolts of cloth in every color and Bernina sewing machines they let you use for free. Maybe she really had needed to get away for a few days, to clear her head.

I took a sip of my drink, savoring the unexpected blend of coffee and chocolate and orange. "This mocha is amazing," I said.

"It's a café Borgia," he told me. "I taught her how to make it." He nodded at Ava.

"Did you invent it or something?"

"No. It was all the rage in Paris in the 1920s. The Frappuccino of its day, I guess you'd say." I laughed, and he went on. "Hemingway said it was the best cure for a hangover that he knew of."

"It sounds like you were pals."

"I don't think Hemingway had any real friends. The only thing he really cared about was his writing."

"I sort of get that," I said. "Maybe, if you can make up really solid characters, it's like they're keeping you company. Not that I'd know."

"But you're a writer," he said. "You wrote that story for class."

I felt myself blushing that he remembered. "Yeah, well. According to Ms. Owen, I should give up."

"That's not what I heard. I mean, she was a little bit harsh," he said, smiling slightly. "But no matter what she says, you shouldn't give up. You're still finding your voice."

"What does that even mean?" I protested, even though it was exactly what Ivy told me when I felt discouraged. "Either you've got the talent or you don't, and clearly I fall in the *don't* category. I mean, Mary Shelley was only nineteen when she wrote *Frankenstein*. She didn't have to find her voice."

"If Mary Shelley had shown her early work to a teacher like Ms. Owen, she probably would never have written another word."

"I'm sure Mary Shelley didn't need a teacher, since she was a natural genius," I said, pushing my café Borgia away.

"Actually, a lot of people think that she wrote *Frankenstein* with her husband. They found notebooks where the two of them collaborated."

"Oh yeah?" I set down my coffee and crossed my arms. "Because a woman couldn't possibly write a novel without the help of a man?"

Jasper's eyes sparkled in amusement. He held up both hands in mock surrender. "He was a poet, and I'll bet he couldn't have written without her help either. Are *you* saying a man and a woman can't write a novel together?" He grinned at me. Was he flirting with me?

I stared at him, too flustered to think of a witty response, and he looked back unwaveringly, like he was memorizing my every freckle. Then he stood up abruptly. "I should probably get going. I need to visit my . . . uh . . . grandfather."

"Okay," I said, getting up too. How had I let myself get sucked in? Here was the first guy I'd ever met who shared my love of books and could hold an interesting conversation about writing. Why did he have to be so good-looking on top of it?

There was absolutely no way he could ever be interested in me. He had those incredible eyes, and that irresistible Mr. Darcy-esque reserve. I had that archipelago of freckles and, I was pretty sure, a zit burgeoning on my chin. I folded my arms over my flat chest. "See you around." I hated myself for thinking that he could be interested, even if it was just one moment. Memorizing my freckles, indeed. Probably wondering whether any of them were cancerous.

"Wait," he said, as I started to walk away. I turned and he raked a hand through his hair again. "When you talk to Ivy, will you tell her to call me?" I could hear the strain in his voice. "I really need to talk to her."

"Sure," I said. "No problem."

Was there a math emergency? I somehow doubted it. Even if they weren't dating, there was more to their relationship than he was letting on. That was clear.

For a second, I considered telling him about my nightmare, how it had felt like I was dreaming as Ivy, and how I couldn't shake the fear that it was connected to her disappearance. But I reminded myself that I barely knew the guy.

He does not want to hear about your dreams.

8.

OUTSIDE, the sky was the color of dryer lint. The day dragged, hour after empty hour to fill. I couldn't bring myself to go back to the trailer yet, where I knew I'd just sit around obsessing over Ivy, so I decided to go visit our friend Skye. I wanted nothing more than to stretch out on the beanbags in her family room, watching a John Hughes movie that we could both recite by heart, with Chewbacca, her ancient Yorkie, curled up in between us.

The Nevermans lived next door to our grandma's old house. Skye was six months older than me and seven months younger than Ivy, and the three of us had been inseparable as kids, spending summer nights camped up in a tree fort that Skye's dad had built according to her blueprint—complete with a dumbwaiter and skylight—while Skye pointed out the constellations and taught us about things like "hypervelocity stars," which rocketed through space at two million miles per hour.

Skye herself was a hypervelocity star. Since middle school, she'd been taking college-level math and science courses online, and by now she probably had enough credits to skip straight to graduate school. But her parents insisted that she come to high school and snooze through a few afternoon classes, so that she could still be a "normal teenager." As if.

The Nevermans were the law-abiding type who would not have approved of me driving without a license, so I parked out of sight of their windows, in front of our old house. There was a bike with a banana seat and pink streamers on the handlebars in the carport where Ivy and I used to leave our bikes. The light was on in our old kitchen. I sat there for a moment, letting the nostalgia fill up my chest.

That was where Grandma used to bake her oatmeal cookies while we sat around the red table. Ivy would sew, Mom would sketch, and I'd write in my journal. We broke the table leg during our move, so now it always tilted unless we wedged the phone book underneath it. Now that Grandma was gone, our family was out of balance too, and I wondered if we'd ever get our equilibrium back.

When I knocked on Skye's door, no one answered, but I could hear a noise out back, so I let myself in with the key they kept under an obvious plastic log. "Hello?" I called out. "Anyone home?" As always, the place was immaculate. Mrs. Neverman had a label maker with which she labeled everything, including her label maker, a fact that Skye and I found hilarious.

Through the window, I caught sight of Skye in the backyard, crouching under the ash tree where our weathered old fort was perched. I hadn't seen her all week, and she'd cut her hair since then—or half of it, anyhow. Skye was elfin and fierce, a tomboy since preschool, and her hair had never surpassed her chin. Now one side was buzzed close to her head while the other hung down to one ear, which was pierced with silver hoops like a spiral binding. She was wearing her dad's gray suit vest and cutoffs over long johns, the look completed by her trademark Converse high-tops. When we were little, I'd gotten in trouble once for scribbling on her new shoes, and she'd saved me from punishment by claiming that she'd begged me to do it. Now it was a tradition. Whenever she got a new pair of high-tops, she'd hand me a marker and tell me to "break 'em in."

"Hey, Skye," I called out as I picked my way across the sopping lawn, stopping when I saw what she was looking at. Inside one of her father's cage traps was a snarling mass of fur. "Whoa!" I said. "Did your dad finally catch a raccoon?" Raccoons were the bane of Mrs. Neverman's existence, constantly sneaking in through Chewy's pet door to mess up her pristine kitchen.

"Hi, Lolo," she said without standing up. "No—this is no raccoon."

I squatted beside her and we both peered at the creature as it whirled around inside the cage. It was the size of a large raccoon, but it had a sharper, foxlike face, a short bushy tail, and long curved claws. As it bared its small yellow teeth and hissed, Skye and I both jumped back.

"What is that?" I said.

"I think it's a wolverine."

"A wolverine?" I turned to look at her, dumbfounded. "I thought they were practically extinct."

She twisted her earrings, a habit of hers whenever she was deep in thought. "They are. I have no idea how it ended up here."

The cage rattled as the animal ran in frantic circles. Watching it, I flashed back to my nightmare, remembering the feeling of entrapment, my wrists bound behind me.

"We should let it out." I reached for the cage, but Skye stopped me.

"I don't think that's a good idea," she said. "I'd better call someone from Animal Care and Control, so they can figure out how it got here and where it belongs."

Normally I appreciated Skye's intellectual curiosity, but I could smell the musk of the wolverine's panic as it hurled itself against the bars, and without thinking, I sprang the trapdoor. We jumped back as the animal burst out, shot up the fence, and disappeared.

"Laurel, what the hell," Skye snapped. "What if it kills more pets?"

I gulped. "What do you mean, *more* pets?"

She looked at me, her eyes moist. "I think it might've killed Chewbacca."

"What?" I felt like I'd been punched in the stomach "Wait— Chewy's *dead?*"

Skye nodded, looking down. "I found him this morning by the trash can, with his throat ripped out." Her voice quavered. "It was pretty horrible."

"Oh my God!" I couldn't believe it. There we were, standing under the fort where we'd pulled the dog up in the dumbwaiter so many times. He'd allowed me to dress him in doll clothes back when I was little, and spent countless hours on my lap while I read. It seemed impossible that he could be gone. Dead. When I looked at the empty trap, I was seized by guilt. "Are you sure that wolverine killed him?"

"Probably, but I don't know," Skye said. "Predators in the wild only kill to eat, but whatever got Chewy left him to bleed out."

"Poor Chewy," I said as my eyes filled with tears.

"An unfortunately prescient name," Skye said, giving a laugh that turned into a sob.

"He was the best dog in the world," I said. "Remember when he saved me from that crazy Doberman by biting its ankles?"

"He was a pint-sized superhero," Skye said. "But if we're going to eulogize him properly, we should admit that he had the world's worst breath."

"And the smelliest farts." We were both laughing now, an aching kind of laughter that reminded me of how it had felt when Ivy and Mom and I put on Grandma's chemo wigs while we boxed up her things, goofing around as tears streamed down our faces.

"Remember how you and Ivy were always fighting over who got to have him in your sleeping bag when we spent the night in the fort?" Skye asked.

I nodded. At the mention of Ivy's name, I immediately felt hollow and panicky.

"What's the matter?" Skye asked. She knew me so well, there was no point hiding the truth from her.

"Ivy's gone," I said.

"What do you mean, *gone?*"

So I told her everything. She looked shocked, until I got to the part about the note.

"Okay, well, I agree it's lame that she took off without telling you, but I'm sure she's fine and she'll be back on your birthday like she said."

I hesitated. I didn't expect Skye to take a premonition from a nightmare seriously, but I needed to tell someone about the dread that I hadn't been able to shake since waking up. "I had this insanely intense dream last night," I said. "I know what you're going to say, but it felt completely real." To my surprise, she began nodding before I'd finished describing it.

"You couldn't move?" she said. "And you felt like you were choking?"

"Yes!" I drew a deep breath. "There was a collar around my neck, shocking me."

"And a guy standing over you? Like a captor of some kind?"

"Oh my God! How do you know all of this?" The crazy thought flashed through my mind that maybe she'd had the exact same dream.

But then she said, "It sounds like you experienced classic sleep paralysis. In conjunction with hypnopompic hallucination."

"Hypna-what?"

"So when we sleep, our muscles are immobilized—otherwise we'd fall out of bed or walk into walls, right? Sometimes we wake up when our muscles are still paralyzed. That's sleep paralysis. And a hypnopompic hallucination is a kind of waking dream—you're half-awake, half-asleep. Imagining that you're tied up or that there's a figure standing over you is really common."

"But it felt like I was Ivy," I said. "I was wearing her pajamas. I was calling for help, but I was calling 'Laurel.' I had memories of things she'd done at camp." Here I paused, because if I wanted her to take this seriously at all, I knew I couldn't share the part about telekinesis. "Don't you think that's weird?"

"Not really. You dreamed you were her because you're worried about her. Your subconscious is trying to digest the stresses of your waking life. In her note, she told you she was visiting a friend from camp, so you imported this detail into your dream." She paused. "Have you ever heard of Occam's razor?"

"Maybe," I said. She rolled her eyes. "Okay, no."

"It's a principle of philosophy that says that the simplest, most logical explanation is usually the truth. If you hear hoofbeats, it's probably a horse and not a unicorn, that kind of thing. If she left a note that she went to Portland, then you should assume that's what happened unless you get real proof otherwise."

I nodded, relieved by her logic. Everything Skye was saying made sense. I'd just told Mom how much Ivy hated that fake arts camp, so naturally I'd been thinking about this while I slept. Everything else—the dungeon, the handcuffs, the shock collar, the man in the mask—was classic nightmare stuff. Hypnogogic something or other. I didn't need to remember the term, it was a relief just to learn that dreams like this were common enough to have an official medical diagnosis.

Skye offered to make us grilled cheese sandwiches for a snack, and as we entered her house, I felt like she'd taken the billowing black mass of the nightmare and folded it over and over, until it became a tiny square, small enough for me to put away and forget about.

For now.

9.

WHEN I GOT HOME, my stomach clenched at the sight of Bryan's old pick-up truck, parked in Spud's spot. Mom and Bryan were sitting at the red table, sharing a joint. The sickly-sweet smoke swirled in the air and the window was wide open, even though it was practically freezing outside.

"Hi, sweetie," Mom said. "How was school?" Through the haze, I could see that her eyes were completely bloodshot.

"It's Saturday," I said.

"Right!" She laughed shrilly. "I know that! How was . . . Saturday?"

She was wearing her tight purple jeans, a low-cut peasant blouse, and cowboy boots, while Bryan—who didn't deign to turn around to greet me—was shirtless as usual, showing off the skeleton riding a Harley that was tattooed across his beefy back.

"Did you just sit around getting stoned all day?" I asked Mom, feeling sick with disgust. How could she act like this when her older daughter was AWOL?

"It's legal," she reminded me defensively. "And it's not like I have some important job I had to get to." She sounded discouraged, but I didn't feel any sympathy. No wonder Ivy had wanted to leave. Just because we were old enough to take care of ourselves didn't make it fair that we should have to take care of her too.

"Well, maybe you should be looking for one," I said.

"That's no way to talk to your mother," Bryan barked, which only made me angrier. Who was he to come in here and pretend like he had any authority over us?

"You know they're reassigning a social worker to our case," I reminded her. "If you don't have a steady job, and you don't even know where your own daughter is, how is that going to look? Do you *want* us to get taken away?"

"It's not like someone is going to show up here out of the blue," she said.

"Let's hope not," said Bryan. He glanced out the window at the corrugated tin lean-to that held Mom's painting supplies. I looked too, and noticed something strange: a line of brightness under the door.

"What's going on in there?" I asked.

"Wouldn't you like to know," muttered Bryan.

"What's that supposed to mean?"

"Forget it. Don't get your panties in a bunch." One corner of his mouth lifted, and the hairs on the back of my neck prickled with suspicion.

Ivy disappeared on the same night she called him a pervert.

What if he'd tied her up in the shed to teach her who was boss? My pulse sped as I sprinted to the shed and flung the door open. Inside, a fluorescent strip light buzzed, illuminating a dozen waist-high potted plants. Their palm-sized leaves glistened, and their swollen purplish buds looked like tiny bruised fists. The smell—one hundred times more potent than the air in the trailer—made my head swim.

Mom caught up, with Bryan huffing and puffing behind her. "You're growing pot on our property?" I whirled to face her, incredulous. "You're a drug dealer now?"

"They're *my* plants," Bryan said. "Your mom just made a small investment."

"How much?" I demanded.

"Just a couple of thousand dollars," Mom said. "But once we start selling it, we can make back every penny in no time."

My fingernails dug into my palms. "That's nearly everything you saved from the museum job! And you still have to finish paying off the fine from your DUI!"

"Why do you think I'm doing this?" she said, reaching for her pendant. "Bryan says it's a fail-proof business."

"But you're an artist! Mr. Sheers gave you that great job!"

She folded her arms. "It *was* great while it lasted, but where am I going to get another painting job in Cascade? I don't have a degree, and I'm sick to death of scrubbing toilets. I need to be realistic about my options." She looked at Bryan, obviously repeating his words. "This is a growth industry."

"If you're nice, there could be a job in it for you too," he said to me. "I could use someone with connections at the high school. Grower's license costs an arm and a leg, so we're going to have to do this under the table for a while."

Without thinking, I grabbed the nearest plant and tore it out of its container. It came out with surprising, satisfying ease, its roots shedding clods of earth. Bryan gripped my shoulders and I dropped the plant.

"Stop it," Mom cried out. "Don't touch her!"

"You know what these things are worth!" Bryan yelled at her.

I twisted free and lunged for another plant. This time he got me in a chokehold. Mom began to sob, tugging at his arm as I writhed and kicked at his ankles, my eyes watering as his forearm crushed my windpipe.

"What is wrong with you?" Mom was screaming now, pounding at him with her fists. "Are you nuts? Let go of my daughter!"

But his grip didn't loosen. "I'm not going to let her destroy my plants," he said.

I gasped for air, trying to elbow him in the gut. But the harder I fought, the harder he held on. I could smell the pot oozing from his pores, and it flashed through my mind that he was so high, he could strangle me without realizing it.

Then I heard a familiar voice in the darkness. "Get your hands off her."

Bryan pulled me closer, his whole body tensing. "Who's there?"

Jasper Blake stepped into the grow light, and Bryan relaxed enough so that I could take one shuddering breath. "Who are you, kid? Her little boyfriend? How cute."

"I said, let go of her," Jasper repeated.

"You think I take orders from a teenager?" Bryan laughed. Instead of answering, Jasper just stared at him—that same focused look he'd given Spud's engine—and a second later, Bryan screamed and let me go.

I stumbled, heaving and rubbing my throat. When I turned around, Bryan was doubled over, cursing. The smell of singed hair filled the shed. I saw a bright-pink patch of skin on his forearm, already blistering.

Mom threw her arms around me. "My baby," she sobbed. "Are you okay?"

I shook her off, keeping my eye on Bryan as he cradled his arm, his face contorted in pain. "What the hell did you do to me, man? This is a serious burn!"

"You should've been more careful. Those grow lamps are really hot," Jasper said. He took a step forward and Bryan backed away, cringing like a beaten dog.

"I need to go to the hospital," he whimpered. "Sheila? Can you drive me?"

"Drive yourself!" Mom spat. "And never come back."

These were the words Ivy and I had been hoping to hear. But instead of victory, I felt a bone-deep exhaustion. My throat ached, and I knew it would be bruised tomorrow.

"I'm going inside," I said, addressing my feet.

"I'll come with you." Mom stumbled after me.

I couldn't even bear to look at her. As we walked to the trailer, I realized that I was now taller than her, even in her boots. But I didn't feel like I'd grown without noticing it.

I felt like Mom had shrunk.

In the Airstream, she sank onto the couch, lying on her side, her bloodshot eyes swimming with tears. "I am so sorry, Laurel. I knew Bryan had anger issues, but I never thought he'd lay a finger on you. I'm so sorry, baby. So, so sorry."

But the more she apologized, the angrier I felt. Like a little kid, she thought saying sorry could erase everything bad. She wanted me to reassure her that I was fine, that she hadn't done anything so terrible, that it was all going to be okay.

But it wasn't.

There was a knock on the door and we both jumped. Mom got there first, opening it just a crack. But it was Jasper.

"He's gone," Jasper said. "I wanted to make sure you were okay." He looked at me.

"I guess." I knew that I should feel humiliated by the spectacle he'd witnessed, but I was too depleted to be embarrassed. I just felt numb. "Mom, this is Jasper. He's a friend of Ivy's."

Mom looked awful, her eyelids swollen, mascara streaking her cheeks, but Jasper offered her his hand as if nothing was out of the ordinary, and she shook it. "Nice to meet you, Mrs. Goodwin," he said.

His formal manner seemed to help her to pull herself together. She dabbed her eyes with the heel of her hand. "Please, call me Sheila. I'm so sorry you walked in on—on that, but thank God you showed up when you did. I've never seen Bryan back down like that. I don't know what you did exactly, but—"

"I didn't do anything," he said. "But if my being there was helpful, then I'm glad."

Mom pinched the bridge of her nose. I felt far away from her, as if she were some old lady who'd fallen on the sidewalk—just some stranger who needed help, from whom I could walk away.

"I'm going to bed early," she said. "Everything always seems better in the morning, you know?"

Keep telling yourself that, I wanted to say, but I bit my tongue.

After Mom went to bed, I made tea for Jasper and myself. I'd hoped that going through the steps of filling the kettle and pulling out teabags would help me feel normal, but the Airstream had never seemed so claustrophobic. I felt hyperaware of Jasper's body, the heat he emitted. He'd taken off his hoodie, and his thin T-shirt clung to his torso, showing off his muscles. I wished he wouldn't stand so still, like he was an animal waiting to spring. Why couldn't he fidget like normal people? I was handing him two boxes of tea to choose from when I knocked against the dinette table and the busted leg splayed out as always.

Jasper got down to help me fix it, and suddenly his face was extremely close. I couldn't help but notice the bump in his nose, and the way his top lip was a little fuller than the bottom one. The kettle whistled and I was glad for the excuse to jump to my feet, my hand shaking slightly as I filled our mugs.

"Thanks," I said, realizing that I still hadn't said this. "Bryan could've strangled me if you hadn't shown up when you did. What did you do to him?"

"What do you mean?" His voice was completely unconvincing.

"Jasper, are you serious?" Suddenly, I was so sick of lies. "You must have done something. He would never have run off otherwise."

Jasper took his tea and went to the window, looking out. "It's finally stopped raining," he said. "Want to go sit outside, so we can talk without waking your mom?"

"Okay," I said, glad to get some fresh air—and, hopefully, the truth.

We sat side by side on the cinderblock stair. The rain had stopped, but it was so cold that our breath hovered in front of us like empty cartoon bubbles. I shivered, and he offered me his hoodie.

"I'm fine," I said.

But Jasper continued to hold it out. "You're freezing. Please take it."

"Then you'll get cold."

"I'm fine," he insisted. "I'm actually quite warm."

I could still feel the heat of his body, even inches away from him. It was clear that he wouldn't give up until I took the sweatshirt, but I draped it over my shoulders without putting my arms in the sleeves. Wearing his hoodie seemed like something his girlfriend would do. I wanted to nestle into it as deeply as I could, to cocoon myself in it, but I forced myself not to. I didn't understand how I could be so frightened about Ivy and so drawn to him at the same time.

"Have you heard from Ivy?" Jasper asked.

I swallowed painfully. "Nope."

"She might have tried to call," he said. "I tried earlier, but no one answered. That's why I decided to come by."

"Sometimes our calls don't go through," I said, newly frustrated at the idea that Ivy could've tried to call home and failed. "Mom had to run a cordless phone line through the refrigerator vent. It's not exactly high-tech. Plus since she and Bryan were busy getting baked, they could've just ignored it even if it did ring." My anger boiled up again and I wrapped my arms around my knees, digging the point of my chin into them. "She is so pathetic," I said.

"At least she told him to leave," he said. "That's more than some people do."

I shrugged. "She'll probably invite him back tomorrow. Besides, she only told him to leave after you hurt him." I turned to face him. "What *did* you do? That was a nasty burn, and he wasn't anywhere near the grow lamps."

He was silent for a moment. "You can't tell anyone."

"Not like I have anyone to tell." I shoved my hands in my armpits. A tingling sensation prickled across my skin, like all my nerves were firing at once.

He took a breath, placing both hands on his knees. "You were right before. I can start fires."

"You can start fires," I repeated mechanically.

"With my eyes."

"Uh-huh," I said. "How?"

"It's just this thing I can do," he said. "I don't know. It's like . . . my power."

I stared at him. Yes, I'd entertained this possibility for a split second after I'd seen him ignite Spud's engine. But somehow, now that he was saying it was real, I didn't want to believe it. I didn't want my world to change any more than it already had. "And when—how long have you been able to—" I couldn't finish. Part of me wanted him to stop talking altogether.

He sighed. "I'd just turned sixteen. I was camping. Ever since I was a little kid, I've always spent a lot of time in the woods. My older brother taught me wilderness survival, and the two of us used to go camping together when he lived at home. But after he moved out, and my mother married my stepfather—let's just say he makes Bryan look like a nice guy—I started going camping on my own, mostly to get out of the house."

He was staring straight ahead as he spoke, and a tiny muscle in the corner of his jaw twitched. He seemed so serious that it dawned on me that he truly believed what he was telling me. Even with his hoodie draped around my shoulders, I started to feel icy cold again. Maybe he was telling the truth.

"Go on," I said.

"So this one day, I was alone in the woods when it started raining. I knew I couldn't last through the night without a fire to keep me warm, and that the rain would put it out even if I did manage to get a match lit, but I refused to give up. I thought I was going to go nuts. Eventually, I just stared at the logs, and I started to get this feeling—like the flame was inside of me. I kept staring, and then . . ."

"And they just—poof—went up in flames?"

"Pretty much," he said, still not turning to face me.

"And that's your power."

He nodded. "I try not to use it. I can usually stop myself. But over the past few days, I've used it three times, which worries me." He paused, waiting for me to butt in again, but I was speechless. "Anyway, there it is. The truth. You asked for it."

I gripped the cinderblock until the edge carved into my palms. Was he completely delusional? But then I replayed the events of the past two days.

The trash can fire in English class.

The way that Spud's engine had mysteriously fired up.

And now, the blistering skin on Bryan's arm.

Every single one of those times, Jasper had been there.

In that moment, I recognized that I was leaving behind the placid shallows of my old life, plunging over a waterfall I hadn't seen coming. Those fires couldn't all be freak incidents.

Jasper had started them.

It was impossible.

And yet it explained so much.

As shock gave way to wonder, it was as if I could suddenly see every tree and blade of grass, the nearly full moon illuminating them in a way that the sun didn't, making them strange and new.

"You have a *magic* power," I said.

Jasper shrugged. "You can call it that. Some people say that humans only use a tiny percentage of their brains. Maybe people like us have just figured out how to tap into the rest."

"'People like us' . . . You mean there are other people with powers?" He nodded. I was shivering hard now. "Who else has one?"

Jasper gave me a hard look, as if trying to decide if I was ready to hear the rest.

"Ivy does," he said at last. "She can move things with her mind."

I felt like my throat was closing up. The dream came back, crashing into my mind with the force of a tidal wave. "But she would have told me," I whispered. "We tell each other everything."

He nodded, looking sympathetic. "She hates to talk about it. It just started over the summer, and she's still really freaked out."

"She told *you*."

"I found out by accident. I get a cup of coffee at Ritual every morning. I happened to show up one day before the place opened, and I was standing outside when I saw Ivy behind the counter, using her eyes to thread a needle. When I saw the thread hovering in the air, I almost couldn't believe it and I knocked into the window. I told her that I know about powers—that I have one too—and I offered to help her learn to control hers. I wasn't lying when I said I'd been tutoring her. That's why we've been hanging out."

I was too upset to even feel relieved to get the truth about his relationship with Ivy. I felt sick again, because so much of what he was telling me matched up with details from my nightmare. I'd thought that the telekinesis in that dream was proof that it couldn't be real. But it was turning out to be the opposite.

"Is there any way she could have sent me a message in my sleep?" I asked.

His head snapped toward mine, his eyes suddenly electric. "What kind of message?"

As I told him about the dream, he stood up and started to pace. "It's possible," he said once. "Under extreme stress, powers can split. She could have developed this additional power to penetrate your subconscious when you're dreaming. Maybe she doesn't even realize it."

My stomach churned. "So you really think she's been kidnapped?"

"I don't know, but I'm pretty sure she's in danger." He sighed deeply. "People with powers are connected. When one of us is stressed, any others who are in the area can feel it. It's like an itch, and the only thing that makes it go away is using our power. That must be why I keep feeling the urge to start fires."

I jumped to my feet. "We have to call the police!"

"What are you going to tell them?" Jasper said gently.

Although my sister left a note saying she's in Portland, I'm convinced she's been chained up in a dungeon. I know this because she's using her magic power to send me telepathic messages in my sleep.

I was pretty sure that paranoia and hallucinations were symptoms of schizophrenia. The police were more likely to take me straight to a psychiatrist than track down Ivy.

I sat back down. "If she was really kidnapped, then maybe she can use her telekinesis to escape?"

Jasper looked sympathetic. "I'm sorry, but I don't think her power is that strong yet, Laurel. If she's actually chained up, I don't think it'll be much help to her."

He was right, I realized, thinking of how weak she'd felt after moving that roll of toilet paper. "Then I'll have to save her," I said.

"*We* have to save her."

That made me feel marginally better. "Okay, but how do we find her?"

He sighed again. "You're not going to want to hear this, but for now, the best move is probably for you to go to bed. It's dark, and we don't know where to look. We could drive around all night without getting any closer."

"Are you crazy?" I wanted to tear my hair out. "There's no way I'm going to be able to sleep now!"

He laid a hand on my shoulder, looking me right in the eye. "Maybe Ivy will send you another dream tonight. Look for any clue that might show us where to look for her, and write down everything that you see in your dream. We can meet at Ritual first thing tomorrow morning and use what you've found to start searching."

I didn't like this plan at all, but I didn't have any better ideas. I was still reeling. Mom's plastic gardening clogs lay at the foot of the steps. They seemed like artifacts from a distant past. I didn't know where I stood anymore—what was real, what was the illusion—but

Jasper was right. My eyes were gritty with tiredness. And if Ivy was sending me messages in my sleep, then I couldn't stay awake just to avoid the nightmare that she was living.

As I drove him home, it seemed laughable that just yesterday, driving without a license had struck me as the scariest thing in the world. Now I found myself operating on autopilot while my mind churned with fear. The heater was broken, but I barely registered the icy air blowing from the vents. On Miner Street, Jasper told me to stop in front of a dilapidated white Victorian with faded red curtains in the bay windows.

"Your family moved in here?" I asked, and he nodded. The house actually had a brass sign on it that read *Headmaster House.* The historic landmark had been deserted for my whole life, those curtains permanently drawn, fading a little more from year to year. Mom always said it was a shame for such a grand old house to stand empty, vandalized by high schoolers every Halloween. Judging by the splattered egg stains on the front door, his family hadn't gotten around to fixing it up yet.

I waited for him to jump out, but he sat there for a minute, looking at me. "I'm really sorry you have to do this part alone, Laurel. I'll be at Ritual at seven, right when they open. Hopefully we'll find Ivy tomorrow."

"Okay," I said, handing him his hoodie.

"Give it to me later," he said. "You're freezing."

"I'm fine," I insisted, trying to stop my teeth from chattering.

"No, you're not." He frowned. "At least let me warm you up before I go."

"What do you mean?"

Instead of answering, he held out his fist. I stared at it, unsure what he wanted me to do exactly. Then he opened his hand. A flame played on his palm, flickering just above his skin.

"Go ahead," he said quietly. "Warm your hands."

I shook my head, though I couldn't stop looking at the flame: a dance of yellow and red with a core of blue. Somehow, giving in to that warmth felt like admitting I wanted him. I was determined *not* to want him. But I also needed to feel comforted, if only just for one moment.

I stretched out my hands and cupped them over the flame.

My frozen fingertips began to thaw. The flame fluttered and danced between them. I reached closer and gasped as heat spread rapidly through my whole body. Maybe I was wrong about him. Maybe he did feel what I felt. I'd thought that our search for Ivy meant we couldn't have any feelings for each other, because thinking about anyone except her was a betrayal. But at the same time, the fact that he was the only one in the world I could confide in right now made him irresistible.

The flame flared up even brighter, its warmth penetrating to my toes. I looked up at him. His lips were slightly parted, his eyes on me. I could have sworn I saw longing on his face. Together, we drew a deep, shaky breath. I had to reach closer, wanting to hold the flame tight, to keep it. It was like a firefly, a reminder of summer's warmth on this rainy, miserable night.

But right before I could touch it, he snatched his hand away, closing his fist over the flame. "I'll talk to you in the morning," he said hoarsely, suddenly in a hurry to get out of the car. The way he'd snatched his hand back—it was like a warning.

Not. Going. To. Happen.

I watched as he slipped into the dark house. I couldn't help feeling the wrench of disappointment.

Then I shook myself. Nothing but Ivy mattered right now.

As I drove back home, a childish longing for a magic power returned to me, stronger than ever now that I knew they were real.

But now, I didn't want to feel special—I wanted to save Ivy.

Instead, the only thing I could do was go to sleep, and hope that she'd find me.

SUNDAY

CREEEAK. *The trapdoor is opening again. I've been alone down here for hours and hours. I don't know how long. I'm starving and desperate to pee.*

I struggle to sit up as he clomps down the ladder. From the back, he looks so normal—the same hiking boots, dark jeans, and forest-green fleece—that it's still a shock to see the black ski mask.

That mask.

Maybe he doesn't want me to see his face so I can't identify him later. Or maybe I know him. Maybe he doesn't want me to recognize him.

It's the same routine. He unlocks the padlock and chain, and then the handcuffs. Once I'm free, he points at the bucket and tells me in a whisper that I have three minutes.

When he returns, he pushes the mattress aside and shoves the chair in its place, in front of the metal ring in the wall. Then he steps behind me and chains me up again. My stomach growls a loud, humiliating gurgle.

You must be starving," he mutters, pulling a brown strip from his pocket. "This is venison jerky. I caught it myself."

I don't care what it is. I'm so hungry, I snatch it out of his hand with my teeth.

I chew and chew but my throat refuses to swallow and I have to spit the stuff out.

"Oh well," he says. "I know you don't usually eat meat. I really shouldn't be giving you any food at all. By Thursday, I need you to be . . ."

"What?" I say softly. "What do you need me to be by Thursday?"

"I need you, Ivy. That's all you need to know. After Thursday, it'll all be over."

10.

I TURNED ON THE LAVA LAMP on the crate between our beds, grabbing my notebook and pen so I could record every detail of that nightmare before it faded. The dawn light was starting to creep in through the widow. I had to do this fast, and then get to Ritual right when it opened.

But once I'd jotted down the entire dream, I felt a sting of disappointment. I hadn't actually seen anything new: no clue pointing to where our search should start. No familiar landmark that we could use to find our way to Ivy.

Reading over what I'd written, it occurred to me that maybe she wasn't really sending me these dreams at all. Maybe they were just hypno-whatsit hallucinations, like Skye had said. She'd said that lots of people had this same kind of dream about having been kidnapped. Jasper didn't *know* that Ivy could send me dreams. All he knew was that she could move things with her mind. He said himself that having a power was freaking her out. Maybe that was why she'd gone up to Portland.

It was easier to believe this than that she'd been kidnapped by a man in a mask who was keeping her chained in a dungeon.

A day ago, I'd been convinced that her note was fake, but now every bit of me wanted to believe it was real.

I threw on some clothes and shoved my notebook in my bag. I'd show my notes on the dream to Jasper. Maybe he would spot some clue that I was overlooking, something that would give us an idea of where to start our search. If not, then maybe I could persuade him to drive up to Portland with me. On that trip we'd taken with Grandma, we'd spent hours at Powell's, a bookstore that filled four city blocks, then gone to a cool shop that sold vintage clothes by the pound. If Ivy was there now, I knew she'd hit those spots again, and I might be able to find her. Or maybe I'd look for that fabric store she loved so much. Maybe this was wishful thinking, but I had to hold out hope.

But when I got to the coffee shop, the place was empty. No sign of Jasper.

"Hey, Laurel—that guy Jasper Blake was in here looking for you a little while ago," Ava told me. "He asked me to tell you that his grandfather got sick. He had to go in a hurry, but he said he'll try to catch up with you later." I nodded, not knowing what to do now. Should I try to make the trip to Portland alone? But then I caught sight of the coffee shop manager, Chad, his bleached hair coarse from surfing, and I remembered that I hadn't talked to him yet.

"Hey," I said, rushing up to him. "Did my sister ask for this weekend off?"

"Nope," he said, frowning, "and you can tell her that it's seriously uncool of her to bail on two shifts."

"Are you sure she never mentioned it?" I asked, as he stepped behind the counter.

Chad nodded, reaching into the biscotti jar and pulling one out. "I hired her to work weekends so I wouldn't have to, and she doesn't get vacation time."

My stomach sank. I couldn't believe that Ivy would have jeopardized her job like this. I was about to leave when I remembered what Mom had said when we first saw that Ivy was gone: maybe she'd met a guy at Ritual. I didn't think she had a secret boyfriend, but since I'd seen her use her power in my dreams, this meant that the other things I was seeing in those nightmares had to be real too, no matter how I might wish otherwise.

Since the man in the mask knew her—knew *about* her—he had to have met her somewhere. He was too old to be a student, and this was where she spent most of her time when she wasn't at school.

"Has anyone weird been hanging around the coffee shop lately?" I asked Chad. "Anyone you might've seen talking to Ivy?"

"This is Cascade," he said with a shrug. "A lot of our regulars are weird."

"How about during Ivy's shifts?" I pressed. "Have you noticed any creepy men checking her out?"

"Lots of dudes check her out," he said, chewing his biscotti. "She's pretty hot."

"What about that guy who came in with the rabbit," Ava interrupted.

"Oh yeah, he's creepy for sure," Chad agreed.

"Tell me about him," I said, leaning closer.

Ava wiped her hands on her apron. "He's definitely one of our weirdest regulars. He usually comes in on the weekends, orders a decaf, and sits right there." She pointed to an empty table near the register.

"He's not here today," I said.

"I don't think he's been back since he tried to give Ivy that dead rabbit," Ava said.

My heart began to pound. "What happened?" I asked, clenching my fists as I leaned forward.

"It was so sick," Chad said, grimacing as he set down the rest of his biscotti. "So this dude comes in with something wrapped up in newspaper. He unrolls it on the counter, and there's a skinned rabbit inside, with the ears still on and everything." He shuddered. "He tells us that he sells game to restaurants. I'm all, 'Dude, this is a coffee shop. We sell, like, muffins and stuff. Put that thing away before I hurl.'"

"But he kept pushing it across the counter at Ivy," Ava continued. "He goes, 'It's for you. You like bunnies. I know you do.'"

"Then she's all, *'Eew! I'm a vegetarian!'*" Chad imitated a high-pitched girly voice that sounded nothing like Ivy's, and I wanted to punch him.

But then I remembered something the man had said in last night's dream.

I know you don't usually eat meat.

"Did you call the police?" My voice was shrill, my guts twisting.

"No," Chad said. "He left, and he hasn't been back since. It was gross, but Ivy didn't seem that worked up about it. Why are you freaking out?"

"Because I think he might have kidnapped her," I said quietly.

"What? I thought you said she was up in Portland visiting a friend," Ava said.

Now they were both looking at me like I was certifiable.

Everything about this guy matched up with details from my nightmares.

Obsessed with Ivy: *check.*

Knows that she's a vegetarian: *check.*

Has a knife that could skin a rabbit: *check.*

I asked if they knew his name, but they didn't. "What does he look like?" I demanded.

"I'd guess he's in his midthirties," Ava said. "He's got brown hair, and he's pretty tall. I don't remember what color his eyes are. Nothing about him stands out."

This was not at all helpful.

But then, all of a sudden, something did stand out. To me, at least. The man had said that she liked bunnies.

Bunnies.

11.

I DROVE STRAIGHT back to our old neighborhood, speeding past Skye's and Grandma's, following the edge of the Klamath River, where every year the banks flood, making the vinyl siding on the houses buckle and rusting the appliances left in weedy front yards. The van careened over potholes, but I barely slowed down as I navigated by instinct, trying to tap into a distant memory of a place I hadn't been back to since I was a kid on a bike.

In my mind's eye, I saw the plywood sign with hand-painted red letters that we must have passed a million times.

Bunnies 4 Sale.
Good 4 Stew.

I could still visualize the skinny gravel path that led from that sign to the back of a dingy yellow house, where a hutch was stuffed with live rabbits. On summer afternoons, Ivy and I used to hop off our bikes and stick our fingers through the mesh, wishing we were brave enough to set them free. Our mom had raised us vegetarian since birth, and somehow it seemed extra cruel to eat something that cute.

Then one day—I must have been nine, so Ivy was ten—we finally worked up the nerve. We'd never seen anyone on the property, and we thought we could do it fast and get away. But Ivy had just cracked the door to the hutch when a man stepped outside, asking just what we thought we were doing. I'd wanted to bolt, but Ivy spoke up. "You shouldn't hurt these bunnies," she'd said, like it was that simple. I held my breath as he strode toward us.

"I don't hurt them," he said matter-of-factly. "I kill them. And they never see it coming." With one hand, he made a sinister chopping motion and we jumped on our bikes, cycling until our lungs burned.

We'd never returned, and seven years had gone by. But to this day, whenever we wanted to freak each other out, we'd make that chopping gesture.

If we remembered him, he could have remembered Ivy too.

After all, I'd remembered him well enough to find my way back here, almost as if in a dream.

But I was wide awake.

The plywood sign advertising the bunnies was still up, faded but legible. I sat in the van, my chest thudding as I stared at the dingy yellow house. The blinds were lowered, and there were no lights on.

What should I do now? It was time to go to the police. I couldn't avoid it anymore. But even if I did, explaining that my sister had been stalked at work by someone she'd met when we were kids, and that I was pretty sure he'd kidnapped her, what proof did I have?

Uh, so I'm following some clues from a nightmare . . .

I still hadn't seen any movement from inside, so I got out of the van, crept up the driveway and pressed my face to a dusty windowpane. Through the blinds, I made out a saggy brown couch facing a big TV, a framed needlepoint hanging on the wall, and magazines fanned across a coffee table. It looked ordinary enough, but weren't the neighbors of serial killers always saying that they had no idea that there was anything wrong with the guy next door?

An oval rug made of braided rags covered the floor. It was definitely big enough to hide a trapdoor. The thought that she could be a few feet away made me reckless.

I jiggled the doorknob. Locked. I rang the bell, holding my breath, but a minute passed and no one came. My body vibrated with fear as I slipped around the side of the house. The back door was locked too, but I saw a large window above a washing machine set out on the deck. Blood thrummed in my ears as I climbed up onto it. I pushed on the windowpane and it slid open easily.

"Ivy?" I said softly. High in a branch, something cawed. "Ivy!" I yelled. But then I remembered the collar. She couldn't yell back without getting a shock.

I was pretty sure I could fit through the window. If this man turned out to be innocent, I'd feel stupid. But I could live with that. *I can't live without Ivy.*

I slipped through the opening and dropped to my feet, landing in some kind of mudroom. Without pausing, I rushed into the living room and yanked back the braided rug. Underneath was a dull linoleum floor, no sign of any trapdoor. I tore through the small house. The two bedrooms had wall-to-wall orange carpeting. I threw open the closet doors and checked under the beds, but found no hidden entrance to a cellar, nothing that resembled anything in my dreams.

I circled the place a couple more times, calling her name and straining to hear a reply. Instead, I heard the crunch of tires on gravel and an engine turning off.

I flew out the back door and around to the front of the house, where a beat-up white town car had parked alongside the van. I was clutching my key, prepared to use it as a weapon. But instead of the man from my nightmares, a gaunt old woman climbed out, leaning heavily on a cane. Her skin was tightly stretched over the bones of her face, the wisps of her hair as fine as cobwebs.

"What are you doing on my property?" she demanded in a voice a lot stronger than she looked.

"I was, uh, l-looking for someone," I stammered.

"It's only me and my boy here." She was standing in my way, so I decided to go out on a limb.

"Is he the one who raises rabbits?"

"That's right," she said, eyes narrowing. "What do you want with Josiah?"

I tried to think of a plausible excuse, but I can't lie to save my life. Ivy always said it was one of my better qualities, but now it was highly inconvenient. "My sister Ivy works at Ritual Roasters," I said.

"She's been gone for a few days, and since she and, uh, Josiah, are friends, I thought he might know where she is."

She shook her head. "Josiah doesn't have any friends, and he never did."

"Oh," I said. "Okay. Well, sorry for bothering you."

But suddenly her expression softened. "Wait—come to think of it, I believe Josiah may have mentioned a girl by that name. Ivy, you say?" I nodded, my stomach curdling. "Yes, I think he did mention her to me. He said she's real special."

"She is," I barely managed to say, trying to conceal the horror I felt inside.

"It's just him and me, and I do worry how he'll make out after I'm gone. It'll take a real special girl to see what I see in him." She smiled, but it didn't reach her eyes.

I tried to force my lips to turn up. I needed her to trust me, so that she'd tell me where her son might have taken Ivy. "I'm very worried about my sister, and I'd really like to talk to him," I said.

"Well, I'm sorry but you can't. He left early on Friday, see, right when the season opened. I expect he'll be gone a week at least."

"Friday," I repeated numbly. *Right when Ivy went missing.* "Where did he go?"

My voice had raised and she was looking at me oddly, but she answered. "Josiah's daddy built a shack in the woods. Every year, the two of them used to spend the season holed up together, catching enough meat to fill the deep freeze."

"He's a hunter?" I asked, picturing that foot-long knife.

"A trapper," she corrected me. "It's in the Strauss family blood. Josiah's daddy always said there wasn't a living creature that boy couldn't catch."

This is venison jerky. I caught it myself.

I could taste that stringy wad of meat.

"Where is this shack?" My voice rang with panic now. "You have to tell me!" The old lady took a step back, but I couldn't control myself anymore. "I need to find Ivy. Tell me where he is!"

"Well, I'm sure Josiah wouldn't know a thing about your sister's whereabouts," she said, all friendliness draining from her face. "Besides, I've never been, since there's no facilities for ladies."

No, I thought. *Just a bucket.*

The rain had turned to stinging hail. I pushed past her and vaulted into Spud, revved the engine, and peeled onto the road. The pavement sizzled and popped as white marbles pelted the windshield. I steered with one hand while I wiped a clear spot on the glass with my fist, but it clouded up again immediately.

Beyond my fogged windshield, the world was a gray and green blur. Gray for the sky. Green for the trees blanketing the foothills. Mile after mile of forest surrounded us in every direction. That hunting shack could've been anywhere. I had no idea what was real anymore, where my nightmares ended or how to use them to find Ivy.

All I knew for sure was that I couldn't handle this on my own.

12.

"I NEED TO FILE a missing person report," I told the cop on duty at the police station. He was short and stocky, with sandy-brown hair and a badge that read Kevin Dougherty, a name that sounded vaguely familiar. "My sister has been gone for three days, and I'm pretty sure she was kidnapped by a man named Josiah Strauss."

"Okay, hold on, kid. Start over." He leaned closer to the partition separating us, so that his breath fogged the Plexiglas. "You say your sister's been missing since Thursday? How old is she?"

"Seventeen." I swallowed hard. "She was gone when I woke up on Friday morning, which is exactly when this man Josiah left for his cabin in the woods."

He frowned. "Then why haven't your parents called to report this? Because I was here all day Friday, and I didn't get a call about any missing teen."

"Ivy and our mom had this big fight the night before," I said. "Our mom thought maybe she took off to give her a scare. But she didn't know about this creepy older man who's been stalking Ivy at work."

"Kidnapping is a very serious allegation," he said. "Why don't you come into my office and tell me what happened from the beginning."

He opened the door leading to the back of the station, guiding me down a tiny hallway to a cubicle with wrestling posters tacked to the walls. He told me to take the seat across from his desk, and after sitting down across from me he picked up a pad of paper, uncapping a pen so he could take notes. So that he'd take me seriously, I tried to talk calmly, focusing on the parts I knew he'd believe.

"Her coworker told me that this guy brought her a skinned rabbit at Ritual," I said. "He was someone we'd met when we were kids. He must have recognized her, and started stalking her after that."

I assumed that as soon as he heard all of this, he would dispatch a search party for the woods immediately—with dogs and maybe helicopters—to find the Strauss family hunting shack. But instead he clicked his ballpoint pen in and out, in and out, and tipped back in his chair, squinting at me. "Maybe he's your sister's boyfriend," he suggested, pausing between every word as if deliberately trying to torture me. "That would explain why he was visiting her regularly at work."

"No way," I said emphatically. "He's really old—over thirty."

The corner of Officer Dougherty's mouth twitched and I gripped my seat, picking at a rip in the vinyl cushion. Behind him hung a framed poster of a wrestler under a halo of stars, and as I recognized a younger, trimmer version of the man across from me, it dawned on me why his name sounded familiar. Kevin Dougherty had been a wrestling legend, going all the way to the Olympics, one of our town's only success stories.

Maybe he's taken too many blows to the head.

"Just last week," he continued, "we had a woman come in nearly out of her mind with worry, telling us that her seventy-five-year-old mother had wandered into the woods, where she could die of hypothermia. In fact, the old lady was on a bus to Reno with big plans to hit the slot machines." He chuckled, then stopped when I didn't join in. "My point being, family members often have the wrong end of the stick. Let's go back to this fight she had with your mom. I'm willing to bet my next paycheck that's why your sister ran away."

"Ivy did *not* run away," I said, but he was on a roll with his theory.

"I'm sure I don't have to tell you that there's an epidemic of runaways in Oregon." He shook his head sadly. "Kids choosing a life of homelessness and drugs. They'd rather live off handouts than finish school and get a job. It's pathetic, really."

Clenching my fists underneath the lip of his desk, I thought of the grungy teens that hung out in front of Price Chopper. Ivy was a neat freak, showering so thoroughly she often emptied our hot water tank. "My sister doesn't even drink," I said. "She never skips class, and she works two jobs to help our mom."

"So why isn't your mom more concerned about her absence?"

"She is," I said quickly, not wanting him to go there. "I mean she was, but then we found a note from Ivy . . ." I trailed off.

"You didn't mention that." He set down his pen. "In this note—did she say where she was going?"

"To Portland," I said. "To visit a friend from camp."

"Well, there you go," he said, looking at me like I was wasting his time.

"But I'm sure that Josiah Strauss forced her to write it!" My eyes filled with tears again. "You've got to believe me! I know she's in big trouble. We have to find her!" I held on to my chair as if he might try to pry me out of it.

After eyeing me for a minute, he sighed and jiggled his computer mouse. "I tell you what I can do," he said. "I'll plug her name in the system. Street kids tend to get a record pretty fast. If she did run away, maybe we can find out where she is."

"I *told* you, she's not a street kid," I said. But I didn't say anything else, because at least he was doing *something*.

His brow pleated as he looked at the screen, and I pitched forward in my seat. "There's nothing on Ivy Goodwin," he announced at last. "But there's a Sheila Goodwin with a suspended driver's license, and an allegation of child neglect." He looked at me. "Is that your mom?"

"I guess," I whispered, my fingers working away at that hole. The fabric tore and foam crumbled onto the carpet. I looked up at him, expecting him to be mad about the chair, and mad that I had wasted his time. But the pity I saw on his face was worse. What if he reported us to a caseworker, and Mom was declared unfit to be our guardian? Clearly I'd made a huge mistake.

"You're what—fifteen?" he asked. I nodded. "Just like my sister Hanna." He clucked his tongue. "You should be worrying about homework and boys, not coming in to file a missing person report. How'd you get here today?"

"I walked."

"Well, I'm going to give you a ride home."

"That's okay," I said quickly. "I like walking, really."

"I insist," he said. "Besides, now that you've made this charge, I'm going to need to talk to your mother."

He had a look of bulldog determination on his face, and I remembered hearing how even after he tore his ACL in the Olympics, he continued wrestling until he couldn't crawl off the mat. Then a phone rang in the distance. "I have to take that," he said. "You wait here, and then I'll drive you home."

I nodded obediently. But the second he was out of sight, I got up and ran, feeling like I was the one who had committed a crime.

"Yes, Officer, Ivy had my full permission to go to stay with her friend in Portland." Mom was speaking into the phone when I entered the trailer. "Yes, I'm absolutely sure. Laurel was just confused. It was a tiny argument—you know how teenagers blow things way out of proportion." She paced, holding the phone in one hand while twisting the chain of her pendant so tightly that I was afraid she might strangle herself.

"I will definitely write down her friend's number the next time she calls. I'm so mad at myself for having lost it. You want to interview Ivy when she gets home? I really don't see why that's necessary, but . . . I see . . . I'd almost forgotten about that." She issued a sound that barely resembled a laugh. "I'm sure she'll tell you that it's a perfectly stable environment, but I guess you can come by and see for yourself. Of course. Anytime."

Finally, she hung up, but she didn't look at me.

"I'm so sorry, Mom." I sank down at the table, wishing the floor would open up and swallow me. "I know I shouldn't have gone to the police, but I've been having these crazy nightmares since Ivy disappeared, and all this stuff in my dreams matches what I learned about this total psychopath who's been stalking her at work!"

Mom sat down beside me, her face pale. "I'm very worried, Lolo."

"Me too!" It was such a relief to hear Mom share my fear. I realized that for once, I couldn't smell pot fumes. Maybe with Bryan gone, she'd stop getting high and start paying attention. Now that I knew the police wouldn't help at all, I felt like I had no choice but to tell her everything.

But I'd barely gotten started when she cut me off.

"You think Ivy's sending you telepathic messages from a dungeon?"

"I know that sounds crazy," I pleaded with her, "but this guy really was stalking Ivy at work, he left for the woods on the same day that she disappeared, and the cop wouldn't even follow up on my lead!"

"Your *lead*, Laurel?" She twisted her pendant again. "I hate to agree with anything Bryan said, but maybe you do read too many novels."

"But you said you were worried!"

"I am," she said. "But mainly, I'm worried about you. Really worried."

"Haven't you been listening to me?" I wanted to scream.

She crossed her arms. "Officer Dougherty also told me that an old lady named Bertha Strauss called to report that a girl was trespassing on her property. There were signs that this girl had entered her house through a window. Was that you, Laurel?"

I shrugged, staring at the bits of glitter embedded in the red Formica.

"I can't believe you'd do something like that." She shook her head. "I feel like you're losing touch with reality."

"You're one to talk," I shot back. "Until yesterday, you acted like Bryan was a knight in shining armor."

I was trying to start a fight, but she didn't take the bait. "You're right," she said quietly. "But you don't have to make my mistakes. What did Grandma always say? 'You've got a good head on your shoulders—'"

"'So use it,'" I finished, wishing more than ever that Grandma were still here with us. I knew that none of this would have happened if she were. I could tell that Mom was thinking the same thing. We were both quiet, and then she started to rub my back in soft circles, the way she used to when I was little and couldn't fall asleep.

"I had an idea," she said. "Of course I'm worried about Ivy too, and it would make me feel so much better if I could just talk to her, hear her voice. I was thinking that we could go and see Pastor Andersen tomorrow. He must have a roster of kids from camp. We could find out which of her friends lives up in Portland, and get a phone number to reach her."

I wiped my sleeve over my eyes. A strange kind of relief—mingled with dread—filled me. If my worst nightmares were real, if we found out that no one from Portland even went to that camp, then Mom would have to take my fears seriously.

"That's actually not a completely useless suggestion," I said.

"Gee, thanks," Mom said, and we both laughed weakly. She held both of my hands between hers. "Gosh, you're freezing. I wish we had a tub. I could run you a millionaire's bath."

I hadn't thought of this in years. A millionaire's bath was something Mom came up with when we were little and feeling sick or in need of some TLC. It consisted of about half a gallon of Mr. Bubble, a bunch of candles, and 7 Up in plastic champagne flutes. The bubbles always billowed over onto the floor, and we felt like movie stars.

She sighed. "Well, instead of a millionaire's bath, you'll have to have a pauper's shower. But at least I can bring you a nice dry robe when you get out."

In the shower, I let my mind drift. I remembered how Mom had tried to teach us about art. She'd shown us that black-and-white picture, the one that can be a vase or two faces in profile, depending on which way you look at it. I'd always been fascinated by it, straining trying to see both pictures at once, but it was impossible. As I let the hot water stream over me, I had this random thought. Maybe families aren't one thing or the other, they're both: happy and sad, resentful and tender, broken and whole.

It's just so much easier to see only part of the truth.

13.

Peyton

AS FAR AS PEYTON WAS CONCERNED, her church youth group was a total drag. But as the pastor's daughter, she could never get out of it. Every Sunday evening, she and her dad drove together to the Faith Center, a converted multiplex, where instead of advertising movie titles, the roadside marquee now read, Coming Soon: Your Salvation or Doom.

Usually, there were just a dozen kids, filling the first rows of the smallest theater. But tonight, folding chairs spilled into the aisles. Her dad must have called every God-fearing family in town, telling them that their kids' eternal souls were at risk.

"Wow, am I ever excited to see so many fresh faces!" Hanna Dougherty squeaked at the podium. Her cardboard-colored hair was pulled back in a French braid, and she was wearing an enormous T-shirt that said *WWPAD. What Would Pastor Andersen Do?* She'd had them made for all the kids in youth group, as a surprise for Peyton's dad's fortieth birthday. Peyton's was balled up at the back of a drawer.

"I'd like to kick off with my favorite verse from Corinthians," Hanna said. "'Do you not know that your body is a temple of the Holy Spirit?'" As she held up her Bible, her gold promise ring flashed, setting Peyton's teeth on edge. Last month, her dad had bestowed this ring upon Hanna in a ceremony in front of the whole congregation, as she vowed to save herself for her future husband.

Like anyone wants to get into those mom jeans, Peyton reflected, trying to resist the urge to scratch her cheek. It felt like a mosquito had stung her on the birthmark that her mom always told her to cover with a very expensive concealer. When it came to her daughter's looks, Peyton's mom spared no expense—probably because that was all she thought Peyton had going for her.

"What's up with Mei?" Peyton asked Stu, who was slumped in the chair beside her. "Have you talked to her since Friday?"

"No, why? Did she say something? What did she say?"

"Nothing." Why was he acting so jumpy? "My dad repossessed my phone because of the party, so I haven't been able to talk to her."

Peyton's father expected her to "set the tone" at all times, which she'd definitely failed to do on Friday night. After driving her home, Mr. Sheers had insisted on escorting her to her front door. She'd cringed when her dad had opened it, a bathrobe flung over his pajamas. She knew she didn't make a pretty picture. Her bra was MIA—still dangling from the stag's antlers—her bare legs speckled with barf. Still, she couldn't believe the look of disgust on his face.

"You said you were spending the night at Hanna's," he'd said through gritted teeth.

"I'm afraid there's more," Mr. Sheers had said. "I hate to tell you this, but Peyton was upstairs when I got home." He cleared his throat. "In Stu's bedroom."

"I was just getting Mei," Peyton squealed in her own defense. "She's Stu's girlfriend. If anyone was getting it on up there, it was her!" But it was obvious that her father didn't believe her, even before what he said next.

I wish Hanna Dougherty were my daughter. At least she's not a little slut.

Actually, he'd whispered it.

Somehow, yelling would have been preferable.

Mr. Sheers was such a nice guy, Peyton had half expected him to defend her, or at least to seem embarrassed. Instead Mr. Sheers had proposed that his girlfriend, Simone Sinclair, come in to talk about the power of abstinence in front of the youth group. "She gets through to kids," he'd said. "I don't know how she does it, but they listen to her. It's a real gift she has."

Now, as the guidance counselor strolled down the aisle, Peyton sat up a little straighter. She hadn't yet been to see her in the office at school, but it was hard not to notice her, since she always looked like she'd just stepped off the pages of *Vogue*. Peyton knew, from eavesdropping on her mom's so-called book group (all they really seemed to do was chug Chardonnay and gossip), that Simone had been in love with Mr. Sheers since high school, pining after him even when he married her best friend. She had to be forty, but she looked good for her age (or any age, really). Way too hot for Cascade, although she had at least managed to nab the town's only "eligible bachelor," as Peyton's mom referred to Bill Sheers, like he was the star of some lame local reality TV show.

Peyton squinted, trying to detect the signs of plastic surgery. Her mom had been shot up with so much Botox that she could barely display a real emotion anymore. But when Simone smiled at the group, her face conveyed genuine warmth. She perched on the table where they served cookies after youth group and crossed her legs, showing off a crimson flash as she swung her foot.

Were those Louboutins? No way could she afford them on a counselor's salary. Mr. Sheers must have bought them for her, along with the diamond pin twinkling from the collar of her black wool sheath—which Peyton recognized from Marc Jacobs's latest collection. Mr. Sheers was certainly treating her right—although the book group ladies had commented on the fact that he had yet to put a ring on her finger.

"I'm guessing most of you were at the big party Friday night," Simone said to the group. "I hear things got pretty wild."

"I'll say," whispered Stu. Peyton glanced over at him, but he was staring down at his lap.

I still can't believe I was in bed with a guy.

"What did you just say?" she choked, certain she must have imagined that he'd spoken those words.

"Nothing," he said, but his face flushed to the tops of his ears.

Peyton frowned, swiveling a pinkie in her own ear. She'd taken a shower right before youth group. Was water trapped in there?

"I've been sent to talk to you about abstinence," Simone said. She looked almost excited, as if she knew a powerful secret that she couldn't resist the urge to spill—an urge Peyton knew all too well. "Now, I know what you're thinking," she continued. "You've heard it before. It's easy for adults to preach about holding back, because what do they know about passion? They're old. They're dried up. And you know what?" She lowered her voice to a whisper. "You're right."

A giggle rippled through the audience. Peyton found herself nodding. Just this morning, she'd heard her mom whisper to herself as she stirred the oatmeal: *I wish Hank were a more passionate lover. I feel like he's just going through the motions in bed.* "Uh, right behind you, Mom," Peyton had said, horrified, and certain that her mother would be even more so when she realized what she'd overheard. But she'd merely spooned a tiny portion of oatmeal into her bowl with a sad plop.

Simone strolled across the stage. "Now I'll tell you another secret. Most adults are scared of you. I know you probably think, 'Yeah, right. They're the ones with the power to ground us or expel us from school.' But you have the power of youth. You remind them of how alive they once felt, and of how much is missing from their lives now."

Hanna's hand shot into the air. "I'm sorry, but what does this have to do with saving yourself for marriage?"

Peyton saw a look of irritation flit over Simone's face. Then it vanished and she smiled again. "I'll get there, I promise. I understand your confusion, Hanna. And I'm sure this talk is probably too late for some of you. I bet some of you have already had sex, and there's nothing wrong with that. It's natural. I'm not here to cast stones. But tell me this: how many of you can say that it was everything it was supposed to be?" She glanced around, but nobody met her eye, not even Elle Jones, who Peyton knew for a fact had slept with three guys—though probably not all at once, like Peyton had told everyone, because that story was so much better.

Simone nodded sadly. "For those of you that haven't had sex yet," Simone said, "listen to what I'm telling you." She hugged herself, her voice a low purr: "The longer you wait, the better it'll be."

Hanna's jaw dropped. Then she stood up. "Uh, thank you, Simone. That was really . . . interesting." She clapped. "Time for cookies, everyone!"

Simone nodded. "Okay, but before I go, I want you all to know that you can come in and talk to me about anything. My office door is always open, and anything you say to me will remain confidential." As her gaze swept across the crowded room, it seemed to touch upon each person, one at a time. Peyton could practically feel it, like a fingertip brushing across her bare skin.

I wish I'd waited.

At first she couldn't tell where this whisper was coming from. She scanned the refreshments table, where Hanna was arranging her M&M's cookies on a platter.

Why did I listen when Remy said that he loved me?

Was that Hanna? It sounded like her voice, whispering. But her thin lips hadn't moved that Peyton could see, and no one else seemed to have heard a thing.

I was so stupid to let him pressure me. He hasn't even texted in weeks.

Yep. That was Hanna, no question. And Remy was the name of their camp counselor. He was cute but borderline pervy, always giving the girls back rubs, letting his fingers wander and linger. In fact, he was the same counselor that Peyton had claimed to have lost her virginity to. She was sick to death of being the pastor's daughter—no guy dared to touch her with a ten-foot pole, lest her father bring the brimstone of his sermons to bear on them—and had hoped that spreading this rumor about how willing she was to give it up might help. But so far there were no takers. She still couldn't believe the way Jasper had brushed her off. She scratched at her birthmark, but this only made it itchier.

It seemed so real at the time, but obviously I meant nothing to him.

That squeaky whisper again! Had Hanna—the blessed virgin—actually done what Peyton had only pretended to? No. Way. Besides, she was standing by herself.

How did that guy get in my bed on Friday night? Where the hell did Mei go?

This deeper whisper came from her left, where Stu was standing with his shoulders hunched up by his ears like he was trying to simulate his football padding.

The room spun as Peyton clenched her fists and squeezed her eyes shut, wishing she could do the same to her ears. Schizophrenics heard voices. Wasn't this the first sign of a mental breakdown? She dashed to the bathroom, locking the door and peering at herself in the mirror. Her cheek was covered with claw marks, cross-hatching her birthmark—it was horrifying. She wished she'd listened to her mother for once and brought her concealer with her. She looked like a crazy person.

This wasn't the first time Peyton had overheard something that she wasn't meant to. No, the first time had been when she was eight years old, sitting in the backseat on the way home from a beauty pageant. Her mom must have thought she was asleep when she whispered to her dad: *It's a good thing she's pretty, because she's not very smart.* Peyton waited and waited for her father to jump to her defense. But instead he'd simply told her mother that it wasn't a very Christian thing to say—which wasn't the same as saying she was wrong.

The fact that she hadn't been meant to hear this whisper only made it seem truer. No wonder it took her so long to learn how to read. By the time she was diagnosed with dyslexia, she'd concluded that her parents were right. She stopped listening in class, and traded gossip instead. Peyton had heard that athletes felt a physical need to exercise. She felt the same need to spread rumors.

Maybe she was going through some kind of freaky gossip withdrawal.

That almost made sense. She hadn't been able to talk to Mei since Friday. That could explain why she was making things up out of thin air.

Youth group was breaking up when Peyton wandered over to the refreshments table. She couldn't remember a day in her life when she hadn't been counting every calorie, avoiding carbs, sugar, fat, basically anything that tasted good, to make sure that she held on to the one thing she had going for her. *Good thing she's pretty.* But today she had no willpower. The cookies were still a little warm and gooey, and before she realized it, she'd polished off three. She caught Hanna eyeing her, nervously spinning her promise ring, and she found herself fueled by the rush of sugar—or something else.

"'Your body is a temple,'" Peyton said, screwing up her face. "Didn't one of the counselors teach us that Bible verse? I can't remember his name, but he was really hot."

"I don't know what you're talking about," Hanna stammered.

"Really? But you guys were together all the time." Peyton snapped her fingers. "Remy! That's it!" Hanna squirmed, her face going pale as her breath came quicker. "Are you two still going out, or was it just one of those camp things that seemed so real?"

"I barely knew him!" Hanna protested.

"That's weird, because I was sure that I saw you sneak off together on the last night, down by the lake."

Hanna's eyes darted in all directions—as if looking for an escape exit in a burning building. Peyton had never seen anyone look guiltier. She felt giddy with power.

"Sweet little Hanna banana," she said, wrapping an arm around her quaking shoulders. "Don't you think you should return that promise ring to my dad?"

"Who told you?" Hanna gasped.

"Who cares? What matters is that we both know it's true."

"Please leave me alone," Hanna whimpered. "I know you hate me."

"*Au contraire!* In fact, I was thinking we should hang out more often."

Dear God, Hanna thought. *Please don't let this be my punishment, even though I deserve it.*

"Yes, you do," Peyton said in a steely tone, so caught up in the game that she forgot, for that moment, to be freaked out.

"Stop it!" Hanna cried.

"No problem. Just as soon as you give that ring back to my dad, and let him know that you're a liar and a—a *little slut*."

Hanna was crying openly as Peyton steered her toward her dad's office. "If you don't tell him, I will. But it would mean so much more, coming from you."

Snot streamed from Hanna's nose, and Peyton felt a twinge of guilt. Then she reminded herself this girl was a total liar as she shoved her into his office and shut the door behind her.

I wish I'd never said that awful thing, her dad would think, after he heard Hanna's confession. *I love my daughter, and I'd never trade her for this hypocrite.*

For the next twenty minutes, Peyton waited in the lobby, which still smelled of stale popcorn from its movie theater days, sitting on her hands to keep from digging at her cheek.

Underneath her excitement, a dark current of fear tugged at her.

Did I just read Hanna's mind?

She tried to squash this question down, visualizing the sour pucker of her dad's mouth as he told Hanna never to return to youth group.

But when the door swung open, he placed a palm on Hanna's head. Hanna's face was blotchy, but she'd stopped crying. "I'm really sorry I let you down," she said.

"You didn't," he replied. "Confession is the righteous path to forgiveness and absolution. That can't have been easy. I admire your courage."

He remained silent as he locked up the church, stalking to the Cadillac so that Peyton had to run to keep up.

He was still refusing to look at her.

"Hanna is not Little Miss Perfect!" she burst out once he was driving. "I don't know what she told you, but she had sex with one of our camp counselors!"

"She made a mistake," he said, eyes glued to the road. "She recognized this, and she confessed."

"Only because I made her!" Peyton raked her fingernails over her birthmark. Her whole face was on fire.

At a stop sign, her father pivoted toward her, wearing the expression of contempt she'd imagined he'd use on Hanna. But as he stared at her, disgust turned to horror. "What the hell did you do to yourself?" he thundered. "Is that a pentacle tattoo?"

"What are you talking about? Of course not!" Peyton lunged for the rearview mirror. Where she'd felt that throbbing heat, there was now a star that shone silver in the middle of her birthmark.

"It's not a tattoo!" she cried, rubbing as hard as she could. "I was just scratching my cheek! I swear to God, it just happened!"

"If I believed that," he boomed in his pulpit voice, "I'd be more scared for your soul than I already am."

Peyton turned away, so he wouldn't see the hot tears coursing down her face. In his darkest sermons, he talked about the demons that could take possession of a person, invited in through sin.

Is that what's happening?

She closed her eyes, leaning her scalding cheek against the cool windowpane as she tried to process the events of the last hour. But her mind wasn't up for the task. None of it made sense. It couldn't be happening.

But cutting through the silence, she heard one last whisper. It seemed to reach her from a distance, weaker than any of the others, and yet far more urgent.

Somebody help me. I need help.

It was a girl's voice, and it sounded familiar.

Somehow, she knew this was one whisper she was meant to overhear, which made it scarier than all the others combined.

14.

I DIDN'T FEEL LIKE EATING, but Mom insisting on "making dinner," which meant dumping a couple of cans of cream of mushroom soup into a pan. I thought the stuff tasted like wallpaper paste, but Mom did most of the shopping at Grocery Outlet, where they sold dented cans a little past their sell-by date for half price, and I guess they had a glut of cream of mushroom. "At least it's filling," Mom said, depressing me even more.

I was sitting on the couch, wrapped in the afghan, when the phone rang, so I got to it first. "Ivy?" I said breathlessly.

"Sorry," Jasper said. "It's just me. So you haven't heard from her?"

Jasper, I mouthed at Mom, my hand over the mouthpiece.

"No news?" he said.

I wanted to tell him everything I'd learned today about Josiah, but after my lecture from Mom earlier about losing touch with reality, I didn't want her to think I was still obsessing. "Yeah, but I can't talk about it right now," I whispered.

"Whatever it is, two heads are better than one," Jasper said. "Come and meet me."

I was scared to drive Spud alone in the dark, but more scared to be alone with what I'd found out about Josiah. Jasper was right—I did need to talk to someone. And what was the alternative? Waiting by the phone while we choked down our soup? "Meet me at the Riverside Diner," I told him. It was a place that reminded me of Ivy. We'd been going there since we were kids.

Mom didn't want me to go out again, but softened when I said I was going with Jasper.

"So that's what this is about?" Her voice softened slightly. "Is it a date?"

"No!" I said. "No one 'dates' anymore. We're just friends."

"Mm-hmm." She nodded, smiling in an extremely irritating, all-knowing way. My face burned as I threw on Ivy's jean jacket and grabbed my keys, but as soon as I was on the road, I relaxed a little, which struck me as funny given how terrified driving made me only a few days ago.

But doing something, anything, was so much better than just waiting.

Jasper was already standing outside the diner when I got there. A hostess in a pink dress and white sneakers showed us to a window booth with a view of the Klamath River. The sight of the water flowing by was soothing—familiar—but my hands still trembled. Thoughts of Josiah made my stomach churn.

"Can I have a pie shake?" I called out to a waitress wiping down the bar. I needed something to calm my nerves if I was going to get through this. Jasper called out his own order: apple pie a la mode. Once the waitress disappeared, he put his hands on the table and leaned toward me. "So what happened today?"

He listened closely as I told him all about Josiah. "I just need to find that shack," I said. "What am I supposed to do now?" I stared out the window at the dark rushing water below. Ivy was out there somewhere, right now, cold and alone in her cell.

Or if she wasn't alone, that was even worse.

"Maybe she's already dead," I said, my voice breaking, although part of me thought I would know if that were true.

"What about your dream last night?" Jasper said. "Were there any clues in that?"

When I described it to him, he repeated the last line. "'By Thursday, I need you to be—'"

"What do you think he needs her to be?" I said.

"I'm not sure. But at least we know he's going to keep her alive until Thursday."

I swiped tears out of my eyes. "So we have until Thursday. Great. What do you think is going to happen then? And why does he need her?"

"I don't know." Jasper worried at the lid of a thimble of half-and-half. "But I want to take you to see my grandfather tomorrow."

Much as part of me felt happy that he wanted me to meet his grandfather, this hardly seemed like the time. "Uh, maybe after we find Ivy?"

"That's the thing. I think he might be able to cast some light on all of this. He's really smart and he speaks about seventeen languages."

"No offense, but I don't really see how that's going to help us now."

Jasper looked around and then lowered his voice. "He used to have a power. He gave it up a long time ago, but he's spent decades researching this stuff. You'd be surprised by how much he knows about just about everything. I've told him about Ivy. I would have taken you to see him today, but he was too sick," he continued. "He had a pretty bad emphysema attack, and his medication really knocks him out. That's why I couldn't meet you at Ritual. Let's go early tomorrow morning."

I did like the sound of getting an adult opinion, especially if that adult once had a power too. Since he knew what Ivy could do, he wouldn't dismiss my fears. The thought of getting his expert guidance suddenly made me feel a lot better. "Can we go see him before school?"

"Definitely," Jasper said. "We'll go first thing. He's at his sharpest then anyway."

The waitress brought our orders and I realized I was actually hungry. I took a long sip from the straw. Jasper dug a spoon into his apple pie.

"What's a pie shake?" he asked, eyeing my frosty cup.

"What it looks like. A slice of pie blended in a milkshake. They only make them here. They're amazing. You should've tried one." He pretended to shudder and I said, "What?"

"That's a violation of the rules."

"What rules?" I said. "The rules of pie?"

He nodded. "It's all about the contrast of hot, flakey pie and cold, creamy ice cream. Blending them together is just plain wrong. It would never happen in France."

"Ooh la la," I said. "And how would you know?"

He smiled. "Sorry, I didn't mean to sound like a snob. I used to live in Paris. That's where I was before I came back to Cascade, which is why I haven't got a driver's license yet. In Paris, I walked everywhere, or took the Metro."

"Wow," I breathed. I'd always wanted to go to Paris—"the City of Light"—but I didn't even have a passport. The farthest Ivy and I had been from Cascade was a trip to Disneyland when we were kids. "But you're from here?" I asked, and he nodded. "So did your family move to France when you were little?"

"No. I went by myself, actually."

"So were you, like, an exchange student or something?" There was a kid in our class who'd gone to Germany for a year. But I didn't remember ever having met Jasper before. Maybe he'd gone to the other middle school.

He shook his head, and when he didn't volunteer any more information, I figured he must have been at a French boarding school. Obviously, he came from money. His parents had bought Headmaster House, the grandest home in Cascade. He'd seen how we lived and probably didn't want me to feel bad. But the silence was awkward now, and I felt relieved when he reached out for my long metal spoon.

"May I?" he said. I nodded, and he took a tentative bite.

"Well?" I prompted him. I could see that he was savoring it.

"I forgot how great pumpkin pie is," he said with a moan. "In Paris, there's a patisserie on every block, but you can't get a slice of pumpkin pie to save your life."

"And it's incredibly good in a pie shake," I said. "Right?"

Instead of answering, he dug in for more.

"Thief!" I said, batting his spoon away so I could take another sip. He grinned. But as our banter faded, I could feel my sadness seeping back in. The pumpkin pie shake was the best flavor yet, and Ivy wasn't here to try it with me.

Jasper looked at me, his stare somehow focused and gentle at once. I knew that I couldn't hide things from him. He paid attention in a way that most people didn't. It felt good to be noticed like that—and also terrifying. But since he refused to look away, I decided to open up a little.

"Ivy and I are on a mission to try all the flavors of pie shake," I said. "We keep this log, pretending to be restaurant critics. What if we never finish?" For some reason, the prospect of this small loss made my eyes flood again, because it made the thought of losing Ivy real. "I'm sorry." I grabbed a napkin. "It's just that she's the only person who fully gets me. I don't know what I'd do if—"

"You're not going to lose her, Laurel." Jasper pushed his pie aside and reached across the table, his fingers encircling my wrist, pulling my hand toward him.

It was comforting for a moment, to feel my hand enfolded in his warm, strong grip.

But then, it wasn't.

Because I wanted more. I didn't want just a friendly squeeze, and as his thumb stroked my wrist, I was certain that he didn't either. I wanted to twine our fingers together and to take his other hand too. I wanted to trail my fingertips over his forearms, up to his shoulder, his chin, and—

Jasper pulled his hand away as if I was the one with the power to burn.

"I can't be with you," he said quietly. "I can't be with anyone."

I could feel my face turn a horrible bright red, and I had to take the cold silver milkshake cup and press it against my cheek for a moment. I was sure he thought that he was making me feel better by pretending he couldn't be with "anyone," that this was his way of letting me down gently, but instead I just felt like a stupid kid, drowning in her big sister's clothes. No way was I his type. His type was probably some chic French girl who clicked around in sexy heels and talked about Sartre.

"Right," I mumbled. I couldn't even look at him. I wanted to slide under the table.

MONDAY

I CAN'T JUST LIE HERE, waiting for him to kill me.

So, I've come up with a plan.

Tonight, when he uncuffs me, I'll wait until he's almost at the top of the ladder. Then I'm going to ram into that ladder with everything I've got.

If I'm lucky, he'll break his neck, or his legs at least. While he's on the ground, I'll run up the ladder before he can catch me.

What if he doesn't fall off the ladder? What if gets mad and tries to kill me?

I don't care.

I have to at least try to save myself.

I take a deep breath as the trapdoor opens.

Showtime.

But tonight, he doesn't unlock my handcuffs. Instead he sits on the mattress, right by my head. I squeeze myself into a ball, willing him not to come any closer. Then I hear the rasp of a match and I smell cigarette smoke. He coughs. The mattress creaks as he leans over me.

"Sorry, doll," he mumbles, "but we're running out of time."

That high, animal shriek doesn't sound like it could come from me, but I know that it is, because every nerve ending in my body is shrieking too, as a white-hot spike drives into my wrist.

15.

I JERKED AWAKE, sweat crawling down my back, and rubbed my wrist. I could still feel the scorching heat of that ember, even though my skin was unmarked. I couldn't stand to be in the bedroomette a moment longer. I threw on some clothes and drove straight to Jasper's.

It was so early that the almost round moon still hung in the sky. It would have been beautiful if I hadn't seen what I'd seen, or felt what I'd felt.

The air on Miner Street smelled like fermented cider from the apples littering Jasper's overgrown front yard. I skidded on a mushy one, almost falling as I rushed up the path to his porch.

I rapped on the big brass knocker, trying to think of what I'd say if Jasper's mom answered, but when the front door opened at last, it was him standing in front of me. He wore his faded jeans and was just pulling on a white T-shirt. His hair was wet, slicked back against his head, so he looked like a silent movie star.

"He's torturing her now," I blurted, breathless from panic. My fear had burned away all the embarrassment of the night before. I didn't care that I'd made a fool of myself. I just wanted to find my sister.

"Slow down," he said. He stepped outside, closing the door and listening intently as I told him about my latest nightmare.

"He's sick," I choked out. "He gets off on hurting her."

"Maybe," said Jasper, "but there could be another reason."

"What?" I demanded.

"It might have to do with, um . . ." Jasper glanced around the deserted street before saying in a lower voice, "An ancient prophecy."

I crossed my arms tightly. "Please tell me you're joking."

"I wish I were. But I promise my grandfather can explain. Let's go see him now."

Jasper grabbed his jacket and we got into the van. He directed me out of town, and onto the highway going east. As the speedometer hit sixty, I felt my pulse speed up to match. But at least the sky was clear for a change, the road dry.

"I've been thinking," he said. "If this Josiah guy was stalking her at Ritual, maybe he saw her using her power. That's where I saw her using it. That might be why he kidnapped her."

"But why would seeing her use her power make him want to kidnap her?" I asked. "What does her power have to do with anything?"

Jasper was silent and I said, "Oh, right. Another question only your grandfather can answer."

He pointed me to the third exit past Cascade, where a narrow road led up to the top of Skinner's Butte. A sign with a drawing of falling rocks told cars to proceed with caution. Thankfully, we took the low road, which wound around the base of the mountain and stopped at a dead end in front of a squat building that looked like a rundown motel. The sign in front read, "Conifers Senior Facility."

"Your grandpa's in here?" I asked. When our grandma got strict with us, we used to tease her with the threat of sending her here someday—*Watch out or you'll end up at Conifers*—but we would never have done it.

He nodded. "I know it's grim, but it's the only place nearby with twenty-four-hour nursing care. I try to visit as much as I can."

He obviously felt bad about it, and I was sorry I'd brought it up. But my opinion of the place didn't change as I glanced around the empty lobby while he signed us in. They'd made a half-hearted attempt to decorate with posters and potted plants, but it was pretty grim.

Even though it was still before dawn, some of the bedroom doors were open, and I could see a few of the ancient residents hunched in front of flickering televisions. My heart sank. How could anyone who lived here possibly be any help in finding Ivy?

Jasper knocked on one of the doors and a voice told us to enter. What I saw inside lifted my spirits a little. The room was lined with bookcases, each tightly packed with leather-bound volumes, with more piled up on top, all the way to the ceiling. An old man was seated in an armchair by the window, so deeply absorbed in the tome on his lap that he didn't seem to register our arrival. He was dressed in a corduroy blazer with elbow patches, and he had Jasper's olive skin and a full head of snow-white hair. His skin was deeply creased, but his eyes, when he looked up, were bright and curious.

"Jasper!" he said. "Forgive me, I thought you were housekeeping."

"Hey, Gramps," Jasper said, grinning. "There's someone I want you to meet."

I stepped closer and shook the old man's hand. He held on with a firm grasp, giving me a shrewd look. His eyes, I noticed, were just like Jasper's: green with tiny flecks of gold.

"So you found the girl," he said to Jasper.

"No. This is her sister, Laurel." Jasper turned to me. "I told Gramps about Ivy's power, and how I was helping her learn how to use it."

"I'm so sorry to hear that she's missing." Mr. Blake was still holding on to my hand, peering up at me as if he were an archaeologist who had just unearthed something totally unexpected. "But I'm sure you'll find her. You have the spark too, don't you?"

"The spark?" I said.

"That's what we call someone with a power," Jasper explained.

"No," I said, wishing that I did.

"My mistake," said Mr. Blake after a moment's pause. "Well, I'm very pleased to meet you, Laurel." He let go of my hand and pressed a button on his armrest. With a whirring sound, his chair-back straightened. "I'm sorry I'm not strong enough to get up and greet you properly. Growing old is hell, I'm afraid. Thankfully, my eyesight still allows me to read, which is all I'm good for these days."

"What are all of these books?" I asked.

"Dust traps," said a nurse in teddy bear scrubs, as she entered with a paper cup of pills. "It aggravates his condition," she scolded Jasper. "I keep telling you, get your grandpa a Kindle."

"I offered, but he thinks they're an abomination," Jasper said.

Mr. Blake laughed. "I never read anything written after the fourteenth century. I highly doubt there's an electronic version of the *Liber Linteus*." He turned to me. "I had a hell of a time procuring that volume. It was written on the wrappings of an Egyptian mummy, but my persistence paid off. It revealed a great deal about people like us."

Jasper cleared his throat and made a jerking head motion at the nurse, but she was too busy giving the old man his pills to pay attention to what she must have figured were senile ramblings. I tried to read the names of the books on the shelves, but I couldn't decipher a single word.

"Is this Latin?" I asked, fingering a volume bound in caramel leather.

"Yep," Jasper said. "And this one is in Quechua, the language of the ancient Incas. It's still spoken today, in some remote parts of Peru. And this here's Gaelic. I hear it was a huge bestseller among the Celts." He and his grandfather both hooted.

"Old books keep me young," Mr. Blake said.

"I'm all done here," the nurse said, "but you two better promise not to tire him out with too much talking."

We agreed, and after she left, Mr. Blake told Jasper to close the door. Once we were alone, their expressions turned serious, and I saw the family resemblance again.

"Now, pleasant as this is, I know you didn't come here for a cozy chat about books," Mr. Blake said.

"Unfortunately not." Jasper pulled up a chair for each of us. "I think Laurel needs to hear about the prophecy, since it concerns her sister."

"I think you're right." Mr. Blake fixed a hawkish stare on me. "This prophecy comes down to us from a nomadic sect of Zoroastrians, who lived in the mountains of Persia three thousand years ago."

"Zoroastrians?" I stared at him, baffled.

"Their teachings are the first place where you find mention of people with powers like ours," Jasper said. "Gramps has been studying them for ages."

"And what does this, um, prophecy say exactly?" I asked, hoping he'd skip straight to the part that would lead us to Ivy. But Mr. Blake was already short of breath. He asked for a glass of water, and Jasper disappeared into the hall and reappeared with a mug in his hand. His grandpa's hand was shaking so hard that he had difficulty holding it. He moistened his lips and set it down. But his voice held steady as he recited these words:

> When forty thousand moons go dark
> As the dead and the living trade places,
> In a town of gold by the western coast
> Druj shall again trade faces.
> As the veil is lifted,
> Evil shall prevail.
> But if he who lost a star
> Is far from there
> And four powers freely link,
> That power cannot fail.

Then they both looked at me expectantly, as if, after hearing this eerie rhyme, I was supposed to have some great epiphany.

"What does that mean?" I asked.

"Basically," Jasper said, "an ancient evil is going to rise here in Cascade on the night of the lunar eclipse, unless four people with powers join together and stop it."

"Hold on," I said. "*Four* people with powers? There's you and Ivy, but who are the others? I thought you didn't have a power anymore." I turned to his grandfather.

"You're right," he said. "Unfortunately, I lost my power, so I can't be part of this linking."

Jasper squeezed his shoulder. Then he turned to me. "Actually, I can't be part of the linking of powers either."

"Why?"

"I'm 'he who lost a star.'"

"How could you lose it?" I asked, more confused than ever.

Jasper looked at the floor. "Because my power caused harm. I didn't mean to, but I did, and this happened." He tugged the collar of his black T-shirt aside, and I saw a pale spot on his clavicle, a divot that looked like a scar, as if something the size of a peppercorn had been scooped out of him. "I used to have a star-shaped mark right there, but it disappeared after . . ."

I felt an icy trickle in my chest, wondering what he'd done that was so bad he couldn't even talk about it.

He stared at the ground. His cheekbones looked even more chiseled than usual. "I'm sorry, Laurel. I wish I could be part of it. I really do."

"I can't believe this!" I was practically shouting in frustration.

"Go easy on my grandson," Mr. Blake said. "He came back from Paris to do everything he could to make the linking happen, even if he can't be part of it. He's been working hard to find the four powers."

"Look, I just want to find Ivy," I said. "No offense, but I don't really care about this linking thing."

Jasper nodded. "I understand. The problem is that the prophecy says that 'Druj'—which means *evil*, loosely translated from ancient Persian—'will prevail,' if the linking doesn't happen. Worst-case scenario, we find her and then Druj kills all of us. Best-case scenario, we find the others and use their powers to locate Ivy."

I took a deep breath. That was something to be hopeful about, at least. "So is Druj a person?" I asked.

"In a way. Druj is a dark force that inhabits a person," Mr. Blake said. "This powerfully dark force has been inhabiting one person after another since ancient times. 'Trading faces,' as the prophecy says."

"Okay, so let me get this straight," I said. "According to this prophecy, four people with powers have to link together to stop some ancient evil force?" A nervous laugh escaped my lips. "How does this dark force get inside people in the first place?"

"There's already a little evil mixed up in each of us," said Mr. Blake, unsmiling. "It's part of the human condition. We all have feel-

ings and desires that are wrong, don't we? Urges we know we ought
to resist?"

"I guess," I said, looking anywhere but at Jasper. I hated this
attraction to him that I couldn't shake, even after he'd rejected me
outright in the diner.

Mr. Blake continued: "The Zoroastrians thought of Druj as a
demon, but not the kind with horns and hoofs. On its own, Druj has
no substance. It's parasitic. It can only operate by taking possession
of a human, getting this person to do its bidding."

He was panting from the exertion of talking. "Do you need to
rest?" Jasper asked, but Mr. Blake shook his head and went on.

"Druj is as strong as the human it controls," he said. "So
throughout history, it has sought to take over someone powerful.
The person it controls must willingly let it in, and it enters by prey-
ing upon the basest human emotions—jealousy, resentment, spite.
It can take something like a smoldering grudge and fan it into life
until it consumes the entire person. That's when Druj takes them
over completely."

I gulped hard. Part of me wanted to crack a joke, make fun of
this absurd scenario. But whether or not any of this was based in
reality, Mr. Blake obviously believed every word. And so did Jasper. I
chewed on the inside of my cheek, trying to figure out how anything
I'd just heard applied to the search for Ivy. "Do you think that this,
um, demon, could be controlling Josiah?" I asked Jasper.

"It's possible. If so, we think it's because he wants to take her out
of the equation, to prevent the linking of powers that's supposed to
happen during the eclipse. That way 'evil shall prevail.' We need to
make sure the linking happens. Then, like it says in the prophecy,
we'll have 'the power that cannot fail' and we can defeat Druj."

I digested this with difficulty, feeling sick as I struggled to keep
track of it all. "So Ivy may have been kidnapped by evil incarnate,"
I said numbly. "Druj." It was just a meaningless syllable, and yet I
could almost taste it, like thick black mud filling my mouth. I cast
around for some way to disprove all of this. "No offense, but how can
you be sure this Zoro-whatever prophecy applies here? It's not like it

says, '*blah blah blah*, all of this will happen in Cascade, Oregon, in the last week of October, this exact year.'"

Ignoring my sarcasm, Mr. Blake said, "No, but this is a former gold rush town. And the ancient Farsi text where I found the prophecy goes on to describe a settlement at the westernmost coast of this continent, nestled in the bend of a river that *cascades*"—he paused, drawing a raspy breath—"from the mountains." He inhaled and exhaled rapidly, his breath choppy. "And a cave painting in the woods here confirms the date as the upcoming eclipse."

"A cave painting in the woods *here*?" I repeated. "Sorry, but how did these ancient Persians get to Cascade?"

"Some members of this sect must have crossed the Bering Strait back when it was a land bridge," Jasper said patiently. "They settled here and intermingled with native tribes. And one of their descendants made this cave painting of moons."

They have an answer for everything.

It would have been annoying, if it weren't so terrifying.

Mr. Blake went on. "The ancients used astronomy to foretell that this linking of powers would happen on the night when, for the first time in forty thousand full moons, a lunar eclipse would coincide with All Hallows' Eve, the night when the barrier between the dead and the living is the most permeable."

"Halloween," I translated. I flashed back to the kidnapper's words from my dreams.

After Thursday, it'll all be over.

Maybe Josiah did know about the prophecy.

I felt the blood drain from my face. Mr. Blake also looked as pale as glue when the nurse reappeared with a tray. She shook her head at us. "Look at how worn out your grandpa is. I told you he needs his rest. You should go now."

But first, Jasper wanted to give his grandfather breakfast, and the nurse agreed reluctantly. "But no more talking!" she said before leaving. Jasper peeled the foil top off a cup of applesauce and then gave him a full spoonful. I could tell that he'd done this many times before by the tender way that he dabbed at Mr. Blake's chin. My heart ached as I thought of my own grandmother, how sick she'd been at the end.

My mind reeled with questions. I paced over to the window and stared down at the empty parking lot. Tears pricked at my eyes again. "Does Druj want to kill Ivy?" It was hard even to say these words, but I needed to know.

"Druj wants to destroy everyone and everything," Mr. Blake said. "Druj wants chaos and death." Mr. Blake was looking at Jasper now, clutching the armrests of his chair. "Remember," he said. "You can't be involved in this linking. When the time comes, you must . . . not . . . be . . . there." He gasped rather than spoke, every word a battle.

"You mean Jasper can't even be *present* when this linking happens?" I said.

"It says right in the prophecy that I have to be 'far from there,'" Jasper said.

"It's the only way," Mr. Blake croaked, fixing his fierce gaze on me. He subsided into a coughing fit, and the commotion drew the nurse back.

"Okay, scram, you two," she said. "It's time for his nap."

Jasper bent down to kiss his grandfather's forehead. "See you soon. I love you."

But his grandfather couldn't respond. His whole body was trembling, and the brightness in his eyes was gone.

16.

IN THE PARKING LOT, I took in deep gulps of the fresh air, a relief after the boiled-cabbage-and-ammonia smell of the nursing home. But however much air I sucked into my lungs, it felt like I wasn't getting enough.

"Did you tell Ivy all of this?" I asked Jasper. "Does she know about the linking?"

Jasper shook his head. "She was already so freaked out, I wanted to give her a chance to get used to her power first, while I looked for the others."

The mountains loomed over us and the cloudy sky seemed to be pressing down. I felt as if I was in a box that was getting smaller and smaller.

All Hallows' Eve. Halloween. Thursday. "We have three days to find three more people with powers," I said, pacing to the edge of the parking lot with Jasper on my heels. I stopped, staring out at the traffic streaming by on the highway. Anger surged in my chest and I whirled to face him. "Why didn't you come back sooner?"

He looked distraught. "I've been here since September, but it's complicated. Cascade is a very, very difficult place for me."

"I'm sorry we don't have enough patisseries or whatever," I shot back, marching to Spud. Jasper grabbed my arm before I could open the van door and spun me around to face him.

"That's not fair," he said. Looking into his eyes, I felt myself soften. It was easier to be mad at him than at the world. But it wasn't his fault that all of this was happening. "We're going to find the others," Jasper said. "And when we do, I think they'll be able to help find Ivy."

"How exactly?"

"It depends on their powers. Maybe one of them will be able to fly, and they can swoop over the forest and find Josiah's shack. Or maybe one of them has bat ears and can listen for his voice."

That did sound promising—and not much crazier than any of the rest of what I'd learned. I got in the van, and he walked around to the other side to climb into the passenger seat.

"But what if we *don't* find anyone else with a power?" I said, gripping the steering wheel even though I hadn't turned the key yet and I had no idea where to go now. "How do you even know that there are others nearby? You're saying we have to find three more people, and I thought that having a power was incredibly rare."

"It is, but there's a reason why those Zoroastrians crossed the Bering Strait to settle here. This has always been a breeding ground for people with powers."

"Seriously?" I said, once again struggling to believe all of this as I watched a truck carrying black-and-white dairy cows careen by. "You mean the way some places have a higher concentration of minerals in the water or something?"

"Pretty much."

I thought about the people in the diner last night: the old woman hunched at the counter warming her hands on a mug of cocoa, the table of guys shoveling down hash browns, the waitress in her white sneakers stuffing napkins in dispensers. What if one of them had a power? How would we ever know?

"You told me it was a fluke that you saw Ivy using her power."

"But people like us are connected. You know how you said that Ivy was being tortured in your dream? Well, that pain you described—when the man burned her wrist?—I'm pretty sure he did that at around half past five this morning." I saw his Adam's apple jump in his throat. "Because that's when I woke up, feeling this uncontrollable itch to use my own power. I know what's behind the itch, but these kids won't have a clue what's happening to them. The only thing that relieves it is using their powers. They won't be able to stop themselves."

"How do you know they're going to be kids?"

"Because people always spark in adolescence. That's when you change most dramatically."

"You mean, you're already getting zits and boobs—well, some people anyway—so why not a power too?"

He laughed drily, but said, "Yeah, exactly."

"And their power could be anything?"

"I don't know about 'anything,' but they can take many forms."

I thought this over for a second. "Then I guess it's a good thing there's only one high school in Cascade," I said, feeling the weight on my chest lift slightly. "So we should watch for, like, someone shooting a spiderweb across the cafeteria?"

"It may not be quite that obvious, but it's true that you know these kids, so you're more likely to notice someone acting unusual. The thing is, we need to hurry, because if Josiah is torturing Ivy, he's probably doing it to make the others spark, so that they'll reveal themselves and he can capture them too. That's probably why he hasn't killed her yet."

"Well, we have to get to them first," I said, turning the key in the ignition. Rain began to clatter on the roof of the van, and something occurred to me. "And then what? How are we supposed to overcome this thing? Isn't it all-powerful?"

"It's like Gramps said, it's only as strong as the human vessel it controls."

"In that case, if we find Ivy and destroy it before Thursday, why do we need to bother with the linking at all?"

"Because the prophecy says the only way to stop Druj is to do the linking. I don't know why. I wish I could talk to the people who wrote it, ask them that. But it's all we have to work with, so we need to follow it."

I pulled onto the road and started driving back into town as fast as I could. As we passed through a grove of trees, I thought about Josiah's shack, somewhere in the forest. I wanted to park Spud by the side of the road and just run into the trees and start screaming for Ivy. But I'd never find Josiah that way.

I wished there weren't so many unknowns. I wished like crazy that I could communicate with her, reassure her that she just had to hang on a little longer and we were coming for her. But I didn't have any choice but to focus on the hunt for these three kids.

They'd better be worth it.

17.

WHEN WE GOT TO SCHOOL, Jasper and I decided to divide and conquer so we could cover more ground in our search. He went to the gym while I marched to the cafeteria, realizing that I'd skipped all my morning classes. But I didn't care. I couldn't have faced another battle with Ms. Owen anyway.

Finally, I had a clear sense of purpose.

I saw an advantage to living in a fishbowl. I had known my classmates forever. Surely I'd be able to detect any supernatural gifts manifesting in my midst.

The cafeteria contained the highest concentration of kids on campus, so I thought it gave me the best odds of spotting someone with a power. What I spotted instead was a tendency for girls to nibble on their glazed poppy-seed muffin tops, leaving the bottom untouched; for boys to consume pizza pockets in approximately two and a half bites, drippy cheese strings clinging to their chins; for kids to stick to their own kind, clustered as they had been since middle school. Stu Sheers and his football buddies unplugged the jukebox every time some guileless freshman wasted two quarters on a song. The Skittles brayed with laughter, every single time.

I quickly realized that in spite of having been in school with most of these kids since kindergarten, I couldn't honestly say if they were acting out of character. Was it weird that Peyton was eating a second bagel slathered in cream cheese? Once, I'd overheard her telling Mei that you could halve the calories if you tore out the insides and only ate the crust. I remembered how Ms. Owen had said that if I wanted to be a writer, I needed to spend more time studying people, trying to understand them better.

She might have a point.

If only we could tear down the posters, advertising the Dark Side Dance on Halloween, and hang up new ones:

Do YOU have a power you're itching to show off?

Now is your big opportunity!

Join a team of four, and link your powers to save the world!

Instead, I trudged out of the gym and over to social studies. Going to class was the last thing I felt like doing, but I had as good a chance of witnessing someone acting unusual in there as any-place else.

Mr. Saunders announced that we were taking a "field trip" to the library, to use the Internet to research the roots of Christianity, Juda-ism, and Islam. I trailed at the back of the pack as we crossed the field, scrutinizing everyone for signs of supernatural itchiness. Instead, all I saw was Mike Mancuso shoving his hand in his jeans pocket to sur-reptitiously scratch his crotch. I felt sick. What if Jasper was wrong? What if there weren't three more people nearby with powers?

What if Josiah had already found them?

"You okay, Laurel?" Mr. Saunders asked, holding the glass door to the library open for me. "Those are some very dark circles under your eyes."

"I haven't been sleeping well," I admitted.

"You kids are under too much stress," he said.

You don't know the half of it.

For once, I was glad that the library was made of glass, so that I could keep an eye on everyone from my study pod. But after ten minutes, I gave up. No one was acting weirder than usual. I hoped that Jasper was having better luck. Part of me wanted to fake cramps and leave, but I couldn't just walk into classrooms at random, scan-ning each group for unusual behavior.

Since I had to do something, and Mr. Saunders had his eye on me, I plugged the words *roots of Western religion* into the search box on my computer, and was startled when one of the first links to pop up directed me to a page on Zoroastrianism, the ancient Persian religion that Mr. Blake had mentioned.

Who needs a superpower when you have Google?

I clicked to a Wikipedia entry.

In Zoroastrian mythology, Asha and Druj—good and evil—are thought to be at war within each of us. In a final battle, also called the "Renovation" (Avestan Drujkoreti), Druj will seek total dominion.

I shifted uneasily. So Druj was real—or at least ancient Zoroastrians had believed in it. I needed to know more about this "Renovation." If I understood what Druj wanted, I might have a better idea of how to stop him. Or it. One of the footnotes linked to a scholarly article, "Apocalypse Then: Zoroastrian visions of the end of the world." Skimming the dense columns of text, one paragraph caught my eye.

The Zoroastrians thought that Druj was limited by the same corporeal restrictions as the succession of human beings it inhabited, obliged to replace its mortal vessel as each one died. Only the undead were thought to live forever. Therefore, the central act of the Renovation is for Druj to reclaim someone from this liminal space. In succeeding, Druj would forge for itself an immortal vessel and prevail over Asha for all eternity.

I struggled to understand the dry-as-dust academic prose. How could you "reclaim" someone? What did *liminal space* mean? And what did any of this have to do with Ivy?

Once Druj has entered its final vessel, the Renovation will be sealed, and the dead freed from death, to overtake the living. As the date of the Renovation approaches, the natural order will begin to fall apart, and the lower beings will be seen to rise from the dead.

"Zoroastrianism?" I jumped as Mr. Saunders peered over my shoulder. "Way to dig deep, Laurel."

"Do you know anything about it?" I asked hopefully.

"Just a little. Nietzsche identified it as the root of all Western religions. He believed that God is a primitive fantasy. He saw no point in goodness, and argued that nothing should stand in the way of a person's quest for power."

"He would've loved high school," I said, eyeing Peyton.

Mr. Saunders chuckled, and patted me on the back. "I know it can be rough," he said, "but you've got your whole life ahead of you."

"Right," I said.

Or maybe I just have until Halloween.

18.

"LET'S GET THIS OVER WITH," Mom said, pushing me back out the door before I made it all the way into the Airstream. She was wearing a collared navy-blue dress that looked all wrong on her.

"Get what over with?"

"We're going to Pastor Andersen's to ask him about Ivy, remember?"

I nodded, though I'd totally forgotten about this plan. I no longer held any hope that Ivy was visiting a friend in Portland, or that Pastor Anderson would give us fresh leads, but I couldn't tell her this, or any of what I'd learned since going to see Mr. Blake this morning, so I followed her numbly to the van.

As I drove back into town, I let myself imagine Pastor Andersen scanning the camp roster before giving us a name and a phone number leading us straight to Ivy. I could almost hear Ivy laugh as I told her every twist of this crazy story.

"You honestly thought I'd been kidnapped by an ancient demon?" she'd ask. "Lolo, you really do read too many fantasy novels."

But I knew that I was letting my imagination run away with me.

Only I was fantasizing about reality as I once knew it.

Luxury SUVs were crammed into the cul-de-sac where the Andersens lived, in a Tudor McMansion nearly identical to the ones on either side of it.

"I haven't been back since Peg fired me," Mom brooded. "She's going to think I'm such a bad mom for not knowing where my own daughter is."

"We could just go home," I suggested, but Mom shook her head.

"We came all this way, and I need to talk to Ivy. I can't believe she hasn't called once." She jabbed at the doorbell.

It took a minute for anyone to answer. From inside, I could hear music and a din of chatter. Then the door opened, and Peyton's mother scanned Mom up and down with the same withering gaze that Peyton reserved for me. "Sheila," she said flatly. "What a surprise." Behind her, waiters in tuxedoes flitted through a crowd, carrying trays.

"I'm so sorry to barge in on your party like this," Mom said, her voice high and nervous. "I was just hoping to talk to your husband for a second about—"

"Sheila! You made it!" Bill Sheers suddenly appeared, his arms flung open. "I was beginning to worry that you didn't get my evite."

"Evite?" Mom echoed uncertainly.

"Of course! We're celebrating the opening of the museum," Mr. Sheers said. "We were supposed to have it on-site, but after the place got vandalized, Peg and Dean graciously offered to host here instead. Didn't you get the message?"

"I—I'm so bad at keeping up with email," Mom said. "But I really came over to ask Dean about Ivy. I'm afraid she's . . ."

"Mom!" I grabbed her by the arm, hissing in her ear, "That's Officer Dougherty!"

She looked panic-stricken as the stocky cop swaggered over. "Mrs. Goodwin?" he said, and she nodded. "You hear from your daughter yet?"

"Just last night," she said, fingering her pendant. "She's having a really g-great time in Portland, isn't she Laurel?"

I managed to nod, avoiding the cop's eyes.

"Ivy went to Portland in the middle of the semester?" Mrs. Andersen asked.

"She's, um, checking out colleges," Mom said.

"They are going to be knocking down your door, begging to give that girl a scholarship," Mr. Sheers boomed. "That girl is a real credit to you, Sheila."

"Both of your girls are," Simone agreed, materializing from the crowd to link arms with Mr. Sheers. She was dressed in a strapless black column of silk that showed off her narrow, creamy shoulders. She looked extra petite beside the tall Mr. Sheers. "It's been such a pleasure getting to know Ivy," she went on. "When she's ready to apply to schools, I will write her an absolutely glowing letter of recommendation." She smiled at Mom, who relaxed as Officer Dougherty finally left, following a waiter holding a tray of miniature burgers.

"Come in and have a glass of bubbly," Mr. Sheers said to Mom. "The museum would be nothing without your spectacular backdrops."

"I really need to get home, Mom," I pleaded. "I have an English paper due tomorrow that I haven't even started."

"Oh, let your mom enjoy herself for a minute," Mr. Sheers said.

Mrs. Andersen turned to me. "Peyton and Mei are downstairs watching TV. I know they'd love to hang out with you."

I knew that the exact opposite was true. But when I looked at Mom, her eyes begged me to go with the flow, and Mrs. Andersen was already leading me to the staircase down to the rec room, her hand between my shoulder blades.

As I descended, I felt like I was walking to meet my doom. I expected to find Mei and Peyton glued to each other as usual, screeching as they sexted some poor guy. But instead they were sitting at opposite ends of the couch. *Project Runway* was playing on TV, but they didn't seem to be watching it. Mei was clenching an empty water bottle so that the plastic popped in and out of shape, while Peyton flipped through *Us Weekly*.

"Girls," Mrs. Andersen trilled. "Your friend Laurel's here!"

"Laurel?" said Peyton, managing to make my name sound like an insult.

"Hey," I said, and they rolled their eyes like I'd just said the dumbest thing ever.

"Make yourself comfortable, dear," Peyton's mom ordered me.

As if.

I sat on the edge of the couch in between them, wondering if Mrs. Andersen had any idea that her daughter and I had been at war since the third grade—or that she herself was partly to blame for this longstanding feud.

Way back in the day, I actually used to look forward to going with Mom when she cleaned the Andersen house. Peyton would let me ride her pony—which she had zero interest in—in exchange for a bag of my grandma's oatmeal cookies. I had to sneak them to her when her mother wasn't watching. Even then, she was already on a diet, expected to stay tiny for the beauty pageants that she wasn't winning anymore.

Maybe that's why she turned mean.

Halfway through the year, I wrote this story about a girl with a pony that had magical powers, and our teacher read it to the class. I never claimed that it was my pony. The whole thing was made up! But I guess she felt like I was stepping on her turf, overstepping my station in life. "Laurel doesn't have a pony," she trumpeted from the top of the monkey bars at recess. "She could never afford one. She doesn't even have a dad, and her mom is our maid!"

Without thinking about it, I ran up behind her and shoved her. Hard.

I felt victorious for about two seconds, until she face-planted.

According to Peyton's mom, her "shattered" front tooth was to blame for the end of her beauty pageant career. Never mind that it was just a baby tooth, or that I wrote a groveling letter of apology. Mrs. Andersen fired my mom, and from that day on, Peyton seized every possible chance to remind me of my inferior station in life.

True to form, the instant her mother retreated upstairs, she lashed out. "What are you doing here? Did you and your mom come to clean the toilets?"

I always told myself that I didn't care what she thought of me, and for once I actually felt that way. To say that I had bigger things to worry about was putting it mildly. But since I was stuck there, I decided to swallow my pride and tell the truth.

Maybe, just maybe, I'd learn something.

"You went to camp with Ivy last summer, right?" I said, and she nodded. "We were wondering if she had any friends from Portland at that camp."

Peyton looked surprised. "No, I don't think so," she said, scrunching her eyebrows. "The Portland kids kept to themselves, and Ivy usually hung around with Simone. Why?"

"No reason," I said. I expected her to keep digging, but instead she returned to turning the pages of her magazine. Mei was still attacking her water bottle. Something was up with them, but I figured that it couldn't have anything to do with me.

Counting the minutes until I could make an exit, I glanced around the rec room. It hadn't changed much since the third grade. There was the white spot at the base of the carpeted staircase, where we'd smeared cold cream to try and cover up a cranberry juice spill. The shrine to Peyton's child modeling career was still standing: a glass case filled with framed pictures from beauty pageants in which the toddler was already slathered in makeup, her smile huge and fake. I used to think that it seemed like fun to get all dressed up and compete in a talent show, but Mom said it was wrong to put peroxide in a little girl's hair and make her parade around in a swimsuit for judges.

A shriek drew my attention to the TV. One of the contestants on *Project Runway* had just won a competition, and was jumping up and down with excitement. I couldn't help thinking of Ivy, whose dream was to be on this show someday.

Why are we wasting our time here? I thought. *I should be out looking for Ivy.*

"Where *is* Ivy?" Peyton asked out of the blue.

"She's in Portland," I said automatically.

"Then why are you trying to find her?"

"Who told you that?"

"No one told me anything." Peyton scratched her cheek savagely. "You said that you were looking for her."

"No, she didn't," Mei spoke up for the first time. "What is up with you, Pey? You're acting so weird!"

"Well, so are you," Peyton snapped, still scratching her face. "You've barely said a word all night. If you don't want to be here, you should just go." She whipped around to face me. "And since you weren't invited in the first place, you should leave too."

"You read my mind," I said.

My words made Peyton crumple. She drew her knees up to her chest, wrapping her arms around her shins like her whole body was curled around something, protecting it. I gaped at her. Did Peyton have a secret? What was she hiding? Replaying our conversation, I started to feel a little bit sick to my stomach, the way that you do when your body senses something before your brain can admit it.

Please, no. She can't be one of them.

I looked at her, trying to keep my face blank. She stared back, and I thought I detected the same effort on her part. She broke eye contact first.

"You're right," I said at last. "I don't know where Ivy is. She's been gone since Friday, and I am looking for her."

"What do you mean?" Peyton's eyes widened. "What happened?"

"I don't know. I woke up and she wasn't there. We found a note saying that she was visiting some friend from camp up in Portland, but I don't believe that she wrote it. I think . . ." I paused, not sure whether to tell them the truth. But if Peyton did have powers—if she was one of the four—maybe I could get her to confess.

I think my sister was kidnapped, I thought.

Peyton gasped, drawing her hand to her mouth. She looked as scared as the wolverine trapped in Skye's yard. She started to gnaw at her thumbnail, just like she used to when we were little. "If I tell you guys something, do you both swear not to tell anyone else?"

Mei nodded solemnly and I did the same, even though I couldn't help but find it ironic that the world's biggest gossip was begging us to keep her secret.

As she told us the whole story about what had happened in youth group, I slid from the couch to the rug. My fingernails hurt, and I realized I was pulling the carpet out in tufts. I'd assumed that the kids Jasper and I were searching for would be special in some way. Special like Ivy was special. Like Jasper. People who deserved to have powers—who could put them to good use. But life wasn't fair. Peyton was rich, pretty and popular. Why not get a supernatural gift too? The same people always got everything. I didn't know why it was taking me so long to grasp this basic lesson.

"Wait—so you're like a mind reader?" Mei asked Peyton.

"So far I only hear the dark stuff," Peyton said. "People's deepest wishes, and their most embarrassing secrets. Things they wouldn't want anyone to know."

I gaped at her, torn between relief and disbelief.

In other words, she'd manifested a gift for hearing gossip.

"You must think I'm totally schizo, right?" she said. Before I could answer, she whirled back to face Mei. "What do you mean, 'Peyton wouldn't believe *me* if I told her what happened on Friday'?"

"I never said that!" Mei gasped.

"No, but you thought it. *You've* got a secret!"

And before I'd had time to absorb the news that Peyton had a power, Mei launched into her own tale of morphing into her drama coach in Stu's bedroom.

"Hold on, so you can *become* people?" Peyton interrupted. "No. Freaking. Way. Like, anyone you want? You just turn into them?"

"I don't know," Mei said. "I've only done it once, but I think I could do it again." She shuddered. "Not that I would. It wasn't exactly fun."

"But how do you do it?" Peyton pressed for specifics while I squeezed back tears. I felt sucker punched. Our quest was nearly over. Here were two of the people with powers that we'd been desperate to find. Maybe Jasper had found the third on his own, and our work was done. But I felt queasy. Peyton and Mei would never do me a favor. They'd never help us find Ivy.

"Omigod," Peyton burst out. "So Stu was suddenly in bed with a dude?" She cackled. "That explains what I heard him thinking in youth group! Does he know it was you?"

"I don't think so," Mei said. "He was pretty drunk."

"Ha!" Peyton cackled.

"You cannot tell a living soul," Mei said. "Promise you won't blab this all over school!"

"Uh, I really don't think anyone would believe me," Peyton said.

"Why is this happening to us?" Mei asked.

"I don't know, but check this out." Peyton licked her thumb and rubbed the pancake makeup off her cheek, exposing a star-shaped birthmark.

"No. Way!" Mei's jaw dropped and she swiveled around, lifting her shirt to reveal a birthmark on her back that looked identical to Peyton's.

And to Ivy's.

This tiny silver star was like a badge identifying them as members of the same club. Reflexively, I checked the mark on my own wrist, but it was just a boring old freckle.

"I can't believe you can *read minds*," Mei said to Peyton. "Do you know how many people have been able to do that in the history of the human race? Like, three!"

"Actually, none," I muttered.

"I guess it is pretty awesome," Peyton said.

As they gushed over their matching powers, I felt an overwhelming urge to throw up.

"You should totally find out who's thinking of inviting you to prom!" Mei squealed. "You could find out what people are really thinking about you!"

Listening to their inane chatter, I realized that I couldn't tell them about the prophecy. I didn't have any idea how to explain the part they would have to play in the linking. Jasper would have to fill them in—or maybe his grandfather could.

"So what's *my* deepest, darkest secret?" Mei asked Peyton, tossing her black hair.

Peyton cocked her head to one side for a moment, then shrugged. "I don't know. I guess I can only do it when I'm not trying. Maybe I only hear what people want to hide."

"Or maybe your power's not that strong," Mei suggested.

"Yeah, it is," Peyton protested. "I hear whispers all the time. You've only used yours once. You might not be able to do it again."

Mei looked irritated. "Of course I could. I'm an actress. I *embody* people. It's the same gift I've always had, only now I've got it times a million."

Peyton shrugged. "Or Friday night could have been a fluke."

I felt like groaning. I remembered when Mei came to school, showing off the designer bag she had received for her birthday—a larger version of the one that Peyton had been carrying for months. Peyton had practically ripped Mei's purse apart, trying to prove it was a knock-off.

I stood up to leave, but as I walked toward the staircase, Peyton suddenly spoke. "Oh my God," she said. "I think I might have heard Ivy."

I whirled around. "What do you mean? When?"

"Yesterday evening, on the drive home from the Faith Center, I heard this one random whisper—a girl calling out for help—and now that I think about it, I'm pretty sure it was your sister's voice."

I threw myself beside her on the couch. "Where exactly were you?"

"I don't know," she said. "My dad was driving, and I was really upset. It sounded like Ivy was whispering right in my ear, but I don't think she was nearby. I could just feel her . . . Like she was reaching out to me or something."

This made sense, given what Jasper had said about people with powers being connected, and able to sense when anyone in the area was stressed. But this message was worse than useless—it was just a reminder that my sister was terrified, and brought me no closer to finding her.

"Maybe Mei could become Ivy," Peyton suggested. "Then you could ask her where she is yourself."

"I don't think it works that way," Mei said.

"How do you know?" Peyton said. "You've only done it once."

"But it's not like I *became* Mr. Dominguez."

"Maybe that's because it was your first time," Peyton said. "Do you think you could do it again?"

"Yeah, but I really don't want to."

"Come on," Peyton urged her. "I dare you. I want to see it happen!"

"Please try," I said, as my mind raced with questions for Ivy. Did she write that note? Did she remember being carried out of the trailer? Did she know that she was sending me dreams? Could she try and send me some clues to help find her?

"I'm sorry, but I don't really know your sister," Mei said. "I was able to become Mr. Dominguez because I see him all the time, so it was easy to visualize him, but I don't think I can picture Ivy well enough to turn into her."

Peyton jumped up and ran over to a bookshelf. She grabbed last year's yearbook and flipped through it until she found Ivy's picture. There she was, smiling the kind of easy, open smile that came so easily to her, lighting her up completely.

Peyton thrust the yearbook onto Mei's lap, and Mei sighed before twisting her long, glossy black hair into a knot. "Okay. I'll give it a shot," she said as she stared at Ivy's yearbook picture and took a few deep breaths, cracking her knuckles and closing her eyes. Her lids fluttered and she clenched her fists, but nothing happened.

"It must have been a fluke," Peyton whispered. "I guess I'm the only one with a lasting power."

Mei's eyes snapped open. "Shut up! I need total quiet so I can focus." She closed them again, murmuring, "I just need to empty my mind . . ."

"That shouldn't be too hard," said Peyton, giggling.

"You're one to talk." Mei pouted.

"Can you please hurry up?" I said.

Mei shook her head. "I'm sorry, but it's not happening."

"Keep trying," I begged her. "You just need to relax."

"What do you know about it?" Mei snapped.

I knew what I felt in my dreams when Ivy used her power, but I kept my mouth shut. She was right. Secondhand powers didn't count, and that was all I had.

Secondhand powers, for the girl with secondhand everything.

Peyton picked up *Us Weekly* and leafed through it. "Maybe you should try becoming someone else," she told Mei, idly turning to "Stars—They're Just Like Us." "Ooh, I know! What about this guy?" She flicked a picture of some tanned movie star walking his dog.

"He is hot," said Mei looking over Peyton's shoulder.

"Oh yeah," Peyton agreed. "Change into him, and I would total-ly make out with you."

"You are such a lesbo," said Mei with a laugh.

"Well, you're the gay dude." Peyton laughed too. "I know. Morph into me. I want to see what my ass looks like."

Mei giggled. "Trust me, that is not something you want to see."

Unable to stand another second of their chitchat, I seized the magazine and threw it across the room. "Just turn into Ivy!" I yelled. "You've done this before. If you can do it, it can't be that hard!"

"Ouch," Mei said, still laughing as she glanced at the yearbook. And then she began to shudder violently. Her features smudged and smeared as if she was something pinched out of dough, being re-shaped by a giant hand. Her chest swelled and her limbs softened, reforming themselves into Ivy's arms and legs. Peyton screamed, and we both shrank back against the couch in fear and awe.

Mei's rosebud mouth widened. Then she dipped her head so her hair hung down in a dark curtain, as if the final letting go of self was somehow too private for us to witness. When she straightened up, blonde curls crackled with static, and a new face snapped into focus.

I gasped. In my nightmares, I was in Ivy's head. I felt her ex-haustion and despair from deep inside her. But it was different to see these things from the outside. Worse, in a way. In just three days, her cheeks had hollowed out, and her skin looked grayish white, like the color of a mushroom. The circles under her eyes were a dark purple, and as she raised her arm to shield her eyes from the light, I saw the angry red welt on her left wrist, where the man had burned her.

With a sob, I flung myself into her arms, shocked to find that she even felt different—thinner, weaker—and she didn't hug me back.

"You're hurting me!" she said, but I just squeezed harder, tears streaming down my cheeks, until she pushed me away.

"I'm not Ivy," she said. "I'm Mei."

But it was Ivy's mouth, producing Ivy's voice.

"Where are you?" I cried. "Help me find you! Give me a clue we can use!"

"I'm right here. In Peyton's rec room. Cut it out!"

I let go, but I still couldn't believe that the girl in front of me wasn't my sister.

Peyton touched her tentatively. "Ivy?" she whispered.

"No! I told you guys! I might look like Ivy and talk like Ivy, but I'm still *me*." As Mei said these words, her hair darkened, as if drenched with ink, and her face began to melt.

"No, no, please, no! Ivy!" I grabbed her shoulders, feeling them give under my hands like Silly Putty.

"Yoo-hoo! Girls!" As Mrs. Andersen opened the door at the top of the stairs, Mei bolted into the bathroom. I wiped my tears with my sleeve as Mrs. Andersen descended the stairs, my mom on her heels.

"What's wrong?" Mom took one look at me and rushed to my side. "What's going on here? Why are you crying, Lolo?"

Peyton looked pretty bad herself, but she managed to speak. "I was just telling a hilarious story," she said. "Laurel laughed so hard I made her pee in her pants."

"If you're having that much fun, you're welcome to stay," Mrs. Andersen offered.

"I have to write a paper," I told her, trying to stop my voice from shaking. "Come on, Mom." I rushed upstairs and pushed through the crowd.

"What's going on for real?" Mom said once we were in the car, but I couldn't begin to tell her.

"Nothing," I said.

Nothing she'd believe.

While I drove us home, Mom told me how awkward it had been—socializing with all of these people whose houses she used to clean. She said that when no one was looking, she'd dropped a chocolate-covered strawberry on the white carpet and ground it in with her heel. Normally this story would've delighted me. But I was so shaken up I couldn't even fake a smile.

"I'm really sorry we couldn't get a number to reach Ivy," Mom said. "Did you happen to ask Peyton if Ivy had any friends from Portland?"

"She said that she didn't."

"Well, I doubt that Peyton would know who Ivy hung out with," Mom backtracked. "I mean, neither of you can stand Peyton, right? Not that I blame you. What a fake, just like her mother."

I was barely listening. I couldn't get over what had just happened in the rec room. I knew that if I so much as tried to tell Mom about it, she'd insist that I turn Spud around and head straight to the nearest hospital for a psychiatric evaluation. There was no way I could persuade her that I'd seen Mei morph into Ivy.

But I couldn't stop thinking about how fragile my sister had felt in my arms, like I could break her simply by hugging her. It reminded me of a time when I'd hugged my grandma, right after she first got diagnosed with cancer. She'd always been a tall woman, big-boned and hearty—she never even got a cold that I could remember—and I'd assumed that she would always be around, at least until I was finished growing up. But after she told me the bad news and then pulled me in for a hug, her bones had seemed as hollow as a bird's, as if they could crumble like chalk. In a way, that moment was worse than anything that came afterward, because I hadn't been prepared for it at all.

When Mom and I got home, I told her I was going to write my paper, but instead I curled up on Ivy's bed. Jasper had given me his number, but I felt too miserable to call him.

My big sister, the person I'd always relied on to take care of me, couldn't do that now. I was in charge, and I had no special gift to help her. No spark.

But that's how life goes: one day we all have to take care of the people who once took care of us.

If only there was some way to be ready for that moment.

TUESDAY

TOUGH AS NAILS. That's what Grandma used to call me, because as a little kid, I never cried when I got hurt.

But she wouldn't say that if she could see me now. My eyes won't stop streaming. The spot where he burned my wrist is still on fire. The pain feels like a black hole sucking me in.

At least this time he left the lantern on. Maybe that was his sick way of trying to make up for hurting me. I shudder, glaring at that ladder as if it were to blame.

Scritch.

I hear the noise—a rasp of metal on brick—before I realize what I've done.

I've moved the ladder. Just an inch. The man wouldn't notice. But I'm pretty sure it happened.

Screech.

I push it in the opposite direction. Again, it moves just the tiniest bit, but I'm sweating as if I'd shoved it with my hands. My burn seems to hurt a little less too.

Scritch. Screech. Scritch. Screech. I push the ladder from side to side. By now my heart is drumming hard, my skin bathed in sweat. I feel exhausted, but I don't want to stop. I take my deepest breath yet, and stare at the ladder until it feels like my eyes could pop out of my head. On my exhale, the ladder lifts in the air.

Clunk.

I'm shaking from head to toe, but it's a rush.

If I can lift a ladder, then maybe—just maybe—I'll be able to use my power to bring down the man in the mask.

Maybe Grandma was right after all, and I am tough as nails.

19.

WHEN I WOKE UP on Tuesday morning, I felt better than usual.

Ivy was fighting back.

Then I remembered what had happened at Peyton's house the previous night. Still in my pajamas, I grabbed the phone and called Jasper, desperate to tell him everything. No answer. Maybe he'd gone to see his grandfather before school. I tried a couple more times, wishing I'd rung last night, and then I had no choice but to go to school as usual, hoping I'd see him there.

There was no sign of him in the parking lot or in the hallway, so finally I stationed myself outside the English classroom, where we both had first period. It was early enough that I hoped to catch him on his own so we could ditch class while we figured out what to do. I was anxiously staring down the hallway when Ms. Owen popped out of the classroom. I gasped—my nerves were so frayed.

"I didn't mean to startle you," she said. "You're bright and early for a change. Since you're here, I'll take your essay now." She beckoned me into the classroom and I had no choice but to follow.

I rummaged through my backpack, pretending to search for my nonexistent paper.

My backpack fell to the ground, spewing books. "I guess I forgot it at home," I said. "I'll bring it tomorrow, okay?" I was definitely going to flunk English—not that it mattered, seeing as the world might end and all.

"Did you take the creative option?" she asked.

"What?"

"To write from the monster's point of view."

I nodded, but apparently she could tell that I didn't have a clue what she was talking about, because she let out one of her Oscar-worthy sighs. "I don't know what's going on with you, Laurel," she said, standing over me as I crouched on the floor gathering up the contents of my backpack. "You say you want to be a writer, but I am beginning to think that's just talk."

I mashed my books and notebook into my backpack, barely able to zip it up. Even though she was attacking me again, I didn't want to cry. I didn't care about anything except Ivy. It was kind of liberating, in a horrible way. "Yeah, yeah," I said. "I have zero potential. I should just give up."

"Zero potential?" She shook her head. "Whatever gave you that idea?"

"Uh, you pretty much ripped my last story to pieces, remember?"

"You're mistaken. I thought it had enormous potential, if you could simply flesh out the characters more."

"Oh," I said, staring at her dumbly. Did she just say my story had "enormous potential"? This would have made my day, on a different day. A different week. Now I looked over her shoulder down the hallway. Still no sign of Jasper, but a few other kids were starting to shuffle in, so he had to be here any minute. I figured I might as well stick around and hear what she had to say. "How do you flesh out characters?" I said.

"Characters come to life when we understand what they want, what their goals are, their fears. Once we know what's at stake for them."

I'd have to think about that—if I ever got the chance.

"You really do have a way with words, Laurel." Ms. Owen peered at me through her glasses. "Frankly, I'm surprised that you'd be so willing to give up your dream of being a writer just because I didn't give you an A on one story. Either you're lazy, and you don't want to put the work in, or else you're afraid."

Oh, right. Back to insulting me—just when she'd made me let my guard down. "I'm not afraid!" I snapped. "I *love* writing. Or I used to."

Ms. Owen nodded. "Exactly. And like any other kind of love, writing is scary, because it requires you to take a risk."

I snorted. "What risk?"

"If you don't try, you can't fail. Isn't that why you want me to tell you to give up? So you can pin it on me?"

Someone knocked against me and I looked around to see Peyton, who didn't seem to realize that she'd hit me with her bag. I tried to catch her eye. Maybe I had a chance to talk to her before class started at least.

"Listen to me," Ms. Owen said. "You need to turn off all those voices in your head that say 'I can't do it, I have no talent, I might as well quit.' Once you silence them, I believe you could do something tremendous."

She stepped away, and I gaped after her.

Something tremendous?

The fact that Ms. Owen had just paid me a compliment seemed as improbable as everything else that was going on.

But before I could move, she'd closed the door. Realizing that I was trapped, my stomach clenched. Jasper wasn't here. I edged toward the door, but Ms. Owen blocked my way. "Take a seat, please," she rapped out, and I didn't have the nerve to defy her openly.

I sank down into a seat that had an empty one next to it and placed my backpack there to hold it for Jasper, but as the minutes ticked by, there was no sign of him. No sign of Mei either. At least Peyton was there. I looked over at her pointedly a few times, but she refused to meet my eyes.

Peyton popped up and shot out the door the minute class ended, but I was right behind her. If Jasper wasn't here to do it, I had to talk to her ASAP, to make sure she and Mei laid low. If Josiah was the host for Druj, and he'd kidnapped Ivy after finding out about her power, in order to prevent the linking, then the same thing could happen to them.

"Hey, Peyton!" I called out, trying to catch her attention in the crowd, but she acted as if she hadn't heard me. *Figures.* For some reason, I'd thought that after what we went through together in the rec room, she might treat me like a human being for a change.

My irritation grew as I followed her into the bathroom, where she was standing at the sink, unloading her arsenal of makeup.

"Where's Mei?" I asked, wishing I could kill two dodo birds with one stone.

"Where do you think?" Peyton peered under the stalls to make sure no one was there and then hissed, "She's home, recovering from what you forced her to do!"

"It was your idea," I reminded her, but Peyton just glared at her own reflection as she began to apply coat after coat of mascara. It was amazing she could even blink under the weight of it.

"Is she okay?" I finally asked.

"She looks like Mei again, if that's what you mean, but I wouldn't say she's close to okay. She passed out in the bathroom after you left. I got her on her feet, but she had to tell her mom she had food poisoning."

"I didn't know using her gift would make her sick," I said, feeling bad for Mei in spite of myself. "I'm sure she'll get stronger with practice."

Peyton arched an eyebrow at me in the mirror. "That's not going to happen, because she's never going to use her 'gift,' again." She put the word in ironic air quotes, then pulled out a tub of concealer and a brush, digging the bristles into her war paint.

I wanted to seize her makeup and stuff it all into the trash. "But she has to practice!" I said. "You both have to develop your powers, and use them to help find Ivy."

"Uh, guess again," she said. "Listen, Laurel, I really do hope you find your sister, but we're not even friends, and Mei and I do not need to get sucked into your twisted little family drama."

"Is that what you think this is?" I was spitting mad now. "Because what's happening is a lot more complicated that you could possibly grasp, and you're a part of it, Peyton, whether you like it or not."

"Sorry," she said, "but we're not."

"What?"

"Maybe *you* can't grasp what I'm saying. Pass. *Nada. Comprende?*"

"*Nada* doesn't mean 'no,' you idiot," I said. "It means 'nothing.'"

"And nothing is exactly what you're going to get from Mei and me," she spat back, fixing her eyes on her reflection. Freezing me out completely, she began painting concealer over the star on her cheek.

So that was her strategy. Cover up and hope it all goes away.

Well, it's not going to work, I thought. *You don't even know the worst part.*

"What?" Peyton's head jerked up. "What's the worst part?"

Now I had her attention, but I was on my way out. Jasper was going to have to be the one to explain about the prophecy, since this girl wasn't going to help me if my life depended on it.

Which it basically did.

20.

STILL FUMING, I stomped over to Headmaster House. "You didn't come to English class," I said, when Jasper answered the door. "Where were you? Did you have to see your grandfather?"

"I was at school. Divide and conquer, remember?" he said. "I hit the weight room to check out the jocks. Didn't see a lot of gifts—supernatural or otherwise—so I came home to shower. I figured if anyone in English class had a power, we would've spotted them already."

"Wrong," I told him flatly. "Peyton Anderson."

"Wait—you found one?"

"Two, actually. Mei Rosen has a power too."

"So why do you look like that? That's great news!" Before I could answer, a woman walked by with a dog on a leash, and he quickly ushered me into a chilly foyer with a black-and-white checkerboard floor. Through the arch of an open doorway, I could see into the living room. The faded red curtains were drawn, keeping it dim so that my eyes took a moment to adjust. It had an elaborate marble mantelpiece and a dark wood floor, but there wasn't a piece of furniture in sight.

"Didn't your family move back in September?" I said, and he nodded. "Where's your stuff?"

"In transit," he said. "Come on, don't leave me hanging. What can they do?"

I scuffed at a mud stain on the checkerboard floor and told him what I'd witnessed in Peyton's rec room.

"A secret-finder and a shape-shifter?" he said. "Those are power-ful gifts. I don't know how exactly, but they have to be able to help us find Ivy."

"But they won't. You don't know them," I said. "Peyton's been my arch-nemesis since elementary school. I swear she gets off on rejecting me. If I tell her about the linking, she'll never help. And Mei is her minion. Plus, she got sick from using her power. We're doomed, Jasper. This is worse than if we hadn't found anyone at all."

"I can talk to them," Jasper said. "Maybe if they hear it from me, they'll come around."

Actually, it probably would help, but the thought of Peyton bat-ting her mascara-encrusted eyelashes at Jasper made me feel worse. I imagined the three of them joining forces to save Ivy while I was left on the sidelines, powerless to help. But what options did I have? I couldn't put my own petty insecurities over my sister's well-being. I collapsed at the foot of the curved staircase, hugging my knees.

"What's the matter?" Jasper said.

"Do you really need to ask?" I stared at the black and white tiles until the grid blurred. "I just feel completely useless."

"You are not even close to useless." He reached down, took my hand, and pulled me back to my feet.

"I don't have a gift," I said, yanking my hand away, in part be-cause his felt warm and comforting and I wanted to keep holding it.

"So? Look at what you've already done without one," he said. "You found these two girls. You found out about Josiah Strauss."

"We have no idea where his cabin is!"

"You're right. But I know you won't give up until we do."

I swallowed. "You just met me. You don't know anything about me. I can tell you that there's nothing special about me. I'll probably just get in the way."

I hunched my shoulders and stared down at the floor, refusing to meet his eyes again. I knew I was being childish and unfair. But it felt like the truth. Jasper reached his hand out and took my chin gently in his fingertips, tipping my face up so that I had no choice but to look him in the eye. My heart thumped. I'd heard they did studies where they found that if two random people stare into each other's eyes for five minutes, they're more likely to fall in love. Sometimes, just staring at each other can make people get angry or laugh or cry. This seemed ridiculous when I read about it. But now I saw how intimate it was to really hold someone's gaze.

No, not someone's.

Jasper's.

I couldn't look anywhere else.

"You're right," he said quietly. "We did just meet, but I already know that you'd do anything for your sister. I know that you're not a quitter. And it's *your* dreams that are helping us find her."

"They haven't shown me anything useful," I whispered. I felt like I could barely breathe.

His fingers gently brushed my cheek. "That's not true," he said. "You don't need a power to be special."

We were still looking at each other. They talk about eyes "locking," but this felt more like something *unlocking*, something twisting and opening up deep inside me.

Then I shook myself. It was a cringeworthy line that Ms. Owen would've crossed out with her red pen. Jasper had told me point-blank there was nothing between us and never could be. Why couldn't I get that through my head?

I blinked the tears out of my eyes and picked up my bag. "We're wasting time. We should go talk to Peyton and Mei. They're all we've got."

"You're right," he said, looking at his watch. "But it's just after eleven. Let's wait for lunch period. We can't exactly pull them out of class."

He was right. In fact, Mei hadn't even been in class that morning, so we'd be lucky if we found Peyton. "What are we supposed to do until then?" I said.

"You should eat something," Jasper said.

I couldn't help smiling. "Why are you always trying to feed me?"

"Did you have breakfast?"

"Just coffee," I mumbled.

"As I suspected," he said. "Look, it's easy to forget to take care of yourself when you're feeling stressed." He paused, catching my eye again. "We don't want another one of those Jane Austen moments."

I had to laugh at that, reminded of how Ivy would tease me about how "hangry" I got. "Point taken," I said. "My low blood sugar is kind of notorious in my family. When I was growing up, my grandma always carried an emergency granola bar for me in her purse."

Jasper smiled. "I don't have any of those, but I can at least rustle up some apples from the tree out front. Why don't you go up to my room while I find something to eat?" I felt the blood rush to my cheeks—*his bedroom?* "Since there's nowhere to sit down here," he added quickly. "My room's the only one that's really functional so far."

I climbed the stairs, curious to see the rest of the house and especially his bedroom. The banister felt cold beneath my palm. The whole place felt cold—like it hadn't been heated in years—and I was surprised to find that the rooms on the second floor were completely empty too, except for the one at the end of the hall, which contained just a large wrought-iron bed covered in a cream wool blanket, and a nightstand stacked with books. I flipped the light switch, but it didn't work. But I was sure that this was his room, because it smelled like autumn bonfires.

Like him.

I loved that smell. I wanted to press my face into his pillow and inhale it. To distract myself, I examined the books on the nightstand. On top was a hardback copy of Hemingway's *The Sun Also Rises*. It looked like another antique. The cover showed a woman in a one-shouldered dress, leaning back against a tree. I opened it, noticing that the paper inside was yellowed, and there was handwriting on the title page.

For my drinking buddy, Jasper B.
The next Borgia's on me. Ernest H.

"Reading? Are you bored already?" Jasper asked from the doorway.

I jumped to my feet, ashamed to have been caught snooping. He crossed the floor, holding a plate of thinly sliced apples. I took it and handed the book to him, still open to the inscription. "Is that some kind of joke?" I said.

"What?"

"The inscription. 'Ernest H.'?"

"No, it's real." He closed the book and set it back on the pile.

"Wait, that's really Hemingway's autograph?" He nodded. "That's amazing! This book must be worth a fortune—not that you'd ever sell it of course. But I don't get it—is Jasper a family name?"

He nodded again, and I bit into a slice of apple as I waited for him to explain. He walked over to look out the window where the rain was striking the glass, the drops chasing each other and merging.

"So my, um, great-grandfather wanted to be a writer when he was young," he said. "He lived in Paris for a while, where he managed to track Hemingway down at Les Deux Magots, this bar on the Left Bank where all the avant-garde writers and artists of the time used to hang out. He showed Hemingway a short story that he'd written, hoping he'd publish it. Instead, Hemingway told him not to quit his day job."

"Ouch," I said. "Your poor great-grandfather."

"I've seen the story, and Hemingway was absolutely right. He saved him a lot of time, which they then wasted drinking together. Or so the story goes."

"Was this his house?" I asked.

"Whose?"

"The first Jasper Blake."

He shook his head, still gazing outside. "I inherited it from my stepfather."

"Wait—*you* own this house?" He nodded. "But I don't get it—where are your mom and dad?"

"Dead," he said flatly, without turning around.

"Wait, what? Both of them?" I pressed my hand over my mouth. "You live here alone?"

Jasper nodded, again just once, burying his hands in his pockets before going on, his voice strained. "When I was very little, my father was killed in a train accident. My mother remarried when I was fifteen, but she died a few months later. Since they didn't have any kids, when my stepfather died, my brother and I were the next of kin."

I was speechless. He'd said all of this in a rush, as if he wanted to get it out fast so that we could move on—as if he found it embarrassing even, this onslaught of bad luck—but I was reeling, my mind firing questions that I didn't know how to phrase, didn't dare ask. How could he live here alone, both of his parents dead, followed by his stepfather? I couldn't imagine living in this huge house by myself—or living anywhere by myself. Even if my family sometimes drove me crazy, I needed them to keep me sane.

He must be so lonely.

"I'm so sorry," I said, thinking that these words had never seemed so inadequate. "My grandma died last summer. I'm not saying it's the same at all," I stumbled on, "but she stepped in after our dad ditched us, and ever since we lost her, I've felt so alone. I think we all do." It was only as I said this to him that I fully realized how true it was.

"Is it legal for you to live by yourself?" I said. "You're not eighteen yet, are you? When your parents died, didn't they assign a social worker to your case or something?"

"No one cares," he said. "On paper, the house belongs to my older brother, Toby."

"You said he's in Europe?" He nodded. "Couldn't he come back and live with you for a while or something, at least until you finish high school?"

"I just came back to Cascade for the linking," Jasper said. "After Halloween, I'll be gone."

"Right." I swallowed. Why had I assumed he was here to stay? He didn't fit in here. I couldn't blame him for wanting to leave as soon as possible. If I'd experienced that much tragedy, I would want to get far away too. Get back to Paris, or someplace even better.

There's nothing keeping him here.

"We'd better go talk to those two girls," he said, his tone all business now, as if all of the personal stuff he'd just told me had driven us farther apart instead of making us closer.

"If only one of them was a time traveler," I said. "Then she could go back to Friday night to stop Ivy from being kidnapped."

"It's not that simple." Jasper's jaw tightened. "Remember how I told you that powers can split?"

I nodded, bracing myself for something else I didn't understand.

"There are true powers, and shadow powers. Those girls have only sparked their shadow powers. The first gift to manifest is usually a shadow power. The true power comes later, if it comes at all. The two powers are connected, but they're also completely different substances—kind of like your body and your shadow."

"So when are they going to get their true powers?" I asked.

"It takes extreme stress," he said. "And it isn't a guaranteed thing."

"What about you?" I asked. "Did you have a shadow power?"

Jasper looked down at the tiles so intently he might have been counting them, and I had a flash of understanding.

"Wait—is *fire starting* your shadow power?" He still wouldn't look at me. The questions rolled off my tongue. "So what's your true power? Do you have it? Can it help us to find Ivy?"

He shook his head. "I can't use it."

"Not as part of the linking," I said. "But why can't you use it to find Ivy?"

"It wouldn't work for that," Jasper said. "Believe me."

Miserable, I stared at the floor. The tiles blurred again, as if the white tiles were disappearing, the blackness claiming every square.

Back at school, we searched for the Skittles all through the lunch hour, and finally one of the volleyball team members told me she thought Peyton had come down with the same bug as Mei and now they were both home sick. Jasper said he would go home and try to call them. Not knowing what else to do, I went to math on the off chance that the fourth person would reveal him or herself.

No such luck. Another dead end. Our quest felt like a tunnel that kept branching into other tunnels, a labyrinth, never bringing me any closer to the way out.

21.

IVY HAD ANOTHER PART-TIME JOB doing alterations at Second Act, the vintage store that our mom's friend Poppy ran on Miner Street. On Tuesdays, which was the one day of the week when Skye didn't have any of her community college classes, the two of us usually tagged along, keeping Ivy company in the back room where she sewed. Poppy would make us into her guinea pigs, getting us to taste the new flavors of homemade kombucha that she brewed to sell at the farmer's market, and we'd drink so much that we'd get tipsy (or maybe it was just a sugar high).

Even though I always looked forward to Tuesday afternoons, it hadn't crossed my mind to go without Ivy. Since Skye knew that she was gone, I wasn't sure what she was doing in the parking lot, waiting for me as usual. She took off her bagel-sized headphones when she saw me. "Hey."

"Hey," I said. "What's up?"

"Do you want to walk over to Second Act?" she said. "I mean, I know Ivy's in Portland, but I thought that if you don't have any other plans, it might be nice to hang out a little bit, and I'll bet Poppy would be happy to see us."

I'd been planning to go to Headmaster House to talk to Jasper, but I didn't feel comfortable sharing this with Skye. "I don't know," I said. It seemed like such a pointless detour. I was going to make some excuse when I realized that I might find some clue at Second Act. Ivy had been spending more time than usual there recently, working on a rush job for a client of Poppy's. I didn't have much hope, but I figured it couldn't hurt to explore any possibility. Poppy was like an aunt to both of us, but she and Ivy were especially close, since they spent countless hours hunched over their sewing projects, side by side in that back room. Maybe Ivy had shared something with her that could be useful.

"I guess we could drop by for half an hour," I said.

Since Second Act was just a few blocks from school, I threw my backpack into the van, then locked it up again and walked alongside Skye, hurrying through the rain, which was quickly turning from a sprinkle to a downpour. I soon regretted deciding to walk. As we rushed to the store, Skye told me that she'd been working on my birthday mix. "I thought I'd kick it off with an old classic. What do you think of this?" She tapped her phone and played Michael's Jackson's "Thriller."

Night creatures call, and the dead start to walk in their masquerade . . .

"Great," I said with a shiver, tucking my icy hands into my armpits.

Skye studied me. "What's up with the monosyllables?"

"Sorry. I just don't have that much to say," I said, thinking: *not much that you'd believe.*

"Huh," she said. "Cause I saw you and that new guy chatting away after lunch. It looked like you were having quite the intense dialogue. What's his name again—Jackson?"

"Jasper." I could feel her peering at me from the corner of my eye.

"Is he a sophomore?" she asked. I nodded. "So, what's going on there?"

"Nothing. He's new, like you said, so he doesn't know many people. I'm just being friendly."

"But you want to be more than that?"

I shook my head, grimacing as I stepped in a puddle so deep that the water splashed up to soak the cuff of my sock.

"Okay, fine, don't talk to me." Skye sounded miffed. I didn't blame her, but I also didn't know how to explain our relationship without supplying a lot of details that she was never going to believe. If I'd regretted giving her the silent treatment, what she said next made me glad I'd held my tongue. "Are you still having sleep paralysis?" she asked. "Is that why you're being so moody?" Her voice was annoyingly gentle, like she was dealing with a child or a mental patient.

"No," I snapped. "But I am still having nightmares that Ivy was kidnapped, and I'm very sure they're real." I had to speak up. But no matter how smart she was, or how many books she'd read on every conceivable subject, she couldn't help me now. This made me feel even more alone, stripped of yet another layer of protection I'd been taking for granted.

We were both silent as we turned into the alley leading to the back entrance of Second Act. The wind was blowing the rain sharply into our faces now, and I had my head down, which is why I noticed that Skye's shoelace was untied. "You're going to trip on that," I said, waiting while she bent down to tie it.

I leaned against the wall, trying to stay dry under the overhang of the roof of the used bookstore next to Poppy's. But water sluiced off the edge of the tiles, splattering at our feet. Skye was still hunched over when I saw something streak by the mouth of the alley, a tawny blur about the size of a Great Dane, although it sure didn't look like any dog I'd ever seen. I leaned forward to get a better look, gasped, and for a split second the creature stopped—I never knew something moving that fast could stop so abruptly—almost as if it had heard my intake of breath. It looked back at me, I swear it did, and as our eyes met, I felt the beginning of a scream gathering at the back of my throat. But before I could let it out, Skye stood up again and the creature, whatever it was, vanished as swiftly as it had appeared.

I wiped the rain from my eyes, blinking hard. "Did you see that?" I asked, my voice coming out funny. I realized that I was shaking from head to toe.

"See what?" Skye said.

"I think it might have been a mountain lion."

"It's not likely," she said, confirming what I already knew. We'd been taught since childhood that while there were still a few remaining mountain lions, bobcats, and foxes high in the Cascade Mountains, these predators were on the verge of extinction, far more afraid of people than we were of them. I'd never seen one before, and we lived right by the state park. They certainly didn't have a habit of roaming into downtown Cascade.

"Maybe it was a dog," she said.

"I guess, but it sure looked like a big cat," I said, shivering again.

"Let's go check it out," she said. "Which way did it go?"

"That way," I pointed. She walked ahead of me on the balls of her feet. I could tell that the naturalist in her had been awakened. Feeling my pulse beating at my throat, I followed her to the end of the alley, turning in the direction where I'd seen the thing—whatever it was—disappear. But there was nothing but a big dumpster there, pushed against a chain-link fence dividing the alley from the back of the credit union.

"There's nothing here anymore," she said.

"I guess it was a dog," I said. "A Great Dane or something—this thing was huge. It must've gotten away."

"A dog can't climb a fence," she said. "And we would've seen it, if it ran back down the alley."

"So you're saying that I imagined it," I blurted out. "Thanks again."

"No, I'm not," she said, but I didn't believe her. And part of me didn't blame her. I hadn't had a good night's sleep in days. It was raining too hard to see clearly. Obviously, my eyes were playing tricks on me. But I felt a chill that didn't pass, even when we stepped into the warmth of Second Act. As she heard the door close behind us, Poppy stepped out from the back room.

"Hi, girls! I didn't expect to see the two of you today," she said. "What's wrong, Laurel?" She was wearing a beaded flapper dress over a pair of jeans tucked into cowboy boots, her gray-streaked hair pulled into a braid that reached the small of her back.

"She thinks she saw a mountain lion in the alley," Skye said.

"But I realize that's impossible," I snapped.

"I said it was unlikely," she clarified. "But if whatever you saw did manage to climb that fence, you could be right. A big cat could do that, I'm pretty sure."

"But why would a big cat be roaming around downtown Cascade?" I asked.

"Maybe it's the upcoming lunar eclipse," Poppy volunteered. "Animals are very attuned to planetary disruptions."

I glanced at Skye, expecting a major eye roll, but instead she frowned and said, "I've been noticing uncharacteristic animal behavior too." She told Poppy about the wolverine, and they started discussing the way that the loss of wilderness spaces was forcing endangered predators out of hiding. Even though she seemed to be taking me seriously for a change, I still found myself regretting that I mentioned having seen anything at all to Skye. Even if a mountain lion had wandered out of the hills and mistakenly ended up in downtown Cascade, what difference did it make? It was simply lost, and would either get hit by a car or find its way back to the wilderness. Normally I would've cared. But nothing was normal right now.

"I wanted to talk to you about Ivy," I said to Poppy. "Did she mention to you that she was going to take a trip?"

"Not once," Poppy said with a frown. "And that is not like her. Your mom said she went to Portland?" Poppy sounded concerned, and I forced myself to nod. "I really can't believe she'd do that without letting anyone know where she was going. She didn't even finish the dress for Bill Sheers, and she was so excited to be working on that project." She sighed. "I guess I'll have to do it myself."

"She's working on a dress for Mr. Sheers?" I asked. "What for?"

"I guess it's a Halloween costume," Poppy said. "He came in a few months ago with this old dress that he wanted repaired, but it was too moth-eaten to put through the machine, so Ivy offered to make a copy. I told her it would be more work than it was worth, but she was excited for the challenge. She must have put fifteen hours into that dress already. Good thing I insisted she charge him by the hour."

Now that she mentioned it, Ivy had told me that she was glad to finally have a real sewing project for a change, and this must have been it. Poppy was a true bohemian, like our mom, which was why they got along. They loved to go thrifting together. Only Poppy had found a way to turn her hobby into a business. She'd scour Goodwills and Salvation Army stores in small towns all over Oregon, looking for cool secondhand clothes that she could resell on eBay. The shop mostly functioned as a workspace to get the used clothes into shape to sell for a profit. Ivy did grunt work—mending tears, hemming jeans, replacing zippers and lost buttons. But occasionally they'd get a commission, and Ivy always jumped at the chance to earn the extra money and put her sewing skills to use.

"Can I see the dress?" I asked.

"Sure," Poppy said, so Skye and I trailed her to the back. Ivy had her own sewing desk, and my throat tightened at the sight of the wooden box where she kept her good scissors and pincushion and seam ripper. The box originally belonged to our grandmother, painted a silvery pink like the inside of an abalone shell. When Grandma died, there was no question who it should go to. I opened the box, hoping to find some note or clue inside, but it only contained her sewing supplies, including a clear plastic pouch of crystal beads that matched the ones on the dress that Poppy brought out to show us.

"This is it," she said, laying on the table a strapless white gown made of tulle, sparkling with crystal beads. I fingered the beads, amazed, as always, by what my sister could make with her hands.

"She had to sew them on in the exact pattern of the constellations," Poppy said. "It took her forever to copy the beading from this one." She pulled a second dress out of a paper bag. The tulle was crumpled and yellowed, but otherwise they looked identical.

"Why did Bill Sheers want an exact copy of an old dress?" asked Skye.

"Who knows?" Poppy shrugged. "Rich people aren't like you and me. They live in a bubble, with enough money to satisfy every whim. As long as he's paying, I'm not asking questions."

"He must have been really happy with how it turned out," I said.

"Actually, he was unhappy with the fit. When Ivy modeled it for him, she could just zip it up. It looked terribly sexy, if you ask me—the girl's got cleavage to die for—but he told her to let it out an inch."

"But Simone's tiny," I said. "Why did he want Ivy to try it on? And if it was for Simone, then it should've been tight on her."

Poppy shrugged again. "Maybe he's got another girlfriend. He never said it was for Simone."

I glanced at Skye, but she looked unconcerned and I told myself that I was clutching at straws, desperate to find any evidence that would lead me to Ivy.

Ivy was always sewing, and Poppy was right about rich people. Besides, even if it was weird that he wanted Ivy to try the dress on, he also wanted her to let it out, so obviously it was meant for someone bigger than her. He probably had girlfriends all over the place.

Poppy took the dress back, and we were just getting ready to leave when the door burst open. It was Logan, Poppy's husband, and he seemed frantic. "You girls okay?" he asked. "I came right away, as soon as I saw the news, to make sure."

"Yeah, why wouldn't we be?" Poppy said.

Logan tugged on his bushy red beard, looking down as he said, "There's been a cougar attack at the playground just a block from here. The thing mauled a child on the seesaw. Then it took off down Miner Street—the rangers have been chasing it and they say they've even put a few bullets through it, but it's still on the loose, last I heard."

"Oh my God," I said, looking at Skye. "I was right! I saw that mountain lion right before we came in here! And it got a little kid?"

"A ten-year-old boy. He's in the hospital with severe injuries," Logan said soberly. "But at least the thing didn't eat him. They think he's going to make it."

I felt so guilty, knowing that I'd been right about what I saw. Maybe, if I'd reported it right away, someone could've caught it before it got that child.

"Let me give you girls a ride home," Logan said. "I don't want you walking around with that thing on the loose. It could have rabies is what they're saying. No cougar has attacked a human in Cascade in eighty years."

I told him that I wanted to drive—mostly because I didn't know how I'd get to school the next day if we abandoned Spud overnight—but didn't object when he insisted on walking Skye and me to the parking lot and seeing us safely into the van. I was shaking again, partly from the news of what had happened to that child, but also from the memory of having looked that wild animal in the face. I kept flashing back to it. Remembering how its eyes had locked on mine. Except the thing was, they hadn't somehow. Even though we only looked at each other for a split second, there had been something unsettling, something off, about that creature's eyes. Maybe it did have rabies, and that was the reason. I'd never seen an animal with rabies before. I'd also never seen an animal that seemed so empty of feeling. I couldn't shake the impression that there was something very wrong with that animal, something more than sickness.

"Are you sure you can drive?" Skye asked as I pulled onto the highway.

"Not really. Definitely not legally. But I think I can get us home."

She half-smiled. Her face was dead white, and I could tell she was freaked as hell too. "Laurel, I'm sorry I didn't listen to you before."

"About the mountain lion?"

"Yeah, that, but also about your nightmares. You really think that they're real?" I nodded, swallowing hard. She didn't sound like she was making fun of me. "Tell me why you think so," she said.

"You didn't believe me the last time I tried."

"I know you never lie. No matter what you say, I'll listen with an open mind."

"And you won't give me some scientific explanation for why I'm wrong?"

"Promise."

She sounded like she really wanted to hear what I had to say, and so before I could lose my nerve, I told her everything. It's like I needed someone from my own world—my world from before—to know what I was going through. I needed to try and build a bridge to this new world, to keep from getting washed away. When we pulled up in front of her house, I finished explaining about the prophecy as we sat in the driveway, facing her kitchen window.

"Wow," she said once I got to the end.

"That's it? That's all you have to contribute to this conversation? Just, wow?"

"Give me a moment to absorb it all." She paused. "You learned most of this from this Jasper guy, right?"

"And from his grandfather."

"Who's in a nursing home."

"I saw Mei turn into Ivy with my own eyes. I'm not crazy, Skye. It happened."

"I believe you," she said. "I'd still like to know why Jasper can't participate in this . . . linking of powers."

"Because he lost his star. I saw the spot where it used to be."

"But how did he lose it?"

"I don't know. He said he did something that caused harm."

"And both his parents are dead. And his stepfather."

"He's not a killer," I said. "I know him well enough to know that much."

"Okay, but to lose every one of them is statistically improbable."

"It's all improbable, but it's happening."

Here we were in Spud, with its stale french-fry smell and bug-splatter-encrusted windshield. Outside, the wind picked up, rattling tree branches. The clouds moved swiftly across the sky to reveal the nearly full moon.

"The linking needs to happen on Halloween," I said. "Which means we still need to find someone else with a power, and Ivy, or else."

"Or else what?"

"Druj wins. Evil prevails. That's what the prophecy says."

She winced at that word. I knew how she felt, but I also knew this was for real. "Let's focus on what we know for sure. This guy who caught you trying to release his bunnies when you were little, Josiah Strauss, is obsessed with Ivy. He's off at his hunting shack in the woods. So the first thing we have to do is find him and see if Ivy is there."

"His mother won't tell us where the shack is. It could be anywhere."

Skye ignored me. "Also, Peyton and Mei need to know everything that you just told me—in more detail." She paused, staring at a point in the distance. "I'll call them tonight and ask them to come to a team-building meeting at Ritual tomorrow morning."

"A team-building meeting?" I mustered a weak laugh. "Come on, Skye. This isn't *Scooby-Doo*. Besides, they already jumped at the chance to turn me down."

"Well, put yourself in their shoes. They don't have a clue what's going on, or why this is happening to them. I'm sure they're completely traumatized."

"So am I!" I didn't see why she was taking their side.

"If I can talk them into coming, can you get Jasper to come?"

"I think so," I said.

"Great. Because I'd like to hear more about it too. It's conveniently murky, if you ask me."

I felt grateful that she wanted to help in spite of her innate skepticism. In the kitchen, Skye's mom dumped pasta in a colander, steam rising around her face. The scene was so cozy and normal, making it almost impossible even for me to believe that any of the things I'd just described could be happening.

But they are.

Even if I didn't have a lot of faith in this so-called team that Skye wanted to assemble, at least she was going to be part of it. She'd built the bridge that I needed, found a way to cross into this new world with me, and I felt less lonely.

"Skye," I said as she got out of the van. "How come you're not insisting that I must be out of my mind? I mean, I still have a hard time believing a lot of this myself, and I've seen my worst enemy morph into my sister."

"Well, I'm not sure I believe the prophecy stuff, but you have no reason to lie. I'm worried about Ivy too. If she's been kidnapped by this creepy Josiah guy, we'd better find her right away."

I swallowed, glad that I'd reached out to her again even if she only half believed me.

WEDNESDAY

NO ONE can make you a victim but yourself.

That's something else Grandma used to say, and I finally get it. I refuse to be his victim anymore. I've almost stopped thinking about food. The burn on my wrist isn't throbbing anymore either.

I know one thing: no one can stop me from using my gift.

Thankfully he hasn't taken the lantern away, so hour after hour I practice. The harder I work, the less drained I feel.

First I unwind the roll of toilet paper, making it unfurl like a long white carpet. Then I roll it back up again, so it looks brand new. I tear off one square, and I make it flutter across the room like a butterfly. It's almost pretty.

Next, I try to build strength. Beads of sweat pop out on my forehead as I move the ladder from side to side. I'm careful not to make a sound, and to set it back carefully, right where it was.

I need to take him by surprise.

My plan is to use my eyes to seize that foot-long knife of his and stab him in the chest before he realizes what's happening. You know in horror movies, how the girl always stabs the monster once and then runs away without making sure that she killed him? And how he always gets one last burst of energy to come attack her again?

That won't be me.

I will plunge that knife into him until I am one hundred percent sure he's dead.

22.

ONCE AGAIN, I woke up feeling a little better. Clinging to the thought that Ivy was getting stronger, I got up and headed to Ritual, where I claimed a table in the back and sipped a coffee I didn't need as my jittery fingers drummed the tabletop. I didn't expect the Skittles to show, so it was a real shock when they arrived on time. They ordered nonfat mochas with extra whipped cream and then plopped down across from me.

"You recovered from your bug, I see," I said. "Weren't you both sick yesterday?"

Peyton shrugged. "We needed to unplug for the afternoon. Where's Jasper?"

Of course seeing him was the only reason she'd come. That explained why her hair was perfectly blown out, and why she was wearing so much makeup that she looked ready to return to the beauty pageant circuit.

"He should be here soon," I said. I'd called him as soon as I got home the previous night, letting him know about this meeting.

And just as I suspected, the moment he walked through the door, she was all over him like butter on toast.

"Jasper, we're back here," she called out, raising one hand and wiggling her fingers. "Hey, so did you really start that trash can fire with your eyes?" she added in a voice that couldn't have been any louder if she'd had a megaphone. "Way to get us out of English class. That book is seriously boring."

"Keep it down," he said, glancing around before sitting next to me. "You can't let anyone hear you talking about powers."

"Sor-*ry*," Peyton said, looking stung, "but I thought you were going to explain everything. I *thought* that was why we had to come here at the butt crack of dawn."

"It is," I said, "we just don't want to be overheard."

"I didn't mean to jump on you," Jasper said, "it's just that you don't know who might be listening, so you have to be careful."

"Why? What could happen?" Mei whispered. As she leaned forward so that her hair fell in her face, I was reminded of the transformation I'd witnessed in Peyton's rec room. Part of me wanted to beg her to turn into Ivy again, just so that I could see her and know that she was still alive, but I knew she never would.

"Can I show you something?" Peyton spoke up again. She pulled back her hair and I gasped. Now I understood why she'd spackled on her makeup like putty. The platinum star gleamed, shining through the thick concealer as if it gave off a true stellar light.

"I have one just like it on my back," Mei said, still speaking in a hushed tone.

"It looks exactly like mine," Peyton added. "Isn't that crazy?"

"It means you've both sparked," Jasper explained. "It happens when your power manifests itself."

"Do you have one too?" Peyton asked. "Can we see it?"

"I'm afraid not," he said, looking down at the tabletop.

"How come?" Her gaze roamed across his torso, and then the side of her mouth curled up. "Wait—is it in a super private place? You can show me, Jasper, even if—"

"There's nothing to show," he cut her off. "I used to have one, but it's gone."

Peyton looked disappointed, but Mei sat up straighter. "Does that mean your power went away too? When? How did it happen?"

"Why don't we start by talking about the linking?" Jasper suggested.

"The what?" Peyton said, but just then, Skye walked through the door. She was wearing red-and-white striped leg warmers under a pair of cargo shorts, and hiking boots. The wind had made modern art out of her asymmetrical hair, blowing long strands over the newly shaved part.

"Hey, guys," she said. "Sorry I'm late, but I had to stop and pick something up on the way."

Peyton and Mei made room for her to pull a chair up in between them. You might have expected the Skittles to pick on someone like Skye, but they'd always left her alone, maybe because she was so unconcerned about other people's opinions of her that there was no fun in attacking her. She straddled her chair backwards, resting her arms on the backrest. "So, fill me in. What did I miss?"

"Nothing," I said. "Jasper was about to explain about the linking."

"Do you have a power too?" he asked her in a low voice.

"Only the power of scientific detachment," she said. "Something that you guys appear to be in serious need of."

"This is Skye," I said to Jasper. "She got the Skit—I mean, Peyton and Mei, to come to this meeting."

Ignoring Skye, Peyton asked Jasper, "So what are people with powers called? There must be a name for us, right?"

Jasper scratched his head. "Well, we've had different names over the centuries, in the different places where we've shown up. One of the names is 'luminary,' which comes from the Latin, *lumen*, or 'light,' and it means 'a prominent person' or 'a celestial body that gives light.'"

Skye snorted. "Full of yourself, much?"

"I didn't say I deserved the name," Jasper said sharply. "I was just answering your question. My grandfather and I always refer to ourselves as people who've sparked."

"That's not very catchy," Peyton said, making me dig my nails into my palms. She was acting like she was presiding over the world's most exclusive club, a role I knew that she relished. "I know, what about 'sparklers'?" she said.

"Sounds like a bunch of cheerleaders," I said, noticing that Skye was looking something up on her phone. "Skye, what are you doing?"

"Research. I found something. 'Squibs.'" She fixed her gaze on Jasper. "'A small firework that burns with a hiss before exploding.'"

"I'm not going to be a squid," Peyton said.

"Me neither," Mei agreed.

I was starting to get really annoyed. "How about 'flares,'" I suggested on impulse. "You know, like those torches they throw on the side of the road when there's an accident? They burn with a super bright light for a really long time, and they protect people from danger." I didn't expect them to take my suggestion, but both Peyton and Mei agreed that they could live with it, which made me feel marginally better for being able to contribute, however microscopically, to their club.

Skye fixed her gaze on Jasper. "Now that that important matter is settled, I'm hoping you can explain to us exactly how this linking is going to work. I know Peyton and Mei have a lot of questions, and frankly, so do I."

A muscle twitched in his jaw and he turned to me. "Uh, Laurel, can I talk to you for a minute?" He paused, clearing his throat. "Alone?"

"Okay," I said. As I stood up, Skye's expression said, *Who does this guy think he is?* I made an apologetic face but I followed him outside. As Peyton's eyes followed us through the window, I felt a slight zing of triumph. She was obviously hot for Jasper, and here he was with me, standing close under a dripping awning. I couldn't remember a time when I'd had something she wanted.

Not that I 'have' Jasper, I reminded myself. *Far from it.*

"I'm not sure we should involve an outsider," he said. "It's already so complicated, and I don't think that girl can help if she's doesn't have a power."

His words stung, but I didn't let it show on my face. "*I* don't have a power, and I managed to find the Skittles." I shoved my hands in the pockets of my jeans. "Look, I know you just met her, but Skye is off-the-charts brilliant. She's like family to Ivy and me, and she's already helped just by getting Peyton and Mei to come here today. Maybe she can talk them into using their powers."

"So you're sure we can trust her?"

"Of course we can," I said.

But can I trust you? The question poked at me, Skye's suspicions getting under my skin. I still didn't understand why he couldn't participate in the linking, what he'd done that was so bad that he'd lost his star. But right now, our priority had to be convincing the Skittles to join us. I resolved to ask him more about what had happened to him the next time we were alone.

Back in the coffee shop, he quickly told everyone about the prophecy, as if speed would somehow make it more palatable. But after he had finished reciting it, everyone looked more confused than ever, just like I'd felt when I heard it (and still did).

"Should I be able to understand that?" Peyton said. "Because maybe I'm dumb or something, but it sounds like gobbledygook."

"You're not dumb," Skye said, and she pulled out a notebook filled with neatly solved equations, flipped to the first clean page, and copied the whole thing down.

"Whoa, did you just memorize that?" Peyton asked.

"Skye has a phonographic memory," I said. "That means that she remembers everything she hears."

"No way! Me too!" Peyton said, but then she sagged. "Except not, like, school stuff."

"Just gossip," I muttered.

Under the table, Skye's foot collided with my shin, reminding me to rein in my scorn if I expected Peyton to do anything for us.

"Why do these alleged prophecies always rhyme?" Skye asked.

I could practically hear Jasper's teeth gritting. "I don't know, maybe to make the prophecy easier to remember. Or maybe that was the translator's decision. The original is long gone by now."

"The words don't make much sense," Skye said. "Peyton's right."

"Thank you," Peyton said, flashing a grin.

"'As the *dead and the living trade places.*'" Skye paused. "Does that mean that corpses are going to rise, in some kind of zombie apocalypse?" She sounded almost eager, reminding me of her weakness for horror movies.

"Only if we don't manage to bring four powers together in the linking," Jasper said, "which is where the two of you can help," he added to Peyton and Mei.

"What does 'Druj shall at last trade faces' mean?" Peyton asked, reading over Skye's shoulder.

"We're not sure," Jasper admitted. "But if the linking happens, it shouldn't matter, so you can see how important it is."

All I could see was that Skye's inner cynic had not been squashed. With her notepad and pen, she reminded me a little of Officer Dougherty, ostensibly interviewing me but so persuaded by his own theories that he could hardly listen to mine. But even though she was being a tad aggressive, I wanted to hear Jasper's answers to these questions of hers—questions I shared.

"It's awfully short on specifics," Skye persisted. "How long have you and your grandfather been studying this thing?"

Jasper folded his arms over his chest. "A very long time."

"Vague again."

"Look," he said, "the prophecy comes to us orally, from a sect that lived in Persia three thousand years ago. Of course it has a few holes. We know they believed that the end of the world was a real possibility—but not an inevitability—and that *if* it took place, it would begin tomorrow night, right here, led by an ancient demon called Druj. We believe that Druj has already taken over a human vessel and kidnapped Ivy, to try and stop the linking of powers. We know this linking has to take place during the eclipse. *If* four powers don't freely link, then—well, I still think the cryptic old prophecy says it best: Druj, or evil, will prevail."

Even though he pronounced all of this in a mocking tone, as if he knew that it couldn't possibly strike the proper chord of terror here in this strip mall coffee shop, decorated for Halloween, with fake cobwebs stretched across the ceiling, black plastic spiders tucked into the gauze—I still felt a chill.

"So you're telling me that demons are real?" Peyton said. "Because I know for a fact that my dad fakes his exorcisms with recordings and incense."

"I'm afraid this one is all too real," Jasper said. "It'll look human, but it will be far more dangerous than any person could ever be."

"Is that why you told us not to talk about our powers?" Mei asked. She was twisting a strand of her jet-black hair around her finger, her fingertip turning paper white. "Do you think this demon could kidnap us too?"

"That's a risk," Jasper said. "You haven't told anyone, have you? Or shown off your powers in public?" Peyton and Mei both shook their heads, looking queasy.

"Good," said Jasper. "Then you should be fine. The linking is tomorrow. We all need to be extremely careful until then."

"And we still need to find another flare," I reminded him. "Four powers have to link."

"I don't get that," Peyton said. "How does it work?"

"My grandfather says that each flare has to participate freely," Jasper told her. "You have to choose to be part of it."

"Yeah, but choose to be part of what? How do we link up?" Mei pressed.

"I don't know. I'm hoping it just happens naturally once you're all together," he said.

"I thought you were supposed to be this huge expert," Peyton said. "Skye told us that you'd be able to explain everything. But I'm not getting a clearer picture at all."

"Thanks for the vote of confidence," he said, darting a look at Skye, "but I'm not an expert, exactly. I'm figuring all of this out along with the rest of you."

"But Laurel said you'd been training Ivy," Skye said, "and that you came to Cascade on a mission to find three—no, four—flares." She paused, giving him a meaningful stare. "Because you can't be part of the linking, right? You lost your star?"

"That's right," he said, looking down at the dregs of his coffee.

"What did you to deserve that?" she asked.

"Look," he said, "I appreciate that you want to get involved, but I'm not sure why you're the one asking all these questions. We don't have time to waste, and you don't have a power, so let's talk about how we might use Peyton and Mei's to try and find Ivy. They've got great powers, but we need to figure out how to use them to locate Josiah."

"Actually, I have a better idea." Skye reached into her pocket and pulled out a folded piece of paper, which she spread on the table.

"What is that?" I said. It looked like a map.

"Directions to the Strauss family hunting shack." She sat back in her chair.

"What?" I wasn't sure whether to hug her or shake her for having taken so long to reveal this. "How did you get this map?"

"From my dad's friend at the Department of Fish and Game. It turns out that Josiah's grandfather got the permit to build the shack before they turned the land into a state park, so it's in the public record. The shack is in the forest, about 10.3 miles from here." She pointed to a spot on the map: the old paper mill, a few miles east of our property. "We can park right here, and from there it should be about a five-mile hike to Josiah's shack, maybe less. If we leave now, we should get there by noon."

I grabbed my jacket, knocking my chair over. Jasper and Skye stood too, but Peyton and Mei stayed seated.

"Come on!" I said. "We have to go rescue Ivy!"

"Are you nuts?" Mei said, crossing her arms. "I'm not hiking into the woods to track down some psycho kidnapper. Sorry, but you need to call the police, Laurel. I'm sure this guy has a gun."

"Or twenty," Peyton agreed, flicking back her hair to show off her gleaming star. "Mei's right. We'd be crazy to go after him unarmed."

"Well, we can't go to the police," I said. "I tried that. It's not like we can tell them what we know about this guy. Did you somehow miss the part about him being," I lowered my voice, "a human vessel for an ancient demon?"

"Actually, I heard it loud and clear," Peyton said. "And if anyone ever told you that you should be a lawyer, you shouldn't listen, because you are so not helping your case with that argument."

"Whatever," I said, my voice tight with anger. "I highly doubt your magical power to *eavesdrop* would be much help anyway." I turned back to Mei, a new plan forming. "Maybe you could *become* a cop! A really big, buff one? What if you pictured, like, the Terminator, or—"

But Mei shook her head. "No way. I told you, I am not using my power again. How could you even ask me to do that? You saw what happened the last time!"

I wanted to scream at her, but I bit back my fury. "Fine," I said, whirling to face Jasper and Skye. "Who cares? I'm sure they'd be completely useless. We're better off without them, right?" I wanted them to agree, for the three of us to charge off without another glance at the Skittles, so it grated at me when Skye turned back to Mei.

"Hang on. You're going out with Stu Sheers, right?" she asked.

Mei shrugged. "Technically. I mean, I haven't broken up with him yet."

"Then can you drop by his house and check out his basement?"

"What for?" Peyton butted in.

"Because Mr. Sheers hired Ivy to sew a dress to give to someone on Halloween, which is the day this linking is supposed to happen."

"So what? I'm sure it's for Simone," Peyton said. "They're, like, pre-engaged."

"But he told Ivy to try it on," Skye said. "Then he said she needed to let it out, because it was too tight on her."

"But Simone is *way* smaller than Ivy," Peyton said, frowning. "She's, like, a negative zero. And Ivy must be at least a ten, with those big boobs." She looked at me, as if wondering yet again how I could be related to Ivy. But Skye nodded, as if Peyton had made an intelligent observation.

"That's why it's a little strange." She turned back to Mei. "If you don't mind, do you think you could just go down to check out the Sheers' basement and see what you find? I'm sure there's nothing, but we don't want to overlook something obvious."

Mei sighed. "I guess so. As long as I don't have to use my power."

"Please don't," Jasper said. "With the linking so close, you shouldn't take any risks. We definitely don't want Mr. Sheers to catch you using it."

"Wait, are you honestly suggesting that Mr. Sheers could have kidnapped Ivy?" Peyton snorted. "He gives, like, a million dollars to my dad's church every year, and he's already got the hottest girlfriend in town! Well, except for me of course." She laughed as if this was all a great big hilarious joke, and suddenly I snapped.

"Could you please, for once in your tragically shallow life, take something seriously? My sister could *die*!"

In the silence that followed, I stared at Peyton. Skye once told me that you can arrange your expression to show the emotion you want to project, but the truth of what you're feeling always shows on your face, if only for an instant. That's why detectives will videotape confessions and then use a freeze-frame to study a suspect's face.

For an instant, what I saw on Peyton's face was pure terror.

Suddenly, I remembered the way I'd felt way back in the third grade, right after I pushed her off the monkey bars—seized with regret as I watched her spit out the tiny rocks embedded in her bloody lower lip. I'd pushed her again, right there in Ritual. When she wouldn't do what I wanted her to, I'd lashed out at her in front of everyone.

But—just like me—she was terrified, and she didn't have a clue what to do about it.

And I had no idea what to say, how to make up with her, or what making up with her even meant. So I said nothing as we left Ritual, each heading for our separate vehicles.

23.

"YOU'D BETTER STOP at home and change your shoes," Skye said, after claiming shotgun.

"What?" I glanced down at my feet. My right one pressed the gas pedal to the floor. I was wearing Ivy's red ballet flats, because my boots hadn't dried out from yesterday.

"We'll be hiking off-trail," she said. "If you fall in those, you could sprain your ankle or worse, and we wouldn't get to the shack."

Groaning, I veered off the highway, knowing that as usual Skye was right. I left Spud's engine running in my parking spot. "I'll be right back," I said. "You guys wait here."

"Do you have anything in there that you can grab for us to use as a weapon?" Skye said.

"A kitchen knife?"

"I guess that's better than nothing."

I was about to remind her that Jasper had a power when he spoke up from the backseat. "Grab as many as you can. We could each use one."

Great, I thought, as I walked toward the trailer. *We were going to battle an ancient demon with dull cutlery.*

But at least we had a map leading to Ivy. I tried to focus on that.

I found Mom seated at the red table, wrapped in the old afghan that Grandma had crocheted, and staring at the phone. I'd caught her doing that a lot over the past few days. At first I thought she was pathetically waiting for Bryan to call, but every time she so much as stepped outside, she'd return and ask immediately if Ivy had phoned.

She looked startled to see me. "What are you doing home? Are you sick?"

I hesitated. Every lie was a brick in the wall that was growing between us, so I tried to be as honest as I could. "I'm going for a hike." I grabbed a box of granola and stuffed it into my backpack.

"Don't you have class?"

"Um . . ." I decided to tell another tiny bit of the truth. "Yeah, but I've been so stressed out, I need to clear my head."

I was desperate for her to look away so that I could take the butcher knife from the dish rack. "By the way, are you sure the phone's working?" I asked. "I tried to call earlier and no one answered. What if Ivy's trying to get through?" As she knelt on the floor to examine the jack, I slid the knife into my backpack.

"It looks fine." She stood up again, frowning at me. "And it was certainly working when I got a call from school yesterday. You missed four periods."

I gulped, shifting from foot to foot. "I wasn't feeling well."

"Honey, I know you're stressed out about Ivy. I am too. But I really don't want you to skip school. This isn't like you."

"I'm fine! Missing a few classes isn't a big deal." I rummaged through the basket by the door for my boots. I was about to leave when she stepped in front of me.

"I said no, Laurel."

Great. She'd finally started acting like a normal mom—exactly when I most needed her to leave me alone.

"I want you to stay out of the woods," she continued. "Poppy told me they haven't found that mountain lion yet."

"I'm going with Jasper," I protested. "We'll be safe together."

"Strong as he may be for his age, I doubt he's any match for a rabid cougar." She paused. "Why don't you two pick something else to do, *after* school? Go to a movie."

"Fine," I said, because I could feel my pulse ticking, every beat another second lost. I reached for the door, grabbing my boots and hoping she wouldn't notice, but she stopped me, tucking a curl behind my ear.

"You look so nice in those flats," she said, taking the boots.

I couldn't fight without making it clear that I wasn't going to any movie. She was going to figure that out soon enough, when I came home with ruined shoes.

But I'll be coming home with Ivy, I told myself.

Nothing else mattered.

We parked behind the old paper mill. The crumbling building was missing most of its windows, and a few shards of dull glass crunched underfoot as we searched the deserted lot, trying to determine which of the overgrown dirt paths disappearing into the trees matched the one on Skye's map.

"I'm pretty sure it's this one," she said, pointing to the steepest path.

"Pretty sure?" Jasper raised an eyebrow.

"We were on the same Girl Scout troop," I said. "She was the only one of us who got her compass badge."

"Still have it," she said, and as she reached into another of her pockets, for a moment I was afraid she was going to whip out her badge. But instead she pulled out her old compass, holding it up and peering at the quivering arrow. "I was right," she said. "This is the trailhead."

"Great." I fell into step behind her, and Jasper took up the rear. I could feel every pebble through the thin soles of my flats, and I kept slipping backwards on the silt covering the path, which got narrower by the minute.

"I'm really sorry," I apologized to Jasper the third time I slid back against him.

"It's okay," he said. "I'd trade shoes, but I don't think those are my style." I managed a smile. The air was damp and icy, the dense foliage blocking what little light there was. Now that we were in the woods, my fear was a thrumming bass beat in my chest, but I kept reminding myself that every step we took brought us one step closer to Ivy.

"What if he has a power?" I asked.

"I think you would've seen him use it in your dreams," Jasper said.

"Assuming these powers are real," Skye added. "Not to mention the dreams."

"Can you please stop that?" I asked her. "You have helped a lot, and I know this whole thing is hard for you to buy, but this is not what we need right now."

We all came to a standstill before a tangle of massive roots. "I just need to see something with my own eyes," Skye said.

Jasper offered me a hand, which I accepted a little self-consciously, hoisting myself over the roots with his help. I thought that maybe he hadn't been listening to Skye, but then he spoke up. "I'm not going to give you a demonstration of my power, just to set your mind at rest."

"I wasn't asking for one," she said.

"Good," he said.

"But just to be clear—you're like, a human lighter?"

I waited for him to lash out, but he just said, "Pretty much. Would've been a hit back in prehistoric times when all they had was soggy sticks, don't you think?"

"Laurel said that you have some other power too, right?" Skye said. "Your *true* power?"

I held my breath, waiting for him to divulge what it was.

"Why don't we focus on the plan for what we're going to do once we get to this shack," Jasper said. "Because we should be there soon, right?"

"Yes," she said, checking her map again. "So we have two things going for us: there are three of us and just one of him, and he doesn't know we're coming. We'll hide in the bushes and wait for him to come out. Then one of us can grab him and hold the knife to his throat while the others go inside to rescue Ivy."

I swallowed, trying not to think of the ways that this could go wrong. I reminded myself that we did have a knife almost as big as his—even if it was so dull that it could barely slice tofu. But at least it was a plan, however flawed. Jasper must have agreed, because he didn't propose any alternative.

As we got deeper into the woods, the path kept disappearing for longer stretches. The rains had caused mushrooms to sprout everywhere; they grew in clumps on fallen trees, peeking between ferns. Curdled-looking yellow fungi like botched omelets. Red toadstools spotted with white like something out a fairytale. Pretty but poisonous.

When we reached an intersection with what appeared to be another trail—although it was hard to say—Skye pulled out her compass and squinted at the map. "I'm almost positive it's this way," she insisted, pointing to the left. Behind me, I heard Jasper sigh loudly as we trudged deeper into the wilderness.

Finally, we came to a narrow log that spanned a rushing creek. It looked slippery, and I wasn't sure I could cross it. Blisters were already forming on each heel, and my blood sugar was plummeting. I pulled the box of cereal out of my backpack, shook out a handful, and then passed it to Jasper, who crammed some in his mouth before passing it to Skye. I glanced at my watch. It was almost noon. "We've been walking for three hours," I said. "Are you sure we're going the right way?"

"Positive," Skye said.

"Let me see that," Jasper said, reaching for the map.

Skye shook her head. "This *is* the right way. The turn-off is in half a mile."

When we reached another slippery log bridge, I grabbed the map, staring at the orderly lines on the page and then at the tangled chaos of the forest. If you stared at the ferns long enough, you could see a path anywhere. "I think this is the same bridge we crossed before," I said, pointing at a bunch of granola scattered on the path.

"You must have just spilled that," she said.

"I did not!" I wanted to hurl her compass into the ferns.

But then a shot rang out.

Some survival instinct kicked in, and suddenly the three of us were crouched on the ground, huddled behind a tall stand of ferns. In my panic, my senses went into overdrive. Every detail stood out fresh and sharp, down to the rows of tiny brown bumps on the fern fronds. At my feet, a wood louse busied itself on a spike of bark.

It seemed amazing that it could go about its business at a moment like this.

The forest was quiet again, except for a bird whose song was a single short note, like the snip of scissor blades. It was obvious that Josiah Strauss had fired that shot and was now hiding behind a tree, waiting for us with a hunter's patience.

Finally, Jasper whispered, "I'm going after him."

"He'll kill you," I hissed, grabbing his arm, but he was already standing up. "Jasper, no!" I leaped to my feet, but something slammed into my chest, a mass of tawny fur that knocked me to the ground. My head hit a rock, and the world fizzed into blackness. Then I heard screaming, and it took a second before I realized it was coming from my mouth. Giant paws were pinning my shoulders down. I could feel the tips of massive claws digging through my shirt. A dripping mouth with inch-long fangs was panting in my face, breath like rotten garbage.

But its glassy yellow eyes were what made me sure.

This was the same beast that I'd seen when Skye and I were in that alley. The one I'd locked eyes with for that moment, that had looked back at me with such glassy emptiness.

Over the top of its enormous head, I saw Skye lunge, holding the butcher knife. As she stabbed it into the cougar's side, it spun around and sank its teeth into her thigh. She screamed, but Jasper managed to wrench the beast off, flinging it to the ground. While the cougar crouched, growling as it prepared to strike again, the three of us stood side by side, a team at last.

"Raise your arms," Skye murmured. "Make yourself as big as you can."

"That won't work," I hissed back, but I did as she said anyway.

"Here comes that demonstration," Jasper said, his eyes fiercely fixed ahead.

Even though I'd seen him use his power before, it still amazed me when tiny flames began to crackle all over the animal's fur. But instead of stopping it, the fire seemed to make it grow stronger. It was a fire-cougar now, with a coat of flame, sparks dripping from its jaws, and glowing embers for eyes. It flattened itself against the ground, ready to spring.

As the cougar leaped, I froze, waiting to feel its weight slam against me again, its jaws snap at my neck. Instead it shot upward, a thrashing ball of fire now hovering several feet above the ground.

"What the hell just happened?" I turned to Jasper. "What did you do? Is that your other power? Your true power?" My knees were like jelly.

He shook his head. "That wasn't me."

We all looked up at the thing, which appeared to be trapped in some kind of net suspended like a hammock between two trees, still snarling and thrashing, still on fire.

"What is that?" Skye said.

"A steel drop net with a radio-controlled electromagnetic trigger." A man stepped out from the trees to deliver this report. He was middle-aged, with neatly parted brown hair, and he wore jeans, a flannel shirt buttoned all the way up to the neck, and glasses. He didn't look in anyone's eyes, but stared at a spot over my left shoulder.

It was Josiah Strauss. I remembered him clearly, from childhood. He still had the same strangely flat voice. And I felt the same terror that I'd felt at nine years old, when he made that chopping motion.

The way I kill them, they never see it coming.

My knife was buried in the body of the flaming cougar, way up in this psychopath's net. Josiah lifted his rifle and I let out a scream. But instead of aiming at me, he shot the cougar again. Overhead, it continued to thrash and growl. Some parts of it were still burning, and it gave off a horribly savory aroma of grilled meat.

"Look," Jasper murmured, gesturing with his chin at a clearing fifty feet away. In the distance I saw a shack built out of gray planks, so weathered and lichen-spotted that it had blended into the forest. "Go get Ivy," he whispered. "I'll grab his gun." Without pausing to think it over, I rushed toward the shack, my lungs straining as I sprinted through the ferns, praying that he'd be able to get that gun and hold Josiah back until I got to her.

I reached the shack and wrenched open the door. "Ivy!" I yelled. It was a single room: scuffed planks strewn with pine needles, a sleeping bag rolled out under the one small window. In a corner lay coils of barbed wire, piles of netting, and a box of canned goods and pasta. I shoved the box aside and ripped the sleeping bag up, but there was no sign of a trapdoor, or any kind of basement dug out beneath the shack. In spots, the wood had eroded to show patches of dirt.

Josiah burst in, with Jasper and Skye right behind him. Jasper was carrying Josiah's rifle, still pointing it at him, but Josiah seemed too agitated to notice. "Everything has its place," he whimpered as he smoothed the sleeping bag back down on the floor and pushed the box of food against the wall.

Jasper looked at him uncertainly, still holding the gun but not pointing it at him anymore, while Skye crouched down and knocked on a floorboard. "It doesn't sound hollow," she said. "There's no cellar under here. There's no foundation at all."

I pressed my ear to the ground, hammering it with my fists. "Ivy!" I yelled.

Josiah stood up abruptly. "Are you searching for Ivy Goodwin?" For the first time, he abandoned his robotic monotone. He sounded scared.

We all whirled around to stare at him, and he seemed to shrink away from our gaze. He stared at his feet, which were pressed tightly together.

"Where is she?" I demanded. "What have you done with her?"

"It's Wednesday, so Ivy should be at school." His arms were pressed against his sides, his fingers curled into fists. "Ivy should be at school," he repeated.

"She's not and you know it!" I shouted.

Josiah hunched his shoulders, like a turtle trying to pull his head back into his shell. He spoke more rapidly, to himself more than to us. "It's Wednesday," he said. "That's a school day, so she should be at school. On Saturday and Sunday, she works at Ritual Roasters, where I always order a decaf, because caffeine affects my sleep cycle." As he spoke, I realized that he didn't sound like the man in the mask. He sounded like there was something wrong with him. "Maybe she's at home," he muttered. "Home sick. You share a bedroom with Ivy, don't you?"

My blood curdled. "How do you know that?"

"I like to trap in the park near there. Your window is low, so it's easy to see inside." He said this matter-of-factly, as if he had no idea that there was anything creepy about it.

True psychopaths have no sense of right or wrong.

"So you came into our trailer and took her on Friday morning?" I asked, backing against the wall, digging my fingers into the wood so that I could feel splinters beneath my nails. He was still refusing to make eye contact and his shoulder kept twitching.

"Oh no." He shook his head, addressing his feet. "Trespassing is against the law. I'd never do that."

"But you took her in the middle of the night," I insisted.

"I did no such thing," he said. "But I did see her leave your trailer."

"What?" I was completely taken aback. "When?"

"At 4:23 on Friday morning," he said. "I track at dawn. That's what I was doing when I saw Ivy walk out your door. I was tracking in the park. I did not expect to see another person. It was still dark. She was wearing pajamas, and she had no shoes on, and she was heading toward town."

Bewilderment replaced the terror that had been paralyzing me. If he'd kidnapped her, wouldn't he deny having been anywhere near our place? There was no reason for him to make up this crazy story.

"Did she look scared?" I asked. "Were you close enough to see her expression?"

He frowned. "I don't know."

"Well, why didn't you ask if she needed help?" My voice cracked. "Who walks out their front door in pajamas and barefoot in the middle of the night? Even if she wasn't running, obviously there was something wrong!"

He shrugged, his shoulders jerking all the way to his ears. "Sometimes girls wear short skirts when it's pouring rain. Sometimes they wear shoes like that in the woods." He pointed at my mangled flats. Then he raised his chin for the first time since I'd started interrogating him. He blinked, and as he took off his glasses to polish them on his shirt, I caught a glimpse of his eyes.

They were brown, not blue like the eyes of the man in my dreams.

I stared at him, not knowing what to think.

Could he wear colored contact lenses when he visited Ivy?

"Excuse me," he said. "I have to go the bathroom now. Please do not touch anything in here." His voice shook a little. I realized something: maybe he wasn't scared because we'd finally caught him. Maybe he was scared because a bunch of teenagers had stampeded into his shack and started yelling at him.

"He's definitely different," Jasper said quietly once Josiah had left, "but I don't think he's a kidnapper."

"I think he might be autistic," Skye said. "Fascination with traps is one of the symptoms. Also, an obsession with schedules and an inability to read faces."

She slid down the wall. When she closed her eyes, the freckles on her lids stood out starkly. Looking down, I saw the dark spreading stain on her leg warmer.

"Oh my God, Skye," I said, kneeling beside her. "You're really bleeding!"

"Let me see that." Jasper crouched down too. Wincing, Skye allowed him to peel off her leg warmer, exposing her blood-smeared calf. He took off his hoodie and used it to blot the wound, revealing a ragged curve of puncture marks.

"It's not that deep," he said. "I don't think you need stitches, but we should keep applying pressure until the bleeding stops."

Josiah returned to the shack, rummaged through his box, and produced a first aid kit. "The cougar is hardly moving now," he reported, as matter-of-factly as he'd shared the fact that he stared into our bedroom window. "Most of it has burned away. I added some lighter fuel to hurry things along." The way he was acting, it was almost like he'd been expecting to catch something like that thing in his net. That was weird. But I had to focus on taking care of Skye.

He laid out everything we needed to finish dressing the wound: wipes, gauze pads, and another bandage. He seemed calmer now. He behaved as if he had nothing to hide, and he seemed to want to help us. What finally convinced me that he had nothing to do with Ivy's kidnapping was something small. He crouched down and carefully opened the package of wipes, pulling one out so that it was ready when Jasper wanted it to blot Skye's legs. Josiah was too gentle to hurt anyone. He wasn't the man in my dreams.

But this revelation brought no relief. I'd been so desperate to find him, so certain that when we did, we'd find Ivy too. Now, our only new clue was this strange story about her walking barefoot, in pajamas, toward town. It sounded like she had been sleepwalking. "You said you're a tracker. Can you track Ivy?" I asked Josiah.

"No," he said. "I track animals by looking for scat, paw prints, and disturbances in the vegetation. Humans don't leave these signs."

"We should probably go to a hospital and get you checked out," Jasper said to Skye. "Even if you don't need stitches, that thing might have rabies."

"It does not have rabies," Josiah spoke up again. "Death kills disease."

"What are you talking about?" Skye said.

"The cougar is dead," Josiah announced matter-of-factly.

Jasper glanced out the window. "No, it isn't, it's still moving up in the trap."

Josiah jerked his head from side to side. "It was dead when it attacked you," he said, and we all gaped at him. "You were smart to set it on fire," he told Jasper. "I think that when it finally burns to ash, it will stop moving."

"I don't understand," I said.

"It's the third one of its kind that I've caught," he said.

"You've trapped three cougars?" Skye asked.

Josiah shook his head in that same jerky way again. "No. First there was a bobcat, then a fox, now this mountain lion. Bullets don't slow them down. I've been trying to track them, but they leave no scat. They kill living creatures, but they don't eat them."

"Just like the wolverine," Skye said. "Rabies would make animals extremely aggressive, and kill without reason, but it wouldn't protect them against bullets. So there's only one logical conclusion." As she rested her head against the wall, closing her eyes, I waited for her to deliver a scientific pronouncement. But when she opened her mouth again, she said, "He's right. These animals are dead."

I wanted to protest that this was impossible. That cougar had seemed pretty full of life when it attacked us. But then I remembered something. When Ivy and I were little, we once found a cat, hit by a car, lying on the side of the road. It died in my arms, and as its body went slack, the light went out of its eyes. The same thing happened to our grandma. We'd been in the hospital room when she died, and it was like there was a dimmer switch inside of her. We'd all watched as she faded, her eyes open but vacant.   Empty.

Just like the eyes of the cougar.

As the dead and the living trade places . . .

Evil shall prevail.

I shivered and wrapped my arms around myself, but the chill I felt was coming from deep inside.

How do you kill something that's already dead?

24.

BY THE TIME WE STARTED BACK, it was almost five. Josiah told us about a shortcut on a fire road and gave us headlamps, but we barely needed them since the moon lit the way, its fullness a grim reminder that the eclipse was tomorrow.

We walked in silence, straining our ears to catch a rustle of the underbrush or the snap of a twig. Before, I'd been scared but also amped up, so sure that we were about to find Ivy. Now, even though the trail plunged downhill, I felt like I was climbing a mountain.

"Maybe the Skittles found something at Mr. Sheers's house," Skye said, when I finally pulled in front of her house to drop her off. "I'll call Peyton and let you know right away if she did."

"Okay," I said dully, certain that Mr. Sheers was not a demon in disguise. They'd gone on a wild-goose chase, just like us. We were facing a force much bigger than any of us, something powerful enough to draw Ivy from her bed and make the dead hunt the living. Now that it was clear that Josiah didn't have Ivy, we had to start from scratch—with only one day left.

We had failed. *I* had failed.

We were almost at Headmaster House when Jasper told me to drive home instead. "I'll walk from your place," he said. "I want to make sure you get inside safely."

"You shouldn't walk through the woods," I said.

"I can use my power if I have to."

"Which one?" I asked, but he didn't answer. I glanced over at him, but he was turned away, gazing out his window.

"I'm sorry we didn't find her, Laurel."

"Yeah," I said. "Me too." Still, I felt like he wasn't doing enough. He'd come back to Cascade with one mission: to find four flares and bring them together for the linking. So far, he'd lost the only one he'd found.

When we pulled up in front of the trailer, the curtain twitched and Mom peeped out the window. I raised a hand and she disappeared again.

"Just tell me this," I said, the anger climbing into my throat. I waited until he looked at me before I went on. "What is your true power? I don't see why you can't just tell me."

Jasper's eyes were as dark as the ocean on a January day. "If you knew the harm my true power could do, you wouldn't ask. Anyway, I told you before, it wouldn't help."

"Why won't you let me be the judge of that?" I was seething now.

"Look, Laurel, I'm doing what I can," he said. "I'm sorry if you're disappointed in me. You're not the first."

"What does that mean?"

"I'm a screw-up. 'Never going to amount to anything.' You should've heard my stepfather. I know I haven't exactly succeeded at this mission." He flung open the van door and got out. "And another thing. After I lost my star, I hated my power, every part of it. I promised myself to stop using it—even my shadow power—which means I should stay away from you."

He started walking toward the woods, but I ran ahead of him, spinning to face him and blocking his path.

"What do I have to do with it?" I asked. "Why do you need to stay away from me?"

When he spoke, his voice was so low that I could barely hear him. "I don't know what it is, if you make me want to show off or—"

Or what? I thought, resisting the urge to reach out and touch him.

He ran a hand through his hair and took a deep breath in. "You've made me break that promise to myself so many times. I want to be able to control myself, not use my power at all, and I can't seem to do that when you're around."

I swallowed. Did that mean he might have some feelings for me after all?

Get real. He just said he wants to stay away from you.

"I didn't force you to light that trash can fire, or ask you to warm my hands," I snapped.

"I know," he said. Even in the bright moonlight, I couldn't read his face.

"The linking is supposed to happen tomorrow, Jasper, and we've only got Peyton and Mei. We have no idea who this other person with a power is. Even if we do find Ivy, we're not going to be able to pull it off."

I wanted him to say, *We will, of course we will.* I wanted him to reassure me. But instead he only said, "I know," again.

"I'm really scared, Jasper. The reversal is already happening, isn't it? The dead and the living trading places?" I scanned the forest, listening for sounds of animals rustling, wondering how many more were out there, clawing their way up from the dirt. "Whatever you did, how bad can it be?" I went on. "Maybe you *can* be part of the linking, if we don't find anyone else." I felt a surge of hope. "We could just ignore the part of the prophecy that says you can't be there. I mean, why do we have to do what all these old dead guys say?"

He sighed. "If it weren't for these 'old dead guys,' we'd have no idea that the world might end. I don't think it's safe to pick and choose which parts we're going to believe and which parts we're going to ignore. We have to trust that they knew more than we do, and that there's a reason for those lines." He gazed up at the small patch of sky visible between the trees. "Besides, even if there wasn't anything in the prophecy about me, I don't *want* my power to be part of the mix. That's the only way to keep you—and everyone else—safe. You have to trust me."

I remembered how I'd held my hands over a flame cradled in his, trusting him not to burn me. "*You* don't trust *me.*" I shivered as the moon slipped behind a cloud. "Otherwise, you would tell me what you did to lose your star."

His eyes were dark hollows in the dim light. "Can't you just drop it?"

But I couldn't. "It's always better to tell someone about your problems. Two heads are better than one. You told me that, remember? So why won't you talk to me?"

"This is different. If I told you, you'd hate me, and you'd be right to." He started walking away again, but I ran after him and grabbed his arm, pulling him to face me.

"No, I wouldn't!" I said, although I wasn't sure if it was true. "Jasper, nothing could be that bad." I kept a tight hold on the front of his hoodie, so he couldn't try to escape again.

The clouds rolled back and the moon shone down again. His eyes looked bright and wet, like there might be tears in them. But instead of saying anything, he pulled me close and wrapped his arms around me, holding me so tightly I could hardly breathe, my face mashed against his chest. The smell of his shirt filled my nose—laundry detergent and toast—but underneath that, there was something else that was just the smell of Jasper, the smell of him and no one else, so intoxicating that for a fraction of a fraction of a second, I forgot everything else in the world.

"Laurel?" Mom was standing in the doorway of the trailer, peering into the darkness. Instantly, Jasper pulled away, leaving my body feeling achingly cold where it had been touching his.

"Wait!" I said, but he was already gone. I ran a few paces after him into the forest, but even with the moonlight, I couldn't see the familiar trail, as if the trees had shuffled from their places, blocking my way wherever I turned.

Mom was waiting for me at the door. "Where's Jasper?"

"He wanted to walk home." Luckily, we'd been standing about ten yards away from the door of the trailer on the edge of the forest, and it was dark enough that Mom apparently hadn't seen us hugging. I dropped my backpack and kicked off Ivy's muddy ballet flats. Mom stared at them, shaking her head.

"Did you go hiking, when I told you not to?"

"Yes. I'm sorry, but can we please talk about this tomorrow?" I said. "I really need to go to bed." I tried to push past her.

"Honey, wait." She grabbed my arm. "Let me fix you something to eat at least." She opened the fridge. "Poppy took me grocery shopping. I got that maple yogurt you like. And I could make spaghetti?"

"I'm not hungry."

Mom sighed. In the harsh light of the open fridge, I noticed her first gray hairs threaded in with the blonde, and flecks of mascara dotting the mauve skin under her eyes. "Please don't shut me out." She took hold of my shoulders. "I wish you'd talk to me, Lolo. I love you. You can trust me."

There was that word again. *Trust.* For a second, I was tempted. What if I took a huge leap and tried again? Told her everything that was going on right now? What if, this time, she believed me? Maybe she could pull it together and help. Maybe she was stronger than I thought. But just as I opened my mouth, Mom said, "Did Jasper do something to upset you on your date?"

"It wasn't a date!" I snapped.

"But you wanted it to be," she said, reaching out to touch my cheek. I didn't have the energy to keep correcting her, so I just stood there. "Well, I'm sorry you're disappointed, but maybe it's for the best, sweetheart. I like him, but he does seem a little old for you."

"He's seventeen," I said. Or was he sixteen? I realized that he'd never told me. Anyway, that wasn't the problem. The problem was that now wasn't the time to be thinking about the way that I could still feel his arms around me.

"He seems very mature."

"And I seem immature?"

"Of course not," she said. "But there's no need to rush into anything serious. I want you to enjoy being a kid for as long as you can."

"Well, so do I," I said, feeling like I had a jagged piece of metal in my stomach.

I went into my room, closed the door, and leaned against it, wishing I could act like the kid I was, bury myself in Mom's arms and sob, tell her everything without worrying about whether she'd believe me or not, let her comfort me, let her take over.

But I couldn't.

You build a wall to protect yourself. Maybe it happens all at once, or maybe it happens slowly, brick by brick. But by the time you realize that you've walled yourself off, it's not so easy to smash that wall down.

25.

Mei

PEYTON WAS GIVING MEI a ride to Stu's house. The plan was for her to wait outside. Mei would tell him that she'd forgotten her sweater in his bedroom on Friday night. While he went to look for it, she would run downstairs. Mei was sure she wouldn't find Ivy, but the thought of going to the basement alone still made her stomach clench.

Peyton parked outside the front gate, where she promised to wait, and Mei reluctantly climbed out of the car. "I'll be right back," she said.

As she rang the buzzer, a sour taste climbed the back of her throat.

Stu's voice crackled through the intercom. "Yeah?"

"Hey, it's Mei!" she said in a perky voice, trying to get into character as the Mei he knew.

Silence.

"Can I come in for a sec? I think I forgot something in your room."

Stu cleared his throat. "I just got out of the shower. Let yourself in and I'll be down as soon as I get dressed."

He buzzed, and Mei wandered through the foyer to the kitchen. No trace of the party remained. The black granite countertops shone like patent leather. The gleaming, stainless sink could've been used as a bathtub. The Sheers' mansion wasn't glitzy, it was just enormous, every room on steroids. There were two of everything: two dishwashers, two Sub-Zero refrigerators, so Stu and his dad never, ever had to share.

Mei idly opened one of the fridges, helping herself to a fortifying swig of Chardonnay. Still no sign of Stu. She remembered how long it took him to style his hair after a game—she'd teased that he like to primp more than she did—and realized this was her chance to run down to the basement to check if Ivy was down there.

The sooner the better, so I can get out of here.

Steeling herself, she slipped down the broad hallway, thankful that the floorboards didn't creak. *There's nothing creepy about this house,* she reminded herself sternly, taking in a collection of snow globes displayed on a console.

Stu loved to show off his dad's wine cellar, and he'd taken her down there before, but she couldn't remember which door led to it. She opened the wrong one and found herself in the museum wing again—the museum Mr. Sheers had created to bring tourists to Cascade and teach people about local wildlife.

Peyton was right. Mr. Sheers was the nicest guy ever, and there wasn't a chance in hell that he had anything to do with Ivy's abduction. But she couldn't help but shiver, remembering that a demon was supposedly behind all of this.

A demon in a human vessel.

Could it hide itself so completely that you could never, ever tell?

A flapping noise, like the beating of leathery wings, made her jump. The ceiling lights were off, and only the track lights illuminated the exhibits, so it took a moment to see where the noise was coming from. She heard it again and caught her breath. But it was just a giant sheet of plastic that had been taped over a broken window, flapping in the wind.

Chill out, she told herself.

But something was different. Several of the dioramas had gaps. Where the mountain lion had been crouching at the base of a potted tree, now there was just some dirt scattered on the floor.

"What are you doing here?"

Mei whirled around at the sound of Stu's voice. He was wearing orange sweats with the OSU logo sprawled across the chest. *Go Beavers!*

"I told you, I forgot my sweater," she said, her heart pounding. "I thought I might have dropped it in here during the party, but I can't find it."

"Okay," he said. "Well, it's probably in my room. Want to check?"

She nodded, but she was in no hurry to return to the scene of the crime. "Um, what happened to the mountain lion?" she said, stalling.

"I guess it got stolen during the party." He frowned. "Can you believe it? They must have taken it through there." He pointed to the broken window. "My dad's making me pay to have the glass replaced."

"That sucks," Mei said, feeling totally unsympathetic. Stu often bragged that he could live forever off the interest from his trust fund, and would never have to get a job. As he led her out of the museum and up the stairs to his room, she realized she'd have to find a way to sneak back down and take a peek later. She was certain that the poor girl wasn't down there—but she had promised.

Once in Stu's bedroom, she made a token effort to kick aside one of the mounds of dirty clothes obscuring the floor. She felt self-conscious as she got on her hands and knees, setting aside her bag as she made a big show of pretending to search under his bed.

He's probably not even watching me, she thought, feeling a resurgence of humiliation as she remembered how *not* turned on by her he was. Everything in his room reminded her of that night: the swimsuit model with her grapefruit boobs, the square of sky visible through the skylight, the rumpled maroon flannel sheets.

"Guess it's not here," she said, standing up. "Peyton's waiting, so I'd better go."

"Uh, Mei," he said, biting his lip. "I'm not really sure what went down in here Friday night, but maybe we should talk about it? Just to clear the air?"

This was a shocker. Stu angling for a heart-to-heart? She stared at the waterbed. She could still feel it bucking and sloshing as he snored on top of her. She could still feel the power of her rock-hard pecs as she shoved him off.

"I don't remember that much," he said. "I had way too much to drink. But did anything weird go down in here?"

"Not really," she said, feeling as uncomfortable as he sounded. "I was pretty wasted too," she lied. "I think we both just passed out."

"Oh, okay," he said. "I mean, sorry." He sank onto the edge of his bed, resting his elbows on his knees and his forehead in his hands, and she sat beside him.

"I feel like you're not that into me," she said.

Stu sighed. "I think I suck at relationships." His voice trembled. "Maybe if my mom was still alive, I'd be different."

Mei was shocked. He'd never talked about his mom before, always rapidly changed the subject if she ever tried to broach it. She was supposed to be looking for Ivy, but . . . she wanted to know more. "What happened to her?"

Stu wiped at his eyes with his forearm. "She had this rare disease that pregnant women can get, where their blood pressure shoots up and their organs fail. She sacrificed her life to carry me to term. That's what my dad always says. Sometimes I think he'd rather I died instead. I think he blames me."

"That's impossible." She placed her hand on top of his. "You were a baby, Stu. How could it be your fault?"

"When it comes to my mom, he's pretty irrational." He shrugged. "'True love never dies.' That's what he always says."

"That's romantic," Mei said.

Stu grimaced. "It's great if you get to be with the person for your whole life, but if you lose them, you're screwed. He still can't move on."

"Isn't he dating that counselor?" Mei asked. "Simone Sinclair?"

"In theory. She kind of threw herself at him. They got back in touch on Facebook, and she moved back to Cascade like a month later. She comes over and cooks dinner for us, but he's always talking about my mom, and asking Simone what she remembers, since they were all in school together. And she totally lets him get away with it, saying what a wonderful friend Bianca was and how much she misses her too."

"Simone must be really crazy about your dad to put up with that," Mei said.

"I feel bad for her. But I shouldn't judge my dad too harshly. I think about my mom a lot too, and I never even knew her." He sighed. "I guess she was pretty amazing."

Mei patted his arm. "She must have been."

"When I was a kid, I used to spend hours studying old pictures of her, trying to imagine what her voice sounded like, trying to see if I looked like her . . ." He shook his head. "Sorry, I don't know why I'm dumping all of this on you."

Mei shook her head. "No, I don't mind at all, and I totally get it. I used to think about my mother all the time too. My biological mother, I mean. I've always wondered if I look like her or like my father, whoever he is. I hate that I'll never know." To her surprise, her own voice was trembling now. She'd never told anyone, not even Peyton, how she'd pined since childhood for a glimpse of her birth parents. It was something that everyone else got to take for granted: knowing which parent was behind which features, not to mention the less tangible qualities that added up to make them who they were.

No wonder it's so hard to turn back into myself, she thought sadly.

"Can I see a picture of your mom?" she asked Stu on impulse.

"Sure." He walked to his bookshelf and pulled out an old Cascade High yearbook. It fell open to a page captioned: *Long Live Bill and Bianca, Prom King and Queen!*

Mei recognized Stu's brown eyes, set in the face of a curvy blonde girl in a strapless white dress. Next to her stood a young Bill Sheers, gazing at her adoringly.

"She's pretty," Mei said.

"I miss her," Stu said. He laughed sadly. "That makes zero sense, right? I mean, how can you miss someone you never even met?"

"I totally get it," Mei said. "I was a week old when my mother left me at a train station in China. There was a note in my diaper, but all it said was my name, *Mei.* It's the Chinese character for beautiful. I always wonder why she named me that and then abandoned me."

"It's the perfect name for you," Stu said, squeezing her hand.

"Hey." She looked at him through her tears. "Do you still want to be with me? Because it kind of feels like you're not that into it."

"I don't know what I want," he said. "But I guess it's true that when we mess around, it never really clicks for me."

"Me neither," she said. "Is it something I'm doing wrong?" she asked. "Do you think I'm a bad kisser?" She braced herself, but he shook his head.

"It's like our lips just don't fit together."

"I know!" she said. Then she paused. "So, um, I guess this is it? We're breaking up, right?"

He gave her a sad smile. "I really hope we can be friends," he said. "I know people always say that, but I mean it. You're a really cool girl, Mei. I've never talked to anyone about this stuff."

"Me neither," she said. "Who knew that breaking up could bring you closer?"

As they laughed, she realized that she was not at all offended, but instead relieved that they could be truthful for once.

"Are you hungry?" Stu said.

"Starving, actually," she said. "But I should get going. Peyton's waiting."

"I could make some quick nachos de microwave," he offered. "It's *mi specialidad*."

"Sure." She laughed again. "Put everything on them. I want the works."

"I'll be right back," he said, and he galloped downstairs.

Mei sat up on the bed, and even though it sloshed beneath her, it no longer seemed so awful. Her gaze landed upon the yearbook, still open to the picture of Bill and Bianca. "Long Live Our King and Queen!"

I wish I could meet her, Stu had said about his mom, the same thought she'd had so many times about her own birth mother. Who knew that they had so much in common? He was like her soul mate, aside from the total lack of chemistry.

I could do this for him.

Chasing this thought, nervous energy coursed through her like a six-pack of Red Bull. But as soon as she felt the shrink-wrapping sensation, she knew what a mistake it was. Stu's mom had been dead for eighteen years. What would he think upon opening his bedroom door to find her standing there? Still a teenaged prom queen? He would be petrified. But Mei couldn't stop what was happening. Powerless before her power, she felt herself being obliterated, as if she were being buried in an avalanche.

"Mei?" Stu clattered back upstairs.

Stay away! she wanted to shout. But her face was as immovable as a shield, and her lips refused to part.

He bounded into the room. She waited for the crash of the plate as he saw his dead mother standing before him. But Stu seemed unfazed.

For a blissful second, she thought she had changed back already. Then Stu walked right by her, knocking on the bathroom door.

He didn't seem to see her at all.

"Mei? You in there?" When there was no answer, he frowned. "Mei?" He opened the bathroom door, looked inside, and then went back downstairs.

Mei wanted to scream, but she couldn't open her mouth. She was freezing, and yet her teeth couldn't chatter. The chill cut through her entire body, paralyzing every cell.

She wondered, *Is this how I'm going to die?*

Then her mind became a frozen cloud, and she stopped thinking anything at all.

THURSDAY

THE MAN CROUCHES *behind me to unlock the cuffs. I hope he can't feel my pulse, which is going a million miles per minute.*

Click.

It's time.

I spin around, flexing my eyes at the knife tucked into his belt. It wriggles free, soaring into the air. For a moment, he just stands there and gapes. Then he lunges. I make the knife dart away, bring it higher than his head. He chases after it, jumps. I swivel the blade so that the tip is pointing at him. His hands fly up to protect his face, then he lowers them to cover his heart.

"No!" he cries out. "Please no!"

I aim the knife at the soft meat of his belly and ram it in and keep ramming it in.

He looks at me blankly. His watery blue eyes are frozen in shock.

I hold my breath, trying to quell the panic rising in my chest. Somewhere up there, he has a life. Maybe there are even people who care about him. But he was going to kill me if I didn't kill him first.

Then, he grabs the handle of the knife, pulls it away from his stomach, and laughs.

"Bravo," he says, still chuckling. "That was quite the performance, Ivy."

There's no blood on the knife. No blood on his shirt. It's not even ripped. But I know I stabbed him. Does he have a power? Is he invincible?

He pushes me into the chair and locks me up again. I'm too stunned to resist. Then he grabs the knife and stabs himself in the chest, over and over. Now I see that it's made of hard plastic, the kind that kids use with their Halloween costumes, where the blade disappears into a hollow hilt.

"You're ready," he says. "I can't wait for tonight."

Then he snuffs out the light, leaving me in total darkness.

26.

SPUD'S ENGINE SPUTTERED TO LIFE, but all I could hear was that horrible laugh. I floored the gas pedal all the way to school. If Mei had discovered Ivy, she would've called. But maybe she'd learned something, seen something, that we could use to find her before it was too late.

The Mini was in its usual spot, but Peyton was alone in the car, staring out the window, which was open a crack, releasing a fragile curlicue of smoke.

"Where's Mei?" I asked, climbing into the passenger seat.

"Gone." Peyton's eyes were puffy, and she hadn't bothered to cover the star on her cheek, which gleamed like a tiny piece of shrapnel embedded beneath her skin.

"What do you mean, gone? Gone where?"

"I don't know." As she went to take another drag of her cigarette, her hand was trembling so badly that I thought she might miss her mouth. "I waited in the car, but she never came out. After an hour, I rang the bell, and Stu told me she'd left without saying good-bye."

"Did she walk home?"

Peyton shook her head. "She lives miles from there, and I would have seen her leave. Besides, she was supposed to spend the night at my place. So at least her parents aren't freaking out. Yet."

My skin prickled. "Have you tried calling her?"

"Like a million times." Peyton sounded anguished. "What if she's really hurt? What if . . ." Her voice trailed off, but I knew where her mind was going, because it was the same place mine returned to when I thought about Ivy.

"Was Mr. Sheers there?"

"Not at first, but I went back later to see if she might have turned up, and he answered the door."

"Did he act guilty?"

"Not at all. He said Stu had persuaded him to take the night off for once and watch the game and they'd just heated up a bunch of leftover Chinese. He even invited me to join them."

I sighed—not that I was surprised. Mr. Sheers was an all-round good guy. I remembered how he'd gone out of his way to put Mom at ease when we walked into the Andersen house the other night, offering her champagne and complimenting her dress. He'd been dressed up for the party too, and he'd joked about how he felt like an undertaker in his suit.

"I'm just a jeans and hiking boots kind of guy," he'd said, laughing.

A sound floated to the surface of my memory.

His laugh.

"Oh my God." A cold noose seemed to wrap itself around my neck. I'd been so blindly convinced that Josiah Strauss had kidnapped Ivy, I'd barely given Mr. Sheers a second thought. Ivy had gone with Mom to work on the murals for a couple of weeks over the summer. Maybe she'd used her power while she was painting, and he'd seen it?

"What's wrong?" Peyton asked, and I realized that I was panting, one hand gripping the handle of the door, the other clutching her knee.

"Mr. Sheers," I gasped. "He has the exact same laugh as the man in my dreams."

Her eyebrows gathered. "So?"

"They're visions from Ivy," I said, quickly filling her in. "Mei must have found her in the cellar, and now he's trapped both of them down there."

"No way he's a kidnapper." Peyton shook her head vigorously. "I've been going to Easter egg hunts at his house since I was a kid. He never misses church, and he puts like a hundred-dollar check in the collection plate every single week."

"A real psychopath can hide it," I said. *And so can a demon,* I didn't add, since Peyton's face was already white. She jumped, and I realized that her cigarette had burned down to her fingers. She rolled down her window and threw it out, leaving the window open so that rain blew into the car.

"If you're sure, then we have to go straight to the police," she said.

"They'll never believe us," I said, remembering how Officer Dougherty had been at that cocktail party too. "He has this whole town in his pocket." I paused, thinking over our options. "We need to talk to Jasper."

"No!" Peyton burst out. "He's not who he says he is, Laurel. He's hiding stuff."

I shifted in my seat. "What do you mean?"

"Remember earlier this week, when we were all leaving school together and I asked if he'd done any modeling?" I nodded, remembering the cheesiest come-on ever. She went on, "I couldn't sleep last night, and suddenly I realized where I'd seen his face. You know how Mei and I have to scan old issues of the *Cascade Trib* for the library's digital archive?"

"Yeah."

"So we found this. I went online and printed it out this morning." She bent over, rummaging through her bag and then handing me a printout of an old newspaper article. My eye was immediately drawn to the photograph of a somber young man with dark hair and piercing eyes.

"He looks just like Jasper," I remarked.

"That's because it is him."

"Come on," I said. The article was dated 1921. "Do the math, Peyton."

"Read the article."

ARSON SUSPECTED IN SCHOOL FIRE

The fire that destroyed The Cascade School may have been intentionally set, according to headmaster James Drexel, whose wife Alice was trapped in the library during the fire and died of smoke inhalation. Drexel has named Jasper Blake, her sixteen-year-old son by a previous marriage, as the lead suspect in what is now a case of arson and manslaughter. "That miscreant always resented me for marrying his mother," Drexel told local sheriff Al Dickson. "I believe he started that fire intentionally, because he wanted to kill me." Jasper Blake has been missing since the night of the fire, and Drexel has offered a cash reward for any information leading to the fugitive's capture, adding, "He must be brought to trial for this heinous crime."

I felt light-headed. The name, the picture, the fire starting . . . So many things pointed to the Jasper I knew—or thought I knew—but there was no way it could be him, since all of this had happened over one hundred years ago.

"Maybe he's a vampire," Peyton said, her voice shrill.

"Come on—there's no such thing."

"Yeah, well, until this week, I would have said there's no such thing as magic powers, but here we are."

"He got his great-grandfather's name," I said, relieved to remember this solid fact. "They must look alike."

"Like identical twins?" She stabbed the page with her finger. "This has to be him, Laurel. I don't know why he's so freakishly young-looking, but he's been lying to us and we can't trust him."

"He's been helping us," I argued. "He came all the way back to Cascade just to find four flares to be part of this linking."

"But one by one, we're disappearing. Maybe *he's* the one who kidnapped Ivy, and then Mei walked right into his trap. He could be Druj!"

I shook my head, speechless. Even though I didn't know what to think about this newspaper article, I still couldn't believe that he had anything to do with Ivy's disappearance—or Mei's.

"I *know* that Mr. Sheers is the man in the mask," I insisted. "The man in my nightmares has his same blue eyes and his same exact laugh."

"Well, what if he has an accomplice?" Peyton sounded miserable, and I knew just how she felt. I took a deep breath, trying to think as rationally as possible.

"Look, you're positive that Mei didn't leave the Sheers' mansion?" She nodded. "You were sitting out there in your car and you would've seen her go. That means she must still be there, probably with Ivy, down in the cellar. Since the police aren't going to listen to us, we need to go and get them out. Now."

With Jasper so determined not to be involved, I didn't think I had a chance of persuading him to join us, and in any case, I'd need to talk to him about the newspaper article before I could trust him. Skye was at one of her classes at the community college this morning, and we couldn't bust into it without causing a scene. On our own, I had no idea how Peyton and I were going to manage it, but I couldn't leave Ivy—and Mei—locked up for a moment longer now that we knew where they were.

"You and me?" she asked, and I nodded firmly, trying to look more confident than I felt. "B-but, what if something happens to us too?" She pulled out another cigarette, but her hands were shaking too badly to work the lighter. She squeezed her eyes shut and tears slipped out.

I felt a twinge of impatience, but I had to get Peyton to pull it together, because I couldn't do this completely alone. I tried to put my panic about Ivy out of my mind and focus on Peyton for a moment. Casting about for the right words, I flashed back to the last time I'd seen Peyton cry, right after I pushed her off the monkey bars back in the third grade. No wonder my mind went there. Without makeup on, she looked about eight years old again, and in bad need of a hug. I reached out and placed a tentative palm on her back. To my surprise, she didn't shrug it off.

"We can do this," I said gently. "You have a magical power, remember?"

"The power to eavesdrop." She sniffed. "You made a point of telling me that it wasn't going to be any help."

"I was freaking out." I paused and admitted, "I'm a little jealous."

"Jealous of *me*?" She sounded incredulous.

"I'd give anything to have a power like yours."

She sniffed. "That's ironic."

"What?"

"Just that I have something you want for a change."

"What are you talking about?" I sputtered. "You have everything and I have nothing, as you've made a point of reminding me since the third grade."

"What are *you* talking about?"

"Okay, I'm sure you don't even remember this dumb story that I wrote about a magical pony, but right before I shoved you off the monkey bars, you blurted to the whole playground that it was a big lie, that I didn't have a horse, or a dad, and that my mom was your maid."

Her mouth fell open. "First of all, I do remember your story," she said. "I remember how Mrs. Gomez was so impressed that she copied it off for the entire class to read. Then, during recess, I actually told you that I thought it was great, and you said, *'I'm amazed that you could read it.'*" She stopped and swallowed hard, as if it was still a painful memory. "I couldn't believe you'd say that in front of everyone, when you knew how embarrassed I was about being dyslexic!"

I gaped at her. Had I really said that? "I didn't know you were dyslexic, I swear."

She shrugged. "It was a mean thing to say."

"It was meant as an honest compliment," I said. "I'm sorry. So that's why you started hating me?"

"I guess," she said. "I'm sorry, Laurel."

I couldn't believe that our war had started over a misunderstanding—or that she was actually apologizing. "I'm sorry too," I said. "And I'm sorry I broke your tooth."

She shrugged, flipping her hair over one shoulder. "At least I got to stop competing in those horrible beauty pageants."

I laughed, and she offered me a tiny smile.

"By the way, I *don't* think your power is useless," I said. "You can hear people's deepest secrets. That's an amazing gift."

My words seemed to give her the boost of confidence that she needed. She sat up straighter. "You're right," she said. "It is amazing.

Let's go get Ivy and Mei." She paused. "But how will we get into the Sheers' mansion?"

I realized that I had no idea. A ten-foot wall surrounded the Sheers' property. There were security cameras mounted over the gate, and an entry code. When Mom worked for Mr. Sheers, he always made sure that he or Stu were there to let her in. Even if we got past the gate, we would need a key to the front door.

I was racking my brains for a solution when a flash of color caught my eye. Simone was striding across the parking lot, swathed in a black trench coat and holding a red umbrella that the wind kept flipping inside out.

"I'll bet she could get us in," said Peyton, following my gaze.

"Yeah, but what do we say? It's not like we can tell her that her fiancé is possessed by a demon, and that he's got a couple of kidnapped girls in his cellar."

"We're not going to tell her that we suspect Bill. We'll make up a better story."

"I'm a terrible liar," I said.

"Well, I happen to be an excellent liar." Peyton reached for the door. "Just follow my lead."

27.

"OUR FRIEND MEI IS IN TROUBLE! We're pretty sure she's passed out somewhere at Stu's house, and we need your key so that we can go look for her."

Peyton and I had burst into Simone's office, which smelled like jasmine. Simone had been standing by the window, swirling tea in a small clay teapot as she gazed at the rain. Now she set it down and closed the door, asking us to start over and tell her exactly what had happened. Peyton explained that Mei had gone over to Stu's yesterday to look for her sweater, and that Stu said she'd left while he was making a snack. "But he doesn't realize that Mei has this weird condition where she randomly passes out."

"A medical condition?" Simone asked, looking concerned.

"Not exactly," Peyton said. "It's just this thing that happens when she gets really stressed. She's got the school play coming up, and she's super nervous about playing the lead. We think she must have wandered into some room to practice her lines in private and then passed out. You know how massive that place is. Stu thought she'd left, so he didn't even try to look for her, but she was supposed to come over to my house and she never showed up. I know she's there, but she isn't picking up her phone." Peyton swallowed. "The thing is, after she passes out, you have to throw like a gallon of cold water on her or she'll sleep for twenty-four hours straight."

Good one, I thought, startled to realize that Peyton was a lot more inventive than I'd ever given her credit for.

"You mean she was trapped there all night?" Simone asked, her eyes widening.

Peyton nodded. "Her parents knew she was supposed to spend the night at my house. I didn't tell them that she wasn't there, because I didn't want them to freak out, but I'm getting really worried and I think we should go and get her. You do have a key, right? We'll bring it right back, I promise!" She held out her hand. "Oh, and we need the code to the gate too."

But Simone didn't offer up her key or the code. Instead she crossed her arms. "What's really going on? Is she on something?"

Peyton shook her head. "I told you—she's just really stressed about the play."

Simone picked up her cell phone. "Well, this sounds serious. I think we'd better call an ambulance."

"No!" Peyton yelled. "I mean, it happens a lot, and she'd be super embarrassed if anyone found out about it."

Simone nodded, appearing to think this over. "I'm going to call Bill then. He's at a construction site today, but I'm sure he'll come right home as soon as he finds out about this." As Simone started to dial, Peyton cast a desperate look at me, and I wrenched the phone from Simone's hand. She looked as shocked as if I'd slapped her.

"You can't call Mr. Sheers," I said.

"Why on earth not?"

"Because he kidnapped Ivy!" I blurted. Once part of the truth was out, I couldn't stop. "He's had her locked her up in his wine cellar all week. We sent Mei to look for her, and he must have trapped her down there too."

Simone's eyes narrowed. "Is this some kind of sick joke? Because I've known Bill for twenty years, and he wouldn't hurt a fly." She held out a hand. "Give me back my phone this instant, Laurel, so that I can call him."

But I clenched it harder, as if holding on to her cell phone would somehow keep her from calling him, even though there was a landline on her desk. In my desperation, I considered making a run for it. But I knew she'd call the police before we made it to the parking lot, and the cops would beat us to the Sheers' mansion and arrest us at the gate.

My arm felt leaden as I handed back her cell phone. But instead of dialing Mr. Sheers immediately, she sighed wearily and then set it down, looking back and forth between Peyton and me.

"Okay," she said finally, "the two of you are obviously very upset, and I always promise kids that I'll to listen to them, no matter what. So I'm going to write a note excusing you both from class just this once. Let's have a cup of tea and sort this nonsense out." She picked up the pot, filled two small iron cups with the fragrant jasmine tea, then handed one to each of us. Peyton and I sat side by side on the love seat, and she pulled out her desk chair to face us.

"Now, tell me everything," she said. "Laurel—where did you come up with this crazy notion that Bill could have kidnapped your sister? And does this mean that she never came home?"

She looked deeply concerned now, and I felt like a total idiot for having come to Bill's girlfriend for help. But now that we'd started down this path, we had to follow it to the end. Besides, there was no one else to turn to. I closed my eyes, reminded by the scent of her tea of the jasmine that grew on a trellis behind our grandmother's back porch, where we used to sit and eat dinner in the summer. It transported me back to a time when I'd felt happy and safe. Maybe that was why I started talking. Or maybe it was because I remembered how much Ivy trusted Simone. Or maybe it was just because of the way Simone looked at me: like she wanted to hear whatever I had to say, and was patient enough to wait until I was ready to say it.

As I told her everything that had happened this week—the story pouring out of me—Simone didn't interrupt with questions or tell me that I had an overactive imagination. She just listened. And I was pretty sure that she believed me by the emotions racing across her face: horror as I told her about the nightmares; amazement as I explained that Ivy had a power, and so did Peyton and Mei, which was why we thought she'd been kidnapped. I told her what I knew about Druj and the linking of powers that was supposed to happen tonight, how we believed that Ivy had been kidnapped in order to prevent it, how we'd yet to find a fourth flare.

"I can't believe this," she whispered, pressing her fingertips to her quivering lips, her dark eyes shiny with tears.

"You don't believe us?" Peyton said.

"Believe you?" Simone fumbled with the zipper of her boot. She was wearing black leggings underneath her smoke-colored sweater dress, and she rolled up one cuff and set her bare foot on the coffee table. "I'm *one* of you!"

We both gaped at what was etched on Simone's ankle.

A perfect silver star.

Peyton jumped up. "*You* have a power too?"

"I think so . . . I mean, I guess that's what it is . . . I've never talked about it!" Simone laughed nervously, even though her cheeks were wet. "I'm sorry, it's just that I've never met anyone like me before. I thought I was the only one." She leaned forward and flung her arms around Peyton and hugged her tightly, and then she pulled back and studied Peyton's cheek. "How could I not have noticed that?"

"I've been covering it up really well." Peyton smiled shyly, reaching up to touch her star. "Mei's got one on her back."

Simone turned to me. "And you?"

"I don't have one," I said, feeling a pang of fresh regret. "But Ivy does, on her wrist."

"And I never spotted it." Simone's face clouded over. "I wish she had confided in me during one of our sessions. She must have thought that I wouldn't believe her. I feel like I failed her." She looked guilt-stricken, but then she made a visible effort to pull herself together. "But you know what? Ivy is one of the strongest young women I've ever met. We are going to find her and Mei, and we will make this linking happen."

"Could you be part of it?" Peyton said.

"Well, I guess so," she said. "I mean sure, if I can help, of course I will." She squeezed Peyton's hand and I felt a prick of jealousy. Ancient magic sang in their veins, while the most ordinary blood trickled through mine.

"What is your power?" I asked Simone.

"Hmm . . . I don't know if there is a name for it." There was a bowl of pale marble eggs on her desk, all different sizes, and she picked one up and rolled it between her hands. "I guess you could say I—well—I draw people to me."

"What does that mean?" Peyton said.

"Well, I draw them to me in different ways. Like this kind of thing." She waved her right hand vaguely, and I wasn't sure if she was indicating the silky jewel-toned pillows on the love seat, or her shiny stiletto boots, or the jasmine-scented tea in the small iron cups. "It's hard to explain." She sat back in her chair, crossing her legs and lacing her fingers around one knee. Her face went blank, and in the lengthening silence, Peyton and I looked at each other, confused. A moment later, the office door opened and the school secretary stuck her head in.

"You wanted to see me?" she asked Simone.

"No," Simone said. "In fact, I've specifically asked not to be interrupted when I'm in a session with students, Janice."

"Then why'd you call me in here?"

"I didn't," Simone said. "Did I, girls?" Peyton and I shook our heads.

"Well, I could've sworn . . ." The secretary left in a huff.

The door had barely closed when Peyton sputtered, "Wow, she can't stand you."

"What makes you say that?" Simone asked.

"I heard her wish that you'd move back to New York, where you belong. She thinks you had a ton of plastic surgery, and Mr. Sheers will never love you like he loved Bianca." She clapped a hand over her mouth. "Sorry," she said. "That's probably more than you wanted to hear."

But Simone didn't seem offended. "You really do have a powerful gift," she said, tilting her head to one side as she gave Peyton a closer look.

"Thanks," Peyton replied, beaming. Then her face crumpled. "But Mei's power is even stronger. She can morph into people. But she actually does pass out every time she does it—I wasn't making that up—and it really is hard to get her to wake up again. I think maybe she used her power when she was hanging out with Stu. I was parked outside waiting for her, and I never saw her leave, so I'll bet that's what happened. What if he saw it happen, and then he told his dad?"

Simone stood up abruptly, reaching for her boots. "I can guarantee that there are no girls chained up in Bill's cellar." She shuddered at the very thought. "But I'm willing to take you over there to look for Mei. The place is ridiculously huge. I keep telling Bill he doesn't need a fraction that much space, but I guess he's attached to the memories . . ." Her voice trailed off. "Anyhow, let's go try and find Mei."

"And Ivy," I reminded her. Suddenly I had an idea. "Or wait— could you just draw her to you? Could you use your power?"

Simone shook her head. "I so wish it was that simple. But I'd have to know exactly where she is. And I am absolutely certain that she's not there."

"Are you sure we shouldn't call the police?" Peyton asked.

"Positive," Simone said. "Bill is *not* a kidnapper. There's nothing whatsoever to be afraid of over there. Besides, don't forget that if worst came to worst, we both have powers."

"But you shouldn't use them," I said quickly. "Not unless you really have to."

Simone raised her eyebrows. "And why is that?"

"It's risky, with the linking tonight. Whoever's kidnapped Ivy could be on the lookout for people with powers, so you need to be careful. That's what Jasper said."

"Who?"

"Jasper Blake? He's been trying to help us find powers for the linking."

She frowned. "Does he have one?"

"Not that he can use," I said.

"What grade is he in?"

"He's a sophomore, I think. He just moved here from Paris."

"Well, no one by that name has ever been to see me, and I meet with all new students to figure out how their credits will transfer."

"I told you!" Peyton said, whipping around to face me. "He's not even a student here. We can*not* trust him, Laurel. Wake up!"

Her words stung. That was exactly what Ivy had said to Mom, when she insisted Bryan was a decent guy. Had I inherited her crappy judgment about men? In spite of everything, I still wanted to trust Jasper. But when I pictured his face now, I saw the stern boy from the newspaper—someone who looked like Jasper, but was a stranger to me.

"We'd better hurry," Simone said as she draped her trench coat over her shoulders, grabbing her umbrella and keys. Peyton and I both followed her out to the parking lot. But then she turned to me and said, "I think you should stay here, Laurel. If Bill happens to come home, I'm not sure how I'd explain being over there with both of you. Peyton dropped her off last night, so I could just say Peyton called me this morning and asked me to come with her to get Mei."

"My sister might be trapped in the cellar," I said. "Obviously I'm going!"

Simone shook her head. "Peyton and I are going to get Mei, but I'm certain Ivy isn't where you think she is. I had dinner there two nights ago, and Bill sent me down to the cellar to get a bottle of wine."

"The trapdoor must be really well hidden," I argued.

"Maybe we shouldn't do this," Peyton said. "What if Mr. Sheers comes home while we're in his dungeon? Then he'd have all of us. Maybe that's his plan."

Simone threw her head back and exhaled sharply. "There is no dungeon down there. There's no need for you to come, Laurel."

"She's right," said Peyton. I bit my lip. "It's going to look weird if you're there too. And if Mr. Sheers does lock us in his dungeon, then we need someone who knows where we are to get help."

I hated admitting that she had a point. "I'm supposed to just wait around and do nothing?" I said, my voice breaking. "Ivy's in handcuffs. How will you get her free?"

Simone gazed up at the clouds roiling overhead, letting the rain fall on her face. Instead of beating her down, the storm seemed to refresh her. When she lowered her chin again, her eyes were bright and focused. "Don't worry, Laurel," she said. "I'm sure that Ivy is not at Bill's, but wherever she is, we *will* find her, and we will free her."

Peyton nodded, and then her hand found mine and we squeezed hard. Simone squeezed my other hand, and for a flickering moment it felt as if some current of strength ran from Peyton into me, and from Simone into us both.

28.

"WE FOUND A FOURTH FLARE," I said to Jasper.

He let me into his house, leading me into the empty living room and raking his fingers through his hair. It was still messy, but it didn't seem adorably disheveled anymore. Looking at him now, all I could think about was his doppelganger in the old photograph, his hair severely parted and slicked to his head. Now, Jasper's bedhead seemed like a disguise, just another way of trying to hide the truth.

I knew that Peyton wouldn't approve of me being here, but I felt like I owed him the chance to explain himself.

But before I could speak, he asked about Simone. "What's her power?"

"She draws people to her." I described what we'd seen her do.

"Sounds like she could be a charmer." When he frowned, he looked even more like the boy in the picture. I could feel the sharp edge of the article, folded up in the pocket of my jeans, but for some reason I felt scared to bring it up—I didn't know if I could take another big reveal.

"Remember how we sent Mei to check out the Sheers' house?" I asked instead, and he nodded. "Well, she never came out. Peyton and Simone are over there right now, looking for her down in the wine cellar. I'm sure Mr. Sheers kidnapped Ivy, so hopefully they're going to find both of them. But if they don't, or if he comes home and traps them down there, then there goes the linking. Poof!"

Unable to stand the dimness, I walked to the window and dragged the heavy red drapes open. The daylight didn't make Jasper wince. His olive skin didn't suddenly start to smoke. I saw him check his watch.

"Do you have somewhere to be?" I asked.

"You heard the prophecy. When the linking happens, I have to be far from here."

I'd conveniently allowed myself to forget about that part of the prophecy. I knew that Jasper couldn't actually be present at the linking, but in my mind he'd been standing just outside wherever it happened, keeping watch. I felt like crying again. "How far away are you going to go?" I asked. "So much is still up in the air. We don't know for sure if Ivy and Mei are at Mr. Sheers's mansion. We don't know if Simone and Peyton can manage to get them out of there before he comes back. We don't know how the linking is going to happen exactly. So much could go wrong still."

"I agree." He cracked his knuckles. "But there's nothing else I can do."

From somewhere deep in the house, I heard the muffled chime of an old clock. *Clang, clang, clang.* It seemed to go on forever. I stared at the elaborate chandelier overhead. I hated the fluorescent lights that flickered and buzzed in the trailer, and I'd always thought how elegant it would be to have a real chandelier. But now that I was actually underneath one, all those crystals looked like tiny daggers, poised to drop.

"So you're just going to run away?" I was picking a fight, maybe hoping he'd be goaded into staying, but he nodded. His eyes seemed sadder than ever. I felt a surge of compassion, but I pushed it down, reminding myself of Peyton's caution.

This guy is not who he claims to be. "I'm leaving," Jasper said. "But there's something I want to give you before I go." He ran upstairs and returned quickly, holding his signed first edition of *The Sun Also Rises.*

"I don't want it," I said, but he pressed it into my hands.

"I read one of your stories in an issue of the Cascade High literary journal," he said. "It made me glad I'd stopped pretending to be a writer. You're the real thing, Laurel. You can't give up."

For a split second, I basked in the compliment. I couldn't believe that he'd tracked down a piece of my writing, that he thought I was *good*. But as I replayed his words, something else struck me. "You never told me that you like to write," I said.

"I was a hack."

I remembered what he'd said about his "great-grandfather," how he'd wanted to be a writer, until Hemingway told him not to quit his day job. My hands started to tremble. The book fell to the floor, falling open to the page with Hemingway's inscription. *For my drinking buddy, Jasper B.*

What had Skye said about Occam's razor? The simplest explanation is usually correct. I reached into my pocket and pulled out the article. I held it out to Jasper and he looked down at it somberly. The boy in the picture had the exact same expression: the one people always had in old photographs, when having your picture taken was a once-in-a-lifetime experience, and you had to freeze in an expression for too long to smile.

"This *is* you," I said. He didn't bother denying it. "But how is that possible?"

Jasper looked shy and angry and embarrassed all at the same time. "It's something that happens when you spark," he said at last. "You sort of—stop aging. That must be why Simone looks so young. I can't explain it. All I know is that my face—my body—have stayed the same, ever since the day I got my power."

"So does that mean you're, like, immortal?" My thoughts turned rapidly to Ivy and hope bloomed in my chest. "You mean people who've sparked can't be killed?"

But he shook his head. "We can be killed, just like anyone else. We just don't age until we give up our power. According to my grandfather, the spark keeps us young because it's such pure energy."

As his words sank in, I felt betrayed, as if he'd been leading me on somehow. Why had he shared so much about his power but held back on this key detail? Many times, the thought had crossed my mind that I'd never met a boy like him before. Well, no wonder, since he wasn't a boy at all.

My brain seemed to freeze, like it just wasn't capable of processing this new truth.

"You should've told me you weren't sixteen. How old are you anyway?"

"I was born in 1905," he said. "And to be fair, I never told you I was sixteen." I started to protest, but he spoke over my objections. "But in a way, I *am* sixteen. Maybe it's because my face and my body have stayed the same all these years, but I really don't feel all that different. The person you are on the inside never really changes."

"Okay, Peter Pan," I said, every word like a hard little pebble I was spitting out. "But you would never have told me if I hadn't found this." I waved the article in his face and he snatched it from me.

"Can you blame me?" He balled it up and threw it in the fireplace. "I didn't want to tell you I was responsible for—" He stopped, and I silently completed the sentence.

His mother's death.

"You set that fire on purpose," I said. "The one that killed her."

"No." Jasper looked at me, his green eyes pleading. "I mean, not exactly. I know you have no reason to believe me, but this was one fire I did not mean to start."

"I don't understand," I said shakily. "Please just tell me everything. Please."

"You'll hate me," he said. "But I guess it doesn't matter, since I'm about to leave and we'll probably never see each other again. You might as well know."

I didn't know who he was anymore, and now—more than ever—we didn't have time for this. Still, the words *never see each other again* made me want to sink through the floor.

Pacing the room, Jasper began to speak. "I was four years old when my father died in a railroad accident." He paused, took a breath, and shoved his hands in his pockets before going on. "My mother needed to support my older brother and me, so she took a job as a secretary at the Cascade Indian School—that was the old name for it—back when it used to be a boarding school for native kids. The original headmaster was a decent man. He let us live in a cottage on the school grounds and take our meals with the students. We didn't have a lot of money, but we never lacked for anything. I remember my early childhood fondly."

Now that he'd come clean about his true age, Jasper sounded different, like he really had been born in another era and was only now letting himself relax into the way of talking that he had grown up with. I finally sat on the floor to listen, leaning my back against the wall, and he continued, still walking back and forth as he spoke.

"Then, when I was fifteen, a new headmaster arrived. James Drexel . . ." He paused, his face hardening. "Drexel was determined to transform our 'humble provincial school' into one that could compete 'with the finest prep schools back east,' as he put it. He swept my mother off her feet with his lofty ideas for how to 'civilize' the native children, who'd been taken from their families, brought to our school to learn English and be forced to conform to our ways." He shook his head. "I never cared for Drexel, but he managed to hide his cruelty from my mother until after they married and we moved in here." He looked around, his face filled with loathing.

"Then what happened?" I asked. Maybe if Jasper told me the truth, I could somehow persuade him it wasn't that big a deal and he could stick around after all and help me save Ivy.

He breathed out sharply from his nose. "He started drinking. Or, I should say, he stopped pretending not to drink. He stopped sparing the rod. When the kids at the school didn't respond to his curriculum, he beat them within an inch of their lives. Pretty soon he started lashing out at my mother too, for anything and everything— if she disagreed with him in public, if she ordered the wrong type of typewriter ribbon, even if she wore her hair a way he didn't like." Jasper swallowed, a muscle firing in his jaw. "At first, he was careful never to hit her in the face. She wore high-necked dresses with sleeves to the wrist. But one morning I saw bruises on her throat. She begged me not to say anything to Drexel. She was afraid he would send me away." He swiped his forearm over his eyes. "She was trying to protect me."

"I'm so sorry," I started, but he shook his head.

"I'm not finished," he said through clenched teeth. "I was completely torn up about it, and I'm sure that's what made me spark. As I told you, extreme stress will do it. After that night in the woods, when I managed to get a campfire lit with my eyes, I started using my power all the time. For a while, it made me feel better. I trained myself to set fire to particular things: Drexel's favorite pair of shoes, the newspaper he was reading. He was suspicious, but he couldn't prove a thing, which only made him more furious. I set fire to his wallet, to his prized copy of Darwin's *On the Origin of Species*. I thought that if I kept him focused on me, he'd leave my mother alone."

I nodded, wrapping my arms around myself. No wonder he'd been so quick to lash out at Bryan, making him leave. Jasper came over where I was sitting, slid down the wall, and sat slumped beside me, continuing to talk as he stared at his knees. "One night, I came to dinner and Drexel was giving my mother grief because the soup was cold. He was sloshed on whiskey as usual, and he pushed her. The back of her head hit the fireplace, he fell on the ground, and she didn't move. I thought she was dead, and I flew completely off the handle. Instead of a spark, I threw a bolt of lightning. Then I realized that the lightning made a kind of doorway."

"A doorway to where?"

"I didn't know." He cracked his knuckles. "But I felt this powerful urge to step through it. When I did, I was still in the dining room, and Drexel was waiting for my mother to serve the soup. It was as if those last few minutes never happened."

"So that's your true power?" I asked, and he nodded, a sharp little jerk. "You can go back in time?"

"It's more like I can turn it back."

"Wow," I said, my heartbeat picking up. "Then what if you could turn back time to before Ivy got kidnapped?"

He shook his head. "It's extremely difficult. It only happens under the most extreme circumstances, and I can only turn it back by a few minutes. About ten is the most I've ever managed." He shoved his fingers through his hair. "It's a stupid power, Laurel. I saved my mother that once—I grabbed the soup and brought it to the kitchen to heat it up—but I should have poisoned it. Then I would've killed Drexel, gone to jail, and that would've been the end of it." He stopped speaking. Outside, the rain redoubled its force, making the pane rattle so hard it seemed likely to shatter in its frame.

"What happened?" I asked, frightened by what was coming next. "How did she die?"

"One afternoon, I happened to pass a classroom where he was beating a six-year-old boy whose only crime was singing in his tribal language." I could feel the fury radiating off him in waves. "Right as Drexel was about to cane him again, I set fire to his rod. He saw me in the hallway, and before I could get away, he grabbed a few other teachers and they threw me in a detention cell under the library. He chained me to the wall and told me he was going to let me rot down there." I could see him having to force himself to go on. "My mother came to visit me in the middle of the night, to bring me a plate of food, when she thought he was asleep. She opened the trapdoor without realizing that he'd followed her."

"Wait!" I stopped him. "This cell under the library had a trapdoor?"

"It was under the old library, but it's gone," he said. "I already checked, and the site was completely razed. They laid a new foundation when they built the new library."

"Okay," I said, disappointed. "So then what happened?"

His voice dropped to a hoarse whisper. "He called her disobedient. He threatened to slit her throat. She was moaning with fear, begging him not to hurt her, but I was chained up so there was nothing I could do. Without thinking about it, I threw another bolt of lightning. I opened another doorway back in time. But I was locked to the wall so I couldn't step through it."

He hunched forward, burying his head in his hands and speaking into his knees. "The lightning burst out of the cell and set the library on fire. All those books went up in flames. I could hear my mother screaming, but I was stuck, still cuffed to the wall. Drexel crawled out of a window and left her behind. The fire came from me, so it couldn't burn me. But it killed her. *I* killed her. And I had to listen to her die." He pressed the heels of his palms into his eyes as if he wanted to grind them out.

He'd told me everything. Now it was my turn. But what was I supposed to say?

You were trying to save her.

You never meant to hurt her.

It was an accident.

All of this was true, and yet I couldn't get a single word out. I could barely breathe. Jasper was still doubled over. The nape of his neck looked pale and vulnerable. I wanted to touch him, but I was also scared to go anywhere near him. And even with the curtains open, the light in that room was so dim, I felt like I was at the bottom of the ocean and I couldn't possibly swim to the surface on time to draw a breath. I didn't know how he could stand it in there, because I couldn't take one more second. And suddenly I was running out the door without saying a single word, not even good-bye.

29.

I TURNED OFF MINER STREET, onto the road winding up to the Sheers' mansion. After hearing Jasper's story, one thing was clearer than ever

You never know when you could lose the people you love the most.

I didn't want to have any huge regrets, the way that Jasper did. What if Simone was blinded by love for Mr. Sheers? Right now, he was our only suspect. And if Ivy was trapped in Mr. Sheers's cellar, then I should be with her. At worst, he would catch me and lock me up with the others.

At least we'll be together at the end.

I was speeding through the final curve, the mansion in sight, when a siren sounded. Red and blue lights flashed behind me, cutting through the fog.

Please, please, please don't let this be happening now.

I half considered speeding off, but I knew I couldn't get away fast enough in Spud, so I pulled onto the gravel on the edge of the road and watched in the rearview mirror as a stocky cop sauntered toward me, already brandishing his ticketing pad. A pit opened in my stomach as I recognized Officer Dougherty.

Just my luck.

He knocked on the window and I rolled it down halfway.

"License and registration," he said.

I fumbled through my wallet. There was my learner's permit, clearly marked with my DOB—which was today. With everything going on, it hadn't even crossed my mind that I was now sixteen.

Happy birthday.

"I'm so sorry, but I think my license is in my other wallet," I lied, hoping that he wouldn't recognize me and that he'd let it go.

"I can look it up from your registration," he said, hand outstretched.

He fiddled impatiently with his holster as I dug through the glove compartment, where I found a coffee-stained piece of paper with the DMV seal. He glanced at it. "This vehicle is registered to Sheila Goodwin. That you?"

"That's my mom," I said.

He took a closer look at me. "Hey, you're the girl whose sister ran off to be with her boyfriend. Did she come home yet?"

"She'll be back tonight," I said, feeling the words stick in my throat.

"Well, you were going forty miles per hour."

"I thought the speed limit was forty-five."

"Not on the curve. On the curve, it's twenty-five. The change is clearly posted."

I bowed my head, trying to look penitent. "I'm really sorry, Officer."

He glanced up at the mountains. "Where were you going, anyway? Only thing up there is the Sheers' place."

"I was just going for a drive," I mumbled.

"Joyride, more like it." He squinted at me. "And shouldn't you be in school? Hey—didn't you say you were fifteen?"

"It's my birthday today," I said. "I just turned sixteen. I swear."

He shook his head and opened the van door. "Well, unless you made it to the DMV this morning, then you're driving illegally. Now get out."

"I promise to get my license right after school," I begged him. "It really is my birthday." I held up my permit as evidence. "Can't you just give me a warning?"

"Out of the question." He took a few steps backwards, scowling at the bumper stickers on Spud's rear bumper. *Question Authority.* "This vehicle will be impounded until your mother pays the necessary fines to release it. And you."

He bound my wrists in front of me in tight plastic handcuffs, and then steered me by the elbow toward his squad car. "My sister Hanna is your age," he said, pushing me into the backseat, "and she'd never pull a stunt like this, because she was brought up to understand that laws exist to protect us, which is clearly a lesson your mother never bothered to teach you."

At the station, he refused to take off the plastic handcuffs. He called Mom on speakerphone, but she didn't pick up. He led me into a bleak little room, furnished with a wooden table and two black plastic chairs that were bolted to the floor. "Make yourself at home," he said, "because this is where you'll be staying until your mom comes to pay your fines."

"You can't throw me in jail!"

He snorted. "This isn't jail. But that's where you're going to end up, if you don't learn to have some respect for the law." With that pronouncement he shut the door, and despair overwhelmed me as the lock clicked.

I never knew that such a little noise could sound so final, like a huge rock rolling across the mouth of a cave.

30.

Peyton

EVEN THOUGH SIMONE HAD A KEY, Peyton still felt like they were trespassing as they let themselves into Stu's place, the cathedral ceiling amplifying their voices.

"Mei?" they called. "Are you in here? Mei?"

Nothing.

In spite of Simone's insistence that Mr. Sheers would never hurt a fly, Peyton's heart felt like a battering ram as they walked down a steep flight of stairs to the cellar. The door was made of stainless steel and there was a keypad beside it, just like the one required to open the front gate. "I should know this," Simone said, frowning. "I just used it a few days ago . . ." She punched in a series of numbers, but the handle didn't release.

"Mei!" Peyton called again, pressing her ear to the cold steel.

"I don't think she's in there," Simone said, but Peyton remained unconvinced.

Why did Mr. Sheers have a locked wine cellar in the first place? Who did he think was going to break into it? What was he hiding? "Maybe she's in there, but she's unconscious," Peyton said. As she closed her eyes, leaning her forehead on the door, she heard a very faint whisper, like a radio caught between stations. *Sssssshhhhh.* Not a single thought passed through the static, and it grated on her nerves.

"I remember now," Simone said, snapping her fingers. "Stu's birthday!"

When Peyton opened her eyes, the noise went away. Simone tapped in the code and swung the door open. It was pitch black inside the cellar, and as Simone groped for the switch, Peyton fought the urge to close her eyes again, less afraid of the darkness than what the light might reveal.

But to her great relief, the wine cellar wasn't creepy at all. She'd expected cobwebs and moldy brick walls, but this was an orderly room with a slate floor, wooden racks filled with bottles, and cabinets holding crystal glasses. There was no sign of a trapdoor, or any floor covering that could've hidden one, and Peyton felt more than a little foolish for having worked herself into such a state.

"See?" Simone said, giving her shoulder a squeeze. "I told you there was nothing to be worried about down here."

Peyton nodded, following her back upstairs. "But we still need to find Mei."

"Why don't you try calling her phone again?"

Peyton did so, expecting to be sent straight to voicemail. But instead, muffled and from a distance, she heard the special ring tone that she and Mei had chosen for each other's calls alone. She dialed again and sprinted upstairs, following the sound to Stu's bedroom, where she dialed one last time. The sound was coming from under Stu's bed. She dropped on her hands and knees, half expecting to find her friend's dead body. Instead, she pulled out Mei's kelly-green designer bag, which she clutched to her thumping chest.

"I was right. She has to be here. She would never have left this bag behind!"

"Then you'd better find her," Simone said.

"Me? But how?"

"We'll do it together," Simone said. "You can hear people's innermost thoughts, right?" Peyton nodded. "So listen for Mei's. Once you hear her, I'll draw her out from wherever she is."

"But I only hear secrets people are trying to hide," Peyton said.

"You don't know what you're capable of," Simone said. "Don't set limits on your power. You're a lot stronger than you give yourself credit for."

Wishing that this were true, Peyton screwed her eyes shut, but she couldn't hear anything but the rain hitting the skylight. When she opened her eyes to find Simone watching her, she was seized by the same frantic feeling that had always come over her in class, whenever a teacher called on her to read out loud and the letters flip-flopped back and forth. "I can't do it!" she burst out. "I told you, my gift's not that powerful."

She sat slumped on the bed, and Simone perched beside her, placing a hand on her back. "Listen to me," she said. "You have an incredible gift, Peyton. If anyone can do this, it's you. I have the fullest confidence in you."

Peyton felt herself blush. She was so used to the low expectations of her teachers and her parents that she'd long ago stopped trying to prove them wrong.

Good thing she's pretty, because she's not very smart.

Maybe Simone understood her better than her mom, who would never have recognized her power for what it was. Maybe she *was* gifted. Closing her eyes again, this time Peyton felt a swirling of energy from her core. Then she heard it for the second time—that staticky noise—but it was louder now, closer. It sounded like a rake scraping across a field of ice. She couldn't make out a single word, and yet the harder she listened, the more convinced she became that this was the sound of a third consciousness in the room—or maybe it was an *un*consciousness—the sound of a mind tuned to nothingness.

"She's here," Peyton said, fear clawing at her insides.

"Where?" Simone's gaze swept the room.

"I don't know. I couldn't pick up any specific thoughts, but I know she's here even though we can't see her." She hugged herself tightly, haunted by that sound. "Simone, something is really wrong with her. We have to find her fast!"

"Okay," Simone said, jumping to her feet. "If you're sure she's here, I think I should be able to draw her out."

"Out of where?" Peyton cried.

But Simone didn't answer. She rolled her head a few times and shook out her arms. Then she caught sight of Peyton staring at her, and she bit her lip. "Do you mind closing your eyes?" she asked. "If you're looking at me, I'm afraid I'll be too self-conscious to focus."

Peyton agreed. But the instant she closed her eyes that horrible noise returned, like a wind howling across a tundra. Maybe this was the sound of Mei's mind shutting down, her brain's last blips as her body went cold. Unable to stand it, Peyton opened her eyes a slit, relieved by the silence, and once she saw Simone in action she found herself unable to look away.

At first, it looked like Simone was doing yoga. She was breathing deeply and her arms were raised above her head, fingers outstretched like she was straining to catch something. Then a vein began to throb at her temple, and her eyes seemed to grow even darker than usual. Her pupils got blacker and blacker until they seemed to turn into a single velvet tunnel, and then it was like the rest of Simone just melted away, leaving Peyton standing on the threshold of a force stronger than anything she'd ever imagined.

At first she resisted it, her body rigid with the effort. But it felt so familiar, like it had been whispering to her all her life, telling her just to relax, just to let go. She already knew just how it would feel to enter that black velvet tunnel: like melting, like flying.

Like falling forever without ever hitting the ground.

"Peyton! Peyton!"

She awoke to fingers snapping in her face. Mei and Simone hovered above her, their disembodied faces pale and ethereal as clouds. Simone looked concerned, and Mei was a greenish shade of white, but she was right here. In this room.

Alive.

Peyton sat up and tackled her friend. "Oh. My. God. I am so, so happy to see you!" she squealed. Then she drew back. "But you're freezing! What happened?"

"I don't kn-know," Mei chattered. "I c-c-can't get warm."

"You poor thing." Simone wrapped Stu's duvet around Mei's shaking shoulders. "You'll warm up soon."

"Wh-what are you doing here?" Mei asked, looking bewildered to see the counselor in Stu's bedroom.

"Simone has a power too," Peyton explained. "She draws people to her. She used it to bring you back from wherever the hell you were."

"I could feel it," Mei said. "It was like someone was tugging on my arms and legs, pulling me out of a dark tunnel. You d-did that?" she asked Simone.

"Peyton deserves all the credit," Simone said. "She's the one who found you."

"I used my power," Peyton said with pride. "So where were you?"

"I have no idea," Mei said. "I had this stupid idea to turn into Stu's mom, so that he could meet her. But I guess I d-disappeared."

"Maybe because you didn't know what she looked like," Peyton said.

"But I was looking right at her!" Mei rummaged under a pile of Stu's clothes until she found the old yearbook. "Look!" She flipped through it until she found the page she was looking for, and then passed it to Peyton. "Maybe it's because Stu's mom is dead," Mei said, her voice dropping. "I think I might have become, like, her ghost or something." She shuddered.

Peyton stared at the picture. A young Bill Sheers had his arms wrapped around the waist of a curvy blonde girl in a poofy white '80s gown. The girl was snuggling into his embrace while he gazed down at her with puppy dog eyes.

"They look so happy together. No wonder he never got over her," she said. But then she caught sight of Simone, and she clapped a hand over her mouth. "Sorry."

"No need to apologize." Simone sighed. "You're not telling me anything I don't already know. They were very happy. They only had eyes for each other."

"Did you like him, even back then?" Peyton asked.

"Yes," Simone admitted. "I was in love with him even then, but they were so lost in each other that neither of them had a clue."

"Is that you?" Peyton pointed at a photo on the other side of the page. But she didn't need to ask, since the girl in the picture—dressed

256   ECHLIN & WATROUS

in a simple black prom dress and standing by herself—looked almost exactly like the tiny woman seated beside her now.

Simone nodded. "I didn't have a date, so they let me share their limo."

"But wasn't that, like, torture for you?" Peyton pushed for details.

"In a way," Simone said. "But at least I got to be with them. I wasn't completely left out. Bianca was my best friend. It was nice of her to include me, I thought."

"Still, you must have hated her in secret," Peyton said.

Simone shook her head. "No one could've hated Bianca. She was sweet to everyone. I got why Bill picked her, even though, sure, it hurt a little. They didn't fall in love to hurt me, and they were so right together—even I had no choice but to see it." She looked at the picture. "But it *was* torture to know that I didn't stand a chance with Bill. I felt like so long as I was here, I'd never develop feelings for anyone else either. So when I left Cascade immediately after graduation, I swore I'd never come back."

"So why did you?" Peyton asked.

"Bianca died. I was terribly sad, but a little part of me wondered if maybe now Bill might start to return my feelings at last. I even sent him a letter, confessing how I felt." Simone fingered her pin, her eyes downcast. "It took sixteen years for him to respond, which is why I believed him when he said he wanted to be with me. But the code to the wine cellar? Stu's birthday?" Her voice faltered. "That's the day Bianca died. He still thinks of her nonstop. He won't let her go. It's time for me to face the facts."

Mei nodded vigorously. "Stu said that his dad can't get over her. Maybe that's why she's stuck."

"What do you mean?" Peyton asked.

Mei pulled the duvet tighter around herself. "You know how people always say that a dead person has 'passed on,' or is 'in a better place'? Well, Bianca is definitely *not* in a better place. She's stuck *here*. I don't know where exactly, but she can't move on."

Studying the photo of Bill and Bianca, Peyton noticed something else. "Hey, Mei," she said, "didn't Skye tell us about a white dress?"

"You're right," Mei said, squinting at the image. "It has the same beading."

"What are you talking about?" Simone asked.

"Skye told us that Mr. Sheers brought an old white dress for Ivy to copy, that it had beads on it sewn to match the constellations."

Simone's forehead pleated. "He couldn't possibly expect me to wear a copy of Bianca's prom dress."

"I don't think it's for you," Peyton said. "He had Ivy try it on, but she had a hard time zipping it up because of her boobs, so he told her to let it out."

Simone looked down at her tiny chest. She seemed to be getting smaller by the minute, her spine drooping. "Bill is a good man," she said, but she sounded less certain now, like she was trying to convince herself. "He's kind and generous. He's such a devoted father."

"Actually," Mei said hesitantly, "Stu told me that they barely talk."

"Well, he's been so busy getting ready for the museum to open," Simone said, but her voice was weak. "We usually have dinner together, but I've barely seen him either this week. He's been working late every night." She brought a fist to her mouth, biting her knuckle. "Oh my God, what if you're right? What if he did do something to Ivy? If he hurt her, I could never forgive myself." That vein was pounding in her forehead again, and she'd gnawed off all of her lipstick. "I don't know what to do," she whispered. "I really can't believe it's possible, but everything you've just told me does make me wonder if I might be kidding myself about him."

Peyton felt a surge of panic. Simone, who was supposed to be in charge here, was clearly on the verge of losing it completely. Meanwhile, Mei was still cocooned in Stu's comforter, her lips blue.

Someone has got to figure out what to do now.

She tried to sift through what she knew. Whoever had abducted Ivy was supposedly possessed by an ancient demon, intent upon preventing the linking of powers during the eclipse. If that was Mr. Sheers, she didn't know why he wanted Ivy to dress up like his dead wife, but that seemed like a trivial detail.

Who knows what a demon gets off on?

The important thing was getting Ivy back from wherever she was.

And then she had a stroke of brilliance. "Aren't you and Mr. Sheers chaperoning the dance tonight?" she asked Simone.

"We were supposed to," Simone said. "He took his tux to the construction site so he could meet me at school. Would you believe that we've never even danced together? I thought maybe at the prom I'd get one dance, but he and Bianca were glued to each other all night."

"Go home and put on your dress," Peyton commanded. "Act like everything is normal. Mei and I will get into our costumes, and we'll meet you at the gym."

Her confidence grew as she explained her plan. It seemed right that she should take charge now. After all, she was the one who had found Mei. She'd figured out how to control her power, tuning into someone else's thoughts instead of waiting for the whispers to come to her.

And she was pretty sure that she could do it again.

31.

IF I PRESSED MY FACE to the window in the door of my cell, I could see Officer Dougherty sitting with his back to me at his cubicle, across the narrow hall. He was eating a king-sized Snickers bar while watching a wrestling match on YouTube. His keys were on his desk, agonizingly close.

I didn't have a watch, but I was sure it couldn't be more than a few hours until the eclipse. I scratched my wrist. With nothing to distract me, the prophecy played on a loop in my mind.

When forty thousand moons go dark
As the dead and the living trade places,
In a town of gold by the western coast
Druj shall again trade faces.

I thought back to what I'd learned in that article about the event the ancient Zoroastrians called the Renovation: "As the date approaches, the natural order will begin to fall apart, and the lower beings will be seen to rise from the dead."

I'd seen the mechanical fury of the wolverine, the cougar with its cold amber eyes. I knew that these animals had come back to life. So it wasn't a stretch to believe that humans could be next, like Skye had said. I didn't want to see corpses walking around with those dim, expressionless eyes. I didn't want to find out what they'd be capable of. Bullets wouldn't kill them. It seemed clear that there was only one way to stop this from happening.

As the veil is lifted,
Evil shall prevail.

Then there was the bit about Jasper. And then it had clearly said:

If four powers freely link,
That power cannot fail.

I hoped against the odds that Simone and Peyton had found both Mei and Ivy and that the four of them could link powers tonight.

But if they hadn't, if they didn't, then there was nothing I could do.

Absolutely nothing.

I remembered a video Skye showed me online, of someone being swept away by a tsunami. Instead of running, this guy just stood there on the beach, watching the wall of water approach. At the time, I couldn't figure out why he didn't at least try to save himself. But now I understood. He would never outrun the water, and he knew it.

I wondered what thoughts had run through his mind in the final moments of his life. I could imagine the physical violence of dying, but I couldn't imagine death itself. My love for the people who mattered to me was too strong—how could it just disappear? Maybe that love would continue in some form, the same way a poem continues to exist even if the book it was written in has been destroyed. This thought comforted me a little. My love might somehow survive me. My love for Ivy, Mom, Grandma, Skye . . .

I didn't want my list of names to be so short.

And Jasper was the next that came to mind.

I felt so badly about the way I'd run out on him, demanding the truth as if it were one correct answer on a bubble test. He wasn't a murderer. I thought about the patient, tender way he'd fed his grandfather applesauce, carefully spooning in each bite. I remembered sipping a pie shake together, telling him about my dream of becoming a writer. I shivered, thinking about how he'd been chained up, forced to hear his mother's dying cries. His description of the detention cell sounded so much like the scene of my nightmares.

"That site was completely razed," he'd said. "They laid a new foundation."

But it was Mr. Sheers who'd built the library, before Jasper came back to town.

Mr. Sheers and his crew who poured the concrete for that foundation.

My whole body tensed up.

The glass structure didn't *look* like it could hide a dirt-floored cellar, but what if Mr. Sheers had come upon the old detention cell when excavating the site, and recognized how well it would suit his purposes? The noise-absorbent cork floor could easily conceal a trap-door. Was it possible we'd been walking right on top of Ivy all week? The idea made me want to pull my hair out.

I tried wrenching my wrists apart, but the plastic cuffs didn't give a millimeter. I seemed to be allergic to them too. An angry red rash was creeping up my right forearm. I pulled down that cuff with my teeth, noticing that my birthmark was puffy, and it itched like crazy.

I stared at it hard. The same thing had happened to the others before they sparked. But what were the odds that I could be sparking now, just hours before the linking?

No way. I was just reacting to the stress.

In bio, we'd watched this video of a snake molting, rubbing against a branch as it pushed out of its papery old skin. I wished I could do that now.

Suddenly I knew what *would* make the feeling go away.

My favorite gel-tip pen gliding across paper. Letters looping across a creamy white page. I longed for the peace that putting the right words to paper always brought: the feeling that the world suddenly made a little more sense. I knew I should stop fantasizing about scribbling in my journal and focus on breaking out of my cell, but I couldn't shake the feeling that the two things were connected somehow.

I got up and stared through the window at Officer Dougherty. I didn't dare ask him for a pen—not like he'd give me one anyway—

but Mom always visualized what she wanted to paint before she began working on canvas. Maybe I could do the same thing, and pretend to write in my head. So I tried it. I pictured a blank page and then, one by one, I imagined words appearing on it.

I feel so itchy I could crawl out of my own skin.

The simple act of constructing a sentence soothed me. As I rested my forehead against the cool glass window, I noticed that Officer Dougherty scratched his arm, digging in hard, like I'd somehow planted the idea of itchiness in his head. But I told myself not to be ridiculous. Solitary confinement was getting to me, that's all.

He finished his Snickers bar and hit "Replay" on his computer. From this close, I could see that one of the wrestlers in the match was skinny but ripped, with a sandy mullet hairdo. He was watching a video of *himself* at the Olympics, and I imagined what was running through his mind, picturing the words looping across a page.

I should have won. I was an amazing athlete. Still am. I'm probably stronger than anyone in this entire town.

It was just a quick little movement, but he held up his arm and flexed a muscle. He might have been loosening up after sitting so long at his computer. But I had the strangest feeling that I had made him do it.

My pulse quickened as I thought about how Peyton, a huge gossip, could pick up on people's darkest secrets. And Mei, who loved to act, could now embody people for real. Ivy had been desperate to sew, and she'd managed to do so without electricity to power her machine. And Jasper had been dying to light a campfire, because he loved being in the woods and didn't want to return home.

Their powers were extensions of things they wanted desperately to do, amplifications of things they loved. I'd always loved to write.

Was I manifesting some kind of writing power?

Had I somehow written in this cop's mind?

But no sooner had the idea occurred to me than I found myself literally shaking my head. It was pathetic how badly I wanted to have a gift of my own. Obviously I was willing to believe anything if I thought it might help me get out of this cell.

But since I was stuck here, what did I have to lose?

What if I imagined that I had a pen and paper and I was writing a story, and he was a character in it, a character I could make do whatever I wanted . . .

I stared at him as I composed another sentence in my mind.

I want to get up and let that poor girl out.

I held my breath, willing it to work, but nothing happened. He just hunkered down in his chair, licking the melted chocolate from the inside of his Snickers wrapper. Unable to bear the sight of him, I turned around and leaned against the door, blinking back stupid tears. Ivy was going to die in her cell, and I was going to die here in mine.

Itching like crazy.

Out of nowhere, Ms. Owen's advice floated into my mind.

If you're serious about becoming a writer, then I suggest you spend more time thinking about what makes people tick. Characters come alive when we know what they want.

I turned back to stare at Officer Dougherty. What made him tick? What did he want? What was standing in his way?

He was replaying that wrestling video again. At the end, he got flipped and pinned to the mat. This must have been the match that he'd lost. I'd forgotten that he pulled his groin and had to sit out the rest of the Olympics. He stopped and hit "Replay," and again the boy on-screen landed hard, one leg twisted beneath him.

I saw him wince each time he watched his younger self fall on-screen. I'd assumed he kept studying the clip to admire his performance, relive the glory, but maybe he was trying to see where he had gone wrong. It probably felt like one day he had been on track for an Olympic gold, and the next he was a traffic cop stuck in his hometown, lurking at a curve on the road, waiting for someone else to mess up.

I'd thought he was just power-hungry. But maybe he wanted to feel important because ever since he got injured, *he* didn't feel like he mattered. Maybe he needed others to respect and admire him, because he didn't think much of himself anymore. Instead of hating him, I found myself feeling just a tiny bit sorry for him.

And I suddenly knew what I should write.

I took a deep breath, and pictured these words on a page:

Maybe I went overboard when I locked this girl up. What if a cop did that to my little sister Hanna? She'd be terrified. Laurel does need to learn to respect the law, but I'll bet she's learned her lesson by now. If I let her go with a stern warning, she'd be so grateful to me for setting her free, I'm sure she wouldn't make the same mistake again. This is my job as a cop: to decide when to enforce the law and when to be forgiving. Now that's a cop you can really admire.

The door nearly knocked into me as it swung open.

"I think you've been here long enough," Officer Dougherty said.

I gaped at him, blinking hard. I hadn't even noticed him getting up and walking over. Hadn't even heard the click of the door unlocking. He didn't have his bulldog face on anymore.

"You've had a chance to think about what you did," he said. "And I'll bet you're dying to get to the dance. My sister Hanna is pretty excited about it. You shouldn't have to spend your sixteenth birthday in here."

I nodded, offering a smile, but not trusting myself to speak as he clipped my handcuffs. "Thank you," I finally croaked. I glanced at my wrist. The hives were gone, and my birthmark still just looked like an ambiguous freckle.

Did I imagine the whole thing?

"I'll let you off with a warning this once," he said. "Get your license tomorrow, and you can come back for the vehicle."

"Thank you so much," I said again, rushing out before he could change his mind.

The clock over the hardware store read 5:58 PM. Overhead, the moon was a sickly yellow, its craters like bruises. I wove between the shuffling Yodas and Disney princesses, already holding heavy bags as they trick-or-treated on Miner Street.

"Hey, watch out!" said a little girl, after I made her drop her candy. As her sister stooped to pick it up, I stopped for a moment to stare at the pair. They could have been Ivy and me, just a few years ago. It felt like there was a band around my heart, squeezing tight as I broke into a sprint, heading straight for the school library.

32.

Peyton

PEYTON NERVOUSLY SCANNED the high school gym for Mr. Sheers. Not that many kids had arrived yet. Black streamers and silver cardboard moons decorated the walls. A disco ball sent a prism of lights swarming across the walls and floor, and her mind swarmed with all the ways that her plan could fail.

What if I can't do it again? Or what if Mr. Sheers doesn't think about where Ivy is hidden? That might not even be his darkest secret. The linking is supposed to happen in less than an hour. How far would he go to stop it?

She felt stupid and overly exposed, dressed up as her star sign—a Leo—in a headband with cat ears and a gold bodysuit with a tail sewn onto the butt. Mei was wearing a toga that was somehow supposed to represent the fact that she was a Libra. And Skye—who'd been filled in over the phone—was apparently dressed as a black hole, which meant she was wearing a black T-shirt and leggings. "We have to show up in costume so that we blend in," Peyton had coached them. "We have to act totally normal." But now she was finding her own advice hard to follow, especially after Mei whispered that Mr. Sheers was here, standing over by the refreshments table.

Peyton turned her head slowly, her stomach seizing at the sight of a tall figure in the shadows. But as he stepped into the light, pouring himself a glass of punch, she relaxed a little. Her mom always said that Mr. Sheers was good-looking enough to play James Bond, and in his tux he looked especially handsome. She saw him clap the football coach on the back. The two of them shared a laugh. As the DJ started to spin, he sipped on his punch while tapping his foot like he couldn't wait to break out some real moves once the crowd thickened.

"He's not acting like he has anything to hide," Mei said. "It's hard to believe he could be some kind of demon."

Peyton had to agree. "Well, maybe he's not." She was second-guessing this whole thing. "I mean, if he wanted to stop the linking, would he be here at all?"

"I don't know," Skye said, her eyebrows gathering. "My dad works for Sheers Construction, and last night, I asked him if Mr. Sheers has any weird habits. At first he couldn't think of anything. But then he told me that Mr. Sheers has one of the guys pick up three hundred liters of liquid nitrogen from Southern Oregon University every month, and deliver it to his house on dry ice. That's a *lot* of liquid nitrogen."

"Sorry, but is that supposed to mean something to me?" Peyton asked.

"It's used in high-tech systems to preserve human tissue, like live embryos," Skye explained.

"Do you think he wants to keep Ivy's body fresh after he kills her?" Mei whispered, looking as pale as the sheet draped around her body.

Skye shivered. "But that doesn't explain why he's been ordering it for years. Peyton, maybe it's something else you could try and find out when you listen in on his secrets?"

Peyton gulped. But before she could answer, Simone strode through the door, dressed in a strapless black silk gown that skimmed the floor. Sparkling from her sash was the diamond pin that Mr. Sheers had given her. The sight of this threw Peyton. If she thought that Mr. Sheers had kidnapped Ivy, then why was she wearing his gift? She'd admitted that he was the only man she'd ever loved, and they hadn't found a thing to incriminate him at the mansion.

Was she backing out?

But then she remembered coaching everyone to dress up and act normal. Obviously Simone was playing her part. Now Peyton needed to do hers.

If Mr. Sheers was guilty, they needed proof, and there was only one way to get it.

A cold sweat broke out all over Peyton's body as she left her friends and wove her way through the crowd to the refreshment table. Thanks to her years on the beauty pageant circuit, she knew how to fake a smile even when her insides were roiling. Nodding to Mr. Sheers, she helped herself to a cup of punch and closed her eyes, preparing to empty her mind. But as soon as her lids lowered, she heard his voice as clearly as if he were speaking into her ear.

No one will find her under the library . . .

She gasped. While she was relieved that her plan had worked, she had the feeling you get when you study for a test, only to find out that it's open book.

I can't wait to see my girl tonight. She's going to look so beautiful in her white gown.

Peyton's cup slipped from her fingers. The punch stained the tablecloth bright red, like blood.

"You okay, Peyton?" Mr. Sheers asked. "Let me give you a refill."

But she didn't wait for him to ladle punch into her cup. She spun around and shoved her way back across the dance floor, oblivious to the protests of the kids whose feet she trampled on in her desperation to put distance between herself and this kidnapper.

This demon.

She almost fell into Simone's arms. "It's him," she gasped. "I'm sorry, but I heard him more clearly than I've ever heard anyone. He's got Ivy trapped under the library, and—the dress, he was thinking about the dress—"

Simone took a step back. "He's coming," she said quietly.

Peyton tried to pull herself together, hoping Simone could do the same. She recalled how Simone had crumpled earlier, when she merely suspected that Bill could be guilty. Now that they knew for sure, what if she fell to pieces? But as he approached, Simone appeared to grow taller, pushing back her shoulders and holding her chin high.

"May I have this dance?" he asked her.

"I'd love to," she told him. "But first, I have to take Peyton home. She's feeling sick—poor thing—must be food poisoning."

"That's a shame," he said. "Why don't you let me give her a ride?"

"No!" Peyton practically screamed.

"We've got some girl things to talk about," Simone said quickly. "I'll be back before you know it. Think you can hold down this fort for twenty minutes?"

Simone wrapped an arm around Peyton and steered her toward the exit. Peyton turned around to make sure that Mei and Skye were following them, and caught a final glimpse of Mr. Sheers, who was practically bouncing on his heels.

She hoped there really was a hell, so that he could roast in it forever.

33.

AS I RACED toward the school, the earth's shadow had mostly de-
voured the moon. By the time I got there, the sky was so dark that I
couldn't see the faces of the kids funneling into the gym. I sprinted
past them, trying to ignore the cramp in my side as the library appeared, a gleaming black cube in the darkness, all those windows
turned into mirrors. I froze as I saw something flickering inside. It
looked like the beam of a small flashlight that someone kept turning
on for just a few moments at a time.

What if it's Mr. Sheers?

Adrenaline coursed through my veins. I knew I was no match for
him, but there was no time to run for help, so I opened the door and
slipped inside, holding my breath as I tiptoed onto the cork floor. It
was cold outside, but the air inside the library felt ten degrees colder.
On the other side of the room, whoever was holding that flashlight
seemed to be inspecting the floor too. Its beam kept methodically
sweeping over the cork, back and forth, back and forth. I'd reached
the photocopier when a shaft of light suddenly hit me in the face
and I froze.

"Laurel?" a familiar voice squealed.

"Peyton?"

From out of the gloom, Skye, Peyton, Mei, and Simone emerged,
as Skye used the flashlight on her phone to pan their faces.

At the sight of them, I went limp with relief. "I'm pretty sure
Ivy's cell is under here," I said.

"We know," Peyton said, explaining how she'd listened in on Bill Sheers's secrets.

"But he really did hide the trapdoor well," Skye said.

"Give me the flashlight," I said.

Now I guided the tiny beam of light over the floor, thinking hard. If I'd learned one thing this week, it was that people often fail to see what is right in front of them. A gleam caught my eye. It was Mrs. Bennett's desk, made of fiberglass: a see-through rectangle that looked like a giant bar of glycerin soap.

Or a tomb.

"Did you check under there?" I asked Skye, who shook her head.

"We couldn't move the desk," she said. "It weighs a ton. But it's see-through."

I tried to shove it aside and couldn't. She was right. But something told me to trust my intuition. I pushed the chair back and climbed underneath. Exploring the surface of the cork with my fingers, I felt a threadlike groove and my heart picked up speed.

"Get down here!" I called. Skye crouched beside me, holding the phone so that she could shine the light while I worked at the crack. A square of floor popped up. When she pulled it away, there was the rickety ladder of my nightmares, descending into a pit of darkness. I swung my legs down into the hole. My feet found the rung of a ladder.

"Ivy!" I cried, straining to see as I lowered myself into the cell. Skye was right behind me. The flashlight beam swung wildly, and then her phone slipped from her fingers, illuminating a slice of grimy brick before it hit the ground and went out.

Pitch blackness.

"Ivy!" I yelled again.

The air in the cell felt rotten, like every breath was infecting my lungs with spores of mold.

Why isn't she answering?

Groping around, I found the lantern on the floor and switched it on, and brightness filled the cell.

Then I saw her: pale and gaunt and dazed, blinking against the glare. She was so haggard that for a moment I thought we were too late.

"Laurel?" she whispered, and the distance between us collapsed.

The next thing I knew, my face was buried in her hair as we both sobbed. Her hands were still cuffed behind her back, and I knew I should be gentle, but I couldn't stop myself from squeezing her as hard as I could, barely able to catch my breath through my tears.

The others crowded around us. Skye set to work trying to figure out how to free her wrists while I yanked the collar from around her neck, flinging it onto the dirt floor.

"Thank God we found you," Simone kept saying. "You poor, poor girl, I am so sorry we didn't find you sooner, but thank God you're alright."

"Just get me out of here," Ivy whimpered.

"We will," I promised. "Hold on." I looked at Skye, who shook her head. Without a key, we couldn't undo the cuff chaining her to the wall.

"Where am I?" Ivy asked.

"Under the library," Peyton told her.

"What?" she cried. "You mean I've been at school this whole time?"

"I'm so sorry I didn't figure it out before tonight," I choked. "I feel so stupid."

While Skye kept yanking at the chain connecting Ivy's handcuffs to the wall, Simone began pacing furiously. "I swear to God, I am going to wring Bill's neck," she fumed.

"Bill . . . You mean Mr. Sheers?" Ivy whispered. "It was him? He did this to me?" I nodded. "Where is he? Is he in jail? Why aren't the police here?"

"He's at the dance," Peyton said, glancing up at the open trap-door before turning to Simone, her eyes wide. "You don't think he'll come down here, do you?"

When Simone didn't answer immediately, Ivy started to shake so violently that the chain rattled. "Wait—you mean he's free? No one even knows that he did this to me? And he's right up there? He could come down here and kill us all!"

"No, he couldn't," Simone said, shaking her head vigorously. "There are six of us, and we are not going to let anything happen to you."

"But he's crazy, and he has a knife! You have to call the police!"

"She's right," Skye said. "We can't get her out of these handcuffs without his key. Besides, this is a crime scene, so we shouldn't tamper with it." She picked up her cell phone, then frowned. "There's no signal down here."

"Mine's in my locker," Mei said. "I'll go up and call 911."

"What about the linking?" Simone said, grabbing Mei's arm. "We need to do it during the eclipse, remember? It's now or never."

"What are they talking about?" Ivy turned to me, her eyes wide with pain and terror. Before I could answer, Simone knelt in front of her and took her gently by the shoulders.

"Listen to me," she said. "I could kill myself for not having known what was going on. But we need you to hold tight and be the brave, strong girl that you are for five more minutes. Do you think you can do that?"

"W-why can't we just call the police?" Ivy whimpered. "I don't understand."

Simone sighed. "Because in addition to being a monster, Bill is a very powerful and cunning man. Even if they do bring him to the station for questioning, he'll get the best lawyer money can buy."

Skye agreed. "You can bet he didn't leave a fingerprint in this cell. There's nothing to prove he was ever down here."

My stomach lurched. Even in my dreams, he'd always been wearing a mask. Not that my dreams would hold up in court. I hated the thought of him getting off. It seemed inconceivable, but I worried that Simone might be right.

"I'm afraid the only way to stop him is to link our powers," Simone said.

"What do you mean? Wh-who else has a power?" Ivy stammered.

"We do!" Peyton piped in.

As Simone quickly told her about the others, I was tempted to add that I had a power too—or at least I thought I might—but then I realized that without me, the four true powers of the prophecy were already accounted for. I didn't want to complicate things, and I had no proof that mine was even real.

"Look," Simone said, tilting her face upward. "It has begun."

Previously, a bit of moonlight had shone through the librarian's translucent desk, but now every particle was gone, the earth shrouded in a kind of darkness I'd never seen before.

True darkness.

I felt chilled to my marrow, remembering that we were up against Druj, not just Mr. Sheers. Even though part of me still wanted to run up for backup, there was nothing a police officer could do to stop an ancient demon. It would be so stupid to find Ivy now, only to let the whole world go up in smoke.

"Simone's right," I told Ivy. "The linking is supposed to create a 'power that cannot fail,' according to the prophecy. That sounds like it will make all your powers stronger. You might even be able to break out of the chains."

Simone flashed me a smile of gratitude. Then she squeezed Ivy's shoulders. "Remember what I told you," she said softly. "Don't be afraid of your gift."

"Okay," Ivy finally said in a small voice. "But fast so I can go home."

"That's my girl," Simone said, standing up.

"What do we have to do?" Ivy asked. "How do we link our powers?"

No one had an answer.

I thought back to our team meeting, recalling how Jasper had said he hoped it would "just happen naturally" once the four powers were in the same place during the eclipse. Apparently that was wishful thinking. I remembered the game Ivy and I used to play as kids, pretending we could activate powers by holding hands. "Maybe everyone could just hold hands?" I suggested.

"I think we need to combine our energies more literally," Simone said. "Perhaps on a cellular level?"

"Blood contains DNA," Skye spoke up. "If your powers are encoded in your genes, then mixing a few drops of blood would combine them."

"Gross," said Mei, grimacing, but Simone was nodding slowly.

"That just might work," she said. "And we could each draw the blood from our stars, since that's where our powers seem to be concentrated."

"But we need a needle," Skye pointed out.

"We could use Simone's pin," Peyton suggested.

"Brilliant," Simone said.

Simone was already removing the pin from her dress. "We need something to mix the blood in, and I think I might have just the thing." She pulled one of her little pewter teacups from the velvet evening clutch hanging by a strap from one wrist. She saw me eyeing her and said, "I'm very particular about drinking tea from my own cup. Now, Mei, why don't you turn around first."

Mei looked queasy. "I really hate needles."

"I don't want to force you," Simone said. "It's your choice." Mei still hesitated, and Simone added in a gentler voice, "Look into my eyes first, and I promise you won't feel a thing."

Mei gazed dutifully at Simone, and an instant later her face went slack. Without being asked, she turned around and raised her shirt, and Simone jabbed her pin into the center of the star. I winced, but Mei didn't even flinch. As Simone pressed the edge of her cup against Mei's flesh and blood trickled into the cup, Mei flung her head back, her tongue running over her lips as if she tasted something sweet.

Peyton held her hair back from her cheek. "Do me next," she said eagerly. Then she too stared into Simone's eyes, and as the pin pierced the star on her cheek, her eyelids fluttered. "Wow," she breathed. "It's crazy how itchy I feel, but in a good way."

"I know, right?" said Mei, who still wore that dreamy expression. "I can feel the itchiness swirling round and round and round . . ." She started twirling in circles, the way Ivy and I used to when we were kids, trying to make ourselves dizzy and fall down. I was becoming uneasy. The mood in the cell was wrong, as if Peyton and Mei had forgotten where they were and why we were doing this.

"I'll do my sister," I said, grabbing the pin.

"Make sure you look in Simone's eyes though," Peyton told Ivy. "It's amazing."

I crouched behind Ivy. It hurt just to look at the welts on her wrists, and it killed me to think of causing her any more pain, but she was gazing at Simone and didn't make a peep as I poked her. Simone came around fast to kneel down beside me, catching Ivy's blood in her cup.

When I stood up, Ivy had the same glazed expression as Peyton and Mei. I shot Skye a worried glance and she returned it. We both watched as Simone stabbed the pin into the star on her own ankle. She drove it so deeply, I was sure she must have hit the bone, but her face betrayed nothing until a crimson drop wobbled over the cup.

Then she smiled.

"Here we go!" she said.

The instant her blood splashed into the liquid, the girls snapped out of their trance.

"Whoa—what happened?" Peyton said, blinking hard. "Did we link? Is it over?"

"I don't feel itchy anymore," said Mei.

"Me neither," Ivy said. "But I don't feel any stronger." She yanked at her chain, which rattled behind her. "Why didn't it work?'

"I feel flat," Mei said. "What's going on?"

Simone didn't answer, transfixed by the cup in her hand. The shadows in the corners of the room seemed to gather and thicken, blending into the folds of her dress.

My stomach cramped with fear, as I thought back to what she'd said to Ivy, as she urged her to take part in the linking.

Remember what I told you. Don't be afraid of your gift.

But she'd claimed that she had never met another person with a power like hers.

The power to charm. To draw people to her.

The way that Ivy had been drawn out of the trailer in the middle of the night.

"Get the cup back," I hissed at Ivy. "Use your eyes!"

Ivy stared at the cup in Simone's hand, and shook her head. "I can't," she said. "It's not working." She looked up at Simone, frowning.

"You tricked us." Peyton burst out, taking a step backwards.

Simone shrugged. "It wasn't personal."

Clomp. Clomp. Clomp.

Suddenly, a figure in a tuxedo began to descend the ladder, something big and white and heavy slung over his shoulder. Skye and I both jumped in front of Ivy, shielding her from Sheers as he turned around.

He didn't seem surprised to see us there.

He hadn't bothered with the mask.

As he slid the sack off his shoulder and cradled it in his arms, I could see now that it was a woman. *Or used to be.* Her head was tipped back at an impossible angle, her arms dangling limply, her skin a grayish white. By contrast, the white dress that Ivy had made looked as bright as fresh snow. It fit her like a dream.

Like a nightmare.

Mr. Sheers looked as giddy as a kid on Christmas morning.

"Wh-what's happening?" Mei asked, as Peyton retched in the dirt and Ivy began to moan in fear.

"We don't need these two," Bill Sheers said, jerking his chin at Skye and me.

"We don't need any of them anymore," Simone agreed, holding up the cup as if to make a toast. "I've got all of their powers right here."

The words of the prophecy marched around and around in my head.

If four powers freely link,
That power cannot fail.

It hadn't occurred to any of us that the powers could be drained. Or that power was not inherently good or evil—it all depended on who wielded it.

And what they planned to do with it.

I was getting a sick feeling that we'd been wrong all along. We should have been trying to *prevent* the linking, not make it happen.

Because now, apparently, it was Simone, not us, that had the "power that cannot fail." I could feel Ivy trembling behind me. Skye edged toward the ladder.

"Stay where you are," Simone barked. "Or I'll hurt one of the others." Her gaze landed on me, and even though she was threatening me, it was almost impossible to look away. I was staring not into a pair of eyes but a long tunnel, and I could feel the presence of something beckoning me at the other end of the velvety darkness.

Now I knew why the three of them had let her draw their blood without whimpering. There was something inside Simone, something calling to all of us, something so ancient that it had lived inside humans since the dawn of mankind.

Something that wasn't trying very hard to hide itself anymore.

Her eyes seemed to be getting bigger and blacker, dwarfing her face, which was collapsing into itself, growing more cadaverous by the second. "Get Bianca ready," she barked at Mr. Sheers, who was gently laying the corpse on its back.

"How can that be Stu's mom?" Mei whispered. "She died seventeen years ago!"

"I've had her in cryogenic storage," Mr. Sheers said, sounding proud. "I always knew someday we'd find a way to bring her back. I gave a fortune to science, expecting the answer to be there. But instead it came in the form of magic, like love itself."

"Oh shut up, you blathering idiot," Simone snapped.

"I thought you loved him," Peyton whimpered. "I don't understand."

"She's all Druj now," I said. Pure evil.

"Cheers!" As if in agreement, Simone lifted the cup of blood to her mouth and glugged its contents. Then she tossed it on the ground, where it shattered as if it were made of glass. She turned to Mr. Sheers, her lips newly red. "Give her to me," she hissed. When he hesitated, she seized the corpse and pressed her lips to Bianca's, her dark hair forming a curtain around their faces. Peyton gagged again while the rest of us gaped in shock.

When Simone finally unglued herself, a smear of blood painted the corpse's lower lip, like the daub of lipstick on a geisha's mouth.

She tossed the body back to Mr. Sheers as if it weighed nothing. He laid it on the earth and felt the neck for a pulse, staring hungrily at Bianca's face.

"It isn't happening!" He held his hand over her mouth as if expecting to feel warm breath, then looked at Simone. "What's going on? You said this linking would create the power to bring her back. You said you would do anything to help us be together again!" He pulled Bianca's head and shoulders up from the ground, trying to shake her back into life, but she remained as floppy as a rag doll. "When do I get my wife back?" he screamed. "You promised! You said! You said!"

"And you believed me." Simone issued a raspy laugh. "Did you honestly think that you and Bianca could gallop off into the sunset and live happily ever after?" A fierce fit of coughing racked her body. "It doesn't work that way, *Bill.*" She spat his name. "This isn't about your petty little love story."

"I don't understand!" He cradled Bianca's head in his arms. "You said you wanted us to be happy again! You said you loved her too! You couldn't believe you had the chance to bring your best friend back to life."

She shook her head. "I hated both of you. You humiliated me."

Bill gaped at her. "You did all this because I chose her? Out of jealousy?"

Simone bent over, coughing. Then she straightened up and when she spoke again, her normal voice was gone. A deep, harsh new voice came from deep inside her. The thing inside her was speaking. "That just helped me get in, you fool! I don't need much to begin with. But I work away at it, making it bigger and bigger, until I control my vessel completely. This one has served me well, but I'm done with it now." She curled forward, clutching her ribcage, muttering unintelligible words. Then her lips opened and closed and a second later, her eyes rolled back in her head so that only the whites showed.

Then something crawled out of her mouth. It was as tiny as a blob of phlegm and it meandered onto her lip, lingering there before it dropped to the floor and continued inching along.

A maggot.

The body that had housed Druj was rotting before our eyes. As Simone's eyeballs shriveled, her limbs withered, and her body caved in, I shrank back against Ivy, wanting to hide her from this sight as I hid against her. My teeth clattered, and some small faraway part of me noted: *Oh, so teeth really do chatter when you're terrified.* From that same distance, I heard Peyton moaning, Mei sobbing, and Mr. Sheers saying, "Oh my God. Oh my God, oh my God, oh my God."

I thought he was talking about Simone, until I saw that he was looking at Bianca.

Her arms were still outstretched, but as we watched, the tips of her fingers seemed to flutter, the way a woman might flutter her fingers to make her nail polish dry faster. He glanced at me as if he expected me to share in his excitement. "Bianca, come back to me. You're so close! We can be together again!"

As he leaned over and began to shower the corpse with kisses, a fresh wave of disgust crashed over me. He kept drawing back between kisses to gaze at Bianca's face. It was as if gazing at her made him want to kiss her, but kissing her meant he couldn't look at her. Her face was no longer soap white—she was merely pale now, her cheeks tinged with pink—as he clutched her close and inhaled her blonde curls. "My sweet girl," he cried. "Bianca, please open your eyes. You can do it, baby, you can do it." Tears rolled down his cheeks as he kissed her.

One last time, he pried himself away to gaze at her face.

And her eyelids clicked open.

But Bianca's eyes were not really eyes at all. They were entirely black now, a black so pure that it seemed to suck in all the color in the room, all the light.

The demon that had been in Simone was in Bianca.

Mr. Sheers drew back and cried out in terror. As if to comfort him, Bianca wrapped her arms around him and grasped his face. Then she twisted his head with no more effort than if she were unscrewing the lid on a jar of pickles. There was a sickening crack, and he went as limp as she had been a minute before. She threw him aside and turned to Mei and Peyton, who were cowering against the wall, too scared even to cry.

"Go!" Skye yelled, grabbing a shard of the cup and stepping in front of them.

Peyton and Mei both scrambled up the ladder, while Skye held the improvised dagger in front of an advancing Bianca. As I looked into those coal-black eyes, utterly devoid of humanity—of life—I remembered Josiah's words.

You can't kill what's already dead.

But I had no time to warn Skye before Bianca lunged at her, grabbing the shard and dragging it across Skye's throat. The gash opened like a horrible red grin. Skye blinked, holding her fingers to the wound, the look on her face one of mild surprise, as if she had walked into a room and found it unexpectedly empty. Then she slumped to the floor. Screaming, I threw myself on the ground and pressed my hand over the blood that was still bubbling, hot and sticky through my fingers. I couldn't catch it. I couldn't hold it in. There was too much, pouring out too fast.

"No!" I sobbed. "Skye! No!"

But she didn't respond, because she couldn't. The blood slowed and got darker, and the light in her eyes quickly dimmed until it was gone.

34.

BIANCA TOOK A STEP TOWARD ME, but then her head jerked up as the first cold ray of the returning moon penetrated the cell. She jumped onto the ladder, landing on it six rungs off the ground, and then she slithered upwards, not like a person climbs, but with a hideous, scuttling motion.

Numb with shock, I set Skye down and went to Ivy, throwing my arms around her and holding her tight, just as I'd done when we first discovered her. I could feel her trembling against me.

A scream from up above tore the air, high and thin. It was a human, I was sure of that, but a human in the grip of sheer animal panic. My ears rang and I thought I was still hearing that first scream, but then I realized there were more screams coming from up there, and layered over the screams were other sounds, whoops like battle calls. Even though these were sounds of exultation, they were far worse than the screams.

Druj had traded faces. She'd found her immortal vessel, and now she was gathering an army. The reversal was happening, and soon there would be hordes of them, the dead taking the place of the living, clawing their way out of the ground to kill and conquer.

I pressed my forehead to Ivy's, wrapping my arms as tightly as I could around her, hoping to muffle her ears, wishing that I didn't have to listen either. Wishing I could go back in time to fix this.

If only I'd stopped Simone from lifting the cup of powers to her lips. If only I'd spoken up when I heard her tell Ivy to trust in her power. If only I hadn't been plagued by self-doubt, and had trusted in my *own* power, maybe none of this would've happened.

Then I raised my head.

The linking was over. The prophecy had said that he needed to be gone then, but there was no rule stating that Jasper couldn't use his power now. If he turned back time, even by just five minutes, that could save everything.

But I had no way of reaching him—wherever he was.

Another whoop of ecstasy came from above.

Maybe one of those undead *things*—I couldn't think of them as people—had already killed him. I couldn't bear the thought that he might die alone up there, believing he'd failed the world. This wasn't his fault. Druj was evil itself, as ancient as the discovery of fire, no match for any human opponent. And in spite of his powers, he was completely human, imperfect and wonderful, strong and weak, just like the rest of us. He had done everything he could to help. He'd come back to Cascade to search for others with powers, even though this town was already his personal hell, the place where his mother had burned to her death while he listened to her crying out in pain. I felt horrible for having run off when he told me that story. For making him feel judged, instead of telling him that there was *nothing* he could've done. That it wasn't his fault.

If only I could say those things now, reach him somehow.

As I scratched at my wrist, I thought of how I'd reached Officer Dougherty, by imagining him as a character, thinking about what he wanted, writing in my mind and somehow reaching his.

Could I reach Jasper like that? Could I convince him to use his true power to turn back time and prevent the linking of powers?

No way, said a little voice in my head, buzzing like a gnat. *You don't know what he truly wants.*

But then it dawned on me that maybe I had been standing in my own way because I was terrified of failing. Maybe my inner critic had been silencing my power, shoving it down so deep inside me, I didn't even know it was there, or what I was capable of.

Something tremendous, Ms. Owen had said.

Ivy was still chained to the wall, and we could hear the howling of the undead growing in volume up above as they gathered in numbers. I knew it couldn't be long before they came down to find us. And then it struck me: *so what if I fail?*

My friend was dead. My sister was changed. Life as we knew it was over. What was left to lose?

So I closed my eyes, visualizing a white page. The words I wanted to put into Jasper's mind were already there. They flowed effortlessly.

That fire wasn't my fault. I was trying to save my mother. I did what I did out of love, and—wherever she is—she knows this. It's time to let go of my guilt. I can't let fear stop me anymore, not when I still have a chance to save people I care about. They're waiting for me in the detention cell under the library. That same cell where I was made to suffer. I can put an end to it now. I need to summon every ounce of power that I have, and turn back time as far as it can go.

I need to stop the linking.

I need to keep Druj from draining their powers.

Instantly, a blinding flash of light illuminated the cell. My arm rose to shield my eyes, and when I lowered it, I saw Skye lunge to pick up the shard of the broken cup, her hand shaking as she held it out toward Bianca.

My stomach clenched, and I tasted bile rising in my throat. We'd done it. I'd written in Jasper's mind, and he'd turned back time.

But not quite far enough.

He'd said that ten minutes was the most he'd ever managed, and that was what seemed to have happened again. Druj had already found its immortal vessel in Bianca. Once again, Bianca was approaching Skye, about to slit her throat with that shard.

"Skye, get out of the way!" I screamed, throwing myself between them. But Bianca wasn't looking at us anymore. She'd whirled around and was glaring at the ladder. I turned too, just as a figure in a black hoodie dropped to the floor and rushed toward us.

Jasper. My heart sped up. No matter what, I felt ridiculously glad just to see him again, when I thought I'd never get the chance. He looked around the cell, taking in the Skittles huddled against the wall, and Ivy still chained in the exact spot where he must have been chained himself so long ago.

"Who are you, boy?" Bianca spat at him. "What are you doing here?"

"I'd ask you the same question," Jasper said coolly, but I could tell by the set of his jaw and the shaking of his hands that he was terrified. As Bianca's gaze drilled into him, with her eyes like black holes, I had no doubt that he recognized the spirit of Druj.

"It's too late, isn't it?" he murmured to me. "I didn't take us back far enough, did I? I couldn't even do that."

"She already did the linking." I tried to think of something to comfort him. "You did your best. You're here. At least we're all together."

"You tried," Bianca cooed in a falsetto. "No As for effort, I'm afraid." She clucked her tongue. "That's the problem with kids these days. Everyone gets a trophy, just for showing up."

I wanted to punch her demonic face. She had no idea what kind of effort and courage it had taken him to do what he just did, to show up here, in the place where he'd watched his mother die as a result of his power, while he was powerless to save her. Just as powerless as we were now. He looked sweaty and pale, holding on to the ladder like he needed it to stay upright. I knew he didn't have the strength to turn back time again. He'd told me how much it took out of him, and I could see that he wasn't exaggerating. We'd both given everything we had, and I was out of ideas.

Bianca took a step toward Jasper. I squeezed my eyes shut, feeling a sick lurch as I waited to hear the snap of his neck. Instead, I heard a snicker coming from behind me. A sound that was totally out of place, but deeply familiar, because I'd been the butt of that particular laugh so many times.

Bianca spun on her heel to confront Peyton. "Is something amusing, you little twit? Do you find it *funny* that you're about to die?"

"No," Peyton sputtered. "Sorry, it's just a private joke between Mei and me." She tittered again, and I heard Mei join in. "You wouldn't get it, Simone—or Bianca, or whatever your name is."

The Skittles were standing shoulder to shoulder, both biting their lips in an unsuccessful attempt to suppress giggles.

"I'm Druj," the demon growled.

"Druj?" Peyton pulled a face. "O-kaaay, but you might, like, want to change that? I mean, since you're going to be stuck with it, like, forever?" They giggled again.

"And you're going to be here for, like, another five seconds?" the demon mimicked Peyton's way of turning everything into a question. "Because I've decided that you're going to be, like, the next to go?"

"Oh, actually, can I go next?" Mei butted in. "Because I don't think I can take it for even one more second."

"Take what?" Druj hissed, her black gaze flicking between them.

"Um, that smell?" Mei said in a stage whisper, wrinkling her nose. "I don't mean to be rude, but did someone fart in here? Because it seriously reeks."

Maybe terror had driven them mad. But they didn't look crazed. They looked like themselves, the girls who'd made my life hell for years. Was it possible that they were seizing their final opportunity to be mean? Maybe they wanted to die in character. Go down in a blaze of bitchiness. I didn't care. It didn't matter what they said or did. We were all going to die, and if this was how they wanted to exit the earth, so be it. If anyone deserved the Skittles treatment, it was Druj.

What amazed me was that she seemed bothered by their teasing. I mean, you wouldn't expect an ancient demon to care what a couple of teenaged girls thought of her.

"What did you say?" she barked at Mei, who elbowed Peyton, a tiny gesture I was pretty sure only I noticed. "I don't smell anything."

Peyton shrugged and said, "Um—I hate to be the one to have to tell you this, Druj, but maybe you don't smell it because it's coming from you?"

"Yeah," said Mei. They giggled again. "But you really might want to invest in some perfume. I mean, if you're going to be around forever, you should probably do something about the, uh, eternal stench."

Bianca didn't actually smell that bad. If anything, she just smelled a little stale, like a chicken breast that had been in the freezer for about seventeen years. I noticed that although Mei sounded for all the world like she was torturing some poor nerd in the cafeteria, she was clutching the folds of her toga in one hand, nervously bunching it up into a knot. She was acting, I realized.

But why?

"Seriously," said Peyton, pretending to gag. "That corpse stink is *not* going to be scoring you points with any zombie guys, unless they've lost their noses."

Bianca stood up straighter, thrusting out her chest. "This body is perfectly preserved," she hissed.

"If you say so." Peyton tossed her hair. "But if I stank like that, I think I'd *rather* be dead."

Bianca made a low growling sound, and my insides knotted. But as she advanced toward the Skittles, Mei caught my eye. She gestured with her chin at Bill's lifeless body, and then looked over at Ivy, and then back at me. I followed her gaze, and then I saw what she wanted me to see.

Chained to his belt loop was a key chain.

Now I looked at Jasper, glancing at the keys and then back at him, and I could tell that he got the message too. He gave a very small nod.

"No wonder you had to kill your boyfriend," Mei kept goading Druj. "You didn't want him to smell your BO and realize what a mistake he'd made."

"I killed him because I had no use for him," Druj spat, so enraged that she didn't notice as Jasper crouched down to unhook the key chain from Bill's belt, then moved swiftly to where Ivy was cuffed and locked to the wall—the same ring to which he'd been chained so many years before—and released her.

"You were too old for him anyway," Peyton said, staring Druj in the face. "How old are you?"

Skye spoke up, her voice shaking. "If she's been around since the dawn of humankind, that places her at around twenty thousand years old."

"Total cougar!" Mei said. The Skittles giggled, and I could hear the hysteria beneath the surface of their make-believe giddiness. Ivy was free now, but we were still Druj's captives.

But the word that Mei had used made me think of something.

The cougar that had chased me had come back from the dead. Josiah had said that the only way to destroy undead creatures like these was to burn them. I looked at Jasper, and as our eyes met again, I didn't have to write in his mind again because I knew that he'd had the same thought. He wouldn't have to rewind time. He could use his other power, his shadow power.

It was worth a shot.

Go, he mouthed, gesturing with his chin at the ladder.

What about you? I mouthed back, but he shook his head. I moved closer to him and he whispered into my ear, "I won't do it while you're all down here. It's too risky."

"We can't leave without you," I whispered back.

"I'm not taking any chances."

I shook my head and he said, "Laurel, let me do this. I have to. It's the only way."

"Over my dead body," Druj hissed, whirling back around to face him.

"That's the plan," Jasper said, drawing himself up straight. He looked at me, and I saw that he meant it. He wasn't going to hurt people he cared about, not after what happened to his mother. But I couldn't stand the thought of leaving him behind.

"Go," he said again. "Now!" Druj's head whiplashed between us. She seemed to be deciding which one of us should be her first victim. Her gaze latched on me and when she lunged, I grabbed Ivy by the hand and yelled, "Go!" to Peyton, Mei, and Skye.

As we flung ourselves up the ladder, I heard a *whoosh* and a horrible shriek. Although I didn't let myself turn around, I could feel the heat at my back as I climbed, my way illuminated by the glow of the fire that cracked and snapped behind me.

Only once I was back on the floor did I allow myself to look down the chute, praying to see Jasper climbing up after us. But instead I saw Druj—or the human torch that once was a demon in Bianca's body. The tulle of her gown melted like sugar, and a shroud of flame enveloped every inch of her as if she'd been doused in lighter fluid.

"Jasper!" I called out, coughing on the acrid smoke now pouring up the chute. I could feel my friends behind me, could hear them saying that we needed to get out of there, but I couldn't bring myself to leave him if there was a chance he was still alive.

Suddenly Druj shrieked again. Sparks flew off her and the flames redoubled in size, as if a log had been added to an already roaring fire. I felt a rekindling of hope. If Jasper was still throwing fire at her, that meant he was still alive. But Druj was now clinging to the bottom of the ladder, setting her foot on the first rung, slow but determined as ever. She pulled herself up, ascended another rung, and then another. A fresh blast of fire hit her from behind, but she just flicked her head to one side, a careless gesture of mild annoyance, the prom queen tossing back her bangs.

She was so close now that I could feel the heat coming off her, blistering, searing my face as I tried to peer around her.

"Jasper!" I yelled.

"Shut the door!" he called back. "Shut the trapdoor!" He was yelling something else too, telling me to shove the desk over the top. It was hard to focus on what he was saying as Druj climbed closer. I could still see her terrible eyes through the cone of flames, as black and soulless as ever, a darkness that couldn't be destroyed, because it was destruction itself.

"Laurel!" Jasper was yelling himself hoarse. "Go!"

"Not without you!" I screamed.

But Jasper had made his decision. He scrambled up the ladder, threw his arms around Druj's waist and pulled her down, landing beneath her on the dirt floor, where they tumbled and twisted, both of them enveloped in the blaze.

I couldn't see them anymore. My fingertips were blistering but I couldn't let go of the edge of the chute.

Then I felt myself pulled backwards as Skye grabbed my shoulders. "You have to let him do this!" she yelled. "Or else it was all a waste. We have to close the door now. Jasper's right. It's the only way to make sure that thing burns to ash."

But I couldn't move. I crouched next to the chute as Skye slid the square of floor into place. Then she grabbed my arm, pulling me to my feet. "We've got to move the desk back now. You heard what Jasper said."

"Not with him still down there!" I said. "He saved us. We can't just let him die."

"But if that *thing* gets out, then we'll all die!" Peyton said, seizing my other arm and trying to force me to my feet.

"Come on, Lolo." It was Ivy now. She wrapped her arm around me. "I don't think he'd want that, do you?"

Black smoke boiled up from the sides of the trapdoor, billowing upwards in a toxic plume. Peyton and Mei and Ivy were all racked by coughs, holding their hands up to try to keep it from infecting their lungs. The cell below was like a kiln now, radiating waves of heat through the floor. But I still couldn't move. I wanted to lie down, press my cheek to the corkboard. I didn't want to abandon him. I wanted to stay as close to him as possible for as long as I could.

Let me do this, he'd said. Maybe he thought that sacrificing himself would make up for having caused his mother's death. For almost one hundred years, he'd felt crushed beneath the weight of that guilt. I wanted so badly to nestle in his arms and let him know how grateful I was, how much I cared about him.

I would never get that chance.

The smoke was filling the library, a black ceiling that was rapidly getting lower and lower. The others were crouched down low too now. As Ivy bent over, hacking on the smoke, I could see the ridge of her spine through her pajamas. She'd lived through a total nightmare this past week. But she'd made it. Thanks to Jasper, and the rest of us too, she was free. If Druj got out now, his sacrifice would be for nothing. Letting that happen would be a bigger betrayal than leaving Jasper behind.

"Okay," I choked out. Every breath I took seemed to be filled with pinpoints of fire as I pressed my back to the desk, joining Ivy and Skye, Peyton and Mei, as together we pushed it over the trapdoor, sealing the entrance to hell on earth.

35.

WE RAN to the middle of the football field, ran as fast as our trembling legs would carry us, ran until the air was no longer tainted with smoke, gasping and breathing in deep, deep breaths, desperate to purge the poison from our lungs. Even though we'd sealed off the cell, it wasn't long before the fire broke free. Flames lapped at the inside of the library windows, filling every inch of the cube, pressing against the glass walls.

Half of the moon now peered from behind its curtain of shadow, but it looked reluctant to emerge fully, as if it didn't want to see the damage that had been done in its absence. *It could have been so much worse,* I reminded myself, although with Jasper gone it didn't feel true. I was shaking so badly that I could hardly stand up.

Kids were streaming across the field from the gym, and the sound of fire engines grew louder, but I could hardly focus on my surroundings, could hardly believe that we'd made it out alive, that the world was still here. We'd made it.

But not all of us.

Even though we'd gotten away from the smoke, stinging tears poured down my cheeks. I felt torn between gratitude and guilt, relief and remorse, and a bone-deep sense of loss. Life was so unfair. I finally had Ivy back, and now I'd lost Jasper, whom I was only just beginning to understand. My friends huddled around me. Ivy wrapped her arm around me from one side, Skye from the other, and then Peyton and Mei joined in too.

Grief is like the ocean. That's what Mom said after Grandma died. A wave will crash over you when you least expect it. I felt wave after wave crash over me now: for Grandma, for Jasper, for Ivy even though she was right here, because only now could I fully let myself feel what it would've been like to lose her. I sobbed and let my body go limp. The only reason I didn't fall to the ground was because my friends and my sister were right there, literally propping me up.

We were truly a team. Every one of us had done everything that we could, combining all of our powers, supernatural and otherwise, to save this world of ours. I wanted to say all of this, but I didn't need to. We'd lived it. We knew what we'd done.

And even though my heart was broken, somewhere deep inside me I felt that I was lucky too. I'd always wondered what it felt like to fall in love. I knew how it felt to love my mom and my grandma and most of all, Ivy. But how does it feel to love someone outside of your family? How do you even know when you've reached that point? And now I understood: you just know. It's not like a thunderclap. It's gentler than that. Your love feels as if it's always been there—just part of the way the world is, like gravity.

I loved Jasper. I wasn't going to try to push that feeling away anymore, or deny it because it was the wrong time or because I was terrified of him not feeling the same way. I felt lucky to have known that love. Even though he'd given up his life for us so that we could have this moment, and the next and the next.

We only broke apart as a procession of fire trucks and ambulances careened onto the scene. Firefighters tumbled from the trucks, hauling long hoses to tackle the inferno, while paramedics rushed toward us. I realized how awful we looked, faces streaked with soot, tears still leaking from eyes that were red from smoke. "Is there anyone else in there?" one of them yelled, and I was about to answer his question when the library windows seemed to curve outwards, as if the glass was melting. I felt rather than heard the shattering.

Kids screamed as glass rained down. Everyone raced in different directions and the paramedics rushed into the crowd, directing students onto the bleachers. One shepherded us toward a waiting ambulance. He tossed a silver emergency blanket to each of us, focusing

on Ivy, who was still coughing and wheezing. He sat her in the open
back of the ambulance and clapped an oxygen mask over her face.

"She's going to be okay, right?" I said

He nodded. "She just needs a little help to get her lungs working again."

Ivy pulled off the mask. "I'm fine. I just want to go home."

"I'll take care of her," I promised, as I wrapped an arm around
her waist so that she could lean on me, still not quite believing that
I had finally found her.

"We'll give you a ride home," Peyton offered.

But the paramedic shook his head. "Sorry, kids, but you're not
going anywhere yet. You were in there. The police are going to want
to get statements from every one of you about what exactly happened. And you too," he said, frowning and taking a step back. "Hey,
wait a minute. Where did you come from?"

I turned around, and for a moment I was sure that the night was
playing a trick on me. The face that I saw was so black with soot that
it was almost as dark as the sky. But set in that face were green eyes
flecked with gold, bright and alive. As alive as Druj's eyes had been
dead. I blinked hard, expecting this vision to disappear. Because it
had to be some kind of hallucination, right? My mind making me
see what I longed to see?

But then Ivy threw her arms around it, followed by Peyton and
Mei and even Skye, each one of them hugging the person who had to
be Jasper, even though there was no way, no way, no way.

"Way," Peyton said, snapping me out of my trance. I hadn't realized that I was speaking those words aloud, fully expecting the appari-
tion to vanish. But now the paramedic was definitely addressing him.

"Were you in the library when it blew?" He looked dazed by this
impossibility.

"No, sir," Jasper said. "I was just walking nearby, that's all." He
was covered from head to toe in soot, tiny pieces of glass glittering
in his hair. But as far as I could tell, not a single strand was singed.

"Well, I'd better take a look at you," the paramedic said.

"I'm completely fine," he said. "Honest." He looked at me as
he said this and I could tell that he was telling the truth. I could've

sworn his eyes seemed even brighter than usual against his soot-blackened face.

"We'll wait for our parents over there," Skye said to the paramedic, who let us go reluctantly. We made our way to join the students huddled on the cold plastic steps, everyone watching the library go up in flames as if it were a Fourth of July fireworks show. The crowd gasped as a geyser of sparks shot from the twisting orange and blue flames and the firefighters blasted the fire with steady jets of water. I wondered if the cell had been decimated at last, or if it still remained, a scorched cavern in the earth.

"What happened? How did you get out?" I asked Jasper once we were out of the paramedic's earshot. I'd hugged everyone else except him. A moment earlier, I'd admitted to myself that I loved him, and but now I felt unsure how to act around him, whether to touch him or not.

"The fire and smoke that I create can't hurt me," he said. "Remember? When you sealed off the cell, Druj couldn't see anymore. I couldn't either, but I got her in a head lock and I shot fire straight at her from close range, flame after flame, until I felt her neck crumble." He paused, shuddering at the memory.

"But the whole place blew," I said.

He nodded. "I was knocked unconscious. When I came to, the top of the cell was gone, and I climbed up a pile of rubble into the library. I couldn't see anything because of the fire but I just kept stumbling forward, hoping I'd get out, and it worked."

"She didn't follow you?" Mei asked. "You're sure?"

"There's nothing left of her," he said.

We were all quiet for a moment. I wondered what happened to the demon when its human vessel was destroyed. Did it fly up in the smoke, hovering overhead until it found another human to infect? I prayed that it was gone for good.

"What was happening when you went up there the first time?" I asked Peyton and Mei. "When Druj got out?"

"What do you mean?" Peyton said.

"That never happened," Mei agreed.

I looked at them and then at Jasper, and realized what must have happened. Because I'd written in his mind, he'd gone back in time and changed those five minutes for everyone else, including Peyton and Mei. Only Jasper and I remembered the alternate version of what happened when Druj got out. For everyone else, that hell on earth was like a rough draft that had been balled up and thrown away. They'd only seen the revision.

"How did you know to show up when you did?" Peyton asked Jasper.

He lifted one shoulder. "I don't know. I just had this feeling." He didn't look at me as he said this, and it dawned on me that maybe he didn't realize I'd written in his mind. It had felt so natural and effortless, as if he'd let me in.

"Yeah, I thought you were never going to use your power," Skye said to Jasper. "What made you change your mind?"

Jasper looked straight at me, his green gaze steady. "I couldn't let fear stop me anymore, not when I still had a chance to save the people I care about."

I felt my face flush deeply. The people he cared about. That had to include me, didn't it? This was a direct quote from the thoughts I'd written for him.

"I did it," I blurted out. "I changed your mind!" In a rush, I tried to explain what had happened to me in the cell, what I could now do. Jasper fell silent as everyone else fired questions. I rubbed the soot away from my wrist with my sleeve. My breath caught as I saw that sure enough, my freckle had become a tiny silver star. Everyone stared at it, exclaiming at how amazing it was that I'd sparked. I was a flare.

Everyone except for Jasper.

Ivy touched my star, and then Peyton and Mei did too. I wanted to feel his fingertips on my skin. But he just stared at me, pressing a fist against his forehead. Then he turned away, facing the dark smoke still hovering like a fog over the school.

I realized that in my excitement, I'd never given a thought to how Jasper would feel, knowing that I'd gone inside his head and changed his thoughts. Maybe he felt like I'd violated his privacy, read his journal—or worse—written in it.

Just then, Officer Dougherty came striding angrily up the steps. "You again?" he called to me. "You really can't stay out of trouble, can you?"

The accusation seemed wildly unfair. *Uh, I just helped save the world?* But I didn't care what he thought. I had Ivy back.

"Is this your 'missing sister'?" Officer Dougherty asked, frowning at Ivy. When I nodded, he asked her, "And why are you wearing pajamas?"

"Costume," Ivy whispered.

"Who can tell me what happened in there?" he demanded. "Were you kids smoking cigarettes? Is that how this fire started?"

"We had nothing to do with it. We were all outside watching the eclipse," Peyton improvised, "and we noticed Mr. Sheers and Simone go into the library. When we saw smoke coming out, we ran inside to help them, but the fire was already out of control."

"Wait, *Bill Sheers* is in there?" Officer Dougherty turned toward the library as if he intended to charge in and rescue Mr. Sheers himself. But the building was just a charred shell by now, a few last rebellious flames refusing to be quenched.

"Someone needs to find Stu and tell him about his dad," Skye said quietly.

"I'll do it," Mei offered.

We watched as Mei and Officer Dougherty approached Stu, who was wearing his football uniform as a token effort at a costume. Officer Dougherty rested his hand on Stu's shoulder. I couldn't hear what he said, but I heard Stu howl and my stomach twisted. He started to run toward the flames, but he got only a couple of yards before Officer Dougherty and one of the firefighters seized his arms. Stu tried to wrench himself free, his body twisting. Beside me, Jasper watched, his jaw set, and I could tell that he was remembering what it felt like to lose his own parents.

"Laurel! Ivy!" I heard a familiar voice call out from the crowd.

"Mom!" cried Ivy, almost falling down the bleachers as she ran toward our mother. She was accompanied by Poppy, who must have given her a ride. By the time I caught up, Ivy and Mom had crashed into each other. They were sobbing and rocking from side to side, and then Mom pulled back, taking in our sooty faces and Ivy's filthy pajamas.

"What happened to you both?" Mom launched into a barrage of questions. "When did you get back from Portland? How did this fire start?"

Peyton, Mei, and Skye had caught up, and I felt relieved when Peyton offered the same story she'd told Officer Dougherty. "Oh dear God, Bill was in there?" Mom looked devastated. "And Simone? They're both dead?"

"We tried to save them," Skye said.

"You went in there?" Mom practically shrieked. "You could have died too! Well, you were heroic. Stupid and heroic." She shook her head.

"What an awful night," Poppy said, shivering. "Poor Stu."

Ivy began to sob and Mom squeezed her tight. "Shh, baby, it's okay. Don't think about it now. It's all over. You did your best to help Mr. Sheers."

"I'm not crying about him!" Ivy's voice contained all of the loathing and terror built up over the week, and I could tell that she was on the brink of telling Mom everything. Part of me wanted her to. Mom should have listened when I'd told her that my dreams were real. But a glance passed between Ivy and me, and I knew we were on the same page. We'd never manage to persuade Mom and everyone else in town of what had happened over the past week. Without proof, it would sound insane. And even if we did somehow convince them, what good would that do? Bill and Simone were dead. Druj had been destroyed. We were safe.

The football field was beginning to fill with parents searching for their kids, and Peyton and Mei gave Ivy and me one last hug before they went off to find their families. The Nevermans claimed Skye, and then only Jasper remained.

"I guess I'd better be off," he said.

"Your parents aren't here?" Mom asked.

"No," he said. "They both passed away some time ago."

"I'm so sorry," Mom said, placing a hand on his arm.

He nodded. "Thank you," he said.

"Well, you're welcome to join us for a bite to eat," Mom said. She wrapped an arm around Ivy. "I think Subway might be open. Poppy, do you mind swinging by on the way home?"

"Of course not. And I've got room for one more," she said to Jasper.

He looked at us for a moment. He seemed tempted, and I thought, *Please, please, please come.* It felt so wrong to say good-bye as if it were any other day, but he shook his head. "That's very kind, but I should get to bed. I'm pretty beat."

"Give us a minute," I told the others, who nodded and gave us some space while I pulled him aside. "Come on," I coaxed him. "You shouldn't be alone tonight."

"I'm used to it," he said. "Seriously. Go and be with your family. I'm fine."

I hesitated, trying to figure out what was going on with him, when he took my wrist. The warmth of his hand made me shiver. He looked at my star. "I had no idea you had a power," he said. "It never even occurred to me that you could have one too."

"I guess I seemed pretty boring and ordinary," I said, my heart sinking as he let my wrist go.

"No. Not at all." Jasper shook his head and a shadow passed over his face. "I liked you before."

I crossed my arms, locking them over my chest.

Liked: as in past tense.

"Time to go, Laurel," Mom called out.

"Okay," I called back. "Well, see ya," I said to Jasper, hoping my breezy tone hid the confusion and disappointment that I felt inside. A few minutes ago, I'd been sure that I loved him, and that he at least cared about me. Now I felt like a silly little girl playing at romance.

"Why don't you stop by tomorrow night," Mom called out to Jasper right before we left. "We've decided to have a little get-together for Lolo's birthday."

"Mom," I snapped, but before I could tell her that I was sure Jasper had better things to do, he confused me again by saying, "Sounds great. See you tomorrow, Lolo."

"Lolo?" Ivy echoed, arching one eyebrow at me as we walked off, arm in arm.

"He was just making fun of Mom," I muttered, but I could feel myself blushing.

"Poor Lolo," Ivy said. "This must be the worst sixteenth birthday ever."

"It could have been worse," I said, and then I added, "a *lot* worse." I squeezed Ivy's arm. Right now, I just wanted to focus on the fact that I had my sister back.

Oh yeah, and the world was still standing.

But Ivy had set Mom off. "It does matter, chickpea," she sniffled. "I never even got a chance to say happy birthday because you rushed off so early this morning. But I'll make it up to you tomorrow. We'll have a real party. I invited your other friends too."

I was about to protest, but I realized that she was talking about Peyton and Mei—and she was right. They were friends now. The thought of seeing them in the Airstream still made me a little nauseous, but I knew I could handle it with Ivy by my side. Tonight put everything else in perspective.

Apocalypses are good like that.

FRIDAY

36.

WHEN I WOKE UP, Ivy was still asleep, curled on her side, facing the wall. Her blonde curls tumbled across her pillow, shiny and smelling like our mom's coconut milk shampoo. Still, I had to peel her quilt back, to double-check that it was really her.

"Hey," she said in a groggy voice. "What's up?"

"I just missed you so much," I choked out.

She lifted up the covers. "Wanna get in?"

"There's no space." Our beds were like shelves, the custom-made mattresses so narrow that one person could hardly roll over.

"Sure there is," she said. "I'll make room." So I climbed in beside her and we held hands, just like we did when we were little, pretending to be activating our super powers, never imagining that one day this would actually happen.

"So what did you dream about last night?" she asked, sounding a little nervous. Before we crashed, I'd told her all about my nightmares. She'd had no idea she'd been sending them to me, was amazed to learn what I'd seen and knew.

"I don't remember," I said, reaching down to pick up Ivy's stuffed lion. I lifted it to my chest and played with its scratchy mane. "Something normal, I think, like not being ready for a math test." I knew it was crazy—here she was, right beside me—but I felt this weird pang of loneliness. It was as if a door that had opened between our minds was sealed shut again, closing off a secret passageway that I'd enjoyed exploring.

"I really don't think I was sending you those dreams," she said. "When I use my eyes to move something, I can feel it. I never felt myself doing that."

"Maybe you did it without realizing it," I said. "Maybe dream sending is your true power."

"It could just as easily be your true power," Ivy argued. "Maybe mind writing is your shadow power and your true power is entering people's heads and seeing through their eyes."

"Whoa," I said. "But if that's true, I had no idea I was doing it either. It always happened in my sleep."

"Maybe because you were in total denial about the fact that you had any power at all."

"So it's like my true power manifested in my subconscious but I haven't really got it yet?" I said, wondering if she could be right. "Do you think if I worked at it, I could see through someone's eyes when I'm awake?"

Ivy plucked her lion from my hands and hugged it. "Don't you dare make me your guinea pig. No offense, but I don't want anyone messing around in my head."

"I would never do that." I felt hurt by the accusation, even though it was the same thing I'd worried that Jasper might think I'd done to him.

"Sorry," she said. "It's just that I want to choose what I share."

"But, Ivy," I argued, "if you hadn't been hiding all these secrets, none of this would have happened."

"What do you mean?" she asked, turning away from me to lie on her side.

"You told Simone about your power." I slid behind her, so our knees lined up.

"She found out on her own." Ivy pulled on the cord that raised the venetian blinds, but it was broken. "She caught me at camp. I thought I was alone in our cabin, and I was using my eyes to straighten the sheet on my bed. It was so frustrating. I didn't even want my power, but I couldn't stop using it."

"Why didn't you want it?"

"It's just . . . scary. It's not *me*. Besides, there's nothing I can do with my eyes that I can't do better with my hands. I want to be a fashion designer." She sighed, smoothing the quilt that she'd made from our grandma's dresses. "I wish it would just go away."

"Are you sure you got it back when the blood spilled out of the cup?" I asked.

Ivy squinted at the blinds, and an instant later they zoomed up, revealing a square of sapphire-blue sky. "I guess I'm stuck with it," she said.

"Jasper's grandfather used to have a power, but he gave it up somehow."

"Really?" she asked. "Find out how so I can too."

"Okay," I promised.

"You like him, don't you?"

"Jasper's grandfather?"

"Yeah, right." She elbowed me in the ribs. "Jasper, you dork."

I swallowed hard. A minute ago I'd been mad at Ivy for holding back, and now I was the one having a hard time telling her the truth. Was it because *like* didn't begin to cover it? I felt a warm glow from head to toe when I thought of him, especially after what he'd done for us last night. But how could I justify the fact that these feelings had formed while she was locked in a dungeon, being tortured on a nightly basis?

"He was there for me from the beginning of this nightmare," I tried to explain. "Mom was convinced by the note she thought you left—" I paused, realizing something. "Which Simone must have forged?"

Ivy nodded, shuddering. "I guess she knew so much about what was going on with me that it wasn't too hard for her to throw in some convincing details." She turned to me. "Nice try changing the subject, by the way. Now back to Jasper."

"Okay." I cleared my throat, knowing that she'd harass me until I told all. "So no one else believed that you could've been kidnapped, but he listened to everything I had to say, and he helped me figure out what was really going on. He was on my side—our side—from the start." I sighed. "He's not like any of the other guys here. He's pretty amazing. So yeah. I guess I do kind of like him or something . . ."

"You know for someone who's usually pretty good with words, this is not your most poetic moment." She laughed. "You have got it so bad, Lolo! Not that I blame you. He is amazing. You're right. And I'm sure he 'kind of likes you or something' back."

"No, he doesn't," I said.

Although maybe he did, before.

I liked you.

Liked.

Maybe, like Ivy, he couldn't stand the thought of anyone messing around in his head. Or maybe he was just detaching himself from me, already planning to go back to Paris as soon as he possibly could, and who could blame him?

"Well, *I* think the feeling is mutual," Ivy said.

"But you saw the way he ran off last night."

"So?" she said. "I also saw the way he was looking at you. And he said he'd come to the party tonight, right? We'll make you look extra hot."

"Stop it," I said, as I felt my face break out in a blotchy blush. Just then, Mom stuck her head in, smiling to find us both in the same bed, letting us know that breakfast was just about ready.

The kitchenette was warm, and Mom was listening to the oldies station, humming along softly to the Beatles' "Here Comes the Sun." She stood at the stove, ladling batter into a skillet, filling it with one enormous pancake, just like our grandma used to make for our birthdays. But as I got closer, I saw that unlike Grandma's fluffy buttermilk pancakes, this one was an ominous grayish color, with little black specks.

"What is that thing?" Ivy asked.

"I put buckwheat flour in the batter," Mom said. "I wanted to make you something healthy." She cast a worried look at Ivy. "You look so worn out, sweetie." She turned away quickly, flipped the pancake onto a plate, then drizzled it with syrup and sliced it into wedges. "There's chia seeds in there too," she added. "They're full of antioxidants. I made this recipe a few times when you were little."

"I don't remember you ever making pancakes for us," Ivy said.

Mom's back was to us as she dribbled more batter in the pan. "When I had you, I'd never followed a recipe. I was so young, I didn't have a clue how to take care of myself, let alone raise a family. Most of the things I cooked ended up in the garbage, and we couldn't afford to throw food away. So I stuck to canned soup and macaroni, where I couldn't fail." She shook her head. "Once we moved in with Grandma, it was a relief to leave the cooking up to her. She loved to cook, and she was so good at it, just like you."

"I'm not that good," Ivy said.

"Yes, you are," Mom said. "But you're still a kid, and I've been counting on you far too much. I want you to be able to enjoy your high school years while they last. So I'm going to take over the cooking." She turned around to give me my plate. "Don't expect me to become Martha Stewart overnight, but I can still learn, right? If you give me another chance?" She stood back, awaiting the verdict as Ivy and I both picked up our forks.

The air felt fraught, as if whatever we decided about these pancakes would determine our family's fate. This wasn't just about Mom's cooking. It was about the ways she'd been failing us as a parent, not listening to us, forcing us to live with her bad choices, turning away when something happened that she didn't want to see. Part of me wondered if she really deserved another chance.

I took a tentative bite. It wasn't as fluffy as our grandmother's pancakes. It was nutty and dense and a little tangy, like sourdough bread.

"These are actually halfway decent," Ivy said, meeting my eye.

"Gee, thanks," Mom said.

"They're different, but they're good," I said. "The chia seeds give an . . . interesting crunch."

Ivy nodded. "But what I'd kill for right now is—"

"Here you go," Mom said, handing her a steaming mug of coffee.

"Oh my God, you know me so well," Ivy said.

"That was the longest week of my life," Mom said in a quiet, serious voice.

"Mine too," Ivy said.

"Mine three," I chimed in.

"Thank God we're all together again," Mom said, and Ivy and I both nodded.   Suddenly, the song on the radio cut off, replaced by the familiar nasal monotone of the school secretary, who always announced snow days: "Due to the fire, there will be no classes today at Cascade High," she said. Ivy and I both stood and gave each other a high five. As we did, one of us bumped the table and dislodged the wobbly leg.

"Whoops," Ivy said, catching her plate in midair.

"I really need to fix that," Mom said, just like she did every time this happened. Ivy and I rolled our eyes at each other, but we were cracking up. We knew Mom probably wouldn't get around to fixing that table, but in the scheme of things, it didn't really matter. Maybe it was a little unstable, but no one else had a cherry-red diner table with a glittery top and matching seats, and there was something beautiful about it—just like us.

37.

WE HAD JUST FINISHED BREAKFAST when there was a knock at the trailer door.

"Hey, Jasper's here already!" Ivy said, staring through the window. As she opened the door, I jumped up, my pulse fluttering. She let him in, bringing with him the smell of fresh, piney air. "You're super early," she said. "The party's not for hours."

"But we're glad you're here," Mom said. "I'll bet you could use some pancakes."

He shook his head. "No, thank you, ma'am. I was actually hoping to take Laurel for a stroll. Unless you're busy?" He looked at me.

"Um, do you need help to get ready?" I asked Mom, trying not to act like it was no big deal that Jasper had shown up and found me in my Eiffel Tower pajamas.

"Go have fun," Mom said. "We've got this covered."

"Okay," I said. "Then I guess I'm up for a stroll."

"Great," he said. "I'll just wait outside while you . . ."

"Slip into something less comfortable?" Ivy giggled. *A stroll?* she mouthed at me and I shrugged, flustered but happy.

I threw on some cutoffs and pulled my hair back, then thought better of it and brushed it out so that it hung in waves around my face. Staring at my reflection in the mirror for a moment, I let myself think that maybe Ivy was right.

Maybe he does like me. Present tense.

I couldn't believe what a gorgeous day it was, almost summery it was so warm. Birds chattered in the treetops, and the air was laced with the scent of wild lavender and mint. After the pummeling rain, every rock and blade of grass seemed freshly washed.

We turned onto one of the park trails that I'd never explored before, strolling through the forest for a mile or so in an easy silence. Then Jasper broke away from the path and began to scramble up a tree-covered slope. "I've got something to show you up here, where this path forks."

We climbed the hillside, pulling our way up outcrops of rock, pushing past giant clumps of ferns. I was happy. There was nothing out here to scare us, and I didn't have to feel guilty about my feelings for him anymore. There was nothing in our way.

He smiled and gave me a hand to help me up over some slippery rocks. His palm felt warm, and I could feel his pulse thumping at his wrist. I wondered where he was taking me and prayed that once we got there he would tell me, at last, what he really felt.

At last he led me up onto a rocky crag that rose clear of the forest. It was flat on top, forming a natural terrace. We could see all the way to Cascade, a cluster of toy houses nestled in a bend of the river. It was the perfect spot for a first kiss. I stopped, hoping he'd think so too. He took my hand again. But instead of kissing me he said, "We're nearly there," and I saw the entrance to a cave in the mountain behind us.

I hesitated. "It's dark." I couldn't help flashing back to the detention cell.

"I can fix that." Jasper's eyes were shining. "Trust me."

I did. I let him pull me into the gloom and then a light flared up, then another, then another, and what I saw took my breath away. Stalactites upon stalactites hung from the ceiling, in more shades of white than I'd ever dreamed existed. Some were the color of antique lace, some as white as ivory. Some were white like the foam on a wave, and some were the creamy white of milk.

"Wow," I breathed, watching as their shadows wavered and danced. The light came from candles, which he was lighting with his eyes, set in rusted coffee cans perched in niches in the rock.

"It's beautiful, isn't it?" Jasper said, and I nodded. The place felt magical, but also peaceful and safe, like a church. He moved slowly along one side of the cave, scrutinizing every inch of it before he stopped. "I can't believe this. They're still here! You have to look at this. We used nails to scratch this on the wall. I never thought the marks would last this long." He grabbed one of the candles and held it up against the rock so I could read what was written there.

Alice Blake
Tobias Blake
Jasper Blake
June 23, 1912

Jasper's name was etched in a slightly rounder, more childish script, while his brother Tobias's handwriting was tiny and meticulous. I stared, marveling at how every letter was perfectly preserved.

"There's something else." Jasper took one of the candles from its niche and led me to the back of the cave where there was a jagged opening about four feet high.

"No way am I going through there," I told him.

"It's worth it. You won't be sorry."

I finally nodded, gingerly squeezing through the opening after him. Now we were in another smaller chamber. The air felt damp, fresh and ancient at the same time. The flame flickered and dipped. Jasper looked sternly at the light until it grew steady, and then he held it up.

An intricate silvery pattern covered the walls, and I realized that someone had etched tiny moons into the rock, growing from almost-invisible crescents to ripe globes, repeating over and over again. The design covered every inch of the surface, thousands upon thousands of moons, marching into the shadows.

I remembered something his grandfather had said. "Is this the cave painting of the prophecy?"

Jasper nodded. "We think it was done a couple of centuries before the first western settlers showed up in Oregon. Looks like they used some sort of flint."

"It must have taken years." I gazed at the wall, awestruck at the thought of these ancient people crouching down in this dark chamber, day after day, patiently chipping away at the wall, never knowing who might find it thousands of years later, of if anyone would be able to make sense of it. Would I have the same drive to write if I knew my message wouldn't matter for centuries?

"I wish we could thank them," I said.

"I know," said Jasper.

"How *did* you discover this place?" I asked as we made our way back to the first chamber.

Jasper looked at the place where he had scratched his name on the wall. "Toby found it. It was the year before he went to Europe and my mother met Drexel. She used to take us on walks in the woods. We would sneak away from the school, and she'd take off her hat and scramble over the rocks with us. In her daily life, she had to worry about putting food on the table and acting respectable, but in the woods she was carefree and happy." He paused and swiped an arm over his eyes. "When Toby found the cave, he knew our mother would love it. He brought the two of us here for a surprise, just like I brought you here today, and we stood for an hour, lighting match after match. My mother had the idea to write our names on the wall with a nail, to show that we were here."

"She had beautiful handwriting," I said. "I can't believe this was written nearly a hundred years ago." I paused, as a crazy thought occurred to me. "Now that I have a power, does this mean that I'm not going to age either?"

"That's right," he said quietly. "Not as long as you have your power."

Whoa. I could hardly fathom this.

"For a long time, I haven't felt any of the optimism and excitement that I used to as a kid," he said. "After what I went through, sometimes just having to wake up day after day felt like a curse."

I nodded. "That makes sense."

Jasper cleared his throat. "But something changed last night. When I woke up this morning, I couldn't wait to show you this place, which is strange because I hadn't thought of it in years." He paused.

"Ever since she died, I haven't been able to think of my mother without thinking about the night of the fire. All of my other memories of her were wiped out. But as soon as I got up, I knew that I wanted to come back here." He paused and added, "And it's because of you, I'm pretty sure."

"What do mean?" I said.

"I don't know what you did exactly when you got inside my head, but it's like you untied some knot."

He reached for my hand, and then he flipped it over. He gently touched the silver star there, gleaming even in the dim light of the cave.

"I don't know why it didn't cross my mind that you could have a power," he said.

I shrugged. "I guess I didn't seem that special to you."

"That's definitely not it," he said, still holding my hand. "Remember how Toby assumed that you'd sparked? I should've known that he was picking up on something. These things can run in families. I mean, he and I both had powers."

"What are you talking about?" But before he could answer, I had a flash of insight. "Wait a minute—is 'Gramps' your brother?"

He nodded, smiling sheepishly. "For obvious reasons, we had to tell the people at the nursing home that he was my grandfather." He let go of my hand. "I guess now you realize what a geezer I am."

"No," I said, but I was reeling. "How exactly did he give up his power? When did he start aging normally?"

"When he was about thirty," Jasper said. "Not long after he fell in love with Emily, the woman he married. Falling in love with her is what made him lose his power."

"You can't have both?" I asked.

He nodded. "The way Toby explains it, your power sparks from your soul's deepest desire. You wanted to be a writer. That ignited your power, and you were able to write in my mind." He paused. "But according to Toby, we only have so much energy. If you channel your desire into a person—if you give yourself over, body, heart, and mind—then your power burns away, and you start aging from that point on."

"And once your power is gone, then that's it? You can't get it back?"

"Not if you lose it that way. But look at this." He pulled the neck of his black T-shirt aside to reveal a perfect star on his collarbone. "It came back last night."

I gasped.

"Seems like those old dead guys did know a thing or two," said Jasper, smiling. "If I'd been part of the linking, Simone would have taken my blood and my power, and then I wouldn't have been able to rewind time or set her on fire."

"So does this mean . . ." I started.

"I've never been in love. After what happened, I could never get close to anyone, because I was convinced I'd hurt them too. That's why I said I could never be with anyone when we were in the diner."

"So what happens now?" I asked. "Are you on the first direct flight to Paris?" My voice caught in my throat.

"Hmm . . . Last I checked, there wasn't a direct flight from Cascade to Paris," he said. "Besides, I need to stay close to Toby. He's my only family left, and I want to spend as much time with him as I can."

"Of course," I said, imagining how I'd feel if Ivy was that old and I knew I could lose her any day. "Maybe my sister could you get a job at Ritual."

"I do make a mean café Borgia," he said, getting closer but still not touching me.

I was so desperate for him to kiss me that for a second I considered trying to write the thought in his mind.

I want to kiss her.

But I wanted him to kiss me because *he* wanted to.

"If you met the right person, would you mind growing old?" I asked.

"With the right person, there's no question what I'd choose."

I nodded, waiting for him to go on.

He's not making a move, so clearly I'm not the right person.

"It's you," he said. "Of course it's you. But you need to be sure too. Think hard. I don't want you to regret it later."

"What do you mean?" I said, turning to face him.

"You just got your power. It's incredible, and you've only had the chance to use it once. What if you want to develop it? What if you need to use it again?"

"I sure hope I don't," I said, but even as I spoke, part of me realized that he was right. *I can write in people's minds.* How could I give that up so quickly? "But you do like me," I blurted out.

"'Like' doesn't begin to cover it," he said, and my pulse jackhammered. "That's why I want you to think about this before you make a decision. This is for real."

Part of me wanted to say that I didn't need to waste a minute thinking it over. But I knew that he was right. I was already falling in love with him—the feeling I'd experienced watching the library burn washed over me again—but what if I did need my power at some point? What if I gave it up without ever finding out what I was truly capable of? I couldn't believe that there was a new barrier between us.

Without kissing me, Jasper moved toward the cave entrance, and I followed him. As we walked back down the trail, more questions plagued me. In spite of what he'd said, would Jasper really be happy being ordinary? What if giving up our powers cast a shadow over our entire relationship, but by the time we realized this, it was too late to go back and fix it?

I trailed after him, wondering if I would ever be able to find my way back to the cave on my own. It seemed tragic that all that beauty was hidden away inside this mountain, never to be seen by anybody, never enjoyed.

38.

WHEN WE GOT BACK, Jasper said that he was going to go home and change for the party.

I let myself get swept up in the preparations, welcoming the distraction. Mom and Ivy and I decorated the trailer, filling our every vase and glass and jelly jar with cosmos, nasturtiums, and marigolds. We put a big pot of cider to mull on the stove, and Ivy baked a carrot cake.

"Now you have to let me dress you," she said, once it was in the oven.

I shook my head. "I'll just change into jeans and a nice shirt."

"No way. This is a special occasion. In fact, I've already picked out an outfit for you." She told me to shower and meet her in Mom's room.

I took my time in the shower before padding into Mom's room in my bathrobe. Then I stopped and stared, slack jawed. Laid across the bed was the most beautiful dress I had ever seen. It had a halter top, silk as iridescent as a dragonfly's wings, and a hem that sparkled with tiny silver beads.

"This is the dress I made for you to wear to the dance," Ivy said. "Poppy's been hiding it. Do you like it?"

"It's amazing!" My fingers stopped short of touching it, as if it might flutter away.

"It is one of my finer designs, if I say so myself," said Ivy.

I seized her in a huge hug. "Thank you!"

"Put it on," Ivy said.

"You want me to wear it tonight? For a party in the trailer?"

Ivy shook her head sternly. "Stop being afraid of standing out. I'll do your hair and makeup. You'll look like a movie star."

I hesitated, thinking how Jasper had never seen me out of jeans. "Okay," I said. "I'm putting myself in your capable hands."

"You won't regret it." Smiling, Ivy twisted my wet hair out of the way with a clip and instructed me to close my eyes. As she began dusting on eye shadow, I fantasized about opening the door of the trailer in the green dress and seeing Jasper's eyes widen. And then he would seize me in his arms and . . .

"I was right, wasn't I?" Ivy said.

"Right about what?"

"About Jasper."

"Please don't tell me you can read minds too."

"Nope," she said. "You're an open book, Lolo. So what happened on your lovers' stroll? Did you make out or what?"

I shook my head, and explained about how your power could burn away.

"So two flares can like . . . flare out?" Ivy exclaimed, coating my lips with lipstick. "Great! There's a way out of this mess, and you already found the perfect guy to flare out with!" She laughed.

"But I might want my power," I protested as she dabbed my lips with a tissue. "It seems like a lot to lose when I don't even know what I can do with it yet."

"It's not like you can go around writing in people's minds. That's creepy. You'd only want to do that if you absolutely had to, which you hopefully won't ever again."

She had a point. For the first time, it occurred to me that it was a good thing I'd gotten this power and not some totally evil person.

Ivy began to blow-dry my hair. "Have you and Jasper even kissed yet?" I shook my head. "I doubt you lose your power the minute you both decide that you like each other. Didn't you say that you have to fall completely in love? That's not going to happen immediately."

"I guess you're right," I said, although I wasn't so sure.

"I know I am." She finished drying my hair and then began to weave a few tiny braids into it, tugging and pulling at it and sticking in barrettes. Once she was done, she helped me to step into the dress, and fastened the button at the neck. Finally, she let me look in the mirror.

I could hardly believe that the girl being reflected was me. The green silk clung to me, giving me curves I didn't know I had. Half my hair flowed down my back, while the other half had been braided and twisted into a gleaming coronet. My eyes, accented with mascara and the lightest dusting of golden glitter, seemed twice as big as usual. I glowed, as if a current of energy ran just below my skin. "Wow," I said. "No wonder you don't want your power when you can do all this without magic."

"Yeah, well," Ivy said. "It's not all my work." She grinned. "You kind of looked like that ever since you got home from that stroll."

I grinned back. At the thought of seeing him again, every cell in my body tingled. Mom was heating the cider on the stove, and the scent of mulling spices filled the trailer.

She appeared in the doorway. "Honey, you look so beautiful and grown up." Her eyes turned misty.

"Pull yourself together, Mom," Ivy said, smiling.

39.

POPPY PLANTED A BIG KISS on my cheek as I let her and Logan in. Skye showed up next, followed by Peyton and Mei, with Jasper right behind them. My stomach fluttered at the sight of him, looking gorgeous as usual in a leather jacket and jeans, and holding a bouquet of lilies.

No one had ever given me flowers in my life. As I walked up to him in my gown, I felt very aware of my bare shoulders and back—all that exposed skin that was usually covered in wool. I worried that I'd look foolish to him, overdressed, but he leaned forward and murmured in my ear, "You look beautiful."

"Thanks," I said, reaching for the flowers.

"That dress is *awesome*," Peyton pronounced.

"Thanks," I said again. They both looked around the trailer and I cringed as I waited for their commentary. But Mei squealed, "This place is super cute, Laurel!"

"It's adorable," Peyton seconded. "Your mom should be an interior designer. I'd hire her to redo my room."

The place did look pretty, I realized as I saw it through their eyes, with our vintage furniture and one-of-a-kind artwork. The fairy lights sparkled over the kitchen cupboards, and candles glimmered on every ledge and shelf.

"We got something for you," Mei announced.

"Right!" Peyton rummaged in her tote and handed me two gifts. "Happy birthday!" they chorused, watching as I tore away the wrapping. The first gift was a deckle-edged journal, its cover decorated with a delicate pale-blue feathery design. I opened the journal so I could touch the thick, creamy pages. The other gift was a rosewood-and-gold fountain pen. I gave them both big hugs, and they glowed.

Mom refreshed everyone's mugs of cider, and we all gathered in the front room, where talk turned to the fire. Logan said that two bodies had been found, one of which had been identified as Mr. Sheers. The other body, a female, had been burned beyond recognition.

Mom and Poppy shook their heads. "Poor Bill, I still can't believe it. And Simone too. It's just too awful."

I edged away, not wanting to fake sadness. Then the sour, familiar taste of fear filled my mouth. Why were there only two bodies? There should've been two women, and one man. Had Bianca somehow gotten away? But I forced myself to snap out of it. She'd burned to ash, that was all, so that nothing was left to identify.

But I couldn't relax. I drifted round the room, sipping a mug of cider, hovering on the fringes of conversations. Skye and Mei sat opposite each other at the table, arguing about whether astrology was bogus. Ivy and Peyton were curled up on the couch, discussing *Project Runway*. Mom was holding court, loudly recounting my "birth story," to Jasper, which ended with her burying the placenta under a redwood tree.

"TMI, Mom," I said.

"Your mom's hilarious." Mei laughed. "She just lets it all hang out."

"She sure does," I agreed.

"You guys are lucky to have such a close family," Peyton said, making me realize that I shouldn't take what I had for granted.

Poppy lit the candles on the cake and Mom switched off the stereo. The two of them launched into "Happy Birthday," and the entire room joined in. When the song came to an end, Mom reminded me to make a wish. Panning my family and friends, my gaze stalled on Jasper, whose face was flickering in the candlelight. Mom held my hair back so I could blow out the candles.

The cake was moist and rich, and as I looked around at everyone, eating cake and laughing together, I saw how much magic there was in ordinary life. With all of this, who needed a power? I caught Jasper's eye, embarrassed when Peyton nudged me in the ribs.

"I'll bet he does kiss you tonight," she whispered.

"Peyton Andersen, stop eavesdropping on my mind!"

"I can't help it," she squealed. "But I won't tell, as long as *you* promise to tell me what happens. Are you ready to flare out?"

"Ivy!" I looked at my sister.

"I had to fill them in," Ivy said. "They need to know how this all works."

"Right," I said, realizing that they would either stay young or flare out too.

"Go outside and make your wish come true," Peyton urged me. "We'll distract your mom."

I looked over at Jasper, who was now standing alone in the kitchenette. He looked back and I knew: this was what I wanted.

I told Mom that I was going to grab some air. Before she could protest, I clutched Jasper's hand. His face lit up and together, we slipped outside.

I shivered in my thin dress. Jasper draped his hoodie over my shoulders, warm from the heat of his body. Heart pounding, I opened my mouth before he could speak.

"I choose you."

Jasper looked at me. "Really?" he asked. "Even if it means giving up your power?"

"Well, it's not like it's going to happen immediately, right?"

"Probably not."

"Because I just turned sixteen—like for real—and I'm not quite ready to . . ." I felt tongue-tied, but it seemed important to lay this out. "Flare out completely," I said finally. "I mean, that's what Ivy calls it. You know what I mean."

A huge smile spread across his face, and he looked at me in a way that made my blush spread down to my toes.

Mom always said that the forest was the safest place on earth, and for the first time all week, this felt true. The moon, still almost full, cast enough light for us to see each other clearly. Jasper stopped where the pines opened out a little into a clearing.

"This is the perfect spot," he said.

"What for?" I said, thinking, *kiss me, kiss me, kiss me.*

"Your birthday present," Jasper said. "Look up."

I tilted my face up at the familiar constellations. Then a star exploded, embroidering the sky with golden sparks.

I gasped with delight. He glanced at me, and the sparks in his eyes matched those in the sky. "You did that!" I said.

"Shh. I need to concentrate. This is harder than it looks." As he gazed upward, a silver bud burst open to reveal its inner petals. Then another exploded, and another, and another, a spectacular cosmic bouquet. I gasped as each star outdid the last.

"It's the most magical birthday present ever!"

Jasper turned to me, taking my hands. "I'm glad, Lolo."

I stood on my toes and leaned in. As our lips met, it felt like a sip of champagne fizzing between us. Like the sparks that we both carried inside us were erupting. I'd never done this before, but I wasn't worried about getting it wrong. For the first time in a week—maybe ever—I didn't second-guess myself at all.

I threw my arms around his neck and felt his encircle my waist. A thrill traveled through me, all the way from my lips to my toes, and all the way back up.

We kissed again and again—soft, gentle kisses—but each one made me long for more. He pulled me in close, kissing my face, my neck, my shoulders. He stroked my back, which my dress left bare. His fingertips felt as if they were leaving trails of fire, even though I knew he wasn't using his power.

This is what ordinary hands can do.

I pulled him closer. I could feel the energy crackling under my skin, as if he were drawing my power out from deep inside me, and I didn't care.

Then the buzzing of his phone interrupted us. I groaned as the buzzing went on and on. "It's got to be Toby," Jasper said, pulling away. "He's the only one who has this number. But I don't understand why he'd be calling. I talked to him this morning and told him everything that happened. Maybe he wants to find out if I got lucky?" He grinned.

"You should pick up," I said. He stole one last kiss before answering, but he kept my body pressed to his, and I heard every word.

"Jasper Blake?" a female voice asked. "I'm one of your grandpa's aides at Conifers. I'm very sorry to tell you that he has had a heart attack."

"What?" Jasper's voice broke.

"We've rushed him to the ER, but he's in critical condition."

"I'm coming right now," Jasper said.

"Wait," the aide said. "Are there any other relatives I should notify?"

"No," said Jasper. "I'm his only family."

"I'm sorry. It's just that before it came on, he was quite agitated. He kept calling out a name—something like Drew?"

Jasper tensed. *"Druj?"*

No. No. No. A cold sweat broke out on my skin.

"Right," the aide said. "Is that a family member?"

"I'll be there as soon as I can," he said. He shoved his phone in his pocket and paced the clearing. "I can't believe it."

"Jasper, I'm so sorry," I said, wishing he'd let me take him in my arms.

"Why would he say that?" Jasper burst out. "Why did he say that name?"

I didn't answer, but we both knew. She—it—could still be out there.

"I have to go," he choked out. "I have to say good-bye."

I threw my arms around him, ignoring the pit of dread swirling in my stomach. He buried his face in my hair and wrapped his arms around me and pulled me in close, so tight it was as if he was trying to melt us into one. Then he pulled away, insisting that I keep his hoodie, and disappeared into the trailer to ask Peyton if he could borrow her car.

As I watched him pull away, I was already nostalgic for the sweet memory of just a few moments before. I wanted to go back to that kiss, to savor our moment of joy, back when I thought it would last so much longer.

A twig cracked in the undergrowth, and I scanned the forest, which no longer seemed peaceful. Still, I didn't want to join the others just yet. I wanted to stay in the spot where we had kissed. I pulled his jacket tight around my shoulders and looked up, hoping to catch the last traces of his fireworks. But they had already faded, leaving only the stars.

At first, when you look at the night sky, the stars dominate, pinpoints on pinpoints of light. But if you look long enough, you begin to notice the blackness, filling every available space.

I walked slowly across the clearing and paused at the edge of the yard, listening to the dance music coming from my home. Everyone I loved was inside. The trailer gleamed in the moonlight, like a fragile silver casket, spilling light into the darkness.